The Carnelian Tree

Anne Pettigrew

Ringwood Publishing

Glasgow

First published in Great Britain in 2022
by
Ringwood Publishing
0/1 314 Meadowside Quay Walk,
Glasgow G11 6AY

www.ringwoodpublishing.com
e-mail mail@ringwoodpublishing.com

ISBN 978-1-901514-81-0

British Library Cataloguing-in Publication Data
A catalogue record for this book is available from the British
Library

Typeset in Times New Roman 11
Printed and bound in the UK
by Lonsdale Direct Solutions

Dedication

To my son, David, and daughter, Susanna, of whom I could not be more proud.

A carnelian tree was in fruit,
hung with bunches of grapes, lovely to look on.
A lapis lazuli tree bore foliage,
in full fruit and gorgeous to gaze on.

The Epic of Gilgamesh IX

(Old Babylonian, c.1800 BCE, trans. Andrew George, Penguin Classics)

Contents

1

A Rude Awakening

January 25, 2003, Oxford

Expectations can be dangerous. They frequently lead to disappointment.

I'd expected my Oxford sabbatical to be a quiet contemplative year. First term had brought some relaxation and re-charging, albeit with sporadic wound-licking after my past traumas, but in the next term everything changed overnight. The outside world intruded on our peaceful college. With a vengeance.

It is a sheltered world, academe. I hadn't realised we were on the brink of war. Ancient kings and modern tyrants were not in my ken. And suddenly, I didn't know whom to trust. Being a humble, innocent teacher in my forties, I was much too old for such shenanigans. I suppose it would be best to start at the beginning.

In the early hours of the twenty-fifth of January – Burns' Day as it happened – I was in bed. Alone. Seconds earlier, I had been lazing on a sandy beach, margarita in hand, a breeze rustling the palms, waves lapping at my feet. A tanned, if maddeningly unidentifiable (though male and bronzed) companion lounged at my side. It was a marked improvement on the usual nocturnal fantasies conjured up by my subconscious i.e., purse-left-at-a-till-in-a-panic, or embarrassed-and-only-half-dressed-at-a-bus-stop. Finding

1

myself thrust into the chilly land of wide-awake, I regretted not buying an electric blanket for this year in college. Replacing the hideous, orange, seventies curtains in my lodge room wouldn't have gone amiss either, they didn't even meet in the middle.

My clock showed 3.30. Middle of the bloody night! My head was throbbing. Unsurprising. For once I had kept up with the girls at the Lamb and Flag. Friday nights with my younger classmates merited declining the shots they consumed between wines. That night, I had not been entirely successful in that regard and might have expected to sleep on past my usual seven o'clock (An annoying ironic fact I'd discovered since coming south – though I'd spent a lifetime setting alarms for seven when in fact I automatically woke then anyway. If I avoided shots.)

I was trying to curl up, wrapping myself in the duvet to doze on, when a noise came from next door. It was unusual to hear anything at night from Cedric's study. He didn't 'live in'. However, Leo's room, on the other side at the front of the Lodge, was a different story. At weekends I often heard full-volume Puccini, though whether it was designed to inflame or drown the cries of passion in Leo's latest conquest, I was never sure. Anyway, that night what I heard was a succession of odd, slow, screeching noises coming from Cedric's study.

They reminded me of the time that I moved our piano and scratched the wooden floor. Steve had gone ape, but if he'd helped when asked, then I wouldn't have been moving the damn thing myself in order to accommodate the Christmas tree. Cedric didn't have a piano. I surmised he might be moving his desk. I also caught muffled voices. The old eighteenth-century Lodge walls were thick. I tried putting an ear to it, then a glass from my bedside table (after drinking the water – I wasn't that dopily hungover). Unlike in the movies, the glass trumpet didn't help much. But, I was puzzled. Surely Cedric had gone home? When I'd staggered in from the taxi last night, I'd noticed the light under his door and minutes later from the loo across the hall I'd heard his alarm-setting bleeps and the front door gently closing. Professor Cedric Gilbert was considerate, a true gentleman. He was said to be a brilliant world authority on ancient Eastern stuff, writing an important book, though I'd been too stressed at the first term welcoming party to register on what. Since then, we'd only chatted about the weather, the day's Guardian, or Tony Blair. Cedric wasn't a fan. Well, his family had an estate in Gloucestershire, so he was bound to be a Tory, but I forgave him. He was still a nice chap. Diligent, often working late. But, I digress. Entertaining at three in the morning was weird.

Via the glass tumbler I did catch drawers being opened and closed and a voice saying 'No!' amongst conversation in a foreign tongue from which the only word I could make out sounded like 'zawjata.' Greek, maybe? Then a louder 'Stop that!', followed by a dull thud, and more foreign chatter sounding cross, then the distinctive high-pitched squeak of Cedric's patio doors being opened. Lucky thing. He had glass doors opening out onto the back garden. My single side window was glued shut by paint.

It went quiet. I returned to bed, expecting to hear the patio doors closing. But, I didn't. Surely, he wouldn't leave via the garden without setting his alarm on the wall outside my room? Might he be drunk? Unlikely. I'd never seen him down more than one beer. At that point I became anxious. Sad to confess it wasn't about Cedric, but me.

Open doors might let more mice into the house. I hate mice. Cedric had a cat, but it was a waste of feline space, being neither fluffily-cuddlesome nor usefully mouse-catching. I'd seen Selassie run out to the garden as mice scampered in to hide under the cookers. Tilly kept leaving the kitchen door open, yet despite shredded cereal packets and health-hazardous 'presents' in the larder, she wouldn't

3

countenance trap-setting. Ridiculous. In my view, PETA didn't apply to feral mice. Sorry, I digress, but this does illustrate how my mind was functioning that morning last January. Badly. I was confused, tired and needed the loo.

Tightening my dressing gown belt, I was halfway across the hall when I heard a groan. I tried to convince myself I'd imagined it. No light was visible around the study door, but I padded over and put an ear to it. Straining, I thought I heard a sigh, followed by a couple of soft moans. Were they rhythmic? Sexual, even? Could Cedric have a woman in there? I had no way of being sure how many voices I'd heard –or their gender. Not that I'd judge. That drawer rummaging might have been for condoms, or the result of furniture moving for a passionate athletic dalliance? Personally, I considered furniture overrated as a prop for passion: another myth from movies. Chastising myself for thinking about sex, likely as I wasn't getting any, I decided it best to leave well alone and continued into the loo, even more freezing than the hall. But, minutes later as I turned off the tap, there was a loud noise from outside the toilet window. A car door closed, gravel shifted, and a vehicle revved off from the driveway. Well, if they'd been 'at it,' they'd re-dressed incredibly quickly! Though I couldn't see quiet academic Cedric having an affair. His wife Anna was stunning. But then, people thought Steve and I were a perfect couple.

Deciding I had to find out what had been going on in the study, I marched back to the door and called out, 'Is everything all right, Cedric?' Getting no response, I knocked on, then tried the door. It was locked. Odd. I hadn't heard it close, nor the alarm-setting beeps. The study was the only Lodge room with security protection. I was sure I'd heard it going *on* before I went to bed, but I hadn't heard it going *off* when Cedric had presumably returned. Or might alarm 'off' beeps have woken me?

By now my pulse was thumping in my ears and I wished

this were a nightmare from which I could wake up – not a reality of beeps, no beeps, things going bump in the night and groans. My forearms tingled. What if those voices weren't Cedric and friends, but intruders? The English voice needn't have been his. My breathing quickened to match my heart

Assuredly, it hadn't been Cedric driving off. He'd never park in the drive as gravel 'wrecked your brake shoes.' He was very particular, a master of neat papers, stacked books and aligned pens. 'Neat desk, neat brain,' as my Chief Superintendent dad used to say. I knew Cedric worked away systematically at his erudite research beside a bust of Socrates, unlike me, struggling for a humble MSc surrounded by messy notes, crisp packets, and a furry monkey in a mortice board declaring, "Good Luck Mum!". Dad would disapprove of my indecision and scattergun thoughts in this situation, wouldn't have hesitated to go in if there was a chance someone might need help. Having heard groans, I knew I should go in. With the door locked, it would have to be via the garden. Grabbing trainers and a coat, I headed for the kitchen door until realisation hit me that exiting that way would mean immediate visibility to anyone remaining in the study. So, I swerved back for my keys, headed out of the front door and crept round the side of the house.

Brushing past dead lavender and skeletal rose beds, I jumped as a police siren screeched from the nearby main road. Should I have dialled 999? To say what? 'Something woke me up?' Och, I was here now. I'd just peek in.

The sky was clear and glittering with stars. Shrubs sparkled with heavy frost. My laboured breath was visible. Two rabbits scampered past, white scuts bright in the full moon. Usually, I didn't sleep at full moons. How annoying that tonight I'd been sound, doing fine till this nonsense. Peering round, I saw the French windows had been flung open widely. All seemed quiet. Slowly sidling forward to peer into the study, I saw no one as I stood on the threshold and shivered.

Inside, the moonlight illuminated a sepia scene of chaos. Books and papers spilled from opened cupboards and bookcases. The heavy Georgian desk was out of place. Beneath it, a fringed silk rug lay crumpled, heaped up at the side. Cedric would be appalled. Beside the desk, something lay glistening and white on the floor. Tentatively, I stepped inside. The object was Socrates, lying on his side, demonstrating he wasn't the solid marble bust I'd imagined, but made of hollow ceramic. His sharp-edged base was darkly splattered and, nearby, splodges of something decorated the carpet. As I bent to look more closely, I cried out when something brushed past my bare ankle. Little Selassie, Cedric's Abyssinian cat, sped past me out into the garden to seek refuge under the rhododendrons. Looking down behind the desk, I saw what he had been guarding.

His master lay semi-prone, silver hair already matted from blood congealed on his temple, gold-rimmed glasses twisted on the floor by his extended right arm. With his flexed right leg, he formed a perfect corpse silhouette for chalking out in a *Murder She Wrote* episode. In a sudden epiphany I realised that this was also the first aid recovery position designed to help preserve life in the unconscious. I wasn't sure if recovery might be possible from such a head injury. Sophie would know, but there was no point in phoning her at four in the morning. I stooped to check Cedric's neck for a pulse and convinced myself of a flutter. Though I didn't have a mirror to check, he didn't appear to be breathing, but he was still warm, and it wasn't long since I *thought* I'd heard moans, so I struggled to turn him onto his back.

It was a lot different from doing CPR on a First Aid class mannikin, but I gave it my best shot. By four-fifteen, Cedric was showing no sign of life and I was as sure as I could be that there was no semblance of a pulse, so I stopped reciting *Nellie the Elephant* for the requisite counting of chest pressures and ceased my resuscitation attempt. Gently, I closed his eyes – as much for my peace as his dignity – and sat back on my heels.

I'd watched dozens of detective films, TV crime series, and read plenty of murder books, but I had no idea what to do beside a dead body. I said a quick Lord's Prayer, which was probably quite inappropriate, but I couldn't think of anything else. It had been some time since I'd been to church. God, corpses made you think about life. And its aftermath, if any. Looking down at the body, perhaps with it being Burns' Day, I thought of his *Epitaph on my own Friend,* where he said, 'if there is another world, he lives in bliss'. Who knew? But I knew my own planned Burns Supper that night was not going to happen.

I admit to sobbing. Mainly in self-pity at being involved, but also in guilt at being totally useless as a first aider. Catching my ghostly reflection in the glass bookcase, I was surprised to see I was shaking. Behind me the garden looked frosty and sinister. A fox scampering past to disappear under the bushes brought fresh palpitations. Dear God, please don't let him eat poor wee Selassie! I rose, heavy hearted. This Oxford sabbatical was not going to be the quiet respite from teaching that I'd planned. Bugger Steve. I wished I'd never left Glasgow. Teaching English to disinterested kids had never seemed so appealing.

2

An Odd Assortment of Souls

I felt as though I was on the set of a movie; something arty, foreign, surreal, maybe by Bunuel. During the last few hours, I'd gone from dreaming of idyllically languishing on a beach to harsh reality, where I'd failed to resuscitate a colleague and was now sitting at a kitchen table. Here, my idiosyncratic housemates appeared to be talking and moving in slow motion, as if rehearsing a scene that I'd witnessed before. Familiar yet not quite. Mustering all my psychology training, I deduced this must be what's meant by *déjà vu,* doubtless brought on by stress and lack of sleep and I tried to reassure myself that despite last night's full moon, I was not a lunatic. Yet.

Out of the window I could see 'scene-of-crimes' police in disposable suits systematically pacing in the garden. Surely not looking for a murder weapon? I wasn't Agatha Christie, but I'd bet my bottom dollar that Socrates was 'it'. Snow was falling. It had been forecast since the start of term. I would need to find my boots today. If I got out.

I drank half of my mug of tea before realising it was coffee. I hate coffee. About to complain to Tilly, the tea maker, I caught sight of her face and didn't. She was pacing back and forth across the room between the door and the two cookers, her wide, distraught eyes reminding me of a kangaroo I once caught in my headlights in the Queensland bush. Steve had snapped, 'Just run over the bloody thing, they're like vermin out here!' Looking back, there'd been so many differences between us.

I set down my Sainsbury's mug, recently bought for its cheerful red poppy design, but now holding a different connotation: death. Not in the wartime Normandy fields, but our peaceful north Oxford college house.

Tilly suddenly whimpered, stopped pacing, and crumpled forward to clutch the edge of the old kitchen dresser. Opposite me, Guy pulled out the chair at his side.

'For God's sake, sit down, Tilly!' He patted the seat. 'Come on, get your ass here!'

Tilly sat down abruptly. 'Sorry, but it's been such a shock, hasn't it? I mean, who expects to wake up and find a dead body in the house?'

'Well, strictly speaking, it was Judith who woke and found it,' Jon pursed his lips.

At this, Tilly clutched a hanky to her face and started crying. I gave Dr Jonathon Wolsey my best glare. He could be such a pedantic prat. Catching my disapproving eye, he leaned over the table to pat Tilly's arm.

'Sorry, Tilly. You're right. It is terrible.' Leaning back, he looked around at us all. 'But what I don't understand is why, apart from Judith, none of us heard a thing?'

The assembled housemates shrugged. We'd been sent in here minutes after the squad car had 'doo-da-ed' up the drive and firmly instructed us not to move until called. That was hours ago. It was now 7.50 a.m. according to the red plastic Westclox on the wall, whose jerking second hand was making a creepy, ominous, theatrical 'tick, tock, tick' that channelled Hitchcockian doom. Apt for this odd assortment of souls closeted together in a yellow brick villa off the Banbury Road while death slumbered next door. We didn't even know if the police had moved the body yet.

Tilly Prendergast was sitting opposite me, her floral silk Kimono wrapped so tightly it was amazing she could breathe. After leaving Cedric cold and still, I'd got Jimmy, the college porter, to summon the police, whilst I rounded up the house. Leo hadn't answered his door. Upstairs, Tilly had taken an age to open hers, and the second I'd told her Cedric was dead, she'd swooned back onto her bed. It had taken all my powers of persuasion to get her up, though she hadn't dressed or brushed her long wavy auburn hair. Despite having a front-facing room, she hadn't heard a thing. But then, she'd admitted taking a 'gelatine-free sleeping capsule.' I wondered why this young D.Phil. student from Bristol researching World War One poets needed sleeping pills at her age, I didn't ask, but vowed to ask my med student daughter Sophie why pills might need to be 'gelatine-free.' Tilly was now sitting beside shaven-headed Guy, who oozed impatience.

The American had one tanned muscular arm around Tilly's shoulder, the other in her lap somewhere below the table. He'd moved in on her immediately after her spectacular break up with Leo at Christmas. I hadn't entirely made my mind up about Guy but didn't think he was good for nervy Tilly; too domineering and controlling. What was she thinking? He was well into his forties with a wife and two kids back home in Virginia.

I thought it odd he'd come to the UK to research the US Air Force in World War Two. And odder still that he was staying in our cramped college accommodation, as I'd seen his huge US house with pool and lush garden in a desk photo. Not short of a bob or two, I'd have expected him to rent a swish apartment or rural cottage while studying. And buy a decent bloody jumper, something better than the awful green, ribbed, military thing he lived in. It was gross. Like the burgers that formed his staple diet, it did nothing for his paunch. Tilly's warning that beefburgers were rich in grated cows' toenails hadn't deterred him, though it put me off McDonald's. My reverie was interrupted by Leo who was sitting next to me. Lycra Leo, as Sophie had christened him, took my hand in his.

'Judith, cara mia - how are you? Such a shock finding the professor's body, no?' He narrowed his eyes in the sexy way only Italian men can.

Reclaiming my hand, I smiled. 'I'm fine, Leo, I just want to be interviewed so I can go and meet Sophie.'

Leo rose to take his croissant from the oven. In profile he reminded me of his D. Phil. subject, though to be honest, I'd only seen Hadrian once, on coins in Glasgow's Kelvingrove Museum. Annoyingly, he was plastering thick butter on his flaking pastry. I'm envious of gluttons who stay whip thin, though admittedly he cycled and 'worked out' in the University Club gym. At thirty, he was the youngest and by far most attractive male in the house. Not that I was in the market. In any case, he changed women like socks; hard to keep up. His was the perfect room for entertaining, large with a forward-facing bay window, queen bed and sofa. Unlike mine: single window and bed, wooden-armed chair, and space to swing a small cat. But I didn't grudge him his amorous success. I wasn't here for romance, but for recovery and renewal. Or knowledge and enlightenment, even. Not sure how well that was going after five months.

A pile of papers thudded onto the table in front of me. I hadn't noticed Jon going out into the hall to retrieve the mail.

'This is mostly for you, Guy. Still no sign of the police coming out to question us. Ridiculous. What kind of a way is this to treat people, I ask you, eh? It's not as if any of us can be sodding suspects! How long is this going to take?'

Even before Cedric's death, Jon had been tetchy. Thursday night I'd heard an altercation at the front door. His partner Ted had shouted, 'That's us finished!' as he'd slammed the front door and left. Pity. I'd enjoyed the odd kitchen drink with Ted. Granted, they'd made an odd couple. Jon, an English Literature lecturer, religious and running-obsessed; Ted an atheist reader of graphic novels and lover of dirty jokes whose main exercise was bending his elbow as a bartender in the Turf. Watching Jon smoothing down his side-parted dark hair and extending his thin neck made me think of Lord Snooty from the *Beano*. My brain seemed to be preoccupied with films and comics.

As Jon started vigorously polishing his flamboyant red plastic glasses, I also wondered about him continuing to room in the Lodge. He was in his early fifties. Cedric had secured him a room here nine months ago after a fire destroyed his Jericho terrace house. Rumour had it there had been mysterious circumstances involving arson and insurer troubles. Typical Oxford gossip. I couldn't be sure what was true.

'I wonder if they'll let me go up to put on my running gear?'

I pointed out of the window. 'It's not a nice day for running, Jon. It's snowing.'

'When you're training for the Commonwealths, you get used to training in all weathers!' He glared, zipped up his grey woollen cardi, picked up Cedric's newly delivered *Daily Telegraph* and harrumphed behind the Review Section.

Typical Jon, never missing a chance to mention his medal. Funny he wasn't more upset about Cedric's death. He'd spent a lot of time with him.

Tilly started sobbing again. 'I don't understand, why would anyone want to kill Cedric?'

Jon lowered his magazine. 'In my opinion, he was asking for it. I told him putting his views in the press was playing with fire. It might be flattering to be asked for comment on Middle Eastern matters but criticising the stances of Western governments and advocating non-intervention is seen as inflammatory in many quarters.'

I was surprised to hear this. 'I thought his research involved ancient stuff?'

'Didn't you read his piece in the Guardian after his last Iraq visit? And then he gave an interview in the Telegraph. Should've stuck to commenting on ancient Babylon. Iraq nowadays is a minefield, or rather it's a big bloody oil field and we're after it!' He laughed at his own joke, though no one else smiled. 'It's oil that the West needs but the place has a dictator that won't play ball. Looks like we are going to get a modern crusade with Blair and Bush taking him out. Now, aren't they strange bedfellows?' He tapped at a frontpage photo of the grinning, hand-shaking pair. 'It will end in tears, mark my words.'

No one responded. I felt a sharp kick in my shin. Jon was directly opposite me and obviously the culprit, yet he neither acknowledged it nor apologised. Doubtless only an involuntarily jerk as he pontificated, but he obviously didn't care whether he'd kicked me or a table leg. Like so many down here, I considered him self-obsessed, arrogant, and opinionated. My hopes of mingling with clever academics altruistically seeking knowledge for the benefit of mankind were dwindling. I rubbed my shin, sat silently, and looked round the table at my housemates. They'd all been given nicknames by my daughter Sophie: Twittery Tilly, Burger Guy, Lycra Leo, and Did-I-Tell-You-I've-Got-a-Gold-Medal-Jon. She thinks her tendency to do this stems from her medical training where every patient's ailment must be classified into a box. I dreaded to think what she called me. But my favourite lodge mate was missing. Abbie. When the doorbell rang, I thought it might be her. It wasn't.

A young police officer ushered in a sobbing figure. I rose to pull out a chair.

'Come and sit here, Gwen.'

Cedric's secretary sat down heavily, her large leather handbag landing on the table, narrowly missing my mug. From films and comics my tired brain switched to theatre: Gwen's dramatic entry evoked Shakespeare at the Globe, all heaving-bosomed heroines declaring love and loss into the middle distance. I'd loved the Globe theatre and resolved to go again soon, but meantime, Gwen was offering plenty of melodrama in the kitchen.

'It's shocking, shocking! Who could want to harm my poor, dear Cedric?' The back of her hand flew to her forehead and tears flowed.

Surprised by her use of 'my Cedric,' I offered a box of tissues from a nearby fridge top. Snatching one, she rushed back out of the kitchen and across the hall. On hearing the toilet door bolt hitting home, I realised all sounds had become very loud to me, which was a worry. In the past, heightened sensitivity to tastes and smells had been precursors to migraines. I hoped that noise wasn't about to prove the same. Flashing lights and a thumping headache would finish me off. I didn't have any migraine tablets.

'Woman needs to get a grip,' Jon sneered, nodding toward the hall.

His mouth couldn't turn down any more at its edges if it tried. 'Don't be so harsh, Jon. She's worked with him for years.'

As his upturning nose revealed a very hairy nasal cavity I hadn't previously noticed, I looked away to Tilly, chewing her fingers and fidgeting. Guy was offering a stream of trite, reassuring platitudes. Leo was tapping on the oilskin tablecloth. Then he snapped.

'Why are English police so inefficient? We Italians would not tolerate this. Where is the magistrate?'

'Er, we don't bring magistrates to scenes of crime here, Leo.' At my answer, he raised his eyebrows. Very thick and dark, they were, more Al Pacino than Hadrian. Steve had loved *The Godfather* as much as I'd hated it. All that violence! I'd walked out of the cinema. Now I longed to walk out of the kitchen. No matter how hard I tried, waves of anxiety were cramping my chest and a blanket of fog was descending on my thinking. I closed my eyes, trying to conjure a yoga mantra, or to take myself to a 'happy place of my choice' as taught, but all that came was a maelstrom of actors and films and dead bodies. What in hell's teeth was I thinking of – a divorced English teacher from a Glasgow comprehensive, coming down here amongst these erudite academics? If only I'd been put in the main college accommodation to room alongside those jolly young undergrads that I'd heard at night singing on the way back from the pub I wouldn't be sitting with this shower next door to a corpse.

The ticking clock had advanced to eight-thirty. What were the police doing? To break the uncomfortable silence, I rose to turn on the radio, selecting Radio 2, usually at this time on a Saturday to be found broadcasting old hits. Hearing the song being played, Jon exclaimed, 'For God's sake!' Guy laughed. I was horrified to hear Marvin Gaye singing, 'Please don't procrastinate. It's not good to masturbate …' Unlikely lyrics that would be approved by the BBC, I'd have thought, but even before I could change channels, Gwen returned, clean faced and slightly more composed until she heard the music. 'What on earth is that?'

I switched it off and sat down again. This waiting about was intolerable. If ever there was a time to wish that *Star Trek's* 'Beam-me-up, Scotty!' machine wasn't science fiction, it was now. Then the doorbell rang again.

Scatty Scholars & Locked Doors

This new arrival didn't require assistance into the kitchen. It was glamorous Abbie, my scatty American Rhodes Scholar classmate.

Ms Abigail Goldman swanned in wearing what Sophie calls the 'clothes of shame'. Mascara-blurred eyes blinked above the diamante necklace, short black velvet dress, and white furry coat of last night's date. They told the story: Abbie had been out all night. She'd told me she was having dinner with a college master. Unfazed that he was thirty years her senior, she'd reassured me her private dinner with him wasn't inappropriate: he wasn't her supervisor. Nonetheless, he *was* from our department. Strolling past, Abbie tossed her sumptuous coat (a Christmas gift from her Manhattan banker daddy) onto the worktop, from whence it slid off onto the tiled floor. While Abbie filled the kettle, I lifted the coat to drape it over the back of a chair.

'Hi, guys. The cops just told me about Cedric. A bummer, eh?' Abbie flicked the kettle switch, poured a large glass of water, and downed it in one. I guessed it had been a long boozy night. 'Say, isn't this like an Agatha Christie movie? *Murder in the Lodge!*' Abbie aped shock with wide eyes and splayed hands either side of her open mouth. She then looked round the room. 'Oh, hi, Gwen. Where's Jared? Isn't he usually in on Saturdays?'

As Gwen now seemed in a trance, I answered, 'No idea.

Haven't seen him for days.'

'It beats me why he's still hanging about. As a Yank with an Oxford doctorate, he should be off to Harvard or out making his fortune,' Abbie shook her head.

Jon put down his paper. 'Nonsense. Being on staff for a year and receiving accreditation in Cedric's 'epic' book is an excellent career move for him. He's been a great asset to us, helping piece together Cedric's final Gilgamesh research, but it is annoying he has disappeared. This week, of all weeks.'

'I hope Jared isn't dead in his room too,' said Abbie, shaking her blonde curls.

Gwen shrieked hysterically. The rest of us glared at our animated housemate.

'Really, Abigail!' Jon looked over his glasses at her. 'Must you be so crass?'

Abbie raised her hands in surrender. 'Sorry! Only trying to lighten things up. I was just wondering if he might be able to throw some light on this … situation.' Her right hand made a flamboyant circle towards the study next door.

'It's shocking, shocking! Who could want to harm poor, dear Cedric?' Gwen shook her helmet of shining black hair.

'For goodness' sake, woman, you've said that already!'

'Shh, Jon! Come on, Gwen, let's get you some tea!' Tilly suddenly re-activated herself and got up to fetch a mug. I wondered if Gwen would actually get tea, but decided that, by the look of her, she wouldn't care if it was coffee.

'Do you know if they've told his wife and kid yet?'

Abbie's question set Gwen off again. 'Oh, poor Anna! Darling Ramin!'

Watching Abbie clattering kettles, mugs, and spoons while opening and closing all the cupboards in turn, I knew she was looking for whatever food she could plunder. Astonishingly, she hardly ever shopped. In fact, I doubted she knew where Tesco Metro was. I'd witnessed her receive couriered meals, but never once touch a cooker knob. Despite asserting her determination to live in college 'for the vibe' rather than 'living out' in a flat, she plainly had no idea about communal living; perhaps Harvard had maids?

'Say, anyone got some cookies?' Abbie looked round the room.

Jon went to the walk-in larder and tossed her a packet of Jaffa Cakes from his shelf. 'Do these pass muster as cookies?'

She smiled sweetly at him. 'Why thank you, kind sir!'

He grunted and disappeared behind the *Telegraph's* Financial Section.

'Miss Judith Frazer?' The question came from a police constable at the door. He lowered his clipboard and looked expectantly from Tilly at the kettle, to Abbie standing munching a Jaffa Cake, to me at the table.

I quietly said, 'Actually, it's not Miss, it's Mrs Frazer.'

'Sorry, madam, please follow me.'

In the hall, he led me into the windowless laundry room opposite mine. We'd suspected the police were commandeering it as an interview room when the faded brown moquette armchairs from beside the front door had disappeared inside it. My interviewer was sitting in one, hunched over a small folding card table I'd seen previously in the switch cupboard between Humphrey Hoover and the fuse box. With his elbows leaning heavily on it, the table appeared ready to collapse at any minute. Raising my eyes to the man himself, I was pleasantly surprised to find him quite young, with an open, smiling face, blonde hair and intensely blue – cobalt, even – eyes. He gestured to the unoccupied chair.

'I'm DCI Keith Steadman. Good morning, Ms Frazer.'

Well, 'Ms' was acceptable. So was he – polite, well-spoken, in a smart navy suit, white shirt, and spotted blue tie. This was no dishevelled Columbo or Frost. I gritted my teeth. What was it with me and films?

'So, I gather you were first on the scene? Can you tell me exactly what happened here last night – or rather this morning?'

My mind blanked. 'Em, from when?'

He smiled. 'Whenever you like.'

Closing my eyes, I took a deep breath, and started. 'I got home late, heard Cedric set the alarm, and presumed he'd gone home. Then I woke later – half past three – heard bumps in the night, then voices, and the sounds of rummaging from his room next door. Then heated discussions in a foreign language, and the patio doors being opened. After a while, it went quiet, and I went to the loo. While crossing the hall, I heard groans. At first, I wondered if Cedric was entertaining, er, a lady friend in – but that didn't seem likely, really. Well, he has a lovely wife.' The DCI raised one eyebrow. 'Then, from the loo I heard a car racing off. Going back passing his door again, I got worried as I thought I heard another groan, so I decided to check the study. With the door locked out there,' I pointed out through the open laundry room door into the hall, 'I headed outside to look in through the patio doors. I was worried anyway that they'd left them open – goodness knows who might come in.' I omitted my fear of mice as frivolous under the circumstances.

'The study door was locked? The attending constable said it opened from the inside.' Steadman frowned.

'Really? Well, it was locked then, I can assure you. It usually opens easily. I've been in many times. When Cedric's secretary is off, I take him a cuppa if I'm making one.'

'Can you tell me why the professor was here so late? Was that usual? And is it common for a professor to have a study in a college lodging house he doesn't live in?'

'Cedric often worked late. He is, or rather was, writing a book. He usually came in around ten am, stayed late, always said his "muse" was best after dark. As to whether a college house study is common for a non-resident, I don't know.

I've not been down here long.'

'I'm not clear why they have you people in here and not the college?'

'This Lodge was built a few centuries ago for another college. When Winston College was built in the sixties, they bought it for their master, but then changed it to lodgings for older postgrads. Tilly says it was originally one of the houses where the old "celibate" Oxford dons accommodated their mistresses and children up-river out of sight of their colleges.' I smiled. 'Our resident Italian, Dr Fabiani, says they were as bad as medieval Popes!'

Steadman grinned. 'Probably. But to finish your story, you went round outside?'

'Yes, and I found the French windows wide open.'

'Did you actually go inside the study?'

'Of course. When I saw him lying there, I checked to see if he was still alive, but wasn't completely convinced he had a pulse – I've got a St Andrew's First Aid certificate, by the way. I tried some CPR for a bit anyway, but really, I knew he'd gone. I mean his head … I thought maybe I'd only imagined the moans. And there was so much blood on the rug. It was a lovely rug from Turkey or Teheran or somewhere that he brought home recently, but his wife didn't like it, so he brought it here.' I paused when I saw he had stopped writing. 'Sorry, that's irrelevant. But to be honest, I felt it was probably hopeless, what with the blood and pink jelly bits on the carpet and the bust, or rather head – why are they called busts?' Steadman shook his head, giving me a small smile as if indulging a child. As he rested his chin on his hand and gazed at me, I was momentarily thrown, and felt I had to fill in the silence.

'It was Socrates, you know. Cedric was given it as some award. Anyway, deciding he had gone, I gave up, ran out into the garden, back in through the front door and called the Porter's Lodge from my room.'

'Not 999?'

'Sorry, no. You don't think properly when you're faced with something like this, do you?' The detective gave me a lopsided grin and flipped his notebook.

I bit my lip, which I always do when nervous, and tried to gather my thoughts. 'Anyway, Jimmy – he's Scottish too – said he'd come straight over. The room was a mess. We didn't touch anything. Jimmy phoned the police, and I went to wake everyone. Then the constables came. Abbie Goldman didn't answer – I now know she was still out. The others, Guy and Jon, got dressed and came down. Tilly came down but didn't dress, she was so upset. Oh, and Leo, Dr Fabiani, on the ground floor front next to me, he wasn't in, but he arrived soon after the others got up.'

'Right, now I know from the college list that Ms Abigail Goldman's a resident, but this other lady who's appeared ...' he looked at the clipboard, 'Gwen Black, who's she?'

'Cedric's secretary. He's also got an American assistant, Jared Kumar, whom we haven't seen all week. Oh ...' Suddenly I felt emotional. 'This is so awful. Have you told Cedric's wife? She'll be devastated.'

'Someone from the College and a WPC have gone to break the sad news. I'll see her later. But lastly, can I ask whether you know if the professor had any enemies?'

'Well, he once told me he'd had angry letters after writing some newspaper article – and Jon mentioned that just now too. But, I thought he always tried to be even-handed; debating, putting both sides of an argument, like a sort of diplomat. I mean, he even wrote in politically opposing papers like the *Guardian* and *Telegraph*. And if I ever overheard the odd, raised voice from his room, he'd always be the one sounding calm and reasoned in reply. That reminds me, I tried to hear what the folk in the study were saying, but most of it was in a foreign language. I'm not sure if there were one or two others apart from Cedric in the room, sorry! And I could only make out one word, *zawjata*.'

'What language is that?'

'Greek, perhaps?'

The DCI shook his head. 'And who usually visited Cedric here?'

'Gwen will know. I'm usually at classes or in the library during the week. And I've no idea about politics – nor what his book's about.' I had to shake my head and expect I wrinkled my nose as I often do when thinking. Steadman was smiling widely at me. He had nice even teeth. Steve's middle gap always annoyed me, but he wouldn't get it fixed. Terrified of dentists, the wimp. Trust me to be ruminating on orthodontics after a murder. 'Sorry, I'm not much help. I'm just a humble teacher taking a sabbatical.'

'Nothing humble about teaching. My wife taught History at Oxford Grammar. Still get cards from her old colleagues on ...' he paused to close his notebook before adding, 'her anniversary.'

My brain whirled again. That hesitation. He'd said 'her' anniversary, not 'ours.' So not a wedding anniversary. Then she must be ... and so he was ... I closed that train of thought guiltily, feeling nauseous and worn out. 'Is that all? May I go now? My daughter will be up in Summertown expecting me.'

'Sure. Here's my card. You know the score, anything else you think of, call me.'

I took it, shook hands, and left. In the hall an ashen Tilly passed me, looking as though she was approaching a noose or sacrificial pyre: arms crossed over chest, quivering hands clutching shoulders, kimono flapping, open-toed sandals clicking. Earlier she'd hinted at running out of Valium. God, she looked like she needed some. I wondered if Sophie could get her any from the hospital. The surgery would be shut. I knew you couldn't buy them in a chemist.

As I opened my room door, I heard the laundry door

quietly close behind Tilly, and felt something fire off in my fatigued brain. In the early hours as I went into my room to phone Jimmy, hadn't I heard a door closing? Not the one for the laundry room, but one further away? Suddenly, I was no longer tired.

Someone else had been up! Steadman was adamant the study door was unlocked, but I'd swear on my father's life it was locked when I'd tried it. Someone must have opened it whilst I was coming back round to phone the porter. Neither Abbie nor Leo had been home, but one of the others must have been out of their room in the wee small hours and I'd heard them closing their door.

But who?

Why unlock the study *after* the murder?

And how come they had a key for it?

4

White Vans, Brie & Joggers

Rushing round my room, I donned boots, coat, scarf, and gloves and went out of the front door. An icy blast of air hit me. I pulled my red woollen scarf up round my ears and hurried down the drive where a solitary woman PC, snowflakes clinging like dandruff to her navy-uniformed shoulders, was pacing at the gate, blowing into her bare hands. She looked frozen, but I suppressed the temptation to run back in to make her a cuppa, selfishly deciding I was already late – and had to get away.

At the crime-tape, I smiled and nodded, indicating I'd like to pass. The constable, who looked younger than Sophie, frowned. 'I am sorry, madam, you cannot leave.' Moving in between me and the gate, she raised an open palm in emphasis, but soon clenched her hand and lowered it into her pocket.

'DCI Steadman says I can go. I've given my statement and I'm late for meeting my daughter.'

The girl hesitated, removed her walkie-talkie, stared at it briefly then clipped it back onto her jacket. I was channelling my best assertive-teacher-mode: locked eyes, brisk nodding, encouraging smile. Eventually she shrugged. 'Oh, very well!' and unwound one end of the tape attached to the railing stumps on the wall.

I'd learned from a TV documentary that few such iron railings removed for 'The War Effort' were ever used for 'munitions.' Had these been sawn off for World War One or Two? Guy might know. Recognising another descent into the meaningless trivia that floods my brain under duress, I briskly stepped forward, comforted by the thought that doubtless some Oxford don had already researched *Utilisation of Railings Removed During World Wars*. Amazing the topics folk make their life's work. I thanked the poor police lass who attempted a smile. I felt sorry for her. Were her absent gloves due to cutbacks? I knew all about them from school.

Out of the gate I turned towards the main road, squelching in the deep, wet slush much churned by the boots of the occupants of the two parked panda cars and large police SOCO van now present. The initial car had been angrily shifted out to the street after Steadman had shouted about 'contaminating evidence,' though I doubted churned gravel would offer clues: I knew from TV's Lewis that farmyard mud was best for identifying vehicle tyre treads.

A plain white van was slowly approaching, its driver wearing a black anorak with the collar zipped up so far that it covered his mouth and nose. Surely it wasn't as cold as that in a modern Mercedes van? It had an odd lump on the roof at the back which I thought might be an aerial or some kind of refrigeration thing. As I watched it accelerate away, I noticed its rear number plate was thickly caked in hard mud, yet its hub caps and sills were clean. Odd. God, everything today was odd! Press, no doubt. Wouldn't be long till the place would be crawling with them. They'd find plenty of informants. I'd sussed academic Oxford was an incestuous society where news travelled like lightning. People in one college knew the goings-on in another often before its own occupants! I turned right into Banbury Road, the main north-south axis of the City, and quickened up. I was forty minutes late.

I had sent Sophie a brief text: 'Going to be bit late, sorry.' Not, 'Found corpse, giving police interview,' which

I'd decided was too alarming. I reached Summertown in ten minutes and was so desperate to meet Sophie that I ignored the pedestrian crossing only two hundred yards ahead and darted across the road between a baker's van and a taxi. It tooted. I stopped myself making a rude gesture: the driver probably had his own problems.

Sophie was sitting inside Summertown's Blue Café, a spent coffee mug beside her, making notes from a huge book which she put on a nearby chair as I arrived. Pointedly, she looked at her watch.

'Hi, Mum. Not like you to be so late!'

I bent to hug her and sat down opposite, my body sagging heavily into the cushioned vinyl chair. As a waitress arrived with a menu, I noted the hand I held out was trembling and tears started welling, so I waved the menu away, snatched down my shaky hand to clasp it in my lap and quickly said, 'I'll just have my usual tea and a bacon and brie panini.'

Sophie handed over her old mug and flashed a smile at the girl. 'Make that two.' As the girl left, she peered at me. 'Mum, are you crying?'

I gave a laugh that came out high-pitched and weird. 'Sorry, darling, don't know why I'm laughing. It's terrible.'

'I've never seen you so pale. You look like you've seen a ghost or something!'

'Maybe I have. Well, not a ghost exactly. A corpse. I found a body next door in the middle of the night.'

'You're kidding me?' Sophie's mouth fell open and her eyebrows disappeared into her strawberry blonde fringe.

'No. I truly found a body on the floor in Cedric's study. Socrates did for him.' As the noisy café suddenly went silent, I realised I'd been shouting.

Sophie waved hands like a conductor hushing musicians and whispered, 'Whose body?'

'Sorry. Prof. Cedric Gilbert, Jared's boss. I thought he'd gone home, but he must have come back, though I didn't hear him put off his alarm coming in. Though again, I might've – I was asleep. But, I heard it going on when I went to bed. It's got bleeps and a long buzz going on and three short ones going off.'

'Slow down, Mum.'

Irritated at Sophie talking to me like a child, I know I raised my voice. 'But when I woke, I heard bumps and groans, thought maybe he'd got a woman in with him, then I thought no, not with him married to lovely Anna, surely? Then a car drove off. I knocked on the study, got no answer. The door was locked – only they say it wasn't. Weird. So, I went outside to look in, as I'd heard the patio doors creak open but not close. Cedric should've got that WD40 … But there he was. On the floor. I tried a bit of CPR, but it was no use. I mean, his head! Socrates has a sharp edge on his base. Lots of stuff on the rug. Well, looked like a lot. How much blood and brain d'you have in your head – is it more than a pint? I did try to revive him, you know. Did my best. It's so horrible seeing a body dead, and blood like that. I do so admire you doing medicine, darling. You'd have known better what to do, I expect. Then I got Jimmy the porter to get the police while I got everyone up. I was questioned first. Everyone else is still there except Jared. Haven't seen him for days. Have you?' I finally stopped to take a breath.

Sophie leaned back and stared. 'God, what a thing! Jared? No, not seen him. I'm a bit cross. Since he went up to the US Embassy in London last Monday, I haven't heard a peep.'

'The embassy? Why?'

'Something to do with emails. He said it was a summons and he had to go. Last Sunday night we had a pizza and beer downtown with friends, but he hardly spoke all evening. He was *well* elsewhere. Walked me home, sat on the edge of the sofa biting his lip, insisting everything was fine when it obviously wasn't. Then he buggered off early leaving half of his beer, very out of character. Just gave me a brief kiss and

27

a muttered, "See you!"'

'Oh, dear. I thought you were getting on so well.'

'Mostly. He is gentle, kind, and funny, but he can piss me off sometimes. Like getting antsy when I can't go to some gig or other. It's all very well for him with his doctorate in the bag, but I'm on the run up to my finals and I'm swamped. Like this…' Watching her lift her three-inch-thick textbook, *Kumar and Clark's Clinical Medicine,* I wondered if the author was related to Jared. His father, Dr Kumar, was an eminent Boston physician. Sophie was shaking her head vigorously. 'You know, arts folk don't realise the sheer volume of stuff we medics have to memorise. They have it easy. I mean, Jared just lists references and makes up theorising waffle for his post-doc research while acting as Cedric's handmaiden.'

I refrained from pointing out that, being myself an arts student, this was mildly offensive. Nor that Cedric no longer had need of a handmaiden. 'Did you ask at college if he's left word about going to a conference or doing research somewhere for Cedric's book?'

'Then why not say so? I decided I wouldn't bother. Like, if he phoned, he phoned. But, by Wednesday I couldn't help phoning. I left voicemails and texts. Zero response. Then today I met his pal Nick outside the Bodleian. He hasn't seen him either. Maybe he's ill?'

'I'm sure there's a perfectly plausible explanation, darling. Why not pop into the college? I'll come with you. If he's there, then I'll leave you to it.' The café's comfortable chatter had resumed: other diners were no longer staring over. The waitress delivered our tea and paninis. I bit into mine, then had to wipe my fingers on a napkin. 'I love melted brie – it's as yummy and comforting as chocolate, only savoury.'

'Likely they stimulate the same endorphins … but, sorry, Mum, we digressed from your body discovery! What d'you think happened? Did anyone else hear anything?'

'Goodness knows. No one heard a thing. Jon wonders if some of Cedric's newspaper articles got folk aerated, but is that a reason for clonking someone stone cold dead?'

'Mummy, what's "tone-cold-dead"?' A toddler's voice at the next table caused his mother to gather up her bag and offspring and rush over to the counter to pay. I'd have done the same: toddler breakfast isn't the time to explain death.

'Och, it's a nightmare. Police are crawling all over the garden being meticulous, there's a frozen policewoman in the drive. I don't want to go home. Why don't we go back to the college, ask after Jared, then go shopping? My treat.' I twisted sideways and crossed my legs.

Sophie started to laugh. 'Maybe we should buy you some new boots?'

I looked down in horror. On my left foot was a brown knee-length boot. On my right, a boot slightly shorter – and black! To compound this insanity, the left boot had a higher heel than the right, although I hadn't been aware of any disparity in gait during my ten-minute walk to the café. I was losing it. No hope. Brain in meltdown.

'Oh, after I was interviewed, I rushed in to pull on boots and my coat. Remind me about my trainers. I should stuff them with paper since they got soaked out in the garden. Or, on second thoughts, I'd best bin them. They got a bit bloody from the carpet. God, I feel such a fool with odd boots. I was so harassed I didn't look in the mirror or put on the big light.' I tugged at my woollen skirt, vainly attempting to pull it down over my knees and hide the disparate boot tops.

'Oh Mum! Let's nip back and get a matching pair before we do anything, eh? You'll put your spine out walking on different heel heights!'

'Tilly's in a right state, you know. Is there any chance you could get her some Valium?'

'Valium?'

'Yes, she's run out.'

'Sorry, no way. Maybe she should see someone?'

Sophie did her best to distract me by chatting about other things. It was almost noon and a second pot of tea later when I called for the bill and my phone rang. The unknown number turned out to be Gwen. Surprising. She'd never phoned me before.

Across the table Sophie was mouthing, 'What's up?' but I waved her to keep quiet, trying to concentrate on the call but at the same time hold my phone away from my ear, as Gwen was shouting.

'Fine, of course I'll take you. Don't worry, Gwen, I'm sure they'll be fine. Calm down. See you soon.'

'Well?' Sophie opened her purse to pay the bill, now on the table.

'It's OK, I've got it!' I put down money. 'There. I've left a tip too. Come on. Quick boot re-assortment and then I'm for the Radcliffe Infirmary. The police found Cedric's wife and son unconscious at home. Seems he was kidnapped from home. The hospital got Gwen's number and she got mine from Abbie.'

At the café door Sophie asked, 'Had they been bashed on the head too?'

Following, I answered, 'No. They got chloroformed, Gwen said.'

'Seriously? Where would they get that nowadays?'

'No idea. I'm not medical, remember, as you're always telling me. Anyway, Anna "came to" and asked for Gwen. They're quite pally, I think. Gwen was in bits this morning even before hearing about Anna. She's right not to think of driving. She's erratic at the best of times – and the only person I know who's got a ticket for driving too slowly!'

'Never!'

'Anyway, I'll get out the Mini and take her to the Radcliffe. Must say it's all very intriguing.'

'Oh, Mum! It sounds more dangerous than intriguing. Be careful. What is going on?'

'No idea. But you go off and see if you can find Jared and I'll mop up the remains of Gwen and take her to poor Anna.'

'Don't say "remains", Mum. Gwen's not dead!'

'Och, Sophie, it's a figure of speech. We lazy arts students like to use them.'

Soon we were at the corner of Hycombe Road where a tall *Leylandii* hedge formed a blind corner. We didn't see the jogger coming, nor did he see us. Head down, jacket hood flopped down over his eyes, as the figure hurtled into me, I staggered and nearly fell.

Sophie yelled, 'What d'you think you are doing? Look where you're going!' before grabbing his arm, twisting it, and spinning him round. Despite the assailant being a head taller, she was able to push him back and tug down his hood.

'Atta girl!' I thought. Sophie's self-defence classes hadn't been a waste of money. Another thing Steve had been wrong about. However, my smile faded when I saw who'd cannoned into us. 'Jon, you bloody idiot, I thought you were a mugger!'

'Watch where you're going. You could have hurt Mum!' Sophie, now stood with one hand on her left hip and the other wagging a finger like a teacher at a naughty schoolchild. I know. I've done it often.

'Sorry, I was running off my anger at the stupidity of the police.'

'Stupidity?'

'Uneducated plods the lot of them. But now I've met you, a word of advice. If you are going home, it might be best to go in the back door. The press are lying in wait at the front of the Lodge. Gwen is waiting for you in the kitchen, Judith. She is devastated about Mrs Gilbert being hurt too.'

'It's awful.' I stretched up and bent forward to retrieve my bag from the slush.

'I hope you are all right.' Jon tentatively patted my arm. 'I am sorry.'

'I'm fine, Jon, just winded. Get on with your run, but please watch where you are going.'

'I will. As if Tilly's hysteria isn't bad enough, Gwen thinks someone is out to assassinate all of us. She is adamant someone was following Cedric – and her too. I suggested it was Mossad, but she said she didn't think that was funny.' He laughed. 'But Cedric ruffled so many feathers. Wouldn't surprise me.' Running on the spot a few times as if winding himself up, he shot off, bright orange trainers flashing up and down, elbows pumping, re-hooded head bobbing as he chuckled and hummed.

Sophie stared after him as he ran full tilt into the swirling snow. 'Why does he think this is even remotely funny? Do you think all academics are mad? I am seriously concerned about your housemates, Mum. I thought Lycra Leo was bad enough.'

I brushed off some slush before re-slinging the wet bag over my shoulder and taking Sophie's arm to hustle her across the road. 'I don't know why Jon's still running at his age. Though I've noticed loads of folk down here do. Are they seeking eternal youth? Suppose he might be after veteran's medals, or something. Then there's Leo cycling the Tour de Oxford daily in that ridiculous bandana. He never wears a helmet.'

'If he came to Casualty and saw the cycling head injuries I've seen, Leo might be less worried about appearing uncool.' Sophie peered round the corner of the street. 'Still, Jon's right about avoiding the front door. There are cars, vans and a gathering crowd outside the Lodge!'

'We can go down to the back lane along the river and round. I've got a garden door key, come on!' I started to walk briskly.

'Slow down, Mum. Ye Gods, how can you walk so fast

when you are waddling?'

I slackened my pace. 'These boots *are* going for my back. I feel imbalanced – not that my housemates are any better! D'you think other elite unis are as full of eccentrics? Who said, "There is no great genius without a hint of madness"? Was it Aristotle? Or Socrates?'

'Oh, Mum, whoever it was, I bet they're dead! Let's get your boots sorted, then you sort out Gwen, and I'll try to find Jared.' Sophie paused to look left at the next road junction. 'Is this the road that connects with the river path?'

'Next one, Sophe. This is a dead end. Ha, you never think about saying "dead" so nonchalantly till something like this happens, do you?'

'No.' Sophie smiled weakly.

'How funny Gwen thought they were being followed. She's never mentioned it to me. Yeugh!' I stopped as I was fulsomely sprayed in slush by a speeding van. 'Hey, I think that's the white van I saw earlier. Bet it's bloody press!' To this driver I did give a single finger.

Sophie laughed, 'Oh, Mum! You're as bad as dad!'

'Well, he's right about it making you feel better!' I managed to brush the slush easily off my coat. 'This Gore-Tex was a sound investment. But oh, dear, your new parka!'

Sophie swiped ineffectually at the muddy splodges. 'Mibbe it'll brush off when it's dried.'

'What a weird day. But seriously, Sophe, who'd be following Cedric? His life was lecture, home, study, home, with occasional sorties to meetings or libraries. What's to spy on?'

'Well, Jared says he goes abroad a lot, especially out East. Maybe he did some spying?'

'Cedric, a James Bond? Now that would be funny!'

I was still smiling when we reached the back garden door of No. 48. Sophie hugged me and hurried on down the riverside towards the college.

5

A Boorach & Anna's Story

Jimmy unlocked the door and looked round before stepping inside. He threw his arm out.

'There you are dearie. Mr Kumar isnae here.'

In truth, when she'd knocked earlier, Sophie hadn't expected to find Jared home, and certainly not now after porter Jimmy had hammered on it with his large fist shouting, 'Hello! Mr Kumar – you in there?'

Jimmy MacTavish returned the master key to his pocket and looked round. 'My God, it's a right boorach in here!'

Hearing her Ayrshire grandmother's word for 'untidy mess' would normally have amused Sophie, but today her heart thumped as she took in the scene while Jimmy poked about. Standard college: cream walls, grey carpet, modern fitted furniture. But chaotic.

'Wi' that *Do Not Disturb* notice hung on the door the cleaners havenae' been in. Ah'll ask them when they last did the room. But they widnae know where tae start the day!'

A right boorach described it. Sophie took in the still made-up bed, bottom end of duvet tucked in as was Jared's way, but the pillows lying at odds with the headboard and the mattress sitting slightly higher at the front than the back. Had it been lifted from its wood-framed base and hastily replaced? There was no knowing when the bed had last been slept in. The floor was home to an untidy mess of papers and press cuttings that looked like they'd spilled off the pile

34

on the desk. Box files lay open, empty. This mess was not one of simple untidiness, and definitely not like Jared. Her anxiety rose by the minute. The phone lay buzzing on the floor. Desk drawers were closed, but when she checked, they were empty. From the chest of drawers beside the bed, a sock poked out of one drawer, a T-shirt from another. The shelf contents were all askew. Jared was super-tidy, a fan of neatly folded jumpers in uniform piles on shelves and socks aligned in drawers. They'd laughed about it. He'd never leave drawers clumsily closed, even if he'd left in a hurry. But why would he have had to? Jimmy was standing pensive, hands clasped behind his back. Shaking his head as she asked him, 'Has anyone apart from me asked for a master key this week?'

He shook his head. 'Naebody's asked me fur wan, but ah've been on nights all week. Should be hame noo but the usual guy's no' arrived and that detective chappie's comin' for me tae sign some statement. Terrible thing. Ye know, Sophie lass, yer mither was brave this morning trying to save the poor professor. Did well. Give her ma best, won't ye?'

'I will. But now I'm convinced Jared is in trouble. He'd not leave this mess. Can you find out if anyone else has been seen coming in here? Or if anyone asked for a key?'

'Ah'll ring roon' the boys. But if someone was locked oot their room, even if we know who they are, the rule is to ask for ID. Could Jared have given someone his key?'

With her heart rhythm now consisting of hopping, skipping, and jumping with an occasional heavy-footed thump, Sophie answered. 'Doubt it.' In his clothes closet, there was nothing missing that she could see. Having stayed over many times, she knew, roughly, the extent of his wardrobe. A few of her things hung in the wardrobe. Ominously, his backpack and suitcase were still in the cupboard behind the door: he hadn't packed to go anywhere. Had he even been back here since leaving for London five days ago? Obviously, someone had ransacked his room – but when and why?

Looking round, she saw that the three pins on his wallboard held only ragged paper shards. She racked her brain. Two photos had been torn off: one had been of Jared with his volunteering team last summer, one with his mum, dad, and brother. And there had been a newspaper cutting about his father winning some award – but why take them? Her brain was churning as badly as her stomach. What to do? She jumped as Jimmy nudged her.

'His laptop's nae here.' He pointed at its lead connected to the college ethernet point.

Sophie bit her lip. 'He'd never take it without its lead. Nor this.' She lifted a black laptop case from the floor. 'He *always* puts it in this. It's a new Apple. Oh, dear!'

'OK. So, I havenae seen him fur days, nor you, nor that pal o' his ye met, eh? Ah'm phonin' the polis.' Jimmy's big eyebrows knitted together as he stooped to pick up the phone on its cord then stopped himself. 'Ah think this is a burglary if nothin' else, so best we dinnae touch anything.'

As Jimmy sped off to his gatehouse lair, Sophie sat on the bed. Tears formed as she whispered, 'Jared, where on earth are you?'

*

After leaving Sophie, I let myself into the back garden of the Lodge. On the grass, the police had left numbered tags that were gradually being obliterated by the falling snow. What could they have found that was worth mapping out? The kitchen door sprang open to reveal Gwen in her customary navy angora hat, belted camel coat, and red leather gloves.

'Hold on, Gwen. I need to get a boot.' I pointed at my mis-matched footwear.

Gwen's worried expression changed to a smile. 'Oh dear! I suppose we are all bit distracted today.' She returned to sit in the warm kitchen, where only Abbie remained.

After I had changed one boot, lifted my car keys, and was returning to the kitchen, PC Clipboard appeared with Abbie, who was chatting merrily. She winked as she passed. Abbie thrived on drama. Going into the kitchen, I shook my head.

Gwen stood up at once. 'Right, shall we go? When we get there, we'll need to check what ward they've put them in. Anna said they'd be moving now they're satisfied her head injury isn't serious.'

'That's great. But hang on, we'll need change for those hospital parking machines.' I had started dipping into my coat pockets and the zip compartments of my bag.

'Ridiculous, profiting from visitors to the sick!' Gwen pulled her fluffy beret down over her ears before opening her voluminous handbag at a wild angle. 'It's fine, I've got lots of pound coins.'

By the look of it she had lots of everything from knitting needles to narcotics. Three pill bottles sat amongst tissues, a torch, and a banana of dubious vintage. Two large spec cases hit the floor. Yet Gwen didn't wear glasses! More oddities. The one I picked up rattled. Sweets, I thought: Gwen was never far from a barley sugar. We hurried out and along the towpath past the punts towards the college car-park.

After sitting out in the cold for a week, it took a while to coax the car into life. I didn't often drive here. After several parking fines from confusing, varyingly ruled zones in the same streets, I'd decided Oxford was not a car-friendly city. Even Jon had sold his Jaguar and now ran or cycled everywhere. Cycling wasn't for me either. First term, after a frightening incident with a taxi, I'd given my new bike to Sophie. I only used my car for weekend runs to Waitrose – and a trip to A&E after slicing my hand instead of a pineapple. That hospital visit had meant another parking fine: I'd underestimated the time it would take for a few stitches. I preferred now to walk everywhere. And buy chopped pineapple.

Driving to the hospital, I asked. 'What's this about Cedric being followed, Gwen?'

'Oh, he thought a funny bearded man was following him – and once I thought he was watching me too – but it was probably only coincidence.'

'Why would anyone want to follow him?'

'No idea. I hoped he was imagining it, maybe being extra-tense as he was near the end of a project. Last week he even accused me of re-arranging his papers – as if! But oh, he was such a lovely man.' Gwen dabbed her eyes. 'His book is lovely too. I do hope we can get his laptop back soon. I suppose police always take computers away to inspect them, don't they? We need his last edit. Mine and Jon's copies are a few weeks old.'

'Surprised Jon wasn't more upset. I thought they were close.'

'Oh, indeed. Did you know they were students together years ago? Cedric did so value his advice, you know. Said there was no one like Jon for editing. But I'm sure Jon is upset. It's just that he's quite a closed person. Probably as grief-stricken as me but doesn't show it.' Gwen sniffed.

I turned into the hospital car-park. 'Perhaps if you asked, the police might give you copies of the files you need?'

The car-park was pretty full, with many cars abandoned over the lines, leaving unusable spaces. Twice, smirking 'smart alecs' nipped into spaces that I was about to reverse into. I eventually bagged a place by getting Gwen to stand in a gap. My mood wasn't helped by skidding in the slush as I got out of the car. But remembering why I was there sobered me: there were worse things than a wet bum. After the reception desk found Anna and Ramin's ward, we wound our way through the corridors to find them.

Anna lay exhausted in bed in a single room. Ramin, wearing an oversized adult hospital dressing gown, sat at her side looking younger than his thirteen years and, with his blue-black hair and russet eyes, very like his mother. Watching him stroking Anna's hand, I felt my throat close.

'Oh, Anna!' Gwen plonked herself down on the white counterpane of the bed. Looking round to see if any officious nurses were in sight to chide her, I saw only a uniformed policeman, lidded coffee cup in his hand, about to sit on a chair in the corridor.

'So good to see you, Gwen – and Judith!' Anna clutched Gwen's arm and turned moist eyes towards me. I awkwardly patted her free hand before taking a chair opposite Ramin.

From her bed perch, Gwen demanded, 'So, what happened? What's this all about?'

'Take it easy, Gwen.' I nodded towards Ramin, looking very anxious.

Anna sighed. 'Oh, it's all right, Judith. Everyone wants to know what happened. But I'm so muddled. I remember waking with a noise. Cedric went down to see what it was. I thought Eli had got out of the kitchen and knocked something over in the lounge as I heard him yelp. Oh, dear, Gwen, I forgot all about Eli – will you go and check him? His food's in the hall cupboard. He has a can a day, split into two servings, a bowl of dry food, and of course water. Could you take him out for a walk perhaps? I hope he hasn't made a mess by now. Or could you take him home till they release us?'

Gwen anxiously nodded. 'Of course. Feed Eli, surely.'

'Jane next door at number six has a key'.

'Fine. But Anna, who were these men?'

'No idea. Couldn't see their faces.'

'So how did you get hurt?'

Anna leaned into her pillows. 'Hearing arguing and raised voices, I got up to go to Ramin's room, trying to think how we could escape if we had to – maybe out onto the garage roof from the spare room? But as I opened Ramin's door, someone hit me from behind. Next thing I knew I was lying on the landing with a policeman shaking me. Then we were in an ambulance coming here.'

'How terrible. And you, Ramin, what did you see happen?'

The boy shrugged. 'I woke up with a man standing over me wearing a dark hoodie and a black scarf up over his nose. He spoke to someone outside the bedroom door in Arabic. Mine isn't good, but I think he said, "Here, take the knife and clean it". Then he pressed a disgusting smelly cloth over my nose and mouth. I couldn't breathe and tried to fight him off. But I blacked out as the other man was tying my hands and feet together. Like Mum, I woke up with a policeman helping me up.' He shook his head. 'I couldn't think straight and had a terrible headache.' Ramin dropped his head. 'They've said the smelly stuff was chloroform. But why did they kill Dad?' He started crying. Gwen crouched down to hug him. I wondered if I should fetch a nurse to get him a sedative.

Anna looked straight at me. 'I heard you found him, Judith. The police won't tell me anything, only that he's dead. What did they put him through? I mean, did they stab him?'

'No. It was probably instant. He was knocked out in the study.' No point in mentioning groans. Nor spilled brains.

Gwen released Ramin and poured him a glass of water from the bedside jug before returning to her perch. 'But what do you think this is all about, Anna?'

'No idea, Gwen.' She shook her head and looked up at the ceiling.

Gwen persisted. 'Judith says the study was ransacked. What were they looking for?'

'I don't know. They made a mess at home too. The police are baffled.'

'Did Cedric tell you someone was following him? He

even had me imagining it!'

'Really? No, he never said. But one thing I do know. The men in the house were arguing with Cedric in Arabic.'

'Did you catch anything they said?' Gwen persisted.

Anna lay back closing her eyes. 'No.' Her chest began heaving. 'Oh, Cedric – what will I do without you?' Tears ran down her cheeks as she turned her face into the pillow.

I leaned across the bed to tap Gwen's arm while nodding towards the door. 'I think we should leave Anna and Ramin to rest now.'

During Gwen's questioning I'd had an uneasy feeling that something other than sorrow had passed over Anna's big brown eyes. Fear? Or was I merely fanciful and overwrought after my own sleepless night? An old memory popped into my mind: young Davie McIvor, that 'eye-avoidance' look he adopted when asked to admit to some misdeed. For him it signified fear his violent father might learn of it. But for Anna, what might she be afraid of? I decided she'd had enough probing questions and moved to practical considerations. 'Is there anything you need, Anna? You can't have had a chance to bring stuff in.'

Anna sat up slightly, gently moving Ramin's head from her shoulder. 'Perhaps toothbrushes and toothpaste?'

Gwen rose to lift her bag. 'I haven't got those, but …' From her bag to my amazement, she produced paper hankies, bottled water, a *Marvel* comic, and a bag of M&Ms. Ramin perked up.

Anna smiled. 'They've said we might get home tomorrow, but we only have these hospital gowns. The police even took our nightclothes away in bags. So clean clothes, please, Gwen? And warm jackets, I think. As I said, Jane has a key. Feel free to rummage in our drawers. And perhaps my handbag from the hall with my phone – it might need charged?'

'Right, leave it to me. I'll come back tonight.'

Anna pushed herself up to sit and hold Ramin's hand. 'Thank you, Gwen. And Judith. I'm sorry, but I am tired now. And the police are coming back later.' She nodded towards the door. 'The nurses tell me we have a guard in the corridor. The police must think we are at risk. They have brought that bed in for Ramin.' She pointed at a folding bed against the wall. 'Everyone has been so kind.'

I squeezed Anna's hand and gave Ramin a hug. As we left, the police officer stood up.

'Names, addresses and relationship to the patient, please?' His pen was poised at a clipboard.

I felt cross. Some guard he was. He'd obviously buggered off for a coffee earlier. I was about to give him a piece of my mind when Gwen beat me to it.

'You're not much of a guard for Mrs Gilbert, are you?' The constable stared. 'So, where were you when we arrived? We could have been assassins!' Gwen growled this in a stage whisper, glancing back to the room in case Anna or Ramin might hear.

He blushed. 'If you would just give me your name, madam?'

Gwen gave him her name and details, plus a diatribe about staying at his post or 'his superiors would be informed'.

Quickly giving mine, I ushered her along the corridor, worried I had underestimated the time we'd need for our visit when buying the parking ticket. We made it with five minutes spare. The gods were with us. Then.

*

Back in Winston Hall, blue-gloved police were searching Jared's room while an irritated Sophie stood outside in the corridor answering the same questions from a detective that she'd already taken from a uniformed constable. 'I told you, Jared last phoned Sunday night, said he was going up to London to the US Embassy in the morning and he'd call when he got back. But he didn't. No, he can't have just gone off on some jaunt as you suggest, his overnight bag and case are still in there, no clothes are missing and, more importantly, his beard trimmer is on the shelf in the bathroom. He'd never go anywhere overnight without it – nor his electric toothbrush. And his expensive Apple laptop has gone, though its connection lead and case are still there. He always takes them with him to the library. Oh, and the porter checked – his distinctive American bike's still chained up outside college, so he's not sped off on that.'

'All right, we'll look into all of this. May I have your contact details, please?'

As Sophie spelled out her name, address, and mobile number, the detective regarded her thoughtfully. 'By any chance are you related to Mrs Judith Frazer over in Winston Lodge?'

'Yes, she's my mother. That's how I met Jared. He works for the professor who's been murdered. She's on an Education Masters, and I'm in Youngman College doing Medicine.'

'Thank you for your help here and tell your mother I hope she's recovered from her upsetting morning. Here's my card if you think of anything else unusual that happened or that you think might be useful to us.' He smiled and walked back into Jared's room. 'Right, lads, anything of note?'

Sophie wondered if she'd heard correctly. Had this DCI Steadman just asked after her mother though they'd only met that morning? Hmmm. Despite the circumstances, she smiled: he was a bit of all right, this guy. No wedding ring either. She'd hoped her mother would find some fun after her rat of a father had done the dirty and departed. In her view, he was more to blame for what happened than Aunt Maggie. Sophie hurried off to the Lodge. Her mother should be back from the hospital by now and should know what had happened to the prof's wife and son. A 'rum do' – like Jared's disappearance.

6

Prowlers & Shadow Whisperers

A search of my freezer drawer only yielded an old M&S lasagne from last term. It would have to do. I was much too tired to go shopping. By six I was worrying there'd been no word from Sophie. Then the doorbell rang. To my delight it was Sophie, armed with carrier bags and a large flat box.

'Hi, Mum!'

'I've been trying to get you all afternoon. What's happened – did you find Jared?'

'No. I've spent the afternoon with the police. But here.' She handed me the box. 'Practicalities first. No idea what you were doing for tea, but I thought we could heat this up with some garlic bread. I nipped along to Marks.'

'You're a saviour, Sophe. Great idea. All I have is a past-its-sell-by-date lasagne!'

'I'm not sure I'm hungry myself.' Sophie went into the kitchen and switched on the oven. While searching for an oven tray, she recounted the state of Jared's room and the missing laptop. 'I think something awful has happened to him. He wouldn't just disappear.'

'It can't be a coincidence, what with Cedric's death, can it?'

'Doubt it. Oh, there's a Chianti in that carrier bag.' Sophie pointed and sat down wearily.

'Good girl, Sophe. I could do with a drink.' I fetched two glasses and uncorked the wine. 'I'll let it breathe for a bit.'

'Sod that, just pour it!' Sophie waved at the glasses.

Putting the giant pepperoni pizza and bread in the oven, I crammed the wrapping into the overflowing bin before sitting beside Sophie and lifting a glass. 'Right, here's to finding Jared safe and well – and catching Cedric's murderer!' I took a sip. 'Speaking of police, did they come to the college, or did you have to go to the station?'

'Your porter friend Jimmy phoned them. He's a lovely bloke, thinks you're a star, by the way! Then I spent ages reciting the same stuff about when I'd last seen Jared et cetera to two different police guys. But, now there's a thing, you've got another admirer apart from the bold Jimmy!'

'What?'

'A nice blue-eyed DCI heard my name, put two and two together, and asked *so* kindly for you. What's that about? Reckon you're on a promise there!'

'Hey, remember I'm your mother! It's about nothing. You don't half talk tosh sometimes, Sophie.' I could feel my face heating up. Inwardly I felt a disquieting warm glow which I tried to suppress. 'I wonder where everyone is tonight?'

'Don't change the subject, that Steadman chap's nice. You could do worse.'

'Leave it, my girl, or we'll fall out.' She might be right, but now was not the time. 'Seriously though, this house is like a morgue tonight.'

Sophie went into peals of laughter. 'Mum, really? A morgue? Don't even joke about morgues. Wait – someone is in!' She pointed to the ceiling. 'No guesses what they are up to!'

I cocked my head to listen. 'First time I've heard anything from upstairs. That's Guy's room.'

Sophie grinned widely. 'He's "at it" with Tilly on that sofa in the corner, I think. I noticed it was on wheels. Very precarious!'

'Well, at least he's not bonking to opera like Leo.' I rose

to get plates and napkins.

'That Leo better watch out you know – with all that tight Lycra he's heading for infertility.'

'Silly. But what's Lycra to do with fertility?'

'Overheating testicles reduces sperm counts,' said Sophie airily.

'Full of fascinating medical facts, aren't you? That reminds me, I meant to ask. Why does Tilly bother that her sleeping pills are gelatine-free? Can you be allergic to gelatine?'

'No, it's a veggie thing. Sort of, *no animal has been harmed in the making of this pharmaceutical.*'

'Right. I wonder if she got any Valium in the end?'

'She'd be better off doing that more often.' Sophie pointed upwards as the squeaking rhythm quickened. 'Sex is less addictive than Valium for reducing stress, I reckon. Though I think she could do better than Guy. I wouldn't trust him further than I could throw him. Something about the way his eyes bore through you, d'you know what I mean? Tilly needs someone more sensitive than Burger Guy.'

'Not sure Lycra Leo was any better.'

'I saw him cycling away from Marks tonight with a bottle of fizz. Said he was off to meet some 'Natalia' in Jericho. But he'll have to watch that tight Lycra – be infertile by the time he's forty. That's why testicles hang down from the body, you know – keeps them cool.'

'Well, you're lucky to be born then. Your dad liked tight jockeys!'

'Mum – too much information!'

I grinned at Sophie's face. 'Anyway, I do wonder where everyone is tonight. They're usually in by now.'

'Abbie'll be out with some old duffer.' Sophie checked the garlic bread. 'Or with a giggling gang holding court, melodramatically describing her police interview.'

'Och, she's OK, I like her.'

'So do I, actually. Come on, Mum, let's escape and do something tomorrow– maybe go for a pub lunch somewhere? I can show you some places I've cycled to with Jared.'

'Sounds good, as long as I'm back in time to finish my essay.'

'Why don't we leave at eleven, have a walk then an early lunch? I've got cases to write up myself. Cancer ones. Bit depressing. Let's watch something on telly tonight – what's on?'

'There's a Morse…'

'Ha! We could do with him!'

The cooker buzzer went. Sophie dished pizza. I poured more wine. Generously. Then I remembered that I'd saved a bottle of Sancerre in my room for special occasions. Deciding tonight was one, I fetched it to chill. As I tackled my pizza, I heard footsteps coming down the stairs and looked out to see Jon walking towards the kitchen before glancing in, then abruptly turning on his heel and exiting the front door.

Looking after him Sophie grimaced. 'Hey, not your number one fan, is he? Snooty git!'

We laughed. In the end, we watched Morse, finished the second bottle of wine, and had a few whiskies. Sophie wobbled home on her bike, and I fell into bed, asleep within minutes.

*

At one o'clock Sophie woke in her empty double bed with an ache deep in her chest. Cedric was dead. Jared was missing. All the wine in the world hadn't salved her distress. She didn't get back to sleep. Next evening, Sophie thought Cowley Road seemed longer than the last time she'd walked home from the city centre. It might be related to the three gin and tonics and bottle of red wine she'd shared with her mother in The Turf. Or the fact that she hadn't eaten much since brunch many hours earlier. Two packets of chilli crisps hadn't soaked up much alcohol, but with her stomach anxiously churning about Jared, she couldn't face the pub chicken and chips enjoyed by her chums and mother. She was glad Mum had come. Chloe and the girls had been a distraction with their 'worst-ever-date' stories that had become wilder and more lurid as the shot tally had risen.

Despite her preoccupation with Jared, she'd admitted to disastrous dates of her own. Like in first year there were Jackson and Gordon: Jackson a New Yorker, Gordon a Londoner. Both, it transpired, annoying, self-centred, keep-fit fanatic fools. Then came Alphonse the Gorgeous, a handsome hairdresser. She'd never looked better, but soon bored of his obsession with society gossip and TV soaps. This time with Jared though, she'd hoped it might be different. He too was nice-looking, but more caring, thoughtful, amusing, and intelligent – everything she now realised she valued. Till he buggered off. Perhaps he was no different from the other dickheads who'd dumped her and were already bunking up with someone new. She felt angry, then cross at herself for caring. But she did.

At her gate, she turned in. She'd not be writing up work tonight; too late, too tired. What a weekend! The house was in darkness with Jackie back in Bristol. Sophie hated being alone, doubtless a factor in her hasty, sequential, mostly disastrous, relationships. But Jackie had had to go home, her gran sounded very poorly. Shame. A girls' chat over a cup of chamomile before bed would have been just what the doctor ordered. She sighed. Life was hard. Lately she despaired of ever qualifying. So much work to get through before finals. And this weekend she'd done diddly-squat.

At the door she swore when her key wouldn't turn in the lock, then panicked she was at the wrong door: these terrace houses all looked the same in the dark. Jackie had once famously caused a ruckus trying to get into next door after a heavy night out. Sophie stood back. Nope. This weedy front garden was theirs: her very own magnificent nettles were poking up through the snow beside that daft gnome Jackie won in a pub quiz. And the door said, '12 and 2 screw holes.' The landlord had never replaced the 6 in 126. She and Jackie were damned if they'd pay for it. Sunny took enough money in rent and still hadn't fixed the broken bathroom towel rail.

Without thinking, she tried the handle. The door swung silently inward. Adrenaline kicked in. Had she forgotten to lock it this morning when heading out to meet Mum? Unlikely. After a spate of local break-ins, she and Jackie had become security conscious. Not that they'd much to nick! She closed her eyes, recalling pocketing her key after locking the door as she had set off. Shit, they must have been burgled! That would put the finish on this awful weekend. Her precious laptop would be gone for sure. Exhaling throatily, she looked round at the street. Loads of folk about. Almost midnight. As a student town, Oxford kept busy till the small hours. She could risk entering. If there was anyone inside, someone outside would hear if she yelled blue murder. Or might it be that Jackie had returned early? She could be in the kitchen with the door closed.

Briskly, she pushed the outside door fully open, stepped into the hall through the inner glass one and called, 'Hello? Jackie, you home?' The light switch didn't work. A loud, 'The fuses gone again?' brought no answer, but there was a noise. From upstairs.

Someone was moving about. But no voice reached her, no lights went on. Glancing back at the street she decided it couldn't be a power cut; the streetlights and the take-away across the road were lit up. Bloody trip switch again! Sunny had to get an electrician. Fires started from dodgy electrics. As a rhythmic creaking reached her ears, a cold tingle moved up her back. Footsteps were hitting the last two loose-boarded steps of the upper flight. Stepping back out over the threshold onto the coir mat she shouted, 'Who's there?' in a voice sounding authoritative and firm. She didn't feel it. A lithe dark-hooded figure was running down towards her with something in their hand. The light from the neon across the road wasn't sufficient to illuminate their face. Her heart stopped.

*

Taking off my boots, I lay on my bed with a groan. What a surreal day. We'd had a lovely drive out to the Cotswolds for a pub brunch, but I knew I shouldn't have agreed to go back out to the Turf with Sophie after we came back, nor left the Mini at college to get the bus down. Meant I'd been too ready to accept drinks with Sophie and her classmate – and abandoned my shots rule again. Problem with tequila is that after the first couple you decide it isn't so bad after all. No point in guilt; done now. And after all the horror of bodies, hospitals and disappearing boys, a bit of relaxation in good company was justifiable. But I wasn't twenty-one anymore, and despite the stodgy bar meal aimed at delaying alcohol absorption, a headache was building, a morning hangover likely. Bugger. Prof. Becker's essay wasn't finished and was due by noon. I dozed for a bit before deciding that to get to proper sleep I'd need to undress and get into bed. And have two paracetamol, which needed a glass of water.

With enormous effort, I switched on the bedside light and slowly rose. Unable to find my slippers, I padded in stockinged feet across the cold hall tiles towards the kitchen. Short of the door I stopped, hearing low voices from within. Male voices. Eavesdropping was getting a habit. The kitchen light wasn't on, but by courtesy of silvery moonlight I could see two silhouettes on the cream wall opposite: one large and bulky, one diminutive with a pointy 'Mr Punch' nose. It was hard to pick up their conversation, but not as hard as it had been to hear through to Cedric's study.

'There has been no sign of him at all. He is very clever.' I

50

didn't recognise the voice, but from the shoulder animation accompanying the speech I deduced the speaker was the whippet-thin shadow. 'He may know nothing, in any case.' There was an accent, but at least they were speaking English.

'Goddamn it, how'd he get away? I need to speak to him. The London guys were useless, got nothing.' Bulky Shadow was easily identifiable in shape and sound: Guy. His shadow blurred and collapsed as a chair leg squeaked across the lino tiles. He must be sitting down.

'He will turn up, Colonel, he must.' So, Guy was a colonel? I strained to hear. 'We need to know what he knows. The Charité doctor may have been in touch.'

'We need to make sure he doesn't make things worse, Baz! It's a bummer I didn't get more outta the old guy before. He mighta been no friend to us when all's said and done, but sod it, with his connections, his death's a blow for intel. There's effing all of use in the files I've looked at so far, though the tape's still being analysed. And you gotta get onto identifying all the guys in that photo. Jesus, what a cock up. Heads will roll for this one. It's a goddamn mess!'

'I have not lost hope …'

'But time is against us and there's still no definite aerials to prove what's going on – only artist mock-ups. Some'll think it's a bit slim to go on, for sure. Not sure it's all kosher myself, to be frank, but we can't risk anyone stirring doubt now they've made their minds up. No loose ends, Baz, or Reith will go berserk. Can't let anything get out that'll spoil the OSP feed.'

'We'll find him.'

'Goddamn it, I hope you're right! You'd best get off now. Where have you parked? You need to keep outta sight round here now. Nosey cops are prowling around with the old guy getting topped.'

Suddenly I was wide awake and disinclined to fetch water from the kitchen. I ran back to my room, head throbbing. But once inside I changed my mind. Why shouldn't I go for some water? Grabbing my last coffee mug complete with dregs, I returned to the hall, banging my door shut and purposely treading on a known squeaky board. Nauseated and with a brain that felt stuck to the inside of my skull straining to burst out, I headed for the bathroom. Though we'd been warned on arrival that its water was 'non-potable' due to lead pipes or tanks or something, I didn't care. I had to have water and painkillers. Closing the door behind me, I noisily shot the bolt. Old houses had plenty of ways to make your presence felt. After running the tap to rinse and fill my mug, I swigged two pills. The banging pipes of the old central heating system indicated it was switching off on its timer: midnight. I flushed the loo and was about to open the door to see if I'd also flushed out the kitchen conspirators when gravel noise from outside told me a car was driving away. Christ, history repeating itself!

Then I remembered that when I'd staggered out of tonight's taxi (I had to stop doing that) there had been a car again out there in the shadows. More a big jeep kind of thing than a saloon, visible end on, sitting at the side to the left of the drive. No one hereabouts had a big vehicle like that. Not sure what colour, but dark. Could it be the black vehicle I'd seen Guy get into a couple of times, and once out of, down at Norwood Road on Thursdays? The day he'd sometimes come back with Harrod's and Fortnum's shopping bags and offer us delicacies? I'd assumed he'd been up researching in the War Museum, but it was puzzling that he never simply got picked up outside our door.

The only other cars ever seen outside here were my Mini, when it wasn't in the college car-park that I preferred to the awkward lodge driveway, or Cedric's Jag, now presumably at his home. Returning to my room, I caught sight of Cedric's police-taped door and felt a wave of grief. Poor chap. I hoped the police knew what the hell it was all about. Tonight's odd goings-on needed reporting. Maybe I should phone that nice DCI? I had his card. Sophie might tease, but Steadman was an approachable person. I'd call him tomorrow – or wait, today! It was tomorrow now! As my hand grasped my room door handle, a voice made me jump.

'Burning the midnight oil, Judith?' It was Guy, switching off the kitchen light as he came out of it, a light not on when I'd gone to the loo. How normal he looked: smiling, relaxed standing wide-legged, Boston Red Sox mug in hand. 'Just came for a caffeine fix to help me finish a paper due in tomorrow.'

I stood mute as he took a few paces forward to peer at me before shrinking back as he pointed with his free hand to under my eyes. 'My, who's had a good night out on the town?' He laughed. 'Taking your mind off things?'

I had noticed in the loo mirror that my mascara was streaked, my lipstick smudged, but who did he think he was to make jokes? How could he laugh when a man was dead, a boy missing, a widow and son grieving? I decided I did not care one whit for Colonel Guy Waller.

'Good night. I'm off to bed. It's been a most upsetting weekend.'

His smile flattened, his eyes hooded, and his face morphed into an expression of sympathy and concern. 'Sure thing, Judith. Terrible, terrible business. Gotta hope those police guys get answers pronto.' Waving his mug at me he ascended the stairs like a lumbering bear.

I stared at his back. He couldn't have a 'paper due in,' he was a visiting scholar with no assignments! I'd always suspected he was a kind of phony. Now, I was sure. Who whispered in a dark kitchen and took a cup of cold coffee to bed? Must be cold – I'd have heard our noisy old kettle or a microwave ding. Not a hint of steam off that mug. Who was he kidding?

What lunatic asylum, or was it a nest of vipers, was I

living in? Guy sounded like a spy, Jon was an insensitive boor, Gwen was paranoid about being tailed, Abbie thought it all a lark, and Tilly was on the brink of a breakdown! Was I the only normal one? Going into my room, I leaned my back against the door and closed my eyes, brain racing, trying to think whether any of them could be connected to the men who'd rendered Anna and Ramin unconscious then killed Cedric.

In truth, though Guy was decidedly odd, it sounded like he was cross Cedric had died – if the prof were the 'old guy' he'd just referred to. Who in heaven's name was 'Baz' who'd just driven off in his big shiny car? Had he also driven off in the gravel after the murder yesterday? Or rather, the day *before* yesterday, it now being Monday. My head throbbed worse than ever, and I was shivering again. Quickly I changed into my PJs and for the first time, locked my door overnight. Amazingly, I fell asleep.

7

Getaways & Haydn

A few hours later, Sophie woke in her cold, dark bedroom on Cowley Road. She lay, mind whirling, before eventually deciding she had to get up. Lifting the duvet, she gently prised off Jared's arm, and ran to the bathroom.

She hadn't slept much, but Jared was dead to the world. There'd been a long kitchen *tête-à-tête*, followed by passionate lovemaking in bed after which she'd gone down to make them hot chocolate. But by the time she'd returned, Jared was snoring. His story was unbelievable, but then everything this weekend had been. Her mother finding Cedric dead, Jared's ransacked room, meeting him on the stairs tonight. She'd been terrified till she realised it was Jared. How could she have forgotten he had a key? He was the only boyfriend that she'd ever entrusted with one. Their first exchange had been angry.

'Where the hell have you been, Jared?'

'Sorry…'

'I was worried sick! Why couldn't you phone?' As Jared had moved in closer, Sophie had been about to punch him, but seeing his exhausted and anxious face, she'd hugged him hard until he was the one to break the spell.

'What's wrong with the lights, Sophe?'

'Oh, hang on.' Inside the hall cupboard she'd flicked all the switches in the fuse box up then down again. When the hall light came on. Jared had dashed to the front door, put off the light switch, closed the door, thrown on the deadlock and leaned back against it.

'What's up with you?' Sophie had shaken her head.

'I'm being followed.'

'Followed? By who, I mean whom? The police? Gangsters? Do you owe money?' She'd never suspected he did drugs or gambled, though from her medical training knew you couldn't always tell.

Jared had shrugged, dropping his head before looking heavenward. 'I don't know for sure, but it's maybe the CIA.'

He'd looked ready to cry. Sophie knew he wasn't joking. 'Have you eaten?'

'Not since breakfast, I was in a boarding house in Jericho but ran out of money and didn't want to risk a cash machine. So, I hid in the Radcliffe Library until it was dark, then came here.'

'Why didn't you take money out?'

'They can trace you. That's why I didn't phone you either. Can you get me a pay-as-you go cell tomorrow and lend me some money? I'll pay you back when I've sorted this out. Or I'll give you my card and pin to use once I'm away?'

'Oh, Jared, what's this all about?'

'Can you please get me toast and a drink first? In fact, you got any of your mum's whisky left?'

In the kitchen Sophie had pulled down the blind and clicked on the downlighters under the wall units before handing Jared, who'd slumped into a chair, a glass and the whisky bottle. She filled the kettle, loaded the toaster, and sat down. 'So, spill!'

'Well, the embassy doesn't like the people I'm associating with online.'

'What people?'

Jared shrugged, shaking his head. 'Just guys from last summer in the refugee camp. A medic from Berlin, a couple of Iraqis, Syrians, and a guy from NYU. We worked together with Médecins Sans Frontières and the Red Crescent as hospital orderlies.'

'So, what's wrong with them?'

'Nothing. We've chatted online on Sunday nights since last summer about helping to influence USAID and lobbying. Maybe occasionally about Arab politics, but nothing much. Like a couple of weeks ago, the Iraqi guy asked if I was going to the anti-war rallies here in Oxford.'

'What rallies?'

'Don't you know? The ones to show Blair and Bush that we don't want war against Saddam Hussein. However terrible a tyrant he is, innocent Arabs will die.'

'But how do they know what you've been talking about?'

'You have no idea, do you? They monitor internet traffic all the time for keywords. Don't look shocked, Sophie, your spooks do it too. But one night we did discuss what Al Qaeda's next plans might be after 9/11. Think that did it.'

Sophie had taken some shallow breaths and twisted her thick long blonde hair into a scrunchie. Sitting on her hands she looked at the floor before looking up to stare at this boy she'd thought she'd known. 'So, Jared, are you anything to do with Al Qaeda?'

*

Miraculously, I woke without a hangover and worked intensely all Monday morning. I didn't feel too bad about the essay that I finally put into Becker's departmental pigeonhole at noon. Resolving to alleviate my 'murder' stress by work, I headed to the College Library, picking up a baguette in South Parade on the way. I'd not bothered with breakfast.

Sitting in a library booth looking out at the snow-covered college lawns, I couldn't concentrate on the *Psychology of Effective Learning*. My brain was preoccupied with the midnight whisperers. First thing, I'd dialled the top number on Steadman's card. It went straight to voicemail. The other number was answered.

'Thames Valley Police, how may I help you? I'm sorry, DCI Steadman is out of office. Would you like to speak to someone else?'

'No, thank you. Could you just tell him I called and would like to speak to him?'

'Of course. You are? And it's concerning?'

Flustered, I left my name and number, said it was about the college murder and rang off. After returning to my room, I idled away the day googling random things in the hope of making sense of prominent words from the whisperers, like 'Reith,' 'aerials,' and 'charity.' Why was Guy concerned about a 'Reith?' The only one I found was the ex-BBC Controller, Lord John Reith, a staunchly Presbyterian chap who'd died in 1971 and who would, therefore, hardly be likely to be getting mad at Guy. Googling 'aerials' brought Argos, TV installers and stuff about DAB Radios: also, unhelpful. Searching for 'charity' yielded acres of rubbish, so I tried adding 'the' to 'charity' (as I thought Guy had) and stumbled on *The Charité*. Though sounding French, it was a Berlin hospital, Europe's largest university one. Perhaps this 'man on the run' knew someone there – who knew? I gave up.

Donning a (matching) pair of boots, I set off to walk along the river past the parked punts. Ducks bobbed and swam in the icy water: they must have well-insulated bums. It was fairly peaceful, but the constant traffic hum from the nearby A14 made me long for my tranquil Scottish hills. Back in the warm kitchen I made tea, and accompanied by a Radio 3 piano concerto, was reading an abandoned Guardian when Jon arrived.

'Good afternoon, Judith, how are you today?' He poured a glass of milk and sat down opposite with a Jaffa Cake. Abbie must have left him some.

'Oh, I'm fine. This week's essay is in, so I'm taking a

58

breather.'

'Glad to find you here. In fact, I was wondering if you'd do me a favour?'

'A favour?'

'Well, I have tickets for a Haydn concert tonight and I thought you might be one of the few people in the house who might appreciate a chamber concert. It's in the Holywell. Have you been?'

'That's kind of you. I'd love to come. I don't know anything about the Holywell.'

'It's in the grounds of Wadham College, Europe's oldest purpose-built music room, dates to the 1740s, I believe. Has acoustics to die for, quite charming. I thought it might be a unique Oxford experience for you.'

'Thank you so much.' I smiled, thinking that with Ted gone, he must be lonely. I didn't think this invite had any other agenda. Plus, for a concert, you didn't need small talk. I was all out of that.

'Shall we meet here at six-thirty, have a bite to eat before we start, and make an evening of it? The concert starts at eight.'

'I'll look forward to it.'

As he left with a smile and nod, I felt guilty I'd misjudged him. Within minutes, Abbie appeared. 'Hi, Jude! Up for a meal out tonight? '

Like buses, are invites. You wait ages with none then get two together. 'Sorry, Abbie. I have a date.'

'Oh? Who's the lucky man?'

'I'm off to the Holywell with Jon.' I dumped my cup in the sink and left a stunned Abbie.

In my room I searched the wardrobe for something suitable for an evening out with a gay, religious, ex-Commonwealth Games medallist to an intimate eighteenth-century concert hall. Thinking we might walk down, and the old place might be draughty, I felt layers might be best.

After trying on several outfits, I was in a navy trouser suit and floral knitted silk jumper when the bell rang. At the second imperious double ring I went out, wondering who'd forgotten their key this time. I got a surprise.

''Mum! Thank God you're in. My, don't you look smart? I need a favour. Hang on though!'

Sophie dropped two heavy carrier bags at my feet in the porch and ran off to pay the waiting taxi. In the kitchen she rattled through her day. 'You know some folk love the sound of their own voices! I mean, these ward teaching rounds are endless with everyone quoting research papers to show how clever they are.' She unpacked the bags. 'Seems to me physicians discuss diagnoses too much while the patient lies ignored in the bed. Honestly, Mum, think I'll specialise in surgery. There, if something's diseased, you just whip it out, job done! Too much waffle in medical wards. Anyway, I eventually got away to dash into town to get stuff for Jared. He's at the house.'

'Really? But why couldn't he go out himself? Has he been hurt?'

'No, thank God! But I had to get him a pay-as-you-go phone with no contract and no name or address recorded, and undies and spare clothes in M&S, and toiletries in Boots.'

'Why on earth? Where's he been? And where's he going?'

'Well, he was in a Jericho B&B but thought it was too dangerous to go back. Later I'll go, pay for his room and collect his things. He's worried that now my place might be under observation too. Says he has to go to speak to someone and time is of the essence. So, I wondered ...'

She knew I wouldn't refuse.

By five-thirty I was sitting in my Mini outside Sophie's terrace. A police car screamed up, siren blaring. I held my breath, but when a police constable jumped out to dash into the takeaway opposite, I relaxed. It was like that lull of bliss after a painful labour contraction, unexplainable to anyone who's never given birth. I even smiled as the copper came out, not with a miscreant, but two polystyrene boxes. The car drove off siren-less, likely to find a quiet munching spot. I now had an insight into Oxfordshire's 'best' and their use of sirens, having puzzled about why we heard them far more in Oxford than back in supposedly 'high-crime' Glasgow! Consulting my watch for the third time in two minutes, I hoped they were getting a move on inside the house. Though dressed, I still had my hair to fix before my Haydn 'date.'

A familiar cream M&S hooded parka came out of Sophie's house. I saw she'd got all that mud off. But it was Jared who dropped into the passenger seat and threw Sophie's old school rucksack into the back seat. I drove off, looking frequently in the rear-view mirror, but saw no discernible consistency in the following traffic. Reaching Oxford Parkway in no time, I stopped directly outside the station and turned to Jared, who looked worried and drawn.

'You know I'm doing this for Sophie, and against my better judgement, Jared. I can't see why you don't just go to the police. Have you done something illegal?'

'No. But it's complex, Mrs F. I'm off to find someone who might help me sort this out. I'll be in touch as soon as I get there. Can you give me your phone number please? They may be tracking Sophie's. I think she should get a new one too.'

I shook my head and fumbled in my bag. All I had was an old M&S receipt. I scribbled my number on its back and handed it over. I looked at what he was wearing: an unlined suede jerkin over a shirt.

'Jared, you'll freeze in that thin jacket! You'll need to get a warmer one.' I didn't care how mumsy this sounded, snowflakes were swirling, and the boy was so thin. He smiled, such a lovely smile. Surely, he couldn't be associated with murder or terrorism? Sophie's garbled account was ludicrous. I forced my red woolly scarf on him. 'Here! Take this at least. It'll be cold on the platform.'

'No worries! I'll get a new jacket up in town. Might be going somewhere warm in the end anyway!' He glanced up at the clock. 'Great timing! There's a Paddington train in five minutes.' He gave me a peck on the cheek. 'I sure appreciate this Mrs F! I owe you one.'

Before I could ask if he'd enough money, he was off into the station. Someone behind me was honking. Through the rear-view mirror I saw a big Audi. Really, some people had no patience. They should have to deal with a bit of real death or disaster and not just a few seconds delay in their mundane workaday. The guy in the silver saloon overtook with a screech and a hand pumping the horn. He got a gesture. Another vertical single finger! I was surprising myself. Two 'fuck off's, a date acceptance and enabling a get-away? Steve would have been appalled. I felt flushed, recalling his parting jibe about women at my '*time of life*' tending to be 'unstable.' God, what a prat! I accelerated out of the Park and Ride back to the Lodge but gathered my wits in time to slow to the speed limit. I had time. No sense in risking a ticket. Which reminded me: Steadman hadn't phoned back.

I enjoyed a nice risotto in an Italian chain city centre restaurant Jon had chosen. He took mineral water with his anchovy salad, but insisted I have wine. Supping the large glass of Soave, I tried to forget my alcohol tally for the week. And it was only Monday.

'Thank you for coming, Judith. I didn't want to waste the tickets. Difficult to get, you know. The Holywell only seats two hundred, and tonight's chamber orchestra is from Heidelberg.'

'I'm sure they'll be excellent.'

'I must confess also I wanted to speak to you about Cedric. I'm sorry if I came over as rather abrasive on Saturday, but his death was an enormous shock. I had trouble taking it in. I was going to talk to you last night but didn't want to intrude when you were entertaining.'

'Oh, it would have been fine. Actually, my daughter was entertaining me.'

'I should say that Cedric and I have been friends for a long time. We came up together in '68 to do PPE.'

'PPE?'

'Politics, Philosophy and Economics. Cedric was a bit older than I, already with a degree in Classics, but his baronet father pushed him into PPE hoping he'd head for public service and Parliament. The course has turned out Prime Ministers every decade since the twenties. We bonded over hating it and left after first year. Made us a tad unpopular, it's such a prestigious course.'

'Why did you hate it?'

'We'd had enough of the British Constitution since 1870, Aristotle, Adam Smith and tedious essays, so Cedric went for his Babylonian obsession, and I took English Literature. Recently – especially with living in the Lodge since my house fire last summer – I've been helping Cedric edit his latest exciting, important book. Sadly, so near completion.'

'What was the book about?'

'*The Epic of Gilgamesh.*'

'I've never heard of it.'

'It is an ancient Sumerian poem from a couple of thousands of years before Christ. Several versions. The later one has twelve sections. It's the first known full narrative story, created in Mesopotamia, the birthplace of civilisation. Sadly, however, that area, which is largely now Iraq, continues to tear itself apart. Though they say Mr Bush is preparing to move in and 'fix' it.' His nostrils flared.

Ignoring the politics (of which I was completely ignorant) I asked, 'Who was Gilgamesh?'

'He was a cruel king. In the *Epic*, Gilgamesh goes seeking eternal life and it's set in a dream world where earth and heaven are juxtaposed. There are moral lessons on law and

63

government, and gods and magical creatures like the Bull of Heaven and Scorpion Men. Think I know a few of those around here!' He laughed. 'And there's a bit of unbridled sex and passion. It's in cuneiform script written on clay and was first translated in London in the 1840s. Pieces are scattered worldwide but some sections are still missing.'

'Sounds fascinating.'

'It is. Cedric recently acquired some new fragments and he wanted to write the book on it to show the enduring lessons it has for us even today, both in politics and saving the planet. In ancient Sumer and Akkadia the world was dangerous and unsettled. Greedy rulers furthered their ends by weaving narratives of false news. Not much has changed!'

'Probably true.' I took a swig of wine.

'But today's battles are not for the cedar wood Gilgamesh pillaged for his great archways and temples, but oil like in Iraq. Did you know Saddam is also building monuments for his own glory – and reburying ancient kings? He tried to consult Cedric, I believe, who did not want to be involved, though he found it hard not to help the university over there.'

'Jon, what do you think about Gwen's suggestion that Cedric was being followed?'

'Perhaps. He's been publicly anti-war. The Americans, for a start, don't like that. Think Bush wants someone to pay for their loss of face after the Twin Towers, and possibly he's decided it will be Iraq.' He shook his head.

'Gosh, not sure I'd grasped that. I haven't been reading newspapers much since I came down. Escaping from the big bad world, really.'

'Ah, Judith, we can't escape the world! I make a point of reading the common room papers daily, including *The Tribune* and *Le Monde*.'

'You speak French?'

'And German. I was partly educated in Switzerland.' He smiled. 'Cedric was brilliant you know. Spoke five languages and had two doctorates. It's been a privilege to edit his translation which captures the beautiful imagery of the ancient text.'

'What will happen to it now?'

He shrugged. 'Anna wants me to finish it with Jared, but where is he? Not cricket, going off like that. Yet he was so excited about the new tablets on the Garden of the Gods section.'

I shifted in my seat, wondering what Jon would think about me aiding Jared's escape. 'The Garden of what Gods?'

'The *Epic*'s Gods have names that you won't have heard of, but like most religions, they had a paradise, a place we'd all like to end up, somewhere beautiful and peaceful. What some students think Oxford might be like – some hope! Interestingly, many Gilgamesh stories recur again later in everything from the *Odyssey* to the *Arabian Nights*, while the Old Testament has its 'Flood' story. Some scholars believe Gilgamesh was Nimrod, Noah's great-grandson.'

'Nimrod? I thought that was a piece by Elgar?'

Jon laughed. The first time I'd seen him laugh. 'I knew you'd enjoy a musical evening! Elgar's Enigma Variations is one of my favourites.'

'Shouldn't we leave soon?'

Jon looked at his watch and waved for the bill. 'It's only a walk along High Street, up past the Radcliffe Camera and round into Holywell Street. You might like to take in one of the Coffee Concerts on a Sunday sometime, too – with coffee in Blackwell's Bookshop.'

Tossing money at the bill as it arrived, Jon told the young waiter to keep the change.

I decided I had misjudged him badly. He was warm, cultured, full of fascinating facts and a generous tipper. As I went to powder my nose, he stayed chatting to the waiter.

The Holywell lived up to expectations. For two hours I forgot about everything. The oboes, horns, and strings were exceptional. Jon explained Haydn's *Piano Trio No.39* had inspired Mozart and Bach. The piece was completely new to me, as was being taken home in a taxi and deposited at my room door with a bow and hand kiss. Extraordinary place, Oxford.

Changed into my pyjamas, I lifted a new A4 notebook and started making lists. On one page, questions. On the opposite, possible answers. At the back random jottings: Gilgamesh, Babylon, Bush, PPE degrees, and Prime Ministers. Thinking how much you learned at Oxford, I put out the light. It was almost Tuesday.

8

Deconstruction & The Hummer Enigma

The feel-good glow from the musical evening lasted until the next day at two o'clock when Professor Becker spoiled it. After reducing young Terry to tears, he picked up my essay paper and tossed it over.

'Pedantic, teacher-centric, reductionist, and unimaginative. It is my opinion you may be unteachable to the level of the qualification you desire, Miss Frazer.'

I was going to correct my marriage status but stopped myself. Without a ring, 'Miss' was a reasonable assumption. Though I'd resisted reverting to my maiden name on divorce for fear of pupil comment, being continually referred to as Miss Frazer was annoying. Suddenly a solution hit me: never mind getting a Masters, I could aim for a doctorate! 'Dr Frazer' sounded better than Ms. But if it were up to Becker, I doubted I'd get on an Oxford D.Phil programme. No matter, I wouldn't mind a common-or-garden 'PhD' from elsewhere. I realised that I was smiling while facing Becker's continuing rant at my stupidity. Terry was gazing at me in bewilderment. Our fellow tutee, Mark, was looking downward at the carpet, which I noted needed hoovering. Perhaps Becker had antagonised the cleaners? I braced myself to stare straight at him and belligerently say, 'So?'

'This week I have prepared you an extra reading list, Miss Frazer. If you could summarise and grasp the main points of theory contained and hand it in by Friday noon, then I may consider letting you continue – if you can demonstrate sufficient insight into your deficiencies, that is.' It was his final barb that banished my continuing attempt at a smile. 'Educationalists must rise above sob-stories as an excuse for lack of attainment in their pupils. You require de-construction, madam.'

My jaw dropped. Unusually for me, I could think of nothing to say. But Becker had more.

'I am drawn to the assumption that you have spent too much time in a sub-standard over-crowded poxy comprehensive up in the wilds of Scotland. If you saw how children were taught in Germany, you might understand how it can be done effectively.'

That did it. Since getting reading glasses, I'd found it easier to speak my mind without my specs, perhaps as the object of my anger blurs at close 'spec-less' quarters. I removed my glasses and took a deep breath. 'Professor, you are free to criticise me all you like, but the children I teach face problems not of their making and I will not have them or their schools full of hard-working teachers dismissed as "poxy" and unworthy of consideration. Nor will I accept derogatory – indeed discriminatory – remarks about Scotland. My analysis of classroom issues is, for them, a valid one, albeit one which I admit may not sit well amongst the paper and textbook norms of this week's elitist reading list. I will be delighted to take on board anything extra you set me, but I will not be insulted. Your attack is tantamount to psychological bullying. Rudeness may cow undergraduates, but not me. I welcome *constructive* criticism, not *destructive*. I thought that was what Oxford was all about. It seems I was wrong.'

With thumping heart, I held my stance as the professor rose to his feet. Satisfyingly, he was shorter than I. Terry and Mark were now grinning. Terry had said nothing in defence of his essay, being a recent Oxford undergrad with little classroom experience who was unable to stand up to a jellybean. I was angry on Terry's behalf as well as mine and felt a rising flush as Becker locked eyes.

'I think we are finished, Miss Frazer. You may go.'

'It is *Ms* Frazer, Professor Becker.'

There was as much a hint of a smile as I'd ever seen in his inscrutable face with its icy, pale, slow-moving grey eyes. For a doubly qualified teacher and educational psychologist he lacked even minimal social charm, but doubtless as a professor at Oxford with life-long tenure, hundreds of published papers, ten seminal books and umpteen degrees, he didn't feel the need to engage with anyone on a meaningfully personal level i.e., be nice. No wonder he wasn't married. Intelligence Quotient? One-hundred and fifty plus. Emotional Quotient? Zero. Thank God his contact with children was now minimal: he only supervised academics. How awful to be a child referred to such a counsellor. He bowed deeply as I snatched up my bag plus his supplementary reading list and my essay bearing his discursive, green pen comments and left Terry and the yet-to-be-deconstructed Mark to it.

Outside, a lemon sun was shining. The road was covered in melting grey slush mashed up by heavy traffic. Going down Norham Gardens, the University Park looked inviting, all pristine white crispness and sparkling holly bushes. During my tutorial, the larger tree branches had shed their snowflake dressing, but the park was still Christmas card pretty. Instead of turning right for Banbury Road and home, I went left towards the park gate. A walk would clear my head. The Cedric business and grappling with esoteric educational theories was too much. In truth, what irked me was that snarky Becker was right: I'd written about specific pupil problems in a theoretical essay set to discuss methods for engaging troubled youngsters. If I did want to progress to a doctorate, I'd need to focus better. Friday was a punitive early deadline, but today I didn't want to rush to the library to collect the reading list. I had more pressing concerns. What had happened to the lovely, unassuming, accomplished Cedric?

Listing questions last night hadn't helped. What could be the murder motive? If Morse was anything to go by, motives were anger, greed, and jealousy. Despite Jon's misgivings, I doubted Cedric would have been belligerent enough to anger anybody. As for greed, was he wealthy enough to merit murdering for money? Then folk could be killed for insurance monies. But if the beneficiary were Anna, surely, she wouldn't have risked being injured? And for jealousy, you needed a competitor. Certainly, workwise, there was that college chap, Manders, whom I'd overheard rubbishing Cedric in the college bar. But what had he to gain? A jealous lover was likely a non-starter: I couldn't see Cedric firing anyone's passion that much! Even I, at the peak of my fury, hadn't thought of killing Steve. For Cedric, none of these motives fitted. The only clues were that his assailants spoke Arabic, knew his home address, and from the mess, had been hunting for something. What? Money? Papers? Letters? An incriminating photo or video? A treasure? I felt that Anna knew something. Her eyes had said it.

In cold daylight, the house crew didn't figure as suspects. Leo and Abbie had been out. Guy was big, strong and more than capable of whanging Socrates, but from the kitchen whispers, he'd sounded cross that Cedric was dead. If the 'old man' he referred to were Cedric, that was.

My head was beginning to ache. I had to sit. Clearing snow from a bench, I plonked myself down, glad of my expensive-but-I-was-worth-it-after-the-divorce   Gore-Tex coat. Apart from a passing dog-walker swinging a poop bag and a young zombified mum with pushchair, I was alone. After sitting for some minutes, I noticed dampness rising up my canvas bag. The bench was very wet. I sighed. Doing a lot of that, yet I hadn't come to Oxford to sigh! No point in sitting here ruining the bag or risking a chill. Time to go speak to Steadman. Something I'd overheard might be of use to the police. Pulling up my furry hood against the chill wind, I trudged off. Walking was easier in matching boots.

Back home, police tapes fluttered aimlessly from the stumpy railings like abandoned party streamers. The police had not returned. As I put my key in the lock, I heard a squeal. Out from under the hedge shot a giant beige and brown rat which gave me palpitations until I saw it wasn't a rat, but Cedric's cat. I threw down my bag in the porch to lift up the poor, shivering, near-furless animal, so ill-equipped for a UK winter. Cuddling Selassie, I closed the storm door and inner glass one, before setting him down. As I unlocked my room, he ran to the study door to scratch and squeak pathetically.

'Sorry mate, he's not there anymore. Hungry? Let's see what I can find for you.'

Scooping him up, I went into the kitchen and filled a saucer with milk. My half-fat was finished, but Guy's blue-topped full-fat wasn't. I used it. He wouldn't miss the calories. Feeling like a primary school kid performing a prank, I topped up the bottle with water and was laughing when Abbie arrived.

'Surprised to see you laughing, I heard you got a roasting from Becker!'

'Who told you?'

'Oh, I met Terry at the Parade Spar. He's sooo disillusioned. Thinking of giving up.' She dumped a bag of groceries on the table.

'Oh, he mustn't do that!' I looked at the veg and fish spilling out onto the table from her carrier bag and pretended shock. 'Hey, what's this, Abbie? Going to cook?'

'I can cook, you know! I'm fed up with burgers, pizzas, and curries. Aim to start eating healthy, take less meat. Been to the Covered Market and the Spar. And joined the gym this morning.'

Out of her bag she took a tin of tuna, which I grabbed. 'Perfect! This'll do for Selassie till I get him some proper cat food.' As I opened it and searched for a dish, Abbie knelt to stroke the lapping cat.

'He seems very thirsty, doesn't he?' After emptying the saucer, the animal looked up with wide unblinking eyes and Abbie picked him and kissed him, ruffling under his chin. 'Sweet boy, aren't you? Even if you aren't furry and cuddly. Don't worry, we'll look after you.' She paused. 'That's odd. Why does he have this inside his collar?' She held up a small rubber oblong.

Setting down the tuna in a soup bowl since Selassie's dishes were still trapped in the locked study 'crime scene,' I peered at it. 'I've no idea. Let's look at it later – just tuck it back in for now. The kettle's on. Time for a cuppa?'

'I'll do coffee. Never sure why you Brits are so hung up on tea! Gonna take the night off. Got great crit for my essay from Toby today. Sorry, not wanting to rub it in. But, jeez, I gotta tell you I saw something real weird earlier. What do you reckon on Guy? I mean don't you think he's kinda odd?'

Soon I forgot all about the rubber oblong in the cat's collar. What Abbie told me prompted me to text Steadman at once.

At four my phone rang. 'Good afternoon, Mrs Frazer. I got your text. I'm sorry your message yesterday went astray, but wondered if you were free to come into the station just now and tell me what's on your mind?'

In minutes, I was in the Mini.

The uniformed desk girl looked impossibly young. After she'd phoned to announce my arrival, another young woman in plain clothes came, greeted me with a 'Hi, I'm Greta,' and escorted me to a nice modern room. It had a polished beech desk and padded chairs. Three walls held old black and white photos of police passing-out parades. The third was a glass partition, through which I saw plain-clothed young men and women on phones or typing at computers. Seeing his coat hung behind the door, I deduced this wasn't an interview room, but Steadman's office. I was standing looking at the photos on the desk when he appeared.

'Thank you so much for coming in, Mrs Frazer.' Steadman extended a hand which I shook.

Firm grip. Nice smile. 'It's no problem.' I was feeling very warm. And still standing.

'Please sit down.'

Greta's head poked back round the door to look expectantly at us.

'Can you get us some coffees, Greta? Or would you prefer tea, Judith?'

Diverted by Steadman's use of my first name, I ignored my usual irritation at women being treated as handmaidens, and responded, 'Tea please, just milk.' Adding, 'Coffee gives me indigestion.' Jesus, as if he cared?

Without looking in it, he took a notebook from the drawer: it was definitely his own office.

'Right, Judith ...'

He'd used my first name again. Disturbing.

'Well, what did you want to tell me? Your text wasn't clear. I presume it concerns the death of Professor Gilbert?' He unfolded the notebook and took a Parker from his inside pocket.

'Well, it might, though there's another matter also ...' I was twirling my dress ring which was loose. Was I losing weight? I noticed my nails needed cut. The index one had a split. I should get them done. Why couldn't I find time for everything I had to do? Now, where should I start with what I needed to say? But I knew I had to stop asking myself questions. There lay insanity.

He tapped the desk with his pen. 'Fire away, I'm all

yours.'

How much should I tell him? Sophie had forbidden any mention of Jared, insistent he needed time to sort himself out. And Abbie's info was hearsay. But with one life down, and Jared's in jeopardy, there was nothing for it. 'Well, it's about a few things.'

Steadman raised one eyebrow. I'd spent futile childhood hours at mirrors trying to do that before gran told me it must be a genetic ability I lacked. He put down his pen and leaned back in his chair. 'Go on. I'm all ears.'

Intelligence shone from his eyes. Like John Thaw as an early Morse. I chastised myself to stop this obsession with crime entertainment: this was real life murder. I suddenly wondered why I'd come: I really didn't want to be involved. 'Er, I'm not sure whether any of my scraps of odd things are important or whether I'm wasting your time.' My mouth was dry. I took a swig of the tea that had arrived: it was coffee. Had I said coffee instead of tea? Thinking it had to *be* no coincidence that the Mad Hatter's Tea Party was conceived in Oxford. I set down the mug, a 'Keep Calm and Carry On' one. Apt.

'Why don't you just tell me everything and let me judge what's relevant? If it isn't helpful, there's no harm done. Anything you have will be great. I don't mind saying we haven't a lot to go on.'

'Well, you asked about Cedric's enemies, and I mentioned his newspaper articles attracted adverse comment and that I'd occasionally heard arguments from the study, but after you left, I remembered a particular door-slamming one last term with Dr Timothy Manders, a college don who, it's rumoured, was miffed at Cedric being made Assistant Master. I mean, I don't think Manders is a killer or anything, but it might be worth speaking to him because apart from anything else, he's always hanging around the Common Rooms. On top of bad-mouthing Cedric, he has a reputation for being a bit of a gossip, knows everything. Not sure he'd have any connection to the men who took Cedric, though. Anna said they were Arabs.'

'You've seen Mrs Gilbert?'

'Yes. I took Cedric's secretary to see her in hospital. Gwen was in such a state she didn't feel safe driving. She and Anna are friends. Poor Anna told us what happened, but that's another thing – I thought she was holding something back.'

'You think she knew these men?'

'Well, I just thought she looked like one of my pupils hiding something or maybe even like she was afraid. A hunch. Don't expect that's much good for a policeman!'

'You'd be surprised. Anyway, anything else?'

'Yes. Guy, the American studying World War Two. He's not doing a Doctorate or anything, says he's a visiting scholar for a year. But – sorry, this is gossipy – I don't think he is as he seems.'

Steadman raised both eyebrows. 'Why?'

'Last night at midnight, I overheard him whispering in the kitchen, in the dark, with a thin short guy he called Baz. They were talking about someone they'd been following whom they'd lost, who knew something about something.'

The detective wrinkled his nose and sat forward, right elbow on desk, chin on his hand. 'Can you be a bit more specific, Judith?'

'Well, I was scared they'd come out and see me skulking in the hall, so I went back to my room and came out again making noises and used the loo.' I omitted the detail about my boozy headache. 'And when I came out, Guy was standing alone at the door of the kitchen, now lit up, with a mug, suggesting he'd just been in to make a coffee, but he has a kettle in his room. Oh, and just prior to leaving the loo, I'd heard the front door closing quietly and a car driving off in the gravel like the other night. Baz, I assumed. The car sounded different from the one after Cedric's thing, though.'

Steadman closed his eyes and pinched his nose. God, I was losing him by prattling like a schoolgirl, but he nodded, the way I often did to encourage a student struggling in an oral exam.

'Baz? Who's Baz? Is he a housemate we haven't interviewed? I thought I'd done you all?'

'You have. He's not. He was the guy in the kitchen whom Guy called Baz. You know they sounded like conspirators; I mean who chats in the dark? They mentioned a Reith, and charity, and aerials and initials OSP or OSC. Oh, and some fleeing person who knew a doctor in a hospital who might have told him something. I wondered if he was talking about *The Charité* – it's a hospital in Berlin I found on Google.'

'Sounds very confusing, if you don't mind me saying, Judith.'

'Sorry. But Guy isn't what he seems – and there's Abbie's story of him and the car.'

'Abbie, the New York, all-night-party girl?'

'Yes. Och, she's all right, you know. Just young, a bit flighty. She's seen Guy get into what sounds like the big, black, long jeep-style car that I've seen him get into, usually parked a couple of streets away in Northmoor Road, near Tolkien's old house – did you know he lived there?'

Steadman was looking amused. He shook his head. 'No, I didn't.'

'I've seen the car several times there on Thursday mornings when I'm walking up to the Summerton shops by Northmoor instead of by the main road. He gets into it, and it drives off northwards towards Kidlington. I know it is Thursdays, 'cos I've no morning classes then, and go up to meet friends for coffee, well for me it's tea …' Now Steadman looked completely bemused. 'Also, it's Thursdays he returns late at night with Harrod's Food Hall bags. But this morning, Abbie saw him get into the car at the end of our street carrying a package. She'd returned to the house as she'd forgotten her tutorial notes. When she went back out, she saw him step out, though he dived back into it when he saw her. She walked on past and didn't look in through its dark windows, but round the corner into Banbury, she peeked back through the hedge to see him dart out and jog back to the house with a different package. Odd, don't you think – or am I being daft?'

'I doubt that. On such small observations can cases be built. Any idea what kind of car it was?'

'It's a massive ugly left-hand drive, black, shiny, squarish thing with three rows of seats and big tyres.' God, I was babbling again. How bad had this idea been?

'And the make?' His pen was poised.

'Abbie says it's a Hummer, her dad had one. Sorry I don't have all the registration, but it included 270 – that's my old room number at school – and a D with more numbers after. Odd.'

'Great.' Steadman was making notes. 'It does sound peculiar. But I can't see how it might be linked to the murder. And it's a pretty distinctive car to use for anything dodgy, isn't it?'

'Oh, I forgot. Guy said it was "a pity the old guy was dead"– Cedric's not that old, but he could've meant him.'

'Right, Judith, I'd like you to make a full statement about that conversation, please. I'll get Greta to come in and take it.'

'Of course.' I had a nagging feeling in the pit of my stomach which I interpreted as fear at being part of this murder investigation, though as Steadman rose to smile at me, I realised there was another emotion simmering – an almost forgotten tingle of that inner body stirring signifying sexual attraction. I smothered it while uttering a swift silent prayer that nothing else awful was going to happen. Especially to Jared. Obviously, no one heard it.

9

Celebration & Tragedy

Greta was a slow writer. I was itching to write the statement myself, thinking it would be much more efficient to tape my answers, transcribe them later and get me back in to read and sign them, but I politely sat and spoke slowly enough for the girl to write down everything. Then I read through it and signed it. I was picking up my bag when Steadman reappeared.

'Sorry, Ms Frazer, but I have one or two more questions.'

Feeling peculiarly crestfallen that he'd resorted to 'Ms,' I sat back down. 'Of course.'

As Greta left, he took out his notebook again. 'The missing boy, Jared Kumar? I believe your daughter's been going out with him for a while. Can you tell me anything about Mr Kumar?'

Mindful of the signs of lying I'd sensed in Anna, I looked him straight in the eye and nodded. 'A lovely boy. I can't see him involved. He was devoted to Cedric, opted to stay on after finishing his doctorate. They were working with Jon Wolsey from the house too, but I expect you know that.' From his blank look, he didn't. 'They nearly had the Prof's book finished. Jon can't understand why Jared's disappeared and Sophie is worried. We've no idea where he is now.' At least that was true.

'Now, the professor's book is on Sumerian poetry, I believe.' Steadman flicked back through his notebook.

'Ancient tablets from Babylon, not sure what they've got to do with it. You know, Jared is a caring person, even volunteered with refugees in his holidays. And he's been exceedingly kind to Sophie.' I felt obliged to labour these points.

Steadman wrote 'Refugee volunteer' and said, 'We're looking into his US background. Eminent medical father, I believe, whom we'll contact. Purely out of interest, anything of note about your other housemates?'

I hesitated, feeling oddly traitorous in answering, 'Oh, they are a motley crew, but none had axes to grind with Cedric. Surely you don't think someone in the house had anything to do with it?'

'Perhaps not, but can you tell me what you know.'

'Well, there's Leo who loves Lycra, bikes and women. He didn't have much to do with Cedric, I don't think. Then Abbie, she's nice, very American, likes older tutors, sometimes cracked jokes at Cedric he didn't get. And Jon? He's for God and men, not necessarily in that order, plus running and Haydn. I suspect postgrads here take to running or alcohol to escape from themselves. Anyway, Jon *is* a bit uptight. And Tilly is an incredibly nervous atheist who loves vegetables, anti-vivisection campaigns and poetry, all pretty normal here in Oxford. Shelley got flung out for being godless, I believe.' Steadman chuckled at this. 'Sorry, this is like a soap opera. I'm sure you don't want to hear this. They're all perfectly nice. It's just Guy, I think, that's hiding something. I don't think he is who he says he is.'

After furiously scribbling, Steadman put down his pen and scratched his head. 'So, basically, Guy whispered with Baz, who had been following someone and lost him. Guy was annoyed – possibly – that someone killed the prof?' I nodded. 'Every little helps I suppose. Your housemates are interesting people, and we always check up on everyone involved at a murder scene. Any secrets will come out.'

'So, you'll be checking up on me?'

'Even you! But if you like you could save me time by describing yourself and your background?'

'I am forty-two, an English teacher in a deprived Glasgow comprehensive school. Divorced last year after my husband of twenty-three years had an affair with my best friend, Maggie. Decided to take off for a year at a whim to do a master's degree down here thinking a change of scene and exercising my "little grey cells" would help get me back on track.'

'You a Poirot fan?'

'More Morse,' I admitted sheepishly.

'Lastly, do you have a partner down here?'

'No. I am currently without a "significant other". The tangled relationships in the Lodge are bad enough! To be frank, I'm not ready.'

Steadman stood and smiled gently. 'I know what you mean. Right, you've got my number. Keep in touch. And thanks for being so honest about everyone and what's happened.'

I gathered my things, looking away, knowing I hadn't been completely honest. Taking his outstretched hand, I shook it and turned to leave before another creeping flush took hold. On the drive back, I reflected on my description of Jared. I didn't think the boy was capable of murder, but until then, hadn't realised how little I knew about him.

Returning to the Lodge, I parked in the drive, brake shoes be damned. It was windy, freezing, and dark. I couldn't face taking the car round to the garage and making the slushy trudge back. Thankfully, the kitchen was empty. I opened cat food I'd picked up at Summertown on the way to the police station and filled Selassie's make-shift dish. The cat was slumbering in the corner on his folded-travelling-rug 'bed.' Sadly, he was a prisoner now unless we let him in and out, the study cat flap being taped off. Drat, I should've asked

Steadman if they could open it. On reflection I decided the DCI was a really nice chap. And he was around my age: almost tempting. First time I'd considered anyone since the *Night of the Revelation*, still raw after two years.

That photo on the floor, tipped from a trouser pocket, had caught my toe at two in the morning, Maggie in a nightdress, smiling seductively, leaning back on our distinctive cane headboard. Stunned, I'd left Steve snoring from his 'late night meeting' to brood in the kitchen. At five I'd phoned Maggie, asked how long 'it' had been 'going on.' The long pause had spoken volumes. By six I'd packed him a suitcase and thrown him out as he was offering feeble excuses – and jibes about unstable menopausal women. A new padded headboard hadn't helped, even with matching bespoke curtains, so I'd moved to the spare room. Some solace had come from dumping his suits at his law practice; not cool for a hot-shot divorce lawyer to be caught out himself.

But that water was well under the bridge. I needed supper. My fridge shelf held only two eggs, four soggy mushrooms, and some spring onions. So, omelette and toast then, followed by online ordering of my new reading list from the library 'stack.' Deciding that I'd collect them from my shelf early next morning and start immediately on a killer essay to impress old Becker, I set to with the eggs. They were very thoroughly whisked.

'Hey. Judith! How are you?'

I turned. Guy looked pensive. 'I was wondering if that lovely girl of yours has seen Jared?' The American swaggered in. He never walked. 'I'm worried. That's a week now he's been gone.'

'I'm sure I have no idea. What's your interest in him?'

'Oh, it's just with the old prof's death I thought it odd he's disappeared.' Guy shrugged, stooping to take a bottle of Budweiser from his fridge shelf. 'Suspicious, even.'

So, Guy thought Cedric was 'old.' 'I'm sure he'd nothing

to do with Cedric's death. But I've no idea where he is. Nor does Sophie.'

'Interesting boy, you know, big heart. Spent last summer in a refugee camp in Iraq helping Kurdish refugees. Saddam's been a bastard to them.'

I remembered Cedric had mentioned Anna was Kurdish. I thought they lived in Kurdistan, not Iraq, but avoiding any admission of ignorance, I merely said, 'Really?'

'The boy's putting himself on the line, disappearing. Cops will want to speak to him. Pass the word to your daughter – he should turn himself in.'

As he left, he flipped his bottle cap on the door jamb. I was livid. That explained those ugly grooves in the woodwork – and this was a bloody listed building! Arrogant bugger with no respect for property, tradition – or people. My opinion of him couldn't get lower. How awful to have been under his command in the Gulf War. If indeed, he had served. How many of his flamboyant tales of derring-do were true? What did Tilly see in him? Why was life now a list of unanswerable questions? Laughing, I dished my rubbery omelette onto a plate, buttered my toast and grabbed a tray.

In my room at my desk with my tea, I abandoned my vow of abstinence to drink a forgotten half-bottle of M&S Chardonnay from my little room fridge plus water, being mindful of my likely struggling liver. Instead of linking into the library on the computer, I found myself googling topics currently piquing my curiosity. 'Colonel Guy Waller' drew two web entries: in one, a Guy Washington Waller graduated Bachelor of Science Degree *cum laude* in 1981 from the United States Air Force Academy in Colorado. It was almost disappointing to find he did have a degree and was listed as being on staff there in 1999. He was also cited on some research papers but there were no references to him for the last four years. He may have been serving right enough. Pouring more wine, I searched for 'Kurds.' Were there many in Iraq? What language did they speak? I found millions of results, but one press report transfixed me.

REUTERS WORLD NEWS
Thousands killed by Chemical Attack in Halabja, Iraq.
Eyewitness report.
March 17th, 1989: 16.30 p.m. by A.M. Pura.

Whilst the horror of witnessing agonising death becomes imprinted on your soul, this report demonstrates that the date 16th of March 1989 should be indelibly imprinted on the world's heart and conscience. I make no apologies for the personalisation of this account.

I owe my survival to my father, who had converted our basement in Halabja into a safe haven with taped ventilators and a sandbagged door. At the first drone of the returning planes that afternoon, he shepherded us downstairs, promising to return as soon as possible after he had fetched one more thing from his workshop next door. As the solid wooden door closed over, I heard him dragging heavy sandbags into place on the other side. It made me anxious, for it would slow his return to us.

There is nothing to describe the fear engendered by falling bombs. The dull thuds. The whooshes, the explosions, the rumbles, and the slow Armageddon sound of tumbling masonry. There had been two swift earlier raids, one causing direct hits on nearby streets. Fires were burning. We watched people running, crying out, trying to pass water buckets in chains and vainly trying to douse the flames. Water was in short supply. After sustained fighting around us for months, we were in a poor situation for survival.

I had volunteered for this assignment as I had family here, including an ailing grandmother, and had spent some days taking photographs and interviewing Peshmerga fighters on the status of the Iraqi War in the area. They believed a retaliatory attack was imminent. No one, especially if they are Kurds, sides with the enemies of the Republic of Iraq.

Tolerance is absent. Revenge is severe. As my family were anxious that I should leave, I had called for my driver. He was due by noon. For once I had agreed that no news story was worth further risk whilst I could still get out. But the car had not materialised when the planes came.

High on one wall of our basement was a narrow window, sealed and criss-crossed with tape. It opened at street level directly onto the wide road near Halabja's Grand Mosque. My younger brother climbed up on a stool to stand and look outside. The call to prayer had gone out and he saw men in the street when the aerial pounding started.

The first wave were MiG-23s, according to my knowledgeable brother. Their bombs thudded down and exploded with grey smoke. Dust followed. Then came smaller planes that he thought were Russian Sukhoys. Thinking how little it mattered what they were, I changed places with him in time to see yellow-white clouds descending. They did not look like dust clouds. Too yellow compared to the grey stone of Iraqi buildings. Too dense. The clouds fell in a peculiarly uniform and purposeful way. The colour was reminiscent of sulphur in school lab fume cupboards. It was not good.

By 5 p.m. the bombing had stopped. I heard wailing. Although I had climbed higher to stand on a pair of packing cases to improve my view at the window, it was now obscured by a young man lying down. He seemed to be gasping for breath but then he started laughing. Or was he convulsing? He had rubbed his eyes which began bleeding. The backs of his hands blistered as I watched. His skin was blackening and began peeling from his fingers. I recoiled in horror, climbed back down to sit on the floor, grasped my stomach, and started praying. What was this hell which had descended from the sky? There had been rumours of what was coming but many thought the government would not dare. My mother sat, head in her hands. My two teenage brothers sat cross-legged and silent. A rare sight.

'Where is Papa?' asked Ahmed.

'He will be back soon,' I said, without much conviction.

The thumps of bombs, or warheads or whatever they were, continued for around forty-five minutes: I had left my watch upstairs. A period of silence – half an hour or more – then ensued before the street came alive with people running and shouting. And then the screaming began.

Soldiers arrived. We heard their vehicles. It was a common, easily recognisable noise. The man, now a distorted body, who had occluded my view was removed. I could make out bent figures in Iranian uniform, and some of our own Peshmergas, lifting up other corpses: men, women, children. Dogs lay lifeless in the dust too. The soldiers returned very quickly each time. I suspected they had lorries to load, but none was in my field of sight. Seeing the soldiers wearing gas masks and huge gloves, I realised our predicament. How long would it be before it was safe for us to leave our sealed tomb?

I poured drinks of water for my brothers and my mother, calculating how long our supply might last. They sipped in a daze and declined my offer of bread. I took nothing. We waited.

With dawn next morning, I resolved to venture forth alone. The boys huddled together. Mother was still sleeping. Having the sandbags on the other side, the door was hard to open. It took all my strength. My father lay at the top of the stairs, his skin peeled and raw. The rictus of his expression showed his death had not been a peaceful one. My anger knew no bounds, but I sobbed no tears. Wrapping my headscarf around my nose and mouth, I stepped over him to move towards the front door of our house and look out into the street. That was not difficult. A pile of rubble and dust had been forced to one side. The house was a shell and the door posts stood proudly erect in splendid isolation: there was no door. A soldier approached, asking if I was well.

'Yes. I have brothers and a mother in the basement.'

'You are in luck. Transport is here. Touch nothing. Bring nothing.' He pointed to a Red Crescent Lorry along the street. 'They will take you. The other one further on is for the sick. He did not have to tell me what the third and fourth lorries were for: they were uncovered and piled high. At that moment, a passing man vomited violently. As the green stream spurted, the soldier pushed me out of the line of fire. 'Please hurry. Get them! Cover their noses and mouths as thickly as you can.' He gesticulated to our basement hole. 'Tell them, we leave immediately.'

I asked him to move my father so that my brothers would be spared the horrific sight. As the soldier shrugged, his epaulettes flapped. A shout wheezed through his mask and snapped fingers brought two Peshmergas who unceremoniously lifted the remains of my rigid, contorted father to carry him to one of the lorries of twisted, once – human, beings. I thought of the pictures of Auschwitz after its relief. Professionally, I should have had a camera. Personally? The thought made me sick.'

Swiftly praying for my father's soul and all others suffering inhumanity from their own states, I sped down to swathe my family's faces and bundle them up the stairs as fast as I could. Fleeting glances up and down the street showed my father's workshop was gone. As was the butcher. And the baker. Adjacent streets had vanished into a bomb crater. My mother was lifted into the lorry. She did not cry, only staring in numb disbelief at a point far, far away.

In history there have been many Bloody Fridays world-wide. Why, I wonder, is Friday a day designated to be marked by atrocities? But this is one of the worst Fridays ever.

As we left, my abiding memory is of the smell of rotten apples. I will never look at an apple without thinking of my brave father as I last saw him. He was clutching a bag of jewellery from the workshop, doubtless thinking we could fund our escape. The soldiers forbade us from taking anything in case of contamination. I was sure someone would take it for their own. But no matter. I would have given it to anyone in order to spare my father and fellow Kurds from this callous genocide.

Eventually, we were taken to Kermanshah. A doctor checked us over and we were assigned to a sports hall with other families. It took me four hours to find a telephone to phone in this report. My mother and brothers are safe now, on the way to relatives. But the world must know Saddam Hussein has used nerve gas against his own people. The soldiers are saying it was mustard gas and sarin.'

What I did not know then, was that the person taking the reporter's dictation praised her courage in reporting the story and offered effusive condolences along with instructions for meeting a driver and assurances that air tickets would be at the airport. Nor did I know of the correspondent's own secret story, whose ultimate outcome she would not know for seven months. What I did know then was that in Oxford fourteen years later, I had tears in my eyes and did no work for the rest of the night. Nor did I sleep.

10

Under the Radar

Friday Jan 31, 2003, Berlin

He had been darting into shops and alleys while watching
out for recurring faces, but so far saw no evidence of being
followed. It had been a rotten night. The small Berlin
hotel was the worst so far. Despite smart public areas, his
bedroom was tired, tiny, with a short lumpy bed and single-
glazed window set yards from the railway track. Trains
had rumbled all night. Suspecting the sheets had not been
laundered, he had not undressed. The breakfast of two small
dry rolls, dubious spread, and artificial purple 'jam' had left
him hungry. He felt he couldn't risk an ATM withdrawal but
vowed to splurge out on a decent coffee and sandwich with
Azzie. Having never had to watch the pennies before, today
he had a fresh perspective on life's priorities.

Pulling up his hood, he trudged along the snow-crusted
streets. With typical German efficiency, the roads themselves
had been cleared. Buses and trams moved freely. He had
a momentary pang of homesickness for New York and
childhood games of demolishing the high snow-ploughed
walls on the sidewalks. Some were as high as six feet. Or
were they lower? He'd been young, innocent, laughing with
his brother, finding joy in simple things in NY and later in
Boston. When life was uncomplicated. And no one thought
you an enemy of the state.

Berlin was busy but Jared knew his way about and understood how the subway worked. Getting euro coins had proved a hassle. The hotel exchange rate was a rip-off and the clerk unpleasant when he'd requested coins rather than notes for his sterling.

He got his ticket at Unter den Linden and negotiated the card-readers to board his U5 train. He didn't mind standing. As the train rumbled on, for the hundredth time he reprised all the discussions he'd had with Azwar Barzinji over the last year, believing there had been nothing incriminatory in any of them, nothing linking Azzie to terrorist groups, no evidence of anti-American sympathies. That 'security' gorilla in London was a deluded fanatic. Jared's faith in democracy had taken a knock. Big Brother was certainly watching.

Arranging this meeting had been hard, needing all the mutual connections he could trawl who weren't on his 'Crescent Task Force' mailing list. Had that name been the problem? *Task Force.* He couldn't remember who'd made it up: it was a joke. They were just friends who'd met in the summer while volunteering. Finding Azzie had necessitated using newly adopted email addresses in internet café PCs with impersonal IP addresses. Tedious. But after that awful grilling by the CIA (or whoever the hell that gorilla at the Embassy answered to) he felt he daren't risk mailing Azzie direct. And he didn't have a mobile number on which to call him with his new 'burner' phone.

The train was emptying. Rubbing his eyes, Jared secured a seat. His life had become a nightmare. Like a Robert Ludlum book. What was the world coming to when a simple Oxford postgrad had to defend and justify his friends? And trying to stay completely off radar was much harder than novels suggested. He'd thought himself clever buying a jacket with his credit card in a Burtons' store streets away instead of near the Eurostar. Bloody naïve. The train guard had asked for his passport. 'They' would now know he was in Europe. But on the second train, from Brussels, no one had asked for identification: he might be home and dry.

Jared was pleased that his cryptic messaging had found Azzie not in Iraq, but back in Berlin. Not surprising perhaps as all he'd talked about during those long nights in the camp had been his fervent wish to return to Germany where he'd happily studied.

Leaving the train, Jared negotiated his way through the milling crowds, leaving the busy station complex, dodging between yellow trams and crossing over Alexanderplatz to reach their old Turkish café haunt just off the main thoroughfare. He chose an outside seat at the corner, glad of his new padded jacket.

Though well after nine, it was still busy with people on their way to work. For them, an ordinary Friday morning, for him, his fifth day on the run. Not that he was in truth, fleeing from 'arrest'. Mind you, he wouldn't put anything past that bastard in the embassy. In the half-hour he waited, no waiter approached, and he wondered why they'd bothered putting tables outside. Then, he spotted Azwar coming across the square. He looked tired, thin and sad, making Jared anxious. His friend walked past him without acknowledgment but paused at the door to turn and indicate by his eyes that Jared should follow him inside. Looking round, Jared waited a moment then did so.

The bohemian café with its scrubbed communal tables bearing diagonal red gingham cloths was empty. Azzie was sitting at the rear beside the toilets, his back to the wall from where he had a full view of the café.

'Hey, man, great to see you.' Jared stepped forward to embrace his friend. He was shocked at how slight he had become.

Azwar looked around. 'So, what's this about, Jared?'

Jared was pleased Azwar was speaking in Arabic: his own

German was seriously rusty, and he knew Azwar's English was limited. Jared's father had pushed for his Arabic tuition; most of his peers had only studied European tongues. Ironic. If he hadn't spoken Arabic, then he wouldn't have been able to volunteer. And wouldn't be here.

The waitress arrived. Jared glanced at the menu and ordered two black coffees and roasted halloumi and veg pittas which he knew Azzie loved.

'Not for me, Jared.' Azzie raised his hand to demur.

Taking in Azzie's old woollen jacket with frayed cuffs and torn pockets, Jared knew money must be an issue. Curious if he was working. Or was he not working as a doctor? He waited until the girl left before saying, 'The food's on me, Azzie. I'm in a shit hotel and had a crap breakfast! But I had to speak to you, if only to tell you that they may be watching you.'

Azwar laughed. 'Someone has always been watching me, my friend! I have been looking to my back for many years. But who is it that you think finds me interesting enough to follow?'

'It's the CIA, I suspect. They have the idea some of our camp buddies are plotting terrorist stuff. I was summoned to the London Embassy and given the third degree.'

'Oh, Jared, none of them will be involved in plots. They are humanitarians like us. Red Crescent volunteers do not kill, they aim to save lives! But I suppose we are living in tough times, and I cannot be sure that some may not be driven to boiling point. At home there is much anger about Saddam, you know – his belligerent actions, the sanctions he has caused. But I became silent after I lost my job for criticising. I had to stop speaking out so I could get work to support my family. Some people are now becoming vocal, incensed about Bush and Blair wanting to serve their own ends by toppling him. Doubt it would help us. Everyone who can is leaving. Sanctions have crippled us.'

'I'm glad you got out.'

'I was so lucky. My girl, Naza, knew someone who got me false papers and a tourist visa for Germany. But she is in prison now. I have no idea where – not knowing is a nightmare.'

'I am so sorry, Azwar.'

'My personal situation is unhappy, but if there is war it will be worse at home. Even amongst the refugees here, some stir trouble and add to the warmongering. I hear things from family and in the hospital which unsettle me greatly.'

'Like what?'

Azwar tensed, looking across the empty café to the door as an old man came in and sat down. Seeing him warmly greeted by the waitress as a regular, Azwar's shoulders relaxed. 'OK, let me tell you about my cousin Zoran. He was in the camp at Zindarf.'

'Where? '

'It is a migrant camp near Nurnberg. He says there was a fool telling the camp organisers about Saddam's dangerous ammunition stockpiles for use against the West. He boasted he managed a weapons facility and swaggered to the other inmates that the intelligence he was supplying would be his passport out of the camp. But Zoran knew the man, a fellow chemical engineering student called Rafiq al-Janabi who barely passed exams and had no friends. Zoran said al-Janabi was a fantasist who would never have been put in charge of a facility in a million years. I have seen the man myself at the hospital recently, brought into the emergency room by the police. He is a drunk, often found confused and agitated in the street. When I treated him, his hospital records showed that in the brief time he had been in Berlin, he'd been sedated several times. The last time, I knew the policeman who brought him. He told me, laughing, that the fellow was boasting he'd given the BND vital intelligence about him running chemical factories and mobile weapon units in Iraq. The policeman didn't believe any of it, considered him a deranged nuisance and wanted him committed. But we found that impossible. My instructions from above were to prescribe sedatives and discharge him. I am sure it is the same man Zoran met. He knew though that Rafiq was interviewed frequently in the camp by BND, and when my cousin left, Rafiq was waiting on asylum papers for freedom. Zoran can't believe the word is out that the Americans believe al-Janabi's BND information and may use it as an excuse for war.'

'Surely not. On one man's story?'

'Who knows? But it is likely they are looking after him. When he came into the hospital, he had a *"Sozialversicherungsausweis."*

'God don't Germans have long words! Is that a Social Security number or what?'

'Yes. But he had no job on record. It is significant.'

'Why?

'Immigrants or refugees usually get the number when they get a job, like Zoran and I did. I suspect the authorities have just given him a number and are paying him themselves.'

'But what are these weapons? The UK press is very vague.'

'Zoran says they call them "mass destruction." They could be biological, like anthrax or nerve gases like they've used in Halabja and elsewhere against the Kurds. Or even nuclear. There is a fuss about UN nuclear inspectors not getting access to sites.'

'I've seen that in the papers too.'

'I never read papers; they are all lies.'

'So where is your Zoran now?'

'In Hamburg. He has his papers, a technical job, and a new wife he met in the camp. Many of my family are also there, but I prefer Berlin. My student years here were happy. I was sorry I went home.' The sandwiches had arrived.

Azwar stopped to eat hungrily.

Jared had a wave of overwhelming sorrow for his friend as he asked gently, 'And how is your mother? Is she with you?' He remembered Azzie speaking fondly of his mother and her struggles to bring him up after his father's early death.

'She is in Baghdad. Sick. I send her as much money as I can for her cancer treatment, but the drugs are in short supply. I did send actual drugs I bought from my hospital, but of course, they never arrived.'

'Your hospital?'

'Yes, I am back in the Charité, the University Hospital. You know I was prevented from working as a doctor at home? They thought me "seditious." I was even in prison for a few months and could only get work as an orderly with the Crescent. Thankfully, back here my German degree has given me asylum and a job from one of my old professors.'

'But in the emails over the winter – why did you hint you were still in Iraq?'

'I decided not to broadcast where I was in case they linked my flight to Naza. But now she is in trouble anyway. I think she may have helped one person too many – a government spy, who knows?' Azwar's voice broke. 'There is one other important thing about this al-Janabi. The day after he left, I received a blood report showing he had macrocytic anaemia, not surprising if he drinks heavily, but I could not file it in his records or contact him for treatment.'

Jared frowned. 'Why not?'

'His records had gone. He does not exist anywhere on the hospital system.'

Before Jared could process this, Azwar glanced at his battered Timex and rose. 'Thank you for breakfast, my friend, but I must go. I have a clinic with the professor at eleven. I hope we may meet again. Please stay safe. *Fi Amanillah!*'

Jared repeated the Iraqi farewell for friends going on a

94

journey whom you may not see again for a long time. They shook hands. Jared watched him go, shoulders down, stooped like an old man. They were the same age. How unfair was life. Such a matter of chance where you were born. Feeling guilty for being born into wealth and security, he lifted his phone to call his father. Once he knew what was best to do, he'd call Sophie. He tried to imagine how he'd feel if she were in a prison somewhere because she'd arranged his escape from Hell. With the heaviness in his heart came a pang of self-realisation: he knew how much he loved her.

11

The Key to the Mystery?

The week passed uneventfully. Buckling down to my essay and extra work, I met the Friday noon 'punishment essay' deadline. That evening, Abbie and I sat in her room, saving the world, and draining the variety of alcoholic beverages we had between us.

Saturday morning, I slept late and woke groggy but managed to stagger safely up out of my narrow bed. Longing for a cup of tea but having run out of teabags, I groaned, grabbed my dressing gown and headed for the kitchen where Abbie sat reading a book, drinking coffee, fully dressed, fully made-up, and immaculately coiffured. Self-consciously tucking a clump of wayward hair behind my ear, I filled the kettle and switched it on.

'Morning, Abbie. You're up early. Not like you on a Saturday.'

'Oh, I couldn't sleep for thinking about poor Cedric, he was such a sweetheart. Good night, last night, though. Say, remind me to get more gin, you certainly tanked it!'

'But surprisingly I don't feel too bad.' Opening the tea caddy, I plucked out a teabag and grabbed a mug. It was that 'Keep Calm and Carry On' one again. Becoming my mantra.

'I have got a bit of a headache, but don't think it's from booze, more from thinking too much about stuff.' Abbie contemplated the ceiling. 'Like, should I go on the wagon? Well, like apart from weekends, of course. Maybe I need to keep sharper – you know? And should I give up men while I'm here, Jude? Reckon this is my time to concentrate on me, what I want. I can get a coupla years more here. Thinkin' I might do a DPhil even.' She was looking uncharacteristically serious. 'You know I wanna make a real difference to the world. Gotta prove to my father I'm not just a silly little girl to be dressed pretty and paraded. Boy, I worked at that Rhodes. You gotta get folk to push you on, you know. I did it. Got a senator even. He said I had grit and intelligence!'

'I'm sure you have.' I was yawning, having trouble grasping any intelligent thoughts as the kettle clicked off.

'So, guys are down the agenda, for sure. Unless, of course, I'm hit by a thunderbolt of passion on the man front. But in Oxford, somethin' tells me that ain't gonna happen. I mean, I like older guys, they're better than my old college classmates who were all dick and no conversation, but I've sure been disappointed over here. Most of these dons are as dull as Minnesota on a Monday.'

Not being sure where Minnesota was or why it might be dull on any day of the week, I didn't comment while selecting a clean teaspoon and sniffing my just-past-its-sell-by milk to pour into my mug and add hot water.

'Say, why do you Brits put milk in first? Ain't that too much?'

'Ha! My ex complained I took baby tea. The "milk first" is historic. According to my gran, you'd crack a fine china cup if you poured in boiling tea straight from a silver teapot.' I stirred milk into the mug then discarded the teabag onto the ever-full bin. I'd tackle it later. As I sat down, there was a scratching at the back door.

'Heck, that's Selassie! I let him out last night. Forgot he can't get back in.' Abbie rose to admit the shivering animal. 'D'you know where we can get him an overcoat? Having a cat like this in England's a crime.' She set Selassie down, emptying out the last of my milk for him. 'Poor wee fatherless thing.'

He lapped the milk hungrily then came to rub himself against my leg. I stroked him, scratching his neck around his collar the way my old cat had liked. Sadly, Selassie had folds of skin and thin fur rather than old Nellie's luxurious coat and my fingers slid easily under his soft woven collar. 'Quite forgot with everything else going on, Abbie. What happened to that thing you found in his collar? Can't feel it. Has it fallen out?'

'Give him here. It's sorta jammed underneath. Funny, doesn't seem to bother him.' Abbie lifted the cat onto her lap and tweaked out a black rectangle from the side of the expandable collar. 'I suppose Cedric got this soft collar 'cos hard leather would've rubbed his smooth skin. It's retained the rubber thing well.' The cat leaped off her knee to head for my proffered bowl of cat food.

Abbie placed the small brown key tray on the table. One side of its rubber was smooth, the other held a trefoil-headed, flat, silver key in a customised depression. We gazed at it as the cat enthusiastically wolfed his chicken Whiskas, clunking the bowl on the floor.

Prising the key out with the point of a knife, I held it up. 'So, what can this be for?'

'More to the point, why stuff it under a cat's collar? Nuts! Not the safest place. Done in a hurry, d'you think, Jude?'

'Another puzzle.'

'I reckon it might be for a briefcase.' Abbie took it. 'Or a desk drawer? A gym locker? Or a left luggage one? It's too small for a room door.'

'It's too fancy for a left luggage locker. I've used plenty of those. And its serrated side looks too complex for a briefcase, doesn't it?'

Turning it sideways, Abbie laughed. 'It looks like the New York skyline! I suppose if it were for a desk drawer it'd have a shorter, tubular, shaft?'

'No idea.' I took the key, replaced it in the rubber tray and tossed it back over to her. 'No marks or clues on the case either. Anna might know.'

'Know what?'

'To do about the cat, Guy,' I retorted, catching Abbie's gaze, and flicking my eyes towards the key. Before she could retrieve it, Guy was over, looking down at the table. Picking up the cat, I rose to stand beside him. 'What do you think we should do with Selassie, Guy?'

Guy wasn't deterred. He leaned forward to pick up the key in its nest. 'So, who has a safety deposit box, then?'

'It's mine,' Abbie snatched it to stuff it into her jeans pocket. 'My father got it for my valuables while I'm in the UK. There's coffee in the pot if you want. Jude and I are off out.'

This was news to me, but interpreting this as a cue to leave, I downed my tea and stood up to head for the door. 'Yes, must get dressed. Time's getting on.'

Moving swiftly past me into the hall, Abbie muttered, 'Be ready in five. Brunch Council of War and a Buck's Fizz on me!' At the foot of the staircase she turned, saluted melodramatically, and took the stairs two at a time.

Inside my room, I leaned back against the door. That had felt like a lucky escape. But from what? God – corpses, cars, keys, and cats! If you wrote this stuff in a novel no one would believe you. I'd intended to collect my books from the library, but it didn't close till one o'clock so I'd still make it even with breakfast out. I expected to have plenty of time for study this weekend to compose a brilliant essay to astound Becker. A glance in the mirror showed a more pressing issue: tangled, fuzzy hair, sticking out at all angles. I plugged in the straighteners. My phone buzzed but I ignored it. I'd managed jeans, jumper, and boots, but had barely unkinked my fringe when Abbie was at the door.

The Blue Café wasn't busy. I was surprised until I saw the

clock on the wall showed it was still only ten o'clock, early for an Oxford Saturday. Abbie peremptorily ordered a stack of blueberry pancakes and coffee for two. I was resigning myself to the fact that I'd need to learn to like coffee, since everyone was so sure that was what I wanted.

Abbie was looking intense. 'Now, the key. Yeh, I should have twigged it was a security box. My dad has ones similar, if bigger.'

'Your dad has bank boxes? Like in heist movies? Why does he need one?'

'Oh, you know, for cash that's not for the IRS, Mum's jewellery, old coins, photos that might be useful, lots of stuff.'

'When are photos useful?' I felt very thick.

'Oh, come on, girl! You never know when you'll need a lever in business!'

'What kind of business is your dad in? He sounds like a gangster!'

Abbie gave a musical laugh, throwing her head back. To my horror I realised the nearest table was again occupied by the woman with the small child who'd asked about 'tone cold dead.' Thankfully, she hadn't recognised me.

'He says all businessmen are kinda gangsters! If you're not, you'll sink. Reckons it's all relative. Dad's pretty legit. Buys and sells shares. On the board of a coupla banks. Goes on US Trade commissions. Well connected. Pally with the Bushes an' all, though they're not my cup of tea. Mum's the intellectual brains. Has degrees from Harvard. Used to teach. But Dad's the money-maker. Think I might speak to him about this. I mean, how do we find out what this key is for? And if it is for a bank, which one?'

'Are we sure it's Cedric's?'

'Come on, girl, who else would've put it in the cat's collar?'

'But why should it be us who investigate it, Abbie?

100

Shouldn't we give it to the police? It might be a clue to the murder. Though I suppose we could ask Anna first? If it is for a box, it must hold something important.'

'You wonder, don't you? Yeh, we have to ask Anna. She'll know which banks he used, for sure. I mean, there's a heap of banks in Oxford. It needn't be here, of course, could be in London, Amman, or Baghdad or wherever he kept disappearing to every few months.'

'I don't even know exactly what he did when he's away. Jon told me he worked on old language tablets, but not why he went overseas. Lectures, maybe? I wish I'd asked Jared.' I stopped, hesitating in case I was implying that I'd recently seen him.

Abbie sighed. 'I'm worried about Jared. Like, could he have been kidnapped too?'

I made a snap decision. If I couldn't trust Abbie, who else was there? 'He's OK. I took him to the station on Monday.'

'You what?'

'I helped him with his, er... getaway!'

'Jude Frazer, I knew you had some spunk! But why has he done a runner?'

'It's to do with the CIA and terrorist emails or something. And he had to go overseas somewhere to sort it all out. He hid with Sophie for a bit as he thought he was being followed and then he took off.'

'Where to?'

'No idea. But he didn't take a warm jacket.'

'So, not Europe then?'

'Well, he was heading for the Eurostar first. He's a worried boy. They told him when he goes home at Easter to the States, they could stop him coming back here. The US Embassy read his emails and called him up. The poor boy said it was all nonsense.' I shrugged, realising how far-fetched it sounded.

Abbie's eyes were wide 'How exciting!' The serving

girl glanced down at the plates of pancakes in puzzlement, obviously wondering why Abbie thought they were exciting. They weren't, but they were tempting. And delicious. Funny how stress like exams, usually put me off food, yet this murder-mystery-key-terrorism hassle had made me ravenous. With three spoonsful of sugar in it, the coffee was almost palatable.

'Judith! Coo-eee!'

As Gwen manoeuvred past and plonked herself down, I snatched up the key from the table and put it in my coat pocket.

'How are you doing? Fancy bumping into you! The police said I couldn't get access to the study for the present, so I haven't been into college, but I've been worried about you all.'

'We're fine. How are you?' Abbie licked maple syrup off her spoon.

'Keeping busy. I've been to see Anna a few times. She's being amazingly brave, but of course with everything she's been through in her life, she's made of stern stuff. Such an admirable woman.'

'Oh?' I didn't like to let this opening pass. 'So, what has she been through?' I tried to sound nonchalant, but heard my voice rise in pitch.

'Well, she was a young correspondent in the Middle East during the Iran-Iraq War. Saw terrible things, like her father being killed. Then her mother and brothers died tragically soon after. Not sure of details. In '87 or '88 perhaps? There've been so many wars out there, haven't there? Another one soon by all accounts. Yes. She and Cedric got married here, then she lost a baby but fell pregnant again soon after. It was a quiet wedding, what with her having no family, of course. And in a registry office. Well, why not? Neither of them goes to church. Or in her case, the mosque. Not sure if Cedric's father came down.'

I smiled gently at Gwen's torrent of disjointed information. 'No family? How terrible. I didn't know. Come to think on it, though. I don't know much about Cedric either.'

'His passion was his Gilgamesh book.'

'Never heard of Gilgamesh before.' Abbie took a sip of coffee.

'It's pre-Biblical.' Gwen nodded knowledgeably. 'There are lots of sections of it in the British Museum, but bits are still missing.'

'Jon told me all about it.'

'Cedric was a world authority on that whole Mesopotamian area. No one knew more. From ancient times to the present. And such a communicator, so in demand by the press for comment on everything that happens there even now, especially in Kurdistan, Iran, and Iraq. Anna was an eminent journalist but since having Ramin she preferred not to work. She won some big journalism award in her day. Her family were Kurds. They're still persecuted. Terrible.' She looked at her watch. 'Is that the time? Must go. My friend will be here shortly. Since it's getting busy, I'll grab that table at the window and leave you to it, girls.' She sped off to sit at a vacant table for two.

'So, Jude, d'you reckon someone did Cedric in because of Sumerian poetry or the coming Iraq War, then?' Abbie looked at me, plucked eyebrows sitting quizzically high.

'I think it's more likely due to whatever is contained in whatever this opens.' I held up the key. 'Let's keep it safe till we've spoken to Anna.' Instead of returning it to my pocket, I took out my purse and tucked it into the zipped coin pocket.

The bill came and I settled it as Abbie was already heading towards the door, obviously having forgotten her promise to buy brunch. But she did hold the door open and started taking charge again. 'Right, then. How about tonight I treat you to college dinner? We'll need to start investigating somewhere. It's the perfect place to find out all about Cedric from the college gossips. You need to book it before twelve.' Glancing at her watch, she said, 'Should manage that.'

Abbie's legs were much longer than I'd realised. I found myself running to keep up. 'I've never been to High Table.'

'Oh, in Winston it's just a Saturday night dinner really, not as much the formal dressy ritual thing they have in the old fusty colleges. Basically, it's loads of men getting drunk on subsidised wine! Can be fun. Time for glad rags and flirting. My treat.'

'Great,' I replied.

Abbie laughed. 'Come on, Jude!'

Trotting back down Banbury Road, I decided I quite liked being called 'Jude.' And I might even quite like another evening with Abbie.

*

After Judith and Sophie had left the café, Gwen's friend nodded through the window at a van pulling away from the kerb outside. 'That van's got a funny bump on its roof. Is it like one of those surveillance vans you see in the movies?'

Gwen laughed. 'I don't know where you get your silly ideas from, Betty! It's just a delivery van. Maybe it's got one of those new satellite thingies I saw on the TV.'

'Oh, I know – it's a BBC licence detector van! They come in plain clothes, so people don't know it's the BBC looking for dodgers.'

'Plain clothes?' Gwen laughed heartily. 'That's for detectives, not vans. You'll be telling me next that it's the CIA!' She called the waitress for more coffee. 'So, what film shall we see this afternoon?'

'Gosford Park sounds good. I can't resist a film with Maggie Smith in it!'

'What's it about, Betty?'

'I think it's a period comedy about a murder in a library …'

Gwen shrugged. 'Oh, well, if you must.'

12

Glad Rags

As I set off for the library to collect my books, Abbie went to book college dinner with the steward. In my view, it was unlikely a dinner would shed any light on her quest to uncover the life, loves, and hates (or haters) of the sadly deceased prof, but I supposed it could do no harm. Since arriving, I'd avoided formal dinners. Although Winston members didn't have to attend in formal academic gowns like older, more traditional colleges, the hassle of getting dressed up to go out for an evening was something I'd decided to avoid during my year of 'escape' from everyday life. Such social functions were stressful reminders of compulsory evenings spent supporting Steve's career. As I walked, I called Sophie who was enthusiastic about the dinner plan.

'Good idea. You should have done one before, Mum. It'll be lovely. Great food, delicious wine. You get interesting folk at the High Table too. We had Oliver Stone at one of ours!'

Unsure who he was, I merely asked Sophie what I should wear. She offered to come and help me choose. At the library, I flashed my card and headed up the stairs to my course shelves to gather the books and photocopy the bits I needed of the ones I couldn't take home.

Back at my desk, I paused before booting up the computer. My tumbler full of pens was sitting to my left though I had no recollection of putting it there and I had to search for my highlighter, curiously in my left desk drawer, not right as usual. I had to get more sleep.

The afternoon went quickly as I read, highlighted passages, and scribbled notes on '*The interplay between generic and subject-specific issues in curriculums.*' I wondered whether taking a sabbatical here had been a mistake? My other post-divorce notion of taking a 'gap' year travelling across Asia might have been easier. I worked on, expecting Sophie's arrival would be a timely reminder for getting ready, but when I heard a knock on the door I nearly died when my watch told me it was six o'clock!

In the doorway stood Abbie, a vision of loveliness in a black silk dress, killer heels, and fur jacket. She looked at me in horror. 'Hey – you not dressed yet? For goodness' sake Jude, we have to be at the table by seven on the dot or they'll not admit us. Come on!' Barging into the room, she flung wide my wardrobe doors and started tossing clothes onto the bed. 'Where are your cocktail dresses?'

'Cocktail dresses?' I mumbled, 'I didn't bring any.'

Abbie grabbed a red, velvet top and black trousers. 'This'll do. You got black heels?'

I shook my head.

Abbie put her foot alongside one of mine. 'Not much difference in size. I have huge feet considering my height! Come on, you get dressed.' She shot out of the room.

I pulled off my jeans, and hastily pulled on the clothes then found I could not get my foot into my only pair of high heels (navy). No wonder. I was still wearing my woolly boot socks. Rummaging in a drawer, I found a pair of pop socks without holes, donned them and slipped on the shoes. They'd have to do. After tipping my makeup bag contents out on the desk, I applied warpaint at the speed of an old school morning. The door banged open again to admit Abbie swinging a large black linen bag in one hand and curling tongs in the other. Plugging in the tongs and switching them

106

on, from the bag she dumped a fistful of jewellery on the desk beside the cosmetics and then held up a pair of black patent heels.

'Think these'll fit, I just bought them but they're a bit big. You Brits sure have weird sizing in shoes and clothes!' She threw the shoes on the floor and shoved me down onto the dressing table stool to fit a shoe on my foot like she was Prince Charming. 'Perfect!' From the jewellery, she selected a pearl necklace, earrings, and a cuff. 'Here! This should perk up your outfit!'

As she looped the earrings in my ears and fastened the necklace, I closed the bracelet clasp, admiring its large sparkling red stone. 'My, is this real?' I asked, then yelped as she caught my upper ear with the hot tongs while twining my hair.

'Sorry – but you gotta keep still!' Swiftly working over my head, she fluffed my hair with a brush before delving again into her black bag to produce a massive can of hair lacquer. Her wild spraying sent me into a coughing fit. Yanking the tongs out of the wall socket, she stood back to admire her handiwork. 'Hmm. Not bad. But you need more lip colour!' From the bag came a red lip gloss she applied over my 'Summer Rose.'

'There!' She lifted me out of the seat and twirled me round as if appraising a child.

I barely recognised myself in the mirror. 'Gosh, Abbie. You are a whizz!'

'An "almost late" whizz. I'll have to pay for our dinners even if we don't get in. Come on!'

Now delving into the wardrobe, Abbie tossed out my red wool coat and a black, red, and silver-embroidered shawl, a present from Sophie I'd never had an occasion to wear.

'Love the scarf, Jude. Wear it as a wrap at dinner. Let's go – drinks will be up!'

Abbie propelled me out of the back door down to the

river path as such pace that I was out of breath by the time we arrived. Tossing our coats into the cloakroom, she marched me into a room I'd never been in before. A steward approached with a tray. Smiling thanks, I took a glass, sipped, then grimaced. 'Ugh! I hate sherry.'

Abbie laughed. 'Don't worry, I've ordered us G&Ts. You need to ask. Sherry's for old maids.' Waving at someone across the room, she put her hand on the small of my back and thrust me towards a vaguely familiar stocky chap in a dinner suit. As Abbie chattered earnestly at him, I mused on how confident she was. Much more so than I'd been at her age – or was even now. She nudged me. 'We were just saying, weren't we, Jude, how awful it is about Professor Gilbert? Especially for you, of course.' She patted my arm. 'Judith found him.'

It was only when he turned to face me that I realised it was Professor Manders, the Assistant Master. Amazing how different folk looked dolled up in glad rags. I usually saw him in the bar wearing a crumpled linen jacket and open necked shirt. He looked concerned.

'Oh, my dear, that must have been most unpleasant.'

'It was. He was a lovely man. Who could do such a thing?' Couldn't believe I was repeating Gwen's irritating mantra, but pathetically couldn't think of anything else to say.

'Well, I suppose he did tread on a lot of toes.' Manders downed his sherry and swiped another from a passing tray. 'He was not universally liked, you know.'

'Oh, gee, why was that?' I worried Abbie was over playing her 'ditzy American blonde' role: bending forward, drawling her words, fluttering eyelashes while sucking on her lower lip. But I had to admit my pupils would have loved her theatrics: you'd never hear this kind of chat in Castlemilk! And that coquettish look as she said, 'I'd have thought the college would've liked having a world authority on the Middle East like Gilbert in their midst?' She looked so innocent. She must have had drama lessons.

'Oh, I wouldn't go so far as to say, "world authority" – he was more a showman. Too ready to pronounce an opinion without the rigours of diligent research, pandering to tabloid jingoism with his over-simplification of world events on which, as an "Ancients" man, he had no right to be commenting.' Manders tutted.

Stepping back, I stiffened. 'Surely everyone is entitled to an opinion?'

He turned to me. 'Excuse me, have we been introduced?'

'I am Judith Frazer, from Scotland. We have met before in the bar …'

'Indeed? Are you a guest?'

'No, I'm taking a sabbatical Masters in Education.' My stomach tightened. We'd met twice. Obviously, I wasn't worth remembering.

'Forgive me. Miss Goldman has a habit of turning up with waifs and strays.'

'And is that such a bad thing?' I was annoyed.

At this Manders took a sherry slug and left abruptly.

I felt my face redden and spoke loudly. 'What a totally, utterly obnoxious man!'

Just then a waiter arrived bearing a tray with two drinks bobbing with ice and lemon.

Abbie winked. 'Here you go, sister!'

Discarding the sherry glass that I'd drained in angry reflex at the 'waif' insult, I lifted a bobbing drink. My burning throat and unpleasantly sticky lips welcomed the clean, cool G&T as I grumped, 'Isn't Dr Timothy Manders a moron?'

Abbie raised one eyebrow. 'Not in the true, educational sense of intellectually-challenged idiot, imbecile or moron since his IQ is doubtless high, but as a high falutin' smug, self-satisfied piece of work, for sure, he's a moron! Since Cedric beat Manders to be Assistant Master, he's bad-mouthed him. He's in Cedric's Faculty, Oriental Studies. Subject, contemporary Middle East, emphasis geo-politics, I believe. Unmarried. Bit of a lech. He made a move on me one night – a clumsy, wandering hands kinda move. When I said I'd come with another guy, he vamoosed. I know his type, thinks he's real special. Probably spoiled by his mama. My therapist would have a field day with him. Aha, there's the boss!' Abbie was off.

Curious why she needed a therapist, I wafted in her wake, sidling between the tutors and students milling about the room. I noticed many diners were like Manders, eyes roving while speaking. Reminded me of Steve, for whom 'socialising' was only a means of assessing net worth or client potential in everyone you met. Never relaxing, never simply enjoying yourself, always collecting business cards. Worse, was his abstention: never more than two drinks a night to 'keep on the ball.' Made me look like a lush. Tonight, I felt old and exhausted, but Abbie was in her element. She was now chin-wagging a dapper silver-haired fellow in a sharply pressed, old-fashioned dinner suit with satin lapels. She nodded towards me.

'I was just telling Judith what an asset Professor Gilbert was to the college. He will be sadly missed, won't he, Professor Gadling?'

'Indeed, Miss Goldman, he will?'

He extended a hand to Abbie who shook it. 'Abigail, please, Professor.'

'And how is your father, my dear? Such a generous donation to the Scholarship Fund! Can we expect to see him soon?' Gadling's eyes came to rest on Abbie's cleavage.

'I'm not sure what his plans are. He's real upset about the murder in my house and kinda thinks I should go home.' This was news to me, but Abbie looked sincere. I sipped my G&T as she continued to press the master. 'If the security here isn't up to it, though, it is a worry. I mean, how can we sleep with a murderer about?"

'Oh, you must stay, Miss Goldman. The murder did not have anything to do with the college – it was merely an unfortunate burglary gone wrong, in my view.'

'But drugging his family was pretty extreme, don't you think? Have you spoken to the police, sir?' That decidedly un-American 'sir' had him almost purring back. Some girl, Abbie.

'Of course, Abigail, as College Head they asked for my opinion. Obviously, Cedric was kidnapped to give them the alarm code. Our systems are connected to the police station, you know. At least I hear his wife and child have recovered. The dog sadly, not so.'

Was this Anna's Eli? We hadn't heard this. I would have to ask Gwen.

Abbie was in again. 'But what was of value in the study? What did they take?'

'Oh, you'd be surprised. Ancient books and artefacts are prized in many quarters. First editions too. I'm told items can be stolen to order nowadays – it's an industry worth millions. Even fake antiques can fetch ridiculous sums. Indeed, rumour has it academics have been offered large sums to validate pieces. But Cedric's secretary said nothing was missing.'

'Don't you think it odd they didn't even take his golden statues?' I asked.

'I think it odder his assistant has vanished. Now what are the implications of that, I wonder? The police echoed my suspicion that he may have had a hand in it. One never quite trusts those of his ...' He twisted his neck, took a sip of sherry, and narrowed his eyes. 'Have you been to India, Abigail?'

Abbie looked startled. 'What?'

I raged. 'Jared is not Indian!' Gadling's blatant prejudice was unbelievable!

He sneered, 'But I know the type – would sell his own mother! And then there's that secretary woman. Well, some say she and Cedric were, you know, close.' He shrugged. 'It happens, long hours together. But with such a comely, slender wife as Anna, would he be tempted by such a frumpy woman? Still, there's no doubt Black carried a candle for *him*. A woman scorned, perhaps?'

Abbie's brow furrowed. 'I'd be careful about inferring that kinda thing.'

'Oh, behind closed doors …' Gadling pouted and lengthened his neck.

I felt a compelling urge to slap his smug face. 'I'm sure the murder has nothing whatsoever to do with Jared or Gwen. The intruders, I heard, were foreign.'

Gadling sneered, 'Yes, but who employed them? Gilbert doubtless made enemies abroad – and up at the British Museum. As I told the police, he was opinionated and acerbic.'

'Really, Master? I found him kind and pleasant. Do people actually commit murder because they are black, have been thwarted in love, or differ in opinion?'

While saying this, Abbie had lowered her glass to her waist, holding it in both hands. I thought for a delightful second, she might throw it at Gadling, but she only tossed him a verbal barb. 'When I speak to my father tomorrow, Professor, I expect he'll be appalled to hear that such poisonous gossip and prejudice exists in the College.'

The Master's face closed as his voice lowered. 'Of course, of course, I am being too flippant. Naturally, I am normally above such things, but I expected you girls to appreciate such titbits. Around such gossip does not the world of women revolve?'

'Not in my experience,' said Abbie as I stood mute with anger.

'Well, in all honesty, I neither know nor care what

112

Professor Gilbert was up to nor what the burglars sought. He translated useless dead languages on broken clay tablets, some of which, apparently, were illegally obtained. In fact, I must tell the police how often he went to Iraq, on occasion neglecting his departmental teaching requirements.' Gadling tutted.

Abbie stood back to look him up and down. 'Can't resist a put-down, Sandy, can you?'

Gadling turned puce. I was thrilled. Tight-lipped, he put his head to the side deferentially though his internal struggle was visible: generous benefactors like Abbie's father were hard to come by. 'You Americans abbreviate everything, I know, but please, it's Alexander, not Sandy.' He then twisted his neck and the conversation. 'In any case, Gilbert was up to something in Iraq. Have you been?'

'No. And in the present climate, I doubt anyone's going there at the moment.'

'How does your father view Mr Bush and impending war, Miss Goldman?'

Abbie was cool. 'He's concerned about the economic implications and putting troops at risk, though there is the question of oil supplies and Iraqi armament to be considered.'

At that a bell sounded. Thankfully, the Chief Butler was announcing dinner. We moved off to the other end of the room. Double doors opened to reveal the dining room. By day, stark sixties minimalist in decor, tonight its long, normally bare wood tables were festooned with white linen cloths, gleaming silver, and sparkling glasses. The candlelight was reflecting magically off the polished wood panelling. Oil paintings of college grandees past and present, albeit insignificant by day, were brought alive by the flickering light. None were female. From tonight's company, I observed patriarchy was still the norm and suspected few colleges, apart from the women-only ones, had many female office bearers.

The diners were taking their places. The women wore long dresses, trousers and silk shirts or mid-length frocks: none very fashionable. Men sported varying attire from dark lounge suits to full evening dress and white tie. There were a few African or Asian faces, but the Top Table, assembling across the end of the room with much bowing, consisted entirely of caucasian males over fifty. Gadling sat centrally, Manders to his right.

'That's where Cedric usually sat,' whispered Abbie, pointing at Manders. 'We peasants have free seating. Hey, there's Guy.' Pointing to him, she waved. 'My, he seems grumpy tonight, Jude. Who's that skinny chap beside him looking chummy? Let's sit with them.'

'No idea. They look like Jack Spratt and his wife from the nursery rhyme!' I whispered, pulling out a seat beside Guy's companion. Abbie sat opposite.

Guy's companion turned to speak. 'Good evening. I do not think we have met?'

I froze. We had never met, but I knew who he was.

Later, we staggered back round the river path to the Lodge.

'That red wine was terrific, wasn't it, Jude?'

'Probably. I wouldn't really know. I just buy whatever's on offer in Tesco's!' I stopped. 'But hey, you know that guy in the kitchen the other night with Guy?'

'What guy?' Abbie sounded completely sober despite her gin, six large wines plus two generous cheese-accompanying ports that I'd declined.

I blurted out loudly, 'That was Baz!'

'Yeh, so he said. You're not making sense.' Abbie lurched towards me exuding port fumes.

'Oh, sorry, Abbie, I didn't tell you about the kitchen conspirators, did I?'

'For Jesus' sake girl I'll have you in that river if you don't stop talking in riddles!'

'No, I've only told Keith. There were whisperers in our

114

kitchen.'

'Whisperers?'

'Guy and that guy, Baz. I think they're spies – or undercover cops.'

'Never!' Abbie bent forward to chortle. 'Guy – a cop? How'd he pass the medical? He must weigh three hundred pounds! Wonder why they left early. He likes his port, ye know.'

'Och, no idea! But they are suspicious. In the kitchen at midnight on Sunday, they talked about tailing someone they lost, lamenting the old boy was dead, aerials, charity and stuff. Made no sense to me. Keith's not sure what it was about either.'

'Keith? Who's Keith?'

'Steadman.'

'Oh, Keith is it, now?' Abbie did a little dance, risky in six-inch heels on a stony path.

'You're as bad as Sophie. Come on, after those toffee-nosed dons sneering at Cedric, Indians, secretaries, and women in general, I need my bed. I don't know who's worse – smug Manders or chauvinist, racist Gadling! And hey, by the way, why d'you need a therapist?'

'Doesn't everyone?' Abbie fumbled with her garden door key.

'No, but I'll need one by the time I've finished here!'

We lurched in. I opened my door to toss in my shoes. 'Night, Abbie. See you in the morning.'

It was morning before I realised that I hadn't needed my key to get into my room.

13

Resolve

I woke next morning on my bed, not in it. The only items of clothing I'd removed were Abbie's shoes. To my mind, it had been a waste of a night. All I'd learned during our drinkathon was that Professor Alexander Gadling hated being called Sandy. And Abbie intuitively knew how to press folk's buttons. Smart girl. God, I had to get up. I was so thirsty.

Once vertical, I heard my phone ringing, but couldn't see it. I had no idea where I'd left it. Had I even taken it out to dinner? I remembered having my handbag in the common room where we'd been till God-knows o'clock. Staggering across the room, I stubbed my toe on my desk chair leg before spotting my Nokia on the desk. My bag lay on the floor spilling out its contents. Relieved, I flipped open the phone to see four missed calls from Sophie. When I hit 'call back,' Sophie answered immediately.

'Hi Mum. You OK? You got me worried. Been phoning you since last night.'

'Sorry, I'm just getting up.'

'Getting up? Its half-past eleven! A good night, then? Sorry I didn't make it to help you dress, Chloe had a crisis. Matt's dumped her. But are you free today?'

'Poor Chloe. Shame. Last night was all a bit of a rush to be honest. I must've left my phone here. Don't worry, Abbie dressed me. Oh, was it you calling when I was wrestling with boot socks? Sorry didn't take time to answer. Sorry.'

'Boot socks?'

'Oh, never mind. Let's meet up today, darling. I've got lots to tell you. But could we meet downtown? I'd rather talk away from here.'

'Really? Get my mysterious mother! OK then, how about I meet you at noon in that nice café beside the Carfax Tower on Queen Street? It's midway.'

'Fine, but mibbe a wee bit later please – I've still to get dressed.'

'Such a slob, Mother! I'll give you till half past.' Sophie laughed.

Ending the call, I opened the curtains. Then wished I hadn't. It was exceedingly bright for February. Trying to avoid a persistent green blob in my visual field from the sun, I narrowed my eyes to grope for towels and head upstairs for a shower. On my towel-turbaned way back down I met Abbie carrying up a coffee.

'You must sleep real deep, Jude. I've knocked on your door twice.'

'It must have been the wine.'

'Great night, wasn't it? Not that you made much sense when we got back. But that Manders is defo a contender for the murder. What a sleazeball! Let's go out for lunch and compare notes on last night.'

'Well, I'm meeting Sophie down in Aldgate at twelve-thirty so …'

'Great! I'll come too. See you in a mo!'

Abbie was off up into her room before I could say anything. Sighing, I continued down to get dressed. Abbie was pushy, but it made sense for her to come. It would save time, letting us mull over our discoveries together while getting Sophie up to date. But Abbie was quite wrong about Manders: he'd not use anything as crude and messy as a bust of Socrates to eliminate a rival. He'd be more a backstabber.

Though I wouldn't put much past that rat Gadling: a heavy instrument might be right up his street. Christ, I was losing it, surmising how different people would kill if they'd a mind to! Feeling suddenly dizzy and headachy, I sat down. After a minute, the light-headedness passed so I grabbed the hairdryer, switching it to full heat to blast my thick shoulder-length hair. Being too tired to style it properly, I only gave it an occasional brush flick. I noticed through the window that icicles were hanging on the brick wall. Excellent! A freezing day needed a woolly bunnet. Solved all hair problems!

*

Sitting in the corner of the small deli bistro, Sophie waved away the girl with poised pencil and pad. 'Sorry, I'll order when my mother comes.' When her phone rang, she smiled broadly at the caller name display. Turning her face towards the wall, she whispered fiercely into the phone, 'Jared! Where are you? I've left so many messages – I thought I had the wrong number!'

'Sorry. Hush, I'll not be on long. Though I hope they haven't found these phones yet.'

'Are you OK? You sound kind of flat.'

'Oh, I'm fine, darling.'

Sophie held in a sob on hearing 'darling.' 'So, how did you get on?'

'I found Azzie. As I thought, he's not involved in anything. But he's a poor soul. In a lot of shit. Doesn't know where his girlfriend is, or even if she's alive. She might be in prison. And his mother in Iraq has cancer. He's got asylum and works in a German hospital but he's sure there is nothing to these allegations about the boys. But I'm sorry I went. He's told me stuff I don't want to know.'

'What stuff?'

'Oh, Iraq stuff. War's coming. I'll tell you soon. But hey, do tell your mum I got a coat.'

'A coat?'

'She nagged me to get one and I did. Glad. It's freezing here.'

'But what about Iraq?'

'Oh, I guess we'll be at war any minute, but it's all based on made-up nonsense from an alcoholic.'

'You're kidding? The news is full of Bush and Blair and mass destruction weapons. What's made up? You're being infuriating. When are you coming back?'

'I might go home for a bit. Oh, but hey, I was thinking about you when I met Azzie in Alexanderplatz. Do you remember us having coffee there before going up the Fernsehturm at Christmas?'

Sophie had to smile. 'The TV Tower? Oh, that was a great weekend! I loved Berlin. And I was so impressed you spoke German. Never met anyone who knows so many languages!'

'Huh, my German isn't great. And remember, some of my tongues like Akkadian are ancient. Kinda easy as we don't know how they were pronounced!'

'Oh, I miss you, Jared.'

'And I miss you, but it's so depressing to be on the brink of war …'

'Oh, Jared, how come you've got mixed up in this?'

'It's unfair. My friends and I were just student volunteers. But maybe Dad was right. I shouldn't have worked with the Crescent. It was Anna who persuaded me, telling me about the awful conditions in the camps.'

'Why did you have to run, though?'

'Yeh, well, that embassy guy was so scary, I'm sure he was CIA, and with Cedric being "taken out" after we'd discussed him, and me being followed. I thought the only thing to do was to go and see Azzie. Sorry, must go, Sophe – that's Dad returning my call. '

'Come back, Jared and get a lawyer. Or see the nice police inspector investigating Cedric's death. Was that the

CIA following you?'

'Not sure. But I often saw a black Hummer at night hovering about. Like outside The Eagle a couple of times. One night it followed my taxi back to college. Probably best now to go home to the US and lie low. Mibbe they'll give up, go away. Don't worry, Dad's got clout. I'll phone soon. Love you, Sophie. Stay safe darling, bye.'

*

There was a socio-cultural gulf between Abbie and me. She'd never been on a bus! I swept past the driver flicking my bus pass, but she faffed with her purse, had no coins, argued with the driver at getting no change from a five-pound note and grumbled the rest of the way. We got off in St Aldgate's opposite the Museum of Oxford and hurried up to the corner where High Street intersects with pedestrianised Queen Street. Sophie's chosen café was a few yards past the Carfax Tower. We found her sitting motionless, staring at her phone.

Pulling up a chair, I touched her arm. 'What's wrong, darling?' Tears fell. She shook her head as I moved my arm to her shoulders.

The waitress came. Abbie glanced at the wall menu and barked, 'Three smoked salmon bagels and three lattes,' and sat down.

More coffee. No matter. I squeezed Sophie. 'What's happened, pet?'

'It's Jared.' She cleared her throat. 'He's gone.'

'Gone?' My stomach churned. This quiet 'restorative' Oxford sabbatical was turning into a nightmare. Sophie looked distraught.

'He's not coming back. It's the CIA. Bush is going to war, all based on lies. Jared's worried he's in danger but hopes his dad will get him home to Boston and it'll blow over.' Sophie accepted a tissue from Abbie, telling her, 'Don't know if Mum's said, but they think some of Jared's friends are terrorists. But he says the worst they did was to suggest George W. Bush is an idiot. They're not planning attacks or bomb-making or anything. I mean, as if? It's all vague supposition on their part. So unfair!'

Abbie sat back. 'So, Jared's disappearance is about Al-Qaeda and the stupid CIA thinking an Oxford postgrad is part of a terrorist cell?'

Sophie nodded, bit her lip, and stood up. 'Excuse me, be back in a bit.'

I leaned my elbows on the table and looked over to Abbie. 'I can't believe a young student was ordered up to the London Embassy, threatened, and virtually chased out of town. And in the UK! What happened to free speech?'

'But understandable, maybe. We Americans feel very violated by Al Qaeda – thousands died in the 9/11 attacks. For most politicians, it's not only the casualties, but the loss of face. Drastic action is called for.'

'But isn't the US supposed to be Western World "goodies"? Surely, they shouldn't go around hounding people for expressing an opinion? They're always condemning "baddy" authoritarian leaders for that sort of thing.'

Abbie looked thoughtful. 'But if you don't know Jared you have to admit it looks suspicious. And we have no idea what other websites some of his Iraqi friends might be posting up on, do we?'

'No, but at least now we can be fairly sure that Jared's disappearance isn't related to Cedric's untimely end. And on that subject, I have to say, I don't think it's to do with Manders.'

'I'm not so sure, Jude. He came over as quite vindictive.'

'OK, he's a rude, patronising creep, but if he'd been going to bump off Cedric, he'd have done it before. It's a few years since he lost the election for Assistant Master. I'd bet on it being enough for him to hang about on the side lines sniping at Cedric, trying to discredit him. So, why bother murdering him in his study – especially using Arabs? And you've forgotten about Anna and Ramin – why would he knock them out and snatch Cedric from his home? Manders could just have popped over from college late one night in the summer break when the house was empty and murdered him then!'

Coffee arrived. I went for my now routine syrupy-makes-it-palatable option, piling in two sachets of brown sugar. If I didn't watch it, I'd be leaving Oxford two sizes bigger. As I was saying this to Abbie, Sophie returned, calmer. She looked at my drink in surprise.

'You started drinking coffee, Mum? I thought you hated it?'

'It's OK if you can't taste it for sugar.' At least that made her smile.

Abbie shrugged. 'Sorry, Jude. I've never met anyone who doesn't drink coffee. I'll get green tea next time.'

'Mum hates that even more! Anyway, we can't do anything about Jared, but what about Cedric – have you any more ideas about what happened?'

I told her about the key in Selassie's collar and Baz at Formal Dinner. 'He was definitely the chap I overheard with Guy in the kitchen last Sunday night. You know, they were talking about someone they'd been following who had disappeared – I wondered if that was Jared?'

'Oh, Mum! You haven't told me any of this—and we've spoken a few times this week!'

'Sorry, but you were so worried about Jared and there didn't seem to be a suitable moment. By the way, at dinner, Guy introduced Baz as, "An old friend from the military over here on holiday".'

'So, they might be military or secret service?' Sophie looked thoughtful.

'Don't know. I told Steadman who said he'd look into Guy.'

'There's something I meant to tell you about Guy as well. He asked me out for a drink last week. As if I'd go out with a loud, opinionated old guy? And he's a fraud. Says he goes out "training"? That's a laugh. I've seen him down at the university parks in sports gear but sitting under a tree on the back path puffing on a fag! He's a chancer.'

'I agree. He isn't kosher. Unlike everyone else here, he never talks about his research. Then there's the mysterious London trips most weeks, getting picked up streets away in a black Hummer thing. Abbie's seen him in it too. I told Keith.'

Sophie knocked over her coffee. 'Hey, Jared was followed by a Hummer! It tailed his taxi from the Eagle and Child back to college.'

I felt chilled despite my big coat. 'Was it a night he'd been out with you?'

'No. Must have been after a night out with the boys.'

Abbie moved aside as the waiter served us bagels and mopped Sophie's spilled coffee. 'I bet Guy only asked you out to quiz you about Jared.' I bit into my bagel and mentioned his demand that I tell Sophie that Jared should return to face the music. Swallowing, I shrugged. 'Guy's CIA, he must be.'

Abbie swigged her coffee and hit the table with her palm. 'Right girls, we need a plan. Can't help poor Jared, but sure as hell we can suss out what Guy Waller is up to. I wonder if Winston College knows he's only pretending to be a visiting scholar?'

'He is listed on Google as having graduated *cum laude* from a US Air Force College.'

'God Mum, you are becoming the sleuth!' Sophie looked admiringly at me.

Abbie waved a finger in the air. 'And we need to see Anna about the key.'

'What key? God's sake, what else, Mum!'

I took it from my purse and showed it to Sophie who asked, 'What's it for?'

'No idea, darling. Possibly a bank box? We thought we'd ask Anna before telling Keith. You know, at first, I wanted nothing to do with this mess, but it's affecting us all, not just Jared. I've started making notes. It's like researching an essay covering dozens of topics which are impossible to form into a coherent argument. Think we'll keep what we've learned amongst us three and Keith. Do you think though we should ask Gadling about Guy, Abbie?'

'No way! Say, I might get my father on it. About time he paid me some attention.'

Just then we paid little attention to the bearded chap with a large backpack who moved into a newly vacant chair behind Abbie. I remembered him later.

14

Spooks & Strategy

Wednesday was bright and sunny. Sophie had a rare day off, so I skipped a lecture at ten, and we went for a leisurely stroll along the canal to Iffley Locks where it's more like a village than an Oxford suburb. A pleasant change from the bustling city.

'How was your tutorial yesterday?'

'I got a grudging "Competent, Miss Frazer".'

'Result!' said Sophie. 'Oh, Jared phoned. He's home, but his mum's not well.'

'Oh?' What's wrong?'

'Breast cancer. She's having chemo.'

'Oh, God. Come on, let's look in here.' We went into the Romanesque St Mary's Church and sat for a while. I lit a candle (my first ever) and said silent prayers for Anna, Ramin, and Jared's mother before suggesting we get lunch in the pub nearby. There Sophie toyed with her cottage pie. 'When are you meeting Anna?'

'Gwen says she's staying with a friend in Norfolk till the weekend. You doing anything Saturday?'

'There's a *Stop the War* march this Saturday. Some of the girls are making placards.'

Mass gatherings make me anxious. Tempers flare. People get arrested. And injured. I'd clashed with Sophie before on her activism, something, along with blonde hair and soulful blue eyes, she'd inherited from her father. Steve would have scuppered his law career after being arrested as a student if his dad hadn't been a Justice of the Peace. But Steve rapidly outgrew his left-wing CND phase: capitalism held more appeal. Divorce law was lucrative.

Sophie pointed her fork. 'We have to protest. Blair's toadying to Bush in backing this nonsense war on Iraq. I'm thinking about resigning from the Labour Party.'

I put on my jacket. 'Darling, it's good to have principles and to follow your conscience – but do take care.'

'Sure.' Sophie pushed away her barely touched plate. 'That's it, I'm done. Let's go.'

'I need to get back anyway. Can't do an all-nighter like last week. Getting too old.'

Laughing, Sophie took my arm, and we walked back to the car.

After dropping Sophie at her college to study, I headed to the library to collect the week's books and photocopies. Back at the Lodge I ruminated on the blessed key. Shouldn't it go straight to Steadman? A familiar tension rose from the pit of my stomach as my heart fluttered. I closed my eyes, inhaled slowly and exhaled deeply while lowering my shoulders to help me relax: a tip from childbirth classes twenty-three years ago. Reminding myself that murder was not my chosen subject of study, I started formulating a cogent, well-argued essay on *Motivating Senior Pupils.*

I stuck 'Post-it' notes at the relevant chapters needing read in the borrowed books, then scanned the photocopies of relevant passages from the books I couldn't bring home. I'd never been able to study in libraries, always distracted by folk moving about or those tempting whispered conversations you could overhear but not quite catch. Early first term Abbie had advocated photocopying pages and articles to take home. Expensive, but allowed study in your own room. Thank God there were only eight weeks in a term, but the two exams and the thesis I had to complete over the summer were a bit daunting. Yet, on balance, I was enjoying Oxford, even with the volume of prescribed reading and pressure of essay deadlines.

Soon it was obvious that a quick scan wasn't enough to absorb the drift of the ten erudite research papers. How could so many people write so much about so little while oft repeating everything everyone else had ever said on their topic? Two were virtually identical! I stretched back. Wine was tempting, but mindful of last week's disaster of jumbled pages knocked onto the floor, first I carefully stapled each article together in page order. Settling for tea and a KitKat, I worked away highlighting, summarising and trying to think of a useful angle. Maybe I should've gone for a more practical course – this 'evidence' was so theoretical, subjective, and prone to bias. And most papers were Oxbridge, all by guys, none referencing 'coal face' classrooms like mine. Hang it all, I would say what I thought. As I'd just told Sophie, principles were worth adhering to – and the blood on the carpet next door had reinforced the idea that life was too short to prevaricate.

I'd managed an outline and a 'starter-for-ten' list of quotes and references when there was a sharp knock on the door that announced Abbie, resplendent in skin-tight violet leggings, green jumper, and matching silk headscarf.

She smiled widely. 'Right, Jude, time for a break! The wine's open and breathing. Howzabout we get in some pizza? I owe you a feed.'

'OK. But let me finish this list and save it.'

'You haven't moved from here for hours. You shouldn't worry as much about these essays, ye know. They ain't gonna fail us – they want our cash!'

Looking out of the window at the dark sky, I realised I'd lost track of time and was suddenly hungry. A pizza would be quick and if I just stuck at one glass of wine then I could manage another couple of hours' work. I stacked my index cards and Post-it notes and clicked 'Save.'

'What do you fancy, Jude – pepperoni?'

'Anything you like. Be up in a minute.'

'Terrific! And we can plan our strategy!' Abbie turned and left singing 'Cry Me a River.'

I tutted. Abbie was singing the wrong tune. I'd never met anyone like her for breaking into song. Though sometimes infuriating, she had so much youthful vim and vigour. And she was brainy, completing essays over two nights. I needed four days. And last week she'd read three novels! Nothing fazed her, but I was struggling to stay on track. Lack of sleep and nightmares were taking their toll. Last night, I woke at four after being chased down a street in Jericho by a man in a trench coat.

I closed down my computer and brushed my hair. God, my face was even more drawn than at the height of the Steve fiasco. Time to get a grip. Put on a good face. I reached for my makeup.

Abbie's upstairs room was warm and welcoming, if untidy. Her heavy green curtains were closed, music played. The room was almost double the size of mine with a large oriel window, new burgundy carpet, and a sofa that she patted.

'Come, sit. You look exhausted, honey. Don't you love this?' She waved at the CD player.

Feeling crushed that make-up hadn't improved my face, I sat. 'Who is this singing?'

Abbie laughed as she poured two glasses of wine. 'Where've you been? It's young Justin Timberlake from Tennessee, my grandma's home state. Doesn't he have a sweet voice? A looker, too. This is *Justified*, his number one album. *Cry Me a River's* my favourite. He's written it with funk and soul …'

'Surely, he didn't write *Cry Me a River*. Someone did it for Ella Fitzgerald in the fifties.'

Abbie flipped tracks and pointed, 'This?'

I was astonished. 'Oh, that's a completely different song – why give it the same title?'

'Why not? But it's good. Hey, that a motorbike?' Abbie broke off, walked to the window, twitched the curtains and peered. 'Right, that's the pizza guy. Back in a mo!'

As she left, I turned down the volume, mindful some housemates might be studying, and heard the shrill old-fashioned doorbell ring and Abbie calling, 'Hold your horses, I'm coming!'

The pizzas were delicious, if huge. One would have done between us, but we managed them bar a few crusts. I even tried my first artichokes. Always something new with Abbie around.

After we'd finished, Abbie poured more wine, strode over to her bed, set her glass on the bedside table, and collapsed down amidst her fringed gold velvet cushions. 'Can't believe it's days since we found the key and we've done nothing with it! Didn't help I had to go to London to see my boring aunt on Monday. So shallow – d'you know she could only talk about how good the shopping is over here? Anyhow, Jude, we'll need to arrange to see Anna.'

'I think we should take the key to the police.'

'Oh, but Anna might be looking for it. It could be to do with something of hers.'

'Don't be daft! Why would it be on Selassie then? I'm worried we'll be in contempt or something for withholding evidence. Let's hand it over.'

'Hey girl, this wouldn't have anything to do with you wanting to see that guy with the hots for you, isn't it?'

I felt my face glow. 'Don't talk crap, Abbie! He's got no such thing!'

'Ah, not what I heard from Sophie! She said that he asked her to give you "his lurve".' Seeing me look daggers she shrugged. 'Well, his regards then! But let's see Anna first. She must be back. Did Gwen say where she stays?'

'I think it's Cumnorhill.'

'Where's that?'

'Out Botley Road, the other end of town, past Seacourt Tower. I have an old uni chum lives there. It's nice. Almost countryside.'

'Cool. Let's arrange to go see her or meet up for coffee or something. But we need her number.' Abbie leaped up, grabbed her state-of-the-art large-screened phone from the desk at the window to tap and scroll before nodding. 'Right, here we are.' With a final tap, she handed it to me with a notebook and pen. 'Ask Gwen, she's got Anna's number.'

Setting down my glass and resting the notebook on the settee arm, I put the phone to my ear. 'Hi, Gwen. It's Judith. I was wondering if you could give me Anna's phone number? Abbie and I thought we'd like to arrange to meet her.' I winked at Abbie then wrote down a number. 'Thanks. How are you doing? Oh dear, that on top of everything? Yes, that must be a trial. Oh, really? So, how about his book then? And Jared as well? That's awful. I am sorry.'

I pressed 'end call' and sat back surprised. 'She's been sacked – and Jared too!'

'Gee, that was quick! That bastard Manders, I bet.'

'You're right. She went to ask if she and Jon could finish Cedric's book, but Manders said it was in hand, asked for her keys and gave her a week's notice. She's gutted. And she's had a house break-in too. Terrible.'

'That's a shame. Wonder if the burglary is to do with Cedric? Hmm. You gonna try Anna now, Jude? You know her better than I.'

As I punched in the numbers from the pad, Abbie offered prompts. 'Ask her how she is. See how soon she could meet us. Tell her we've found something important of Cedric's.'

I waved her to shush. 'I know, I know. It's ringing.'

'Anna? This Is Judith Frazer from Winston Lodge. How are you?' I paused to listen. Abbie nodded encouragingly from her bed. 'I am glad you managed a break. You're back tomorrow? Great! I'm ringing because my colleague Abbie – you remember the American girl – found something in the cat's collar we'd like to talk to you about. Could we meet?'

Abbie was up crouching, head down at my ear trying to listen in. I shrugged her off. 'Fine. Noon on Friday. At your house? Oh, if you'd rather.' I nodded at Abbie. 'University Park, second bench. OK. See you then.'

'Why didn't you say we had a key? And why meet in University Park? Sounds like a Cold War movie – a *park bench*?' Abbie laughed.

'She was oddly cagey at the hospital, you know. I suspected she was holding something back. But now, I'm sure. She looked over at the open door every time she spoke – especially after that policeman guard came back. Maybe they told her not to say anything? Or is she wanting to meet away from her house because she thinks it's bugged?'

'So, like Gwen, she thinks there's been surveillance too?'

The heater was at max and the room warm, but I felt a chill at my back. Little things were swirling into focus. It was Abbie saying 'surveillance.' That white van – I'd seen it at various points in the street, at college and outside the Lodge. If it were workmen on a job, why did it keep appearing near us? And if it was owned by someone living nearby, why wasn't it usually parked in the same place? Come to think of it, as I'd looked out at Abbie greeting the pizza boy, there had been a white van outside tonight – was it the same one that splashed Sophie and I the other day? And then, there was that bearded young man with a large Adidas backpack I'd seen trailing behind us as we walked back from the café last weekend, though he did saunter on when we turned in the gate. I thought it was the same guy I'd noticed hovering outside the department a couple of times on Tuesdays after our tutorials. He usually had a phone to his ear, but I'd not seen him talk into it. He definitely wasn't one of the Education students we'd met at first term receptions. Another niggle arose. At that Formal Dinner, Baz had mentioned my M.Ed. course, but I hadn't mentioned it. How did he know? I shivered.

'Abbie, now I think on it, I'll take that back. We might have been tailed. I'm not sure we should go on with this on our own. By all means let's see Anna since we've arranged it, but straight after we'll go to the police.'

'You are kidding about being tailed?' Abbie sat up suddenly, legs over the edge of the bed.

I listed my worries about the van, Adidas man and Baz. Abbie got up to look outside. 'There's no van now. I've never noticed your backpack guy. Did he look like a bomber?'

'God, what does a bomber look like? Mind you, think how many people in Oxford have backpacks. He was swarthy, had a kind of chin-edge Henry VIII beard. I remember now he was in the Carfax café, sitting a few tables away before moving to one behind us. He got up as we faffed before leaving. We were chatting so much that I hardly bothered. But he did follow us. And had a heavy backpack.'

'Truly? Gee, worrying. Could this guy be linked to the one following Jared? Jesus. I know the States have gone all a-twitch since 9/11, but that does it, I'll get onto Dad. He's got friends in high places. Maybe after Jared's experience though, I'd be better doing an email in the morning from the internet shop downtown, not use my laptop or phone.'

'Isn't that a bit much? But do contact your dad if you think he can help find out anything about Guy. Pity we have to wait till Friday to see Anna.'

Abbie walked across the room and raised the music volume before whispering, 'Do you think our rooms might be bugged?' Her eyes swivelled from the pictures on her wall to me. 'Are they watching everyone in the Lodge, I wonder?'

'Och, let's not be daft.'

'Hmm. Why don't we have a drinks party Friday night, Jude, see what everyone's thinking?'

'Och, Abbie, let's not be too hasty about discussing this with anyone, but if you must, it's my birthday Sunday – there's an excuse.'

'Done deal, Jude, let's party! Mibbe a spooks' angle is over dramatic, but there's one thing for sure, Cedric's murder isn't any old robbery gone wrong.' She peered behind all her pictures and examined the telephone before opening another bottle of Zinfandel.

15

Art & Dead Kings

I loved Thursday nights in Oxford. Life Drawing class. I'd attended various art groups over the years, but on seeing the Life Class poster on the Winston College notice board, I'd signed up immediately, unable to resist quality tuition from a Ruskin Art College tutor.

I'd never done life drawing before. It was challenging. The nude models changed pose every fifteen minutes for the first hour, necessitating intense concentration to get anything recognisable down on paper in the time. You had to switch off your busy brain in order to process visual impressions and transfer them into the sweep of your hand. No time for dwelling on intrusive worries about looming essays. Or murder suspects. I preferred it to Sunday evening yoga class which I'd dropped out of after three sessions. Apart from worrying about the leader's flagrant disregard of college 'no-candles' safety rules, I wasn't quite on Tabitha's wavelength. Her exhortation to wind down by 'visualising myself as a fluffy cloud,' was a step too far.

But Art Tutor Madeleine was another matter. A blonde similar in age to me, she was encouraging and patient, helping me to convert disastrous scribbles into recognisable drawings. At the mid-evening common room coffee break we'd discuss art in its wider sense. Tonight, the debate centred on the best 'anatomical' painters. Two Italian girls extolled Leonardo and Michelangelo. I countered with

Dürer, remarking that his apostle's praying hands were astonishing.

'Yes Judith. Dürer – the Leonardo of the North. He's from my hometown, Nurnberg. Have you seen the hands?'

'No, Madeleine, only photos, but I love them. So detailed, so real, almost 3D.'

'A genius. He even made his own paper. The drawings are in Vienna. You must go.'

The class resumed. I struggled with the night's voluptuous subject. Somehow folds of adiposity were more difficult to portray than the muscles of our last handsome, toned male model. Soon, it was nine, time to pack up my charcoals and unclip my drawing to roll it up. My nearby Italian classmate's drawing was formidable. 'That's great, Natalia!' The girl smiled. She was gorgeous, young and talented. I was more depressed than ever. Why was I bothering trying to draw, never mind coming down here to Oxford at my age?

Madeleine took my last sketch and uncurled it. 'A valiant effort. You are improving.' She nodded towards the dressing model in the corner. 'Giselle is not an easy model to capture. Now, please take this.' She held out a sheet torn from a notebook. 'Some homework. But leave the Ashmolean till next week, please. I'll need to arrange your visit. Then you'll go to the desk, give your name and leave your bag outside. And whatever you do, touch nothing without wearing their gloves – it is a capital offence!'

'Thank you.' I was touched.

'You seem a bit down, no? You need inspiration! If it's a tutor upsetting you, forget him. They are mostly idiots.' She winked and left.

I looked at the note, quaintly labelled 'Oxford musts to be seen.'

University College – Shelley Memorial.
Magdalen - the chapel, Addison's Walk, and the deer.
Pitt Rivers – everything!

Ashmolean – you won't believe what's in the basement ...
Christ Church – the Gallery, their Dürer if it's out.
Will have more next week after I've had a think! Maddy x

I put it in my bag and returned to my room, heartened by Madeleine's kindness, if not by my feeble artistic accomplishments.

Friday morning brought a seminar on *'From Module Outlines to Effective Teaching'*. Afterwards, Abbie and I went for a coffee and, for a change, discussed our course. I bought Abbie her first ever cheese scone. I had carrot cake, justifying the calories by knowing I was walking far more down here than back home in Glasgow. We sat in one of our favourite haunts, a vaulted old church-café conversion in Radcliffe Square. With its bare wooden floors, stone and oak walls and no soft furnishings, my phone echoed loudly when it rang. The call was brief. 'No problem. Of course. See you then.'

Abbie had scoffed her warm scone in three bites. 'My, these are good! Who was that?'

'Anna. She can't make noon.' I licked some buttercream topping from my fingers.

'Bummer! Why not?'

'She has to pick up her new car at lunchtime, so she's asked to meet at three outside the Dragon School before she picks up Ramin. '

'But I've got a hair appointment – and Popham's in the Parade is so popular I doubt I'll be able to change it for weeks.' Reassuring her I'd manage alone, she added, 'Don't you just go giving her the key without finding out what it's for, though.' She wagged a finger at me.

'Of course not. But you know, everything that was Cedric's is Anna's now, so strictly speaking, it's up to her what she does with it. Though I do think we need to tell the police.'

'I suppose.' Abbie frowned.

Draining my tea, I patted Abbie's hand and stood. 'Come on! Last night I got a list of interesting things to see in Oxford. How about Shelley's tomb?'

'Sure, why not? I've got time for that. Where is it?'

'University College.' Taking out my *Oxford Handbook 2003* with map, I led her out into the crisp sunny day, 'It's down off High Street and the oldest college here, founded in 1249.'

'Gee? That's sure old!'

'You know about Shelley?'

'Of course. I'm an English Major, right? Wrote a paper on him once. He was a radical atheist and a vegetarian. Never went to lectures.'

'Really?' I stopped abruptly.

Abbie stopped, placed her left hand to her breast (she'd definitely done drama) and loudly recited, 'My name is Ozymandias, King of Kings – Look on my Works, ye Mighty, and despair!' before throwing out her right hand as if demonstrating a view.

As a woman passer-by stared at this jean-clad, fur-jacketed, blonde's theatrics, I whispered apologetically, 'Sorry, she's American!' At which the woman nodded knowingly and moved off, shaking her head. I took Abbie's arm. 'Oh, come on, you're as mad as a brush. I'm more a fan of his *'To a Skylark,'* myself.'

'I like it too. Poor chap. His love life was nuts then he drowned. Short and tragic.'

She didn't speak again till we were in Shelley's shrine. Stained-glass windows flanked his marble statue on its bronze plinth with poetry plaques above.

'My!' Looking at the recumbent nude figure, Abbie knotted her brows. 'Gee, whose idea was it to have him lay here for an eternity with that weeny pecker lying loose?'

I consulted my book. 'Says his daughter-in-law wanted

the statue to show him as he was found, washed up on a beach after a storm sank his boat off Venice.'

Abbie was unimpressed. We strolled round the college until she had to head off in a taxi. Prompted by carrot-cake-guilt, I set off to walk home, wondering who'd modelled for the statue. I hadn't told Abbie that Shelley had been so decomposed he could only be identified by a poetry book in his pocket. Drowning must be horrible. But was being smashed on the head preferable?

It was almost two by the time I got back. Sipping hot chocolate, I read a few papers before walking to the Dragon School Lodge gate for three. I could hear cheering, likely from a team game being played out of sight. At school, I'd hated sport, unable to see the point of hanging upside down on wall bars or shivering on a hockey pitch. Today was cold too. I was stamping my feet with my hands stuffed in my pockets to keep warm when a bright yellow Mini drew up and tooted. A smiling Anna leaned over, opened the passenger door and gestured me to sit inside.

'Sorry to change the arrangements, Judith, but I've been waiting on this car for weeks. It was my birthday present. Cedric was cross it was so late. Still, he'd be pleased I have it now.'

I thought she looked far better than I would have in the circumstances. Even with dark shadows under her eyes, the woman was stunning. 'Abbie sends apologies, she had a prior engagement. It was she who found this inside Selassie's collar.' I unzipped my purse to hold up the key. 'Do you know what it's for?'

'No. I have never seen it before. In the cat's collar? How strange.'

'Abbie thinks it looks like her dad's bank security box key. Did Cedric have one?'

'He never mentioned it. But if he did, I know what he might have put in it.'

138

'What?'

'Have you told the police about this?'

'No, but why should that matter?'

Anna slumped back on the headrest with eyes closed. 'I knew it was about the tablets.'

'What tablets?' I was shocked: I'd never suspected drugs might be involved.

'Precious ancient script tablets my cousin Mahmoud gave Cedric on his last trip over.'

I twisted round to face Anna. 'Jon mentioned them.'

'*The Epic of Gilgamesh.* An old set of stories from Mesopotamia that Cedric felt said everything that's always been true about politics, sex, power – even the need for conservation. But it's not well known except to scholars.'

'But why would he put tablets in a bank box and not keep them in his department?'

'It's complex. Mahmoud is a historian, though not an Assyriologist like Cedric. He bought these clay pieces, many of which regularly turn up from the desert. Western sanctions are causing hardship. People are selling anything they can. Who can blame them? They have to eat. There's a great black market in artefacts.'

I shook my head. 'But why did Mahmoud give them to Cedric?'

'He thought them significant, being found at ancient Nineveh. When Cedric was lecturing at the University in Baghdad last September, Mahmoud gifted them to him as a thank you for him taking out medicine for his sick son. Drugs are in short supply at home. As Cedric was only there for a few days, he gambled he might not get a permit in time and worried the pieces might disappear. Corruption is rife. Being so excited by the tablets, he stupidly sneaked them home hidden in his dirty laundry. They turned out to be missing pieces of Tablet Nine which he has translated with Dr Clark at the British Museum. Clark had a break-in recently which worried Cedric. Perhaps he thought it wise to put them in the bank until he could legitimise them. He was preparing to record the translation online if they had to be returned. It is possible someone else wanted them badly.'

I handed the key to Anna. 'So, you think this is for a security box containing the tablets?'

Anna nodded. 'Though I'll check to see if it fits anything else at home. It should have told the police about the tablets before. I mean, others like Clark are aware of them.' She sighed heavily. 'I worry about repercussions for Mahmoud if someone in Baghdad knows he gave the tablets to Cedric.'

'If there is a box, where do you think it might be?'

'Cedric had an account in Coutts private bank at their Oxford branch.'

'If it's there, will they let you open it?"

'The estate isn't settled, so I think I'll need to take the lawyer. But I'll contact him and let you know. Thanks for taking time to bring me this.'

'It's no problem. Did the police have any idea what the Arabs were after?'

'No, nor their nationality. But that Detective Steadman now thinks that whatever it was, after ransacking our house, the study and Gwen's home they know we don't have it, so they've decided Ramin and I are not in danger and took away our protection.'

'That's something. A shame though that Cedric didn't manage to finish his book.'

'The University Press still wants the manuscript by the end of March. Jon wants to finalise it but incredibly, the college has sacked Gwen and Jared. Did you know? I am worried about him too. Where could he possibly have gone?' Anna looked tearful.

'I know about the sackings, Anna. But don't worry about Jared. He's gone home.'

'That's a relief. Gwen thinks the college is being very

disrespectful to Cedric, as do I.'

'The Master, Gadling, knew about the new tablets, you know.'

'I thought he might. Gadling and Manders are gossipy jealous old women. How I wish we had stayed at Harvard! But Cedric wanted Ramin educated here.' She hung her head then lifted it. 'Oh, Judith, what was I thinking of, not telling the police about these things? Foolish.' She brushed off tears with her palm. 'Right, once I'm home I will phone the lawyer, arrange a visit to the bank, and call Inspector Steadman.'

As Anna sat forward to look at approaching chattering children, I noticed she was wearing a striking broad silver ring with a blood-red polished stone.

'What an unusual ring! What gem is that?'

Anna smiled, turning the ring. 'It's a Carnelian set in silver that Cedric had made for me. The cuneiform letters mean "Love and Life."'

'I've never seen a Carnelian before.'

'They're from India and have been prized in Iraq since Gilgamesh's time. You know people were trading over great distances even two thousand years before Christ.'

'Goodness!'

'In fact, jewels feature largely in the segment of the *Epic* revealed by the new fragments. There is a Garden of the Gods with jewelled trees, especially carnelians. Goethe wrote a lovely poem on carnelians.'

'Goethe wrote poetry?' I felt so uneducated.

'Cedric loved it. Carnelians were said to "drive away evil things". Looks like it didn't work for him, Judith, did it?' She bit her lower lip.

'I hope this key helps unlock what happened to Cedric.'

'So do I. Here's Ramin now, so much taller than the others.' She smiled fondly. 'He's been accepted for Oxford Grammar after the summer. Remarkable as he is dyslexic and found it difficult transitioning to the UK school system. How I worried about him as a baby, guilty in case my poisoning would have damaged him. But dyslexia is his only problem.'

'Poisoning?'

'Gas. I was exposed on my last assignment for Reuters. It was to Halabja, my old town and I was newly pregnant. I lost that baby, a girl. We were barely mourning her when I fell pregnant with Ramin. Such a miracle.' She wiped away a tear.

I squeezed her hand. 'I am so sorry you've been through so much. You've got my number now, Anna. Ring anytime.'

As I exited the car, Ramin came up to stroke the yellow bonnet. 'Cool car, Mum!'

I walked away, sad, but with my mind whirling with all this info. Cedric's demise might well be connected to this Gilgamesh *Epic*. A modern murder linked to ancient history? It was some place, Oxford, constantly throwing up questions. And exposing my ignorance. Who knew Goethe was a poet? I felt another Google session coming on. A decent cup of Tetley's and a sit-down was needed.

Walking back, I suddenly remembered about that Reuters article I'd found on Google – the awful story of gassing Kurds in Iraq. Had Anna been there – or even was she that journalist A. Pura? My main thought was that I needed to speak to the lovely DCI Steadman again. Did he know about these ancient tablets? I doubted loyal Gwen would have mentioned them.

Back at my desk, as I booted up my computer, my mind flitted to Abbie's downtown recitation on Ozymandias. Was he real? Randomly, I keyed him in first. And wished I hadn't.

"Nothing beside remains. Round the decay of that colossal wreck, boundless and bare. The lone and level sands stretch far away."

Death and decay everywhere, much like my desk, currently strewn with a browning banana skin, digestive

142

biscuit crumbs and random essay ideas on index cards and Post-it notes. Depressing. Dead kings, dead poets, dead professors, and a degree I was worrying might end up dead in the water at the rate I was going! I should look to refresh myself with the words of *To a Skylark*. Blithe spirits were in short supply.

Internet searches offered too many ways to procrastinate from work, too many random interesting facts. Ozymandias was the Greek name for Pharaoh Rameses II whose statue had been due in London in 1818 when Shelley wrote his poem to highlight that even the greatest rulers and their empires faced decay into oblivion. And Carnelians? Egyptian Kings revered them as signs of the setting sun. Jewish priests wore them to represent one of the twelve tribes of Israel. Mohammed had a carnelian signet ring. Queen Victoria loved them. Wearing them was said to increase confidence. I could do with that.

As for Gilgamesh, I discovered he was real. Procrastinating further, I scribbled down multiple new facts into my existing 'murder musing' journal, putting 'R' beside the probably relevant and 'C' beside the curious but not immediately so. I now had three pages of notes. And a troubled heart. Hearing my gran saying, 'a trouble shared is a trouble halved' – metaphorically of course as she'd been dead twenty years – I lifted the phone and called Steadman, who wasn't in. I left a message. Fifteen minutes later he rang back.

'Ms Frazer? I hear you're looking for me?'

'Yes, thanks for getting back to me. Think there are more things that you might like to know.'

'Anything in particular?'

'Quite a few. Perhaps best if I come and see you in the morning?'

'Sadly, it's my first weekend off for a month. You could see a colleague at the station tomorrow?'

'I suppose,' I said, sighing.

'Or perhaps you might join me for a spot of lunch? You could tell me your info, and then we'd see whether you'll need to come in on Monday to make a formal statement or whether I can just log it and get you in later if it leads to anything?'

I hesitated. What 'anything' might it lead to? Was lunch wise? Wasn't I a discoverer of a murder victim, with whom he shouldn't be fraternising? But in different circumstances would I hesitate? He was nice. God, I had to stop posing myself questions!

'Have you been to the Randolph?' His voice was rich and warm.

'No, I haven't, as a matter of fact.' I tried to rein in my enthusiasm – the poshest hotel in Oxford, favourite haunt of my idol Morse and his author, Colin Dexter!'

'OK, how about twelve-thirty in the Morse Bar? You can tell me your information then I'll treat you to a bit of Oxford history and lunch. Will I need a notebook?'

'Well, I've made a list myself, trying to make sense of a number of things.'

'Good, it's a date then. Well, not a date, I mean a meeting. You know where the Randolph is, I take it, opposite the Ashmolean Museum?'

'Of course. But won't you get into trouble fraternising with a murder witness?'

He laughed. 'Don't worry, there's no harm in a meeting in public, open and above board. Now it might be different if *you* were buying *me* lunch!'

'What? Oh, I see, that'd be bribery!' I gave a silly schoolgirl laugh. Pathetic.

'Till tomorrow, then? Bye Judith.'

Judith. Not Ms Frazer.

16

An Awkward Party

Half an hour later, Abbie breezed in and made me gasp. 'Gracious, Abbie!'

'Do you like my new image? David thought it confident, striking, no-nonsense.'

'Well, it is short.' Seeing Abbie's pout, I added, 'But it has a lot going for it. I mean, it is very neat. And it'll be easy to keep, need less blow drying. It'll soon grow, anyway.'

Abbie frowned. 'No. I intend sticking with this. No more "blonde, bimbo" curls. High time I re-invented myself – tougher, edgier, spiky hair, in control. Think I might get a tattoo next.'

Unable to follow that logic, I countered, 'Shall I make us dinner tonight?'

'No need.' Abbie lifted two carrier bags. 'This is my new Vidal Sassoon hair stuff, and this has M&S lasagne, garlic bread, salad, wine, plus some nibbles for the drinks. I did little cards this morning and put them under everyone's doors.'

'Cards?'

'Drinks party! I put seven till eight, allows them to honour any other plans later. Said it was your birthday.' I must have looked vacant as she looked exasperated. 'You've forgotten, haven't you? The drinks party plan to suss out what everyone's thinking?'

'Right, of course, yes.'

Abbie gave me the food bag. 'Can you put the lasagne and bread in the oven and stack the rest in the fridge? That'd be swell. I'm off to clear up my room, then we'll have tea and a full Anna de-brief in here. I worry those kitchen walls have ears.'

Over lasagne in my room, I rattled through my meeting with Anna and her plan for a bank visit and then the police.

Abbie clapped her hands. 'See, I knew that key must be for something important!'

'And by the way, I phoned Steadman. He's taking me out to lunch tomorrow.'

'Result!' Abbie was enthusiastic. 'A date's a fantastic opportunity, Jude. Not just ye know, 'cos he's kinda fit, but it's a chance to find out where they've got to in the investigation.' Abbie was sitting on my bed hugging her knees, dinner plate precariously balanced on the edge of the bed shedding tomato-sauce-laden lettuce onto the floor. I swiped it up with a tissue. The mark remained. Abbie didn't notice. 'So, like, when *was* your last date, girl?'

'This isn't a date, Abbie. It's just a chat,' I insisted.

'Don't be ridiculous. He wouldn't have asked you for lunch unless he was interested, especially not to a five-star hotel! Give it your best shot, even if you don't get much out of him.'

Thinking I heard a noise from the hall, I sprang up to open the door. There was no one there. 'Sorry, Abbie. Guy was hovering in the hall earlier. Thought that was him again.'

'Forget him. He's a sleazeball. I'm gonna tackle Tilly – she'll spill anything she knows.'

'Och, he'll have been trained to keep schtum. She'll not know anything. She's only his bit on the side.'

'Where do you Brits get these expressions? I'll love that – "bit on the side"! Tried phoning Dad to find out more about Guy, by the way, but he's at a conference. Mom'll get him to call when he's back.'

Abbie took our plates to the kitchen, and I returned to summarising a couple of papers for the essay, so far lacking any cohesive argument. Changing into a loose blue Wallis shirt and black trousers, I added gold hoop earrings, slapped on makeup and was up at Abbie's door by five to seven.

She had flowers on her coffee table and tumblers and wine glasses laid out. All new: the clue was the crumpled boxes in her waste bin. The room was lit by a desk lamp. Fragrant candles wafting scents of lilies, rose and vanilla. Bowls of crisps and nuts were scattered about, and she'd brought up two folding metal garden chairs from the switch room to supplement her seating, plonking tasselled bed cushions on them. While I sat on one, Abbie fiddled with an ice bucket, bottles and cartons at her desk and Justin Timberlake played softly in the background.

'Hey Jude, here you go!'

I accepted a lurid striped, orange, red and yellow drink complete with purple paper umbrella. 'What's this?'

'You never had a Tequila Sunrise?' Abbie looked surprised.

I sipped, then took a proper drink. 'Oh, that's nice! Cheers, Abbie.'

The door opened to admit Tilly, wavy hair braided into one thick back plait and one thin encircling her head like a coronet. She never wore makeup and in tonight's candlelight looked even more ghostly. I marvelled that she never tanned despite hours on her allotment. Charms jingled from wrist and ankle bracelets as she walked. Her arms looked painfully thin beneath her chiffon sleeves as she offered a tissue-wrapped gift. 'Happy Birthday Judith.'

Accepting it without disclosing it wasn't yet my birthday, I gave her a hug and sat to open the parcel which contained a photo frame embroidered with purple and pink flowers.

'Oh, that's lovely! Thanks, Tilly.'

'I made it.' She looked at Abbie's offered drink. 'Sorry, if it's got alcohol in it, I can't.'

Abbie replaced it with a glass of pure orange juice.

'That's really kind, Tilly.' I set the present down on the floor beside me. 'I didn't know you embroidered.'

'It's tapestry actually. You get kits. It's relaxing.'

I thought she was looking better today. Then Abbie asked, 'So where's Guy?'

Tilly stiffened and looked down at her drink, shaking slightly. Her ice cubes clinked. 'I haven't seen him since yesterday. He must be busy with his project.'

At that precise point, Guy arrived with a large, expensive, bouquet that he presented with a bow. 'Lovely flowers for a lovely lady. Happy Birthday!'

They were at least twice the size of any I'd ever had from Steve. 'I love roses and lilies. Thank you, Guy.'

'Thought you'd need brightening up after everything. So, how old are we today, Jude?'

'A gentleman never asks a lady their age.' Tilly looked crossly at Guy.

'Sorreee! It was only conversation. Don't get your knickers in a twist.' Ignoring the space beside Tilly on the sofa, he sat on the other garden chair.

'I'm sure Guy didn't mean any offence, but I'll be forty-three, if you must know.'

Guy accepted a beer from Abbie. 'Yeh, well age is all relative, isn't it? So, guys, how are we bearing up after Cedric? Anyone seen Steadman around?' Guy leaned over to the coffee table and grabbed a handful of crisps. 'Potato chips, great!' He munched while speaking. 'So, Jude, your girl heard from Jared Boy, yet?'

'I believe he's in Boston.'

Guy stopped with his bottle halfway to his mouth. 'Well, you don't say? Still think he shoulda stayed here and faced the music.' He got up to browse Abbie's CD collection. 'Let's get the party started. We need something livelier than

Timberlake.'

'I like him" said Tilly.

'Too bad.' Guy swapped Abbie's choice for Nirvana, increasing the volume. 'This is more like it. *You Know You're Right.* Great song.'

As I winced at the loud grating guitar riffs, Tilly rose to lift the flowers, whispering, 'It's warm in here. These'll wilt without water. I'll go and put them in a vase.' She crept off, head bowed, in a jingle of bells as Guy was strumming an imaginary guitar with his eyes shut. As Abbie turned the volume down, Jon arrived. Unwrapping his gift, I found an illustrated Penguin paperback.

He nodded towards it. 'By Andrew George, out just before Christmas. Fellow's from the School of Oriental and African Studies in London and takes a different slant to Cedric, but it'll give you an idea of the Gilgamesh story. Thought you might like to understand why we're so passionate about it and its themes of family, friendship and rulers' duty that speak to us even today.'

'Yeh, well the world's much more dangerous now. We can destroy the planet with nukes.' Guy put down his empty bottle, walking over uninvited to snatch a fresh one.

Abbie ignored him to ask Jon what he'd like.

'A beer's fine, Abbie. But Guy, in ancient Assyria, slightest disagreement with your rulers and they'd cut out your tongue – or worse! Aren't we more civilised today?'

'Don't kid yourself. They still do that nowadays, those Air-abs. Medieval. Saddam's a bastard. Secret police everywhere, watching everyone. Tortures enemies and gets his sons to watch. And women have no rights – they're all owned by men. Everyone has to toe the line!'

Jon frowned. 'Friends, can't we chat about something lighter for Judith's birthday? And may I have some of those nuts, Abbie? Walnuts are good for the heart, they say.'

'Really, Jon? That's interesting.' I took some from

Abbie's offered bowl.

Guy swallowed another handful of barely chewed nuts. 'Ashkenazi Jews don't eat nuts on some religious holidays, you know. They are taboo from Rosh Hashanah to Yom Kippur.'

'Oh? Is it like a Lent sort of thing?' I turned to Abbie, knowing her father was Jewish.

'I believe it's to do with the Hebrew word for nut, *egoz,* having the same numerical value as *chet*, which means sin.'

Jon leaned back on the sofa. 'It's not only the Chinese who have a thing about numbers, is it, Abbie? The Jews time their Sabbath from a candle, lit not fourteen nor nineteen minutes, but exactly eighteen minutes before Friday sundown till three stars appear in a Saturday sky. During that time, you are forbidden to work, drive, or do much except read scriptures. Don't you think Judaism is much more taxing than Christianity?'

'Hey, though, what about Muslims – all that praying to Mecca five times a day? What a drag!' Guy's nose wrinkled.

From the sofa beside Jon, Abbie looked round at us. 'My father is Reform Jewish. My mother converted on marriage. I've chosen not to continue with it, but we should respect everyone's beliefs. If we did, the world would be a more peaceful place. Makes me wonder with their different faiths, where Cedric's funeral will be?'

Jon shrugged. 'And when. They'll have to wait till the police release his body. He's Church of England, although not married in their eyes according to know-it-all Professor Manders over in the college. Anna hasn't mentioned anything about a funeral yet.'

'You are in touch with her?' Guy wrinkled his forehead.

I was fascinated by his rapidly changing facial expressions. His jaw was firmly clenched.

'Of course. We spoke today about getting Cedric's book published, though I wish Jared was in touch – think he has the last proof copy. Gwen's laptop was stolen when she had a break-in.' Jon set his beer on the floor. 'I have a next but last version that may have to do, but Dr Clark may know. He saw Cedric the morning before he died. I've left him a message.'

'Dr Clark?' queried Guy.

'British Museum fellow.' Jon answered.

I asked Jon, 'Do you think it was the manuscript those men were after?'

'I cannot see why, for it will be published soon and there's nothing controversial in it that anyone would want to suppress.'

Guy looked at Jon intently. 'Has Anna said anything about the police investigation?'

'No. She's just back after a few days away.'

'*Buona notte!*' In strode Leo, who, to my discomfiture, was obviously just off his bike. His constrained nether regions drew the eye, Lycra delineating every little anatomical detail. I tried to imagine Guy in Lycra: perhaps best not. Only his arms were remotely toned. Leo extravagantly presented me with a silver wine bag. '*Buon Compleano, bella donna!*'

'Prosecco, Leo! Thank you, how kind.' I stood to accept it and his triple kisses then sat back, placing the present down beside Jon's.

'Drink, Leo?'

'*Birra, per favore,* Abbie. Ah, Azurro, how excellent!' He gave Abbie a thumbs up.

'What's keeping Tilly? She's taking a long time to find a vase.' Abbie put down her cocktail and headed out. In the ensuing awkward silence, I searched for something to say and turned to Leo. He at least, was looking cheerful. 'And how's the Hadrian research coming on?'

Leo needed no excuse. We listened politely till Guy butted in. 'Bet you're not including his genocide, are you? Forget Hitler or Arafat, Hadrian was one of the original Jew haters – wiped out half a million of them in 134 AD. Bar Kohkba revolt, you know it?'

'Surprised you know about that. Not sure that's the correct numbers, but it was a significant event. The Jews thought their leader, Simon Bar Kohkba was the Messiah.' Leo sat legs wide apart, elbows on thighs, beer bottle swinging back and forth below his muscular thighs. 'They got that wrong. But as a general, Hadrian was more interested in conserving his borders and stability than genocide.'

Guy chipped in. 'For sure though, he couldn't subdue your countrymen, Judith, could he? Had to build a wall to keep them out!' He laughed.

'Aye, us Scots are fierce!' I attempted a bent elbow and flexed biceps. 'I've walked part of Hadrian's Wall. Bits are still visible – and there's a good museum near Hexham.'

'Yes. Many good archaeological finds are still being made there.' Jon looked at his watch. 'I hope Tilly is all right. Abbie has been gone a while.'

'Damn fool girl, what's she up to now?' Guy slammed his empty beer bottle down on Abbie's desk and left.

'Not one for manners, our American friend, is he? But I am afraid I must love you and leave you too, Judith, if you don't mind. I have another engagement.' Jon gave me a peck on the cheek and left.

Leo laid down his beer and opened his arms. 'Ah, Judith, now we are alone! Might I take you out for a birthday drink once I have changed?'

'Thanks Leo, but I'm a bit tired. I'd like an early night.'

'No problem. *Tanto auguri*!'

'What does that mean?'

'All good wishes. But could you speak to Tilly? She is a lost soul and needs more than poetry of the dead for comfort. Guy is not good for her. He is pushy, thinks himself so clever. She needs a friend, no? It cannot be me, sadly.' He kissed me on both cheeks and left.

Lifting his prosecco bottle, I felt the cool glass. He must have just bought it from the fridge at the Spar. I popped the cork and was filling a glass when Abbie came in. She looked round in confusion.

'Where is everybody?'

'Well Jon had a prior engagement, Guy had a go at Leo about his hero Hadrian causing some ancient holocaust and left, then Leo asked me out for a drink before retreating disappointed.'

'Jesus, can't leave you for a minute, can I? But get any info of note?'

Filling another tumbler and handing it to Abbie, I crammed the prosecco bottle into the melting ice bucket and sat down with her on the sofa. 'Nope, but *salut*!' We chinked glasses. 'That's about the only Italian I know. Got it from a Sicilian I dated before Steve. 'Four-dates-Nico.' Not a goer. Too fond of mirrors.'

Abbie giggled. 'A 'goer'? I love you, Jude. But wait, I have info. Poor Tilly.'

'What about her?'

'She's a mess. Guy's been supplying her with bloody pills, uppers and downers. Seems when she was an undergrad, her fiancé – on being told he wasn't getting a First – threw himself off the Biochem tower. Afterwards, she had a month in a psychiatric hospital before graduation, then got better and started her D.Phil. But last term, after some sexual fling with a married tutor, she went to bits again. Her doc sent her to another shrink, who wanted so much salacious detail about her sex life, she was appalled, thought him sleazy. She then had a bit of a relationship with Leo who wanted her to stop taking Valium. They fell out, then her family practitioner stopped her prescriptions, and she lost it. Finding her crying one day, Guy told her he could get her all manner of pills. He moseyed in as a gallant knight and got his leg over. I don't think she's that physically attracted to him, but she's needy.

153

And now she's panicking because he's told her he might be going home soon.'

'Why? Thought he was here for the year?'

'She's heard him whispering on the phone during the night when he thinks she's sleeping. Thinks he's usually on to the Pentagon, repeating things like "yes siree!", "duty calls" and "heading home".'

'The Pentagon? God. Poor lass. She needs help. Why doesn't she change her doc?'

'Exactly what I said. Going to take her to mine in Jericho. She needs a shoulder to lean on, for sure, but Guy's not a good one. She's also cross at him for always badgering her to spill what we all talk about.'

I refilled our glasses. 'Ah, so she's a bit on the side whom he can fuck in exchange for pills and use as a stool pigeon? Nice one Guy!' I lifted my glass in mock toast.

'Jesus, Jude. Didn't think you swore.'

'It's not unknown for us Scots to stoop to ancient Anglo-Saxon! You know this fizz makes me see things more clearly. Think I'll buy some proper champagne and glasses tomorrow for my real birthday!'

'Bottoms up!' Abbie chinked our glasses again and pulled over a garden chair to put her feet up on. 'So, to recap, don't you think we now know everyone's secrets? Tilly's mourning a long-lost lover, has a hopeless taste in men and needs a shrink. Jon is kinder than he looks and wants to help Anna finish the book. And Leo still carries a bit of a candle for Tilly. She'd be better off with him, narcissist though he be.'

'They've all got egos bigger than the Empire State, haven't they, Abbie?'

'Except Tilly. That's her problem, no self-worth. And on that topic, Jude, as part of my reincarnation as a new woman, I've been thinking what to get tattooed. What would you have? A butterfly? A dragon? A bird? And where?'

'I'd have the evil eye on my bum!'

'Oh Jude, you kill me!' Abbie emptied the bottle into our glasses and upended it in her bucket. 'It'll have to be neat gin next. Luckily, I've got more. The tequila's finished.'

17

The Randolph

Next day, walking down Woodstock Road towards St Giles, I was edgy. Ridiculous at my age to be feeling nervous on a date, especially as Keith had pointed out it was not, in truth, a 'date'. I crossed Beaumont Street towards The Randolph with its four regal flagpoles waving their massive Union Jacks. Opposite was the Martyrs' Memorial where a babbling crowd of students and grey-haired folk in woolly hats and anoraks bearing CND badges milled about. People queued to sign a large open book as Sophie proffered leaflets to folk passing. Placards proclaiming, '*Stop the War*' and '*Make Tea not War*' sat atop a table which was fronted by a banner saying, '*Stop the War Coalition.*' At the side was a supersized photo of Prime Minister Blair labelled *'B-Liar.'* I tried not to worry about Sophie's involvement: it was her choice. It was perhaps ironic they were gathering at the gothic memorial where sixteenth century dissidents had been burned for heresy. Free speech has always brought trouble, but crossed fingers, there'd be none today.

The Randolph was an imposing Victorian Gothic building of attractive pale brick with rows of pointy windows and an arched entrance. Wrought-iron balconies gave it an air of a French chateau. Oxford is awash with buildings from many eras. I'd just discovered (via Jon) that the actual university was founded in the twelfth century after Henry II forbade English men from studying in Paris. Cambridge

156

was a later spin-off by Oxford scholars who fell out with the townspeople in a 'town and gown' dispute. I'd learned a lot this term.

The Randolph front door was whisked open by a smiling uniformed doorman. I found Steadman in the panelled lounge resplendent in an open-necked blue shirt and blazer. He rose to pull out a seat for me. *Steve never once did that.* The waiter arrived before I'd descended into it.

Keith Steadman grinned. 'What would you like to drink, Judith?'

'Er, I don't know ...'

'How about white wine?'

'Lovely.'

He asked for Sauvignon and turned back to me. 'Right. Table will be ready in half an hour. Let's get business out of the way first.' He lifted a reporter's notebook and pen.

I took a deep breath. 'Firstly, Jared. He's phoned Sophie and is home in Boston. The US Embassy accused him of colluding online with terrorists, but he insists they were only students he met volunteering last summer. The embassy were especially interested in an Iraqi doctor in Berlin, whom Jared says has no *jihadi* links and is preoccupied with worries back home. For what it's worth, neither Sophie, nor I, think Jared had anything to do with the prof's death. I mean, with so much to gain from being cited in the prof's book, he had no motive.'

Steadman made notes. 'Shame about Jared. Your daughter must be upset he's gone.'

'She is. And Cedric's college rival, Assistant Master Professor Timothy Manders, has already had Jared and Gwen sacked. He's a bit of a so-and-so, but you should speak to him. I know you spoke to the Master, but Manders is actually in Cedric's department and will know more about what he was up to.'

'Good idea. Anything else?'

Judith sighed. 'Most importantly, Guy. Don't know if you've looked into him, but he is weird. Abbie and I keep finding him skulking about. Couple of days ago, I opened my door as Sophie was leaving and he was on all fours right outside, maintaining he'd lost a contact lens. Rubbish. Abbie's heard him boast about his twenty-twenty vision necessary for the Marines. That's another anomaly: he told me he'd been an air force pilot. I've confirmed online he graduated from a Colorado Air Force Academy, but there are gaps in his online history. Amazing what you can find nowadays, isn't it? But he needs a serious look at.'

Steadman reviewed his notes as I took a breath. 'So, I've got – Jared's gone, Manders is a bastard but may know stuff, Guy says he's a marine – or pilot – and snoops. Is there more?'

'Oh, yes. Guy's been supplying Valium and stuff to Tilly who needs psychiatric help. She's had a sad time that I won't go into, but she complained to Abbie that Guy was always pumping her for info about our house chat. Though she's panicking that he's going back to the States soon, says it's to do with the Pentagon.'

'The Pentagon?' Steadman looked incredulous.

'Apparently. She said he speaks to them during the night. Not sure exactly how she knows to whom he's speaking – and suppose too he might be boasting to sound important.'

'But she's a bit mad, you say?'

'Not mad, more anxious. Definitely sincere and truthful, though. Unlike Guy, who does those odd trips to London in a black Hummer that picks him up away from the Lodge as I said – though it's a mad, conspicuous car to use for anything shadowy. And he is always going on about where Jared is and his pal Baz knew what degree course I was taking, though I suppose Guy might've told him so that's probably not important. But he did quiz me about what Cedric used to talk about. He and Guy are definitely up to something, Mr

Steadman.'

'Oh, do call me Keith outside of the station.'

'Keith. Right then.' I was aware of a couple passing towards the dining room and from the corner of my eye thought the man looked back at us, but I didn't turn to look myself as Keith was again summarising.

'So, Guy's dodgy, dishes out drugs. Baz knows things but we have no idea who he really is.' He flipped over to a new page. 'Anything else?'

'Cedric had a wee cat with a soft woven collar. Abbie found a key in it that she thinks might be for a security box. In fact, Guy saw it and thought that too. She told him it was hers. I've given it to Anna to see if it fits anything in Cedric's home study and if not, she's going to his bank with her lawyer on Monday to see if he had a deposit box there.'

'What bank, do you know?'

'Coutts' High Street branch, a private bank. Gwen says his family, the Gilberts, are rich landed gentry in Worcester, big charity benefactors. Incidentally, talking of charity, it was Anna who got Jared his Red Crescent refugee camp volunteer placement last summer. I discovered the Red Crescent is kind of a Muslim Red Cross. You've no idea how much I've learned in the last couple of weeks!'

Steadman underlined phrases on his pad. 'I'm certainly learning a lot myself today.' He was scribbling fast, flipping over sheets. I wondered if policemen were like doctors, developing obscure scrawls only they could read? But with my own bad handwriting, I had no right to be so critical. It was then I remembered my typed list. I fished it out of my bag. 'Sorry, this summary might help.'

'That's great, Judith, thanks. Think I should be putting you on the payroll! Now, did Mrs Gilbert have any idea what might be in whatever this key's for?'

'Clay tablets.'

'Come again?'

'She thinks there *is* likely to be a box, and it will contain ancient clay, or terracotta cuneiform bits of an epic dating back centuries I've been told about by Gwen, the dons and Jon. Iraq is full of them. They turn up in the desert.'

'But why put them in a box and not in a museum?' Keith took a slug of the wine he'd ignored whilst talking. Putting down his pad, he leaned back. 'And what's cuneiform?'

'I looked it up. Looks like little trumpets carved into clay and baked hard. Not hieroglyphs but an early alphabet of syllables. Anna told me yesterday her cousin Mahmoud gave Cedric some bits of the *Epic of Gilgamesh* as a thank you for taking medicine to Iraq for his son. Only naughtily, he didn't get an export licence. The *Epic*'s a poem everyone keeps telling me is amazing, a precursor of the *Iliad*, *Arabian Nights*, and Noah's flood in the *Bible*. Jon gave me a book on it for my birthday I haven't had time to open yet.'

'This case just gets stranger and stranger. Are these old tablets worth much?'

'I don't know. They are very old. The *Epic* goes back three-thousand years, but according to my research last night, the main versions are from 1800 and 1300 BC.'

'Or BCE, as we call it now.'

'Sorry, I know, Gwen told me.'

Keith laughed. 'History's my thing, by the way – I'm a Balliol history grad. Today's police aren't all uneducated plods, you know. But my topic was the Tudors.'

'Oh, really?' I savoured a large mouthful of wine.

Keith lifted his glass. 'Happy Birthday – whenever it was!'

'Tomorrow!' I felt my face warm as the waiter arrived.

'Sir, madam, your table is ready.'

As I stood, I caught Keith's arm. 'Oh, lastly, Anna said there was a guy from the British Museum, Clark I think, who was helping Cedric translate. You might speak to him. She said Clark's department had a burglary that worried Cedric

160

and might've made him put the tablets away safely till he could see how to legitimise them before publishing the book. As for that, Jon's determined to finish it, but the latest edited version was on Cedric's study computer. I don't suppose you could get copies of the book files off it for him?'

Keith stopped in the middle of the hotel lobby. 'We don't have a study computer of his.'

'What? Gwen said it wasn't there when she walked round the room with you looking for missing items. She thought you'd already taken it.'

It was Keith's turn to colour. 'We have his home laptop and a PC we took away after her tour of the room. Been checked. Nothing of note.'

'Was it a fancy silver American PC?'

Keith exhaled slowly. 'No. Just an ordinary HP.'

'Gwen's then. Not Cedric's.'

Once in the dining room, we passed a man who pulled his chair round to face the wall, though there was plenty of room. I ignored him as Keith ushered me on and helped me into a seat by the window. I felt relieved for the first time in days. I'd shared everything I knew and felt all responsibility now rested with Keith. Outside on Beaumont Street passers-by huddled into furry hoods. Snow was falling. Inside we were warm and cosy. I accepted a menu of mouth-watering choices. Bit pricey. But I wasn't paying. Oxford wasn't so bad.

'Not sure what you like. I recommend the ale pie – it's tremendous. Will we have a bottle of chianti? Or another white? Happy to have a glass of red with my main if you want fish.'

'I do love fish.' As I swithered between halibut and lemon sole, my stomach felt uneasy. I closed my eyes, recalling the mess of the study when I'd gone to call for help. Cedric's neat thin computer with its large, graphite-edged screen balanced on top had been there. It was unusual, lacking the large hard

161

drive case of most desktops. And I last saw it on the desk when rising from my futile CPR. By then, the 'robbers' had gone. But the computer had not.

'What do you think of this Chablis, is it OK?' Steadman was tasting the wine. 'Now enough murder mystery, let's get to the serious business of the day – lunch!'

The waiter poured me a glass which I sipped. 'Delicious. But sorry, Keith. Cedric's computer – was definitely there when I went to fetch Jimmy. Someone must have been in the study between my leaving to phone him and your guys arriving.'

Keith narrowed his eyes. 'Surely that's impossible – can't have been long.'

'Cedric's unusual Packard PC was on his desk as I left – I'm positive.'

The notebook came back out. More questions followed before he patted my hand across the table. 'Enough. Let's have a nice afternoon and talk about something else.'

I tried to enjoy being spoiled. It had been a long time. I ate every scrap of the delectable lunch and consumed the best part of the bottle of Chablis. Keith had two more glasses of red.

18

Mata Hari

Back at the Lodge, Abbie was down at my door before I had my key out.

'So, how was it? You seeing him again?'

'Calm down Abbie. We're not sixth formers after a school dance!'

'What's a sixth former – is that a twelfth grader?'

'I've no idea!' Laughing, I threw my furry jacket onto the bed and sat to unzip my boots.

'You look happy anyway. A few glasses of wine, eh?' Getting no reply, Abbie added, 'So, what did he make of our investigations? Who does he think did it?'

'He just wrote everything down. What did you expect? I don't think they've made much progress, but I doubt he'd say if he had, would he?'

'Why not – especially with him having the hots for you. You made another date?'

'No!'

'He'll call though, mark my words …'

'Och, quit your havering and go put the kettle on!' I put my wet boots under the radiator. The snow had been quite deep in the University Gardens by the time we'd taken a walk after lunch. He was full of Oxford stories. Like the students who, convincing tourists the Martyrs' Monument was the steeple of an underground church, took money for taking them to a nearby flight of steps that actually led down to public toilets! I changed my socks and headed for the kitchen where I recounted the Martyrs' story. 'Gullible Americans, I'd reckon!'

'Well, excuse me!' Abbie stood hands on hips, feigning indignation.

'I'm joking, but then again, you have to admit…'

Abbie lifted a saucepan.

I put my hands up in surrender. 'Anyway, Keith brought me home in a taxi.'

'Result, girl!' Abbie held out a palm for a high five. 'You betcha, this'll go places. Aim for dinner next time, more romantic.'

'I will whack you in a minute.'

'Aw, you gotta live a little, Jude! He will call.'

Although I hoped he might, I'd no illusions: there was an unsolved murder between us. I dunked a teabag in a mug Abbie filled from the kettle. 'Where is everyone?'

Abbie depressed her cafetière. 'Lycra Leo's at the gym. Jon's out for a run with a new bloke called Caleb. That Jewish chap Izaak, who was here last term, is upstairs packing 'cos he's finally given up his room to go live with his fiancée, Miriam and her parents till the wedding.'

'Och, I'm pleased for him. And Tilly and Guy?'

'She left at ten towing a weekender. Guy left just after. Hasn't returned. You did remember to tell Steadman about him spying on us?'

'Yes, but I've been thinking since we saw him eavesdrop in the hall – it means our rooms mustn't be bugged, Abbie.'

'True. Talking of spying, no white van sightings today.'

'Good, but let's not get paranoid. Drat, forgot to tell Keith about the van – and the beardy guy. Think they're on the list I gave him, though. I'll check. But one curious thing, turns out neither the robbers nor the police have Cedric's PC. It is missing.'

'Gwen said the police have it.'

'No, she only assumed that. According to Keith, there was no computer on his desk when the police went in, but there was before I went to phone Jimmy.'

'So, what does that mean?' Abbie stopped mid-munch of a Jaffa Cake.

'It means, someone here unlocked the door and pinched the computer whilst I came back round outside the house.'

'I've been wondering about that. Why didn't you use Cedric's desk phone?'

'Heavens, obviously I wasn't thinking straight after finding Cedric's blood-soaked body.'

'Sorry, Jude. So, who nicked it? Jesus, they must have been bloody quick off the mark.'

'Yes, and they didn't have time to relock the door, so the police found it open.'

Abbie looked heavenwards, thinking. 'Leo's nearest.'

'But he wasn't home. Unlikely he could've returned without me seeing him.'

'So, whose window overlooks the back garden who heard you yell, saw you run out the back and came down in the speed of lightning? What did Keith think?'

'Don't think he has a theory.' I poured milk into my tea from a carton labelled with an orange sticker saying, 'Jon'. I no longer cared. 'But you know, it was nice to be out today, Abbie, away from here, good food, classy wine, a walk, a laugh. Keith's good company.'

'I'm glad. You deserve a break, girl! Shall I go and get a bottle?'

'No thanks. I'm off to read some notes and not waste the day completely.' Back in my room I lay down with a notebook. Soon, I was sound asleep, my soundest sleep for a fortnight.

Just after seven, I wakened to the noise of a helicopter. But looking out, I couldn't see any. Though there was an airfield nearby, nothing usually flew over us. I supposed it to

165

be a police helicopter chasing someone or an ambulance one for another crash on the busy A14 from where a siren wailed. It was dinner time, but after smoked duck, halibut with samphire and celeriac mash followed by a decadent sticky toffee pudding at lunch, I decided a piece of toast would suffice. I lifted my jar of hot chocolate (which mysteriously emptied itself if left in the larder) and headed for the kitchen.

Guy was sitting at the table, today's Telegraph before him, empty mug at his right elbow, a notepad and pen at the left. A southpaw, like Steve. I was beginning to feel like Sherlock Holmes.

'Good evening.' He leaned back in his rickety ladder-back chair.

'Hello, Guy. Not out with Tilly?'

'She's gone to Bristol for her sister's thirtieth.'

'Oh, weren't you invited?' Cruel maybe, but I wasn't feeling warmly disposed to this drawling fraud from across the Pond.

'Of course, but I'm not keen on moving the relationship to that level.' His face was blank.

'Well, I suppose with your wife at home …' I turned my back, filled the kettle, took out a mug and teaspoon and headed towards my breadbin.

'She's got someone new, wouldn't care. We've been legally unshackled for a year. How come you know I was married?'

'The family photo on your desk when I took you up that parcel.'

'Oh. At the moment that family group is the best one I have of the kids. I'll see them soon and get a new pic. They'll be growing like weeds.' He sighed, walked over to rinse his mug before inverting it on the draining board. 'Say, are you doing anything tonight?'

The toaster popped. 'Pardon?'

'How about I stand you dinner and we get to know one

another? Nice neighbourly meal.'

Heavens, a third invite within twenty-four hours! About to decline, I hesitated. 'I'm busy tonight, sorry. But how about lunch tomorrow?'

'Sure thing. Twelve?' At my nod he added, 'It's a date!'

Back in my room I wondered what had come over me. Essay concentration being impossible, I picked up Jon's book only to be simultaneously fascinated and appalled. It was explicitly sexy in places – and Gilgamesh was a horror!

Next day, reading my third serious menu in three days, I considered what it would be like to be a food critic. Might be fun. Granted, only last week I'd fantasised about being a detective, though that may have been influenced by recent intimacy with one particular detective. Not that it was *intimacy,* exactly. My thoughts were interrupted.

'Jude?'

'Sorry?'

'Is that OK?'

'Sure!' I'd no idea what I'd agreed to but reckoned that in Gee's whatever was being offered would be fine. I'd passed here many times, admiring the displayed menu but considering its prices well out of my range except for special occasions. Cost wasn't fazing my companion as he discussed the wine list with the maître'd.

'We'll have number 47, the Premier Cru.' The immaculate manager trotted off.

Guy spoke as I looked at the menu. 'I haven't brought Tilly here. She's more a lentil roast, veggies, and organic seaweed kinda gal, but I come when I need a good steak. The quality's good, but my, you Brits eat them small! You need to go to the States and see what we call a steak, Jude. Now, Texas and Arizona – they're the places. You been?'

'I've been to New York and Florida. But to be honest, I thought US food helpings were too much.' I smiled apologetically, mulling over how to handle this interview, as

167

I'd decided it was. 'I prefer seafood.'

'Say, you had New England clam chowder? Can't be beat. And razor clams? Food of the gods! I should show you New England in the fall!'

The waiter took the order, retrieved the menus, and left.

'So, girl, what makes you tick?' Guy leaned over.

Though it was barely noon, I sensed an unmistakable whiff of beer across the table. 'I've come here to learn new ways of teaching disadvantaged kids, spend time with my daughter and forget my cheating husband. My original degree was interrupted by getting pregnant. I finished it as a mature student when Sophie went to school. How about you, Guy?'

He ignored my question. 'So, what did you major in?'

'If you mean Honours, I got a double first in English and Psychology at the University of Glasgow, then after teacher college, taught English. And you?'

The wine waiter arrived. Guy paused, swirled, sniffed, and sipped a taster of white wine before waving it away. 'Too warm, Edward. Let's start with a glass of Moet. Keep the starters till that's chilled. And get me a glass of Montrachet with the steak.' The waiter put the white wine in a floor-standing ice bucket and scampered off. I regarded Guy with new eyes: he had some refined tastes.

'Sorry, Guy, I don't want to drink much. I've got work to do this afternoon.'

'Relax, it's the weekend. Hey, it was you who suggested lunch today. So, who was the lucky guy you were out with yesterday?'

'Oh, just a colleague.' I tried to bat my eyelashes before looking him straight in the eye. Lying was easy once you started. 'Pretty boring. Like most men down here.'

'You in the market?'

I gritted my teeth. 'No. I'm here for a Masters. But why are you here? I haven't seen you much in the library. What's your thesis on?'

'I thought you knew. No thesis. I'm on sabbatical, a visiting scholar researching a book.'

'What's the book about?'

'World War Two Allied cooperation, particularly US and British air strategy, 1941 onwards. After Pearl Harbour.'

'Why Oxford?'

He shrugged, gulping champagne. 'Why not? It's near London.'

Hardly a line the University Press Office would be using. 'Did I hear you'd been a pilot?'

'Yep. Then Special Services.' He put a finger to his lips. 'Shhh, can't talk about that. Don't ask or I'll have to shoot you!'

'I won't, then!'

'So, tell me about your daughter.'

'Sophie? She's at Youngman College, final year medicine. Smart, dedicated. What are you dedicated to?'

'Freedom.' He reached over, lifted the white wine bottle, and felt it. 'Improving.'

Clenching my hands in my lap, I thought drawing teeth was easier than this. How had Mata Hari got her information? Was it all pillow talk? That would be a step too far. But this lunch was a useless mistake.

19

Wackaloon

With difficulty I tried to steer Guy to disclosure. 'So, where did you do your undergrad degree?'

'The Air Force Academy.'

'I don't mean school, I mean your *college* degree. What university were you at?' I knew the Academy was one but feigned ignorance. I couldn't think of any other question.

'The USAF Academy is a university. It's in Colorado, churns out military grads after four years of education, physical training, and character building. Very prestigious. A tough call to get in. The four-year degree courses cover everything from social sciences to engineering. My major was psychological warfare.'

'So, you were an officer in the Air Force?'

'Yep.' He sat back looking pleased with himself. 'Still am!'

'Should I call you Lieutenant Waller?'

He smiled. I was beginning to discover how many smile types there were. This one was grade-four smug. 'Nope, Colonel. Whether lecturing at Fort Bragg or the NATO college in Rome, I'm Colonel Guy Washington Waller.'

'What do you lecture on?'

'Global Security Challenges.'

'Big League, important stuff!' I tried to look impressed.

'It is, especially at present state of play.' He looked about before lowering his voice. 'I'm also linked with Pentagon committees and vet stovepipe intel with the Office of Special Plans, advising the military.' He winked. 'And the President. Best say no more.' He tapped the side of his nose.

I itched to ask what the hell 'stovepipe intel' was but worried he'd clam up. God, he'd gulped his champagne in two swigs and had almost finished a glass of white wine he'd poured. I was only halfway down my champagne. Guy tore into his plateful of whitebait on a bed of spinach, eating American style, fork only, with occasional fingers.

My smoked trout was beautifully presented. I ate a mouthful before asking, 'So, it's a tricky time in the world, isn't it?'

'Sure thing. Al Qaeda and the threat of *jihad* looms large. Goddam Air-abs.' As before, I considered his pronunciation of 'Arabs' offensive, rippling with contempt. 'But George Dubya's gonna be takin' action soon. Goin' for Iraq – The Axis of Evil.'

'But isn't Afghanistan the problem? You've still got troops there, I mean, Bin Laden …'

'Come on now, Jude, let's leave the politics. I'd rather hear about your lovely daughter. And her boyfriend. Wedding bells there d'you think?'

'I shouldn't think so. He's just lost his job.'

'That so?'

'Apparently, Prof. Gilbert wasn't too popular in college. They've binned his support staff. Jon's manfully trying to save the book Cedric spent years researching, but the last version was on his study computer …' I watched him closely. 'Which the murderers stole.' He showed no response whatsoever. But if he wasn't the lodge sneak thief, who was?

He poured himself more wine. 'Did you talk to the prof much? Like, did he tell you what he did out in Iraq?'

I found his pronunciation of Iraq as 'Earak' also irritating but forced a smile. 'We mainly chatted about cats and the weather.'

'You Brits and the weather! What's that about?'

'Well, we do get a lot of weather here. Like this!' I pointed to the glass ceiling being battered by rattling hail. 'Snow yesterday, today this. Treacherous. I'll not be walking home!'

'No worries, Jude, I'll get us a cab. How was the trout?'

'Delicious.' I looked up. 'There are those helicopters again. Must be some police thing.'

Guy smirked. Eyes darting about, he leaned forward whispering, 'No, it's Clinton. Here to see Chelsea – you know his girl is over here presently doing International Relations?'

'Yes. Didn't hear her father was in the UK, though.'

'He likes it low key, but the SS have 'copters and cars and God Knows Who monitoring him and the family. Once a president, always a liability, as we say in the trade.'

'Talking of family, where are yours?'

'After the divorce, Bekka moved up to Carolina Beach. She hated Fort Bragg. Suppose I was away too much. We drifted apart.' He shrugged, his mouth turning down into an arc with lower lip protruding like a petted child. 'While I was overseas, she met another guy. He's in real estate, got a high-end house with a pool and horses. Kids love it. See them when I can. Todd's eight, and Samantha's ten now.' As he poured a third glass. I kept my hand over mine. 'So that's me. Footloose and fancy free at forty-two. Yeh, and tired of special ops, I don't mind saying, so when this sabbatical was offered, like, 'You wanna go study somethin' military in England?' I jumped. For sure, there's the odd special assignment here and there still, but I reckon I'm due this as R and R in compensation for the Gulf horrors. Wounded in action, ye know. But hey, offered a chance to eat, drink and be merry in an Oxford College was a no-brainer. Cheers! Or don't ya say "slangee" in Scotland?'

'Phonetically it's "slanjava." I spelled out S*làinte mhath.*

'Means "good health."' I clinked my glass to his. Seeing his upside-down sneer of a smile, suddenly I'd had enough and went for the jugular. 'So, you do special assignments? Does that mean you are a spook or a green beret?' Not that I was exactly sure what a green beret was …

'Gee, you're direct for a Brit! But hey, I like that. I reckon I've been a bit of both. Who's to say? Here's our food. Glory be – a ten-ounce blue ribeye! That'll do.' Taking his glass of red, he nodded at the wine waiter, 'Tell Edward to cork the bottle. I'll take the rest home.'

Tucking into my shredded duck and pomegranate salad, I toyed with asking about Baz, but settled for asking how he was enjoying the college.

Guy responded with a rundown on our housemates. 'The Lodge sure is some place, isn't it? Now Tilly,' he burped, 'is swell company sometimes, but nutty as a fruit bat. Leo? A narcissist stuck in the dark ages. Cedric was a bit of a wild card. Crazy ideas, like insisting we should keep outta the Middle East. He didn't get it - there are times when a man's gotta do …' He refilled his glass, waving aloft the empty white bottle for more. I was shocked at the pace of his drinking: four of white, one of red and a champagne. Surely risky for a spook?

'And Abigail – why'd she come here? With a Rockefeller papa, she doesn't need degrees. And how come she got a Rhodes? She doesn't need no financial assistance either!'

'No idea. Actually, I like her.'

'Sure, sure,' he slurred. 'Then Jon, he's a May-jor dickhead! Religious nut who buggers barmen? Sure as hell heading for damnation!'

Not joining in with his laughter, I aligned my knife and fork across my empty plate and dabbed at my lips with a linen napkin while looking at my lap as Guy was talking with his mouth full and dribbling grease down his chin.

'So, babe, who d'ya think did for Cedric?'

173

No one had ever called me 'babe' before. Thankfully. Sipping wine, I shrugged.

'Howzabout Donut Gwen? God, she sure had the hots for him. But he was oblivious – think she coulda lost it?'

'That's ridiculous. There were intruders.'

'Sure, so they say. Anyway, I'm with Jon – it's political. The old guy upset some powerful Air-abs. Do you know he was cosy with summa Saddam's inner circle? Turns out the Iraqi boss man's keen on the ancients, thinks he's the reincarnation of some fuckin' old king – Gogglemouth, or Nebuchadnezza or whoever. Can you believe the guy, in this day and age? Sick sayin' it, but we should've carried on and done for Saddam after Kuwait. Biggest lost chance in all of goddam living military memory.'

I felt unable to process this gem but deduced the alcohol was hitting home. Guy's language was becoming more barrack room, his tongue loosening. I mumbled, 'You don't say?' God, the lingo was catching.

'Cedric should've stayed out of it, hunkered down in his dreamin' spires. For sure, I bet one of Saddams's lot got to him. Ruthless buggers.'

The waiter appeared. 'Did you enjoy your steak, Colonel Waller?'

'Sure thing, but maybe I'll skip dessert today. Judith, you want one?'

'Oh, no thanks, I've had enough.' I was losing the stomach for more than food.

'You know we should do this again, Jude. Nice talkin' to someone without a rod up their ass spouting goddam opinions on issues they know diddly-squat about. These dons and journos – debating shit, diggin' up controversy? Oxford's outta step. Goddamn, if they'd seen what I've seen. Kids and guys with legs blown off by IEDS.'

'IEDS?'

'Improvised Explosive Devices. Bloody Air-abs stash

'em inside goddam animal carcasses roadside to get our boys or in fields where kids run.'

'How awful.' I wanted to go home.

'Things are what they are. Endless wackaloon doesn't keep the world safe, does it?'

Now too disengaged to enquire what 'wackaloon' meant, I watched Guy scrub his mouth with a napkin, abandon his ketchupped fork on the clean cloth and snap his fingers. 'Hey, two coffees and two brandies, over here. No, make it two Armagnacs.'

I caught the waiter's eye as he lifted our dirty plates and shook my head. 'Sorry, just tea for me.'

'OK, OK, party-pooper!' Guy leaned over to pat my hand.

I took it back into my lap. 'Do you think a brandy is wise? Won't you be taking Tilly out tonight?'

'Yeh, well, it's big elbow time. The incompatibility index has finally blown its limit.' He downed his wine in one gulp and gazed at the empty glass. 'Call this Dutch courage! D'you know where that came from? They'd get Dutch soldiers pumped up on beer before battle. There's more to warfare than training and strategy. Yep, tactics be damned, you gotta have balls. We give our boys speed, ye know. You tried amphetamines? Better than booze. But I like booze! You know, on special ops, not drinking's the hardest part. Almost tougher than killing.' He laughed, burped, and rose to weave unsteadily across the restaurant to the gents.

I sat for a few seconds before folding my napkin. Never in my life had anyone opened up to me about so much awful stuff. At first, I'd almost warmed to him, hearing about his kids, but his was an alien world. Shocking that he'd let loose secrets. I wondered how much was true – or was it bombast to impress?

As we waited in the lobby for our ordered taxi, Guy leaned in to aim a kiss and clumsily grope my breast. I removed his hand. He whispered directly in my ear, 'Howzabout we send away the cab and get us a room?'

Hearing the toot of the taxi, I sped outside without answering and succeeded in sitting at the far side before Guy stumbled in. As the driver pulled away from the kerb, Guy was muttering. 'You know I'd like just fine to get off the bandwagon ...' I removed his hand from my thigh and breast several times. 'Ye know, I like you, Jude. I like fishing too. You like fishing? New England's the place...' Almost at once he fell asleep on my shoulder.

On arrival at the Lodge, I woke Guy and paid the driver. With difficulty, I guided my unsteady lunch companion (clutching the remains of his expensive claret), up the drive and the stairs. At his door, he lurched to balance with his back to the wall, mouth agape, eyes unseeing. With him making no effort to get his key, I stuck my hand in his coat pocket and fished out his keyring. The first of its three keys worked, but as I opened the door, he slid down the wall to rest on the floor outside, head flopped forward. I despaired. How was I going to get him up?

20

One Mystery Solved

Having possibly heard Guy hit the floor, a handsome young man emerged from Jon's room next door. He had a grade four smile displaying dazzling teeth.

'Need a hand?'

'Oh, yes, please!'

'Hi, I'm Caleb. What's happened to your friend?' He sniffed. 'Drunk? It's not four o'clock!'

'He's had a pretty liquid lunch. Can you tell?'

Between us we got the mumbling American to his feet and half-dragged him towards his bed onto which he fell face first.

'Can't have that, my lad.' Caleb expertly lifted Guy up, divested him of his coat and inner jacket, and laid him back on the bed in the recovery position, before fetching a towel from the washbasin to put under his head. 'He's likely to be sick. I'm a nurse, in case you wondered. If you leave the door open, I'll check on him now and again, make sure he's OK. Think this chap's got a problem. Does he do this often?'

'No idea. My first lunch with him. And it'll be the last! I'm Judith – I live downstairs.'

Jon appeared carrying a tray of sandwiches and beer. 'What's happening?'

'Just sorting out your neighbour. He's trollied!' Caleb laughed.

Tutting, Jon returned to his room. Caleb patted my arm.

'Don't worry, he'll be fine.'

Appalled to realise I didn't care, I went back downstairs, pulled out my key and opened my door. Hanging my coat on its hook, I flopped onto the armchair in relief. That was it! No more sleuthing. I was finished. It was now up to the police. Time to concentrate on myself and my course.

Getting up after a few minutes to switch on my laptop, I sat down at the desk. As I moved my keys over to reach my notebook, I suddenly panicked: my car key was missing. There were only three ordinary keys on the ring. It took a few seconds for me to grasp that there was no car key because it was not my keyring! Delving into my coat pocket, I found mine, Winnie the Pooh still held four keys: car, front door, room door and garden door. The other keyring was Guy's. But it had opened my door! I compared the two sets of keys. Guy's ring had Uncle Sam's head, not Winnie's. One of his keys was identical to one of mine – the front door one. His other two resembled each other and my Yale room key. I tried his Yale keys in my lock. One didn't work, the other did. I strode across the hall to Cedric's study door, still taped over but accessible. Again, one of Guy's keys didn't work, the other locked it. I was staring at it when Abbie fell in the front door laden with carrier bags.

'Fabulous sales on! What's wrong – you seen a ghost?'

'No. But I've got a skeleton!' I lifted the keyring aloft.

Abbie narrowed her eyes and dropped her bags. 'Whose are those?'

Holding up the enamelled Uncle Sam with pointing finger, I asked, 'Guess who has a master key?'

'Guy? Jesus! Come on, let's try it on my door!'

At Abbie's door upstairs, I reprised my unlocking and locking efforts with Guy's keys before going in to sink on her sofa.

'This is shocking,' said Abbie.

'Damn right it is! Now I understand how things seemed

to have been moved around and why I've found my room unlocked a few times. He's been searching our rooms, the bastard!'

Abbie bared her teeth. 'Yeh. My journal's gone. Bloody fucker! Where's he now?'

'Snoring in his room, smashed.'

'Maybe we should look around while he's out for the count?'

Caleb appeared at the door. 'Sorry, heard your voices. Judith, your guy got up suddenly, went to the loo, locked the door. Think he's being sick.'

'Serves him right. Thanks Caleb, but he's not my guy!'

Caleb made a face and returned to Jon's room, closing the door.

After asking me who Caleb was, Abbie took Guy's keys from me. 'Should we keep them to look around his pad when he's out again? Or confront him?'

'No, Abbie. I've left Cedric's study locked to show the police there is a master. Let's not get involved.' Grabbing the keys, I crossed the hall, threw them towards Guy's empty bed, and returned.

'So, how come you had his keys?'

'When we came back after lunch, he was so drunk I had to open his door. He fell over. Caleb helped me get him in. Nice chap. Said we should leave Guy's door open, and he'd check on him. Caleb's a nurse from Ghana. I must've put Guy's keys in my pocket without thinking. And God, lunch was awful. Guy said he'd been wounded in the Gulf, but even so, he's hell-bent on this new bloody Iraq War. He admitted connections to the Pentagon – and he's an objectionable racist.'

'You look done in, Jude. Want a brandy?'

'No! I'm going to get some tea and lose myself in work. Tomorrow first thing I'll speak to Keith. He's going to love this.'

179

As I passed the bathroom, I heard retching. Served him right. Back in my room, I sat anxiously at my desk. What an awful birthday! But at least I now knew why the study door was locked, then wasn't, how Cedric's computer had disappeared before the police arrived, how objects in my room had mysteriously moved and why after the college dinner my room was unlocked. Anger supplanted anxiety. How had this character, a man who thought killing was easier than alcohol abstinence, ended up in our Lodge? I ached to phone Keith, but it was Sunday, and I knew he was off. In any case, it was now five o'clock and I had only nineteen hours left to finish my essay.

Typing up a heading, *Comparative Studies in International Education,* was a start. But I needed an angle. I was shocked at how brutally different Guy's world view was from mine. I wondered if his education had affected it? From my paper mountain I selected US education research articles. They started school older, did general subjects longer, and in less depth by Abbie's account. Did beginning the day hand on heart, pledging allegiance to the Stars and Stripes, affect them? And gun laws allowing multiple US school shootings and massacres? True, the UK had the one-off Dunblane, but armed guards in Bronx schools must alter your attitude to violence. I was deep in thought when Sophie rang.

'That's me just finished my stint in casualty. Sorry I couldn't come earlier, but I'll be over shortly. Have you had a nice quiet birthday?' I laughed out loud. 'What's so funny, Mum?'

'Ignore me, Sophie. Please come. It'd be lovely. You can help with my essay. I've nothing in the fridge, but just get something for yourself. I had a big lunch.'

'OK.'

As Sophie rang off, Abbie's head popped round the door. 'Sorry, know you want to work, but had to tell you Dad's getting on to Uncle Felix.'

'Who's Uncle Felix?'

'Dad's younger brother. He's in the State Department, a mover in higher echelons. Love that word, don't you? Anyway, he's brilliant, handsome. We love seeing him at every family funeral, wedding, and bar mitzvah.'

'So, you like him, then?'

'Don't diss me, girl! But, like, when my sister and I graduated, he gave us an all-expenses paid trip to Vegas. Mum went ape, but he's cool, knows everybody worth knowing in the Capitol.'

'You graduated with your sister? Did one of you drop back a year with illness or what?'

'Nope.' Abbie grinned. 'She's my younger sister by fifteen minutes! We're identical twins. She's in Hollywood, or rather, she is writing scripts at Berkeley. Her name is …' Abbie held out a palm to me. 'Guess?'

'What?'

'Judith! Ha, ha! Must be why we two get on so well. See you later, sister! Gotta go sum up my own brilliant essay then do drinks with some Rhodes' guys at eight.'

Sophie arrived with a curry carry out. While nibbling onion *bhajis*, I summarised lunch. 'Guy can't hold his drink, admits he's in special forces, and has a master key that opens all our rooms!' I decided to omit his pass at me.

'Wonder how he got that?'

'No idea. But he's dumping Tilly, praise the Lord!'

'Great! The way he talks to her – so controlling. Why does she put up with him?'

'Drugs. He told me the US military dish them out to combatants. Presumably that's his access. Gives them to Tilly. He even offered me some!'

'You're kidding? You should've said yes and taken them to the police.'

'I'll tell Steadman about that and the master key tomorrow. I bet Guy has Cedric's PC, which was there after the intruders had gone, but missing when the police went in. I suspect he was up or wakened at my scream discovering Cedric, looked out, saw me go back into the garden, belted downstairs, unlocked the door and grabbed the computer before I came in the front door. It was lighter than most PCs and it was easy to run upstairs with it. I was fumbling with my key outside as I'd stupidly shut it behind me going out.' Wiping my greasy fingers on a paper hanky, I twisted my chair back towards the computer. 'Now, to important stuff. I'd like you to listen to this argument and give me your comments.'

'OK, but first please open your presents!' Sophie picked up her bag of gifts. The first was Neal's Yard lavender bath oil, the second Twining's Calming teabags, the third a navy hoodie top with a Winston College logo, and the fourth a bottle of prosecco.

'Thanks darling. All thoughtful. Could do with a bit of calming lavender and herbal tea!'

'The sweatshirt was reduced,' Sophie confided. 'Spotted it in Shepherd and Woodward's window. They've got a big sale on. Girl said their sales slump in Hilary term. In Michaelmas, newbies buy loads of scarves and sweatshirts, and, in Trinity, departing grads buy mementoes before they go.'

'I'll not need mementoes of Oxford after this term's shenanigans!'

'OK, let me take this rubbish away and fetch glasses. Prosecco might give us inspiration!'

Sophie left at ten to cycle home. I worked on till one o'clock then set my alarm for five-thirty when I was grateful for my room kettle. Setting to work again with tea and shortbread, I cross-referenced, re-arranged, added brilliant conclusions (well, conclusions), typed references in Harvard convention, and spell-checked. By half-ten, after a last proofread, I was happy, so sped upstairs for a shower. Blasting my hair, I tied it back and dressed. It was raining heavily. The pavement slush looked a nightmare, so I called a taxi. As I arrived at the department, I found Abbie coming out.

'Hi, Jude! Essay in with time to spare, eh?'

'Not much! Up half the night. Too old for this.'

'Go stuff it in Becker's pigeonhole and I'll treat you to lunch!'

'You're on. I could eat a horse!'

I ran up the stairs to the office to dump my work on the existing pile, reflecting these essays could easily be submitted electronically. Was there a sadistic element in Becker's insistence on hard copies? Students had to trail across town to physically lodge them. Or was his 'bag' the need for wads of paper to deface with green ink and flourish dramatically at tutees? As I left, I passed Terry looking ill. Refraining from offering a hug as he didn't look far off a meltdown, I smiled reassuringly. 'Morning!' He nodded and trudged on up.

Outside Abbie was talking to a young man who, as he moved off, slipped something into his pocket. 'Who's that?' I asked.

'I'll tell you later.'

I let it go. We traipsed along under Abbie's umbrella to our favourite downtown Turkish café where you could smoke through hookah jars. We didn't, but loved its exotic feel, it's delicious food, and herbal tea strewn with hibiscus petals served in long-handled copper pots. At five-foot nine, I found its low, embossed leather pouffes seating at filigree-engraved copper tables uncomfortable, but willingly suffered it for spiced tea, kebabs, and delectable pastries.

Abbie ordered our usual and started. 'Guy told me this morning he'd had a lovely lunch with you. I must say I was surprised he was as chipper after being so out-of-his-skull.'

'Bet he's used to it. But och, it was a bloody nightmare! He ate like a Neanderthal and made a gross pass. Still, I found his master key, and got a drunken confession that he was a kind of spook.'

'As indeed he is!' Abbie folded her arms to sit tall and proud, almost falling off her squishy leather stool in the process. Her smile was grade five smug.

21

Baklavas, Yellow Cake & Floppy Discs

I had never seen Abbie so smug. 'What?' I had to ask.

'Uncle Felix came up trumps! Papa called this morning, even though it was the middle of the bloody night for him, warning me to be careful. Guy is one mean critter. Felix told him that at first, he had trouble finding out anything about Waller other than he'd been a colonel in the Air Force during the Gulf War. But Felix has got a pal who owed him, someone high up in the IRS. D'you know tax guys have more legal powers of access than ordinary law enforcement? I didn't. Anyway, he discovered Guy's a protégé of one Douglas Jay Feith.'

'Feith? Oh, it must've been *Feith* Guy talked about in the kitchen with Baz, not *Reith,* who's an old BBC controller. So, who's Feith?'

'Under Secretary of Defence, said to favour...' she looked up to her right, *disseminating alternative intelligence assessments and avoiding departmental consensus committees*, if I recall Dad's words correctly. Sorry, I made notes but left them 'cos by the time I'd taken down all his info I was late and had to dash out with my essay. Felix says there's a Zionist agenda. His dad was in a concentration camp, I believe. Seems he's made two *War on Terror* departments. One feeds biased news into foreign media to bolster US support or diss other agencies – that's *Strategic Influence* or something. The other's an *Office of Special Plans*, Pentagon

185

based, where Guy's a big cheese. Felix reckons Guy's over here on a mission. The Pentagon lot – who are sorta separate from the CIA – are the ones with the information from some Iraqi dissident in Germany that Blair and Bush are parading as an excuse for war.' Abbie sat back triumphantly.

'Heavens! Worse than I thought. How could the university let that kind of man into our little postgrad house?'

'Dad doubts they know, but, you betcha, he'll tell them. Wants me on the next flight.'

'Oh dear, Abbie.' The kebabs arrived. We ate in anxious silence until I had to ask, 'But why should Guy come *here* particularly?'

'Ah, I forgot. Felix's CIA sources suggest Cedric was a "person of interest", known to have been in contact with some of Saddam's inner circle. Felix even wondered if the CIA might've tried to recruit him. Maybe they asked and he said no?'

'Not sure I believe all this. Anna was a Kurd. Saddam's trying to exterminate them, so why would Saddam's lot be chummy with Cedric, who is married to a Kurd?'

Abbie shrugged. 'Dunno. But Anna hasn't been back home for years. Doesn't use her old name, either. I phoned Gwen last night to see how she was and tell her you'd given Anna the key. She said Anna's maiden name was Alya Pura, though all her papers over here have her as Anna Gilbert. The Iraqis mayn't know about her. She and Cedric met in the US'

'I actually guessed she might be the 'A. Pura' who authored a Reuters' article on an Iraqi gas attack. But God, we find out one thing and six more oddities pop up. It's not like this in Morse!'

'I know it's shallow, but Morse influenced me, you know. The university seemed so cool, historic, all clever people and old traditions, like the epitome of English eccentricity.'

'That I can vouch for!'

'Dad was against it. Then Felix told him a qualification from Oxford was like a passport to writing your own pay cheque back home, so he agreed I could come, but he wasn't for stumping up, said I had a degree. Hence the Rhodes' deal.' At that, Abbie jumped up. 'Oh, look – seats at a higher table, come on!'

I gratefully moved over to a standard-height chair and stretched my back.

Abbie recommended kebab munching. 'If Guy's in an offshoot of the CIA, then he's probably not researching anything except Cedric and Jared.'

'D'you think it was Guy's offshoot CIA, who challenged Jared?'

'Could be. They'll be looking at any terrorist possibilities. Felix hinted that the government's been monkeying around with other intel against Saddam in the past, like a plot about African Yellow Cake – that's a kind of uranium he needs for A-bombs.'

'Enough, Abbie! I'm getting a headache. Are you going back to New York?'

'Like hell, I am! I might've in the past if I'd needed Dad's cash, but Grandma died at Christmas, leaving everything to Judy and me, so I don't.'

I hugged her. 'I'm glad. This place wouldn't be the same without you.' As Abbie was pouring the last of the fragrant hibiscus tea into our little pottery cups, my phone went. 'Anna! How did you get on? Oh, great! Yes, good idea.' I gave Abbie a thumbs up. 'Of course. Abbie's here too. Four? Right, we'll be there. Take care.'

Now it was my turn to look smug. 'She's got them. '

'What?'

'The Gilgamesh tablets, plus two floppy discs and other stuff from a bank box. Wants us to meet in Jon's room at four.'

'Jon's?'

'She doesn't have a computer now, so she called Jon, who said we could look at the stuff on his, copy the important files, which he hopes include the latest book version, then call the police. Pity we're meeting in the Lodge. Guy could be breathing down our necks.'

'Och, we can lock the door.'

I laughed. 'So that he can open it with his master key?'

'Oh, haha! But what'll we do till four?' Abbie looked at her watch.

I pulled out Maddie's list. 'How about the Pitt Rivers Museum and its shrunken heads?'

'Oh, no! Anything else?'

'Oxford's oldest college for the chapel and deer?'

'Where's that?'

I unfolded my map and pointed. 'There, Magdalen College, pronounced "Maudlin".'

'Magdalen sounds nicer than Maudlin! But let's have more tea first.' Abbie ordered apple and rosehip tea and pistachio baklavas. While waiting for them, I remembered about the boy I'd seen her with outside the department earlier.

'Hey, did I see you give money to that boy you were chatting to this morning?'

Abbie reprised her smug 'cat with cream' look. 'Excellent deduction, Mr Holmes! That's Nigel, a psychology undergrad from my Pilates class. A bit sweet on me, I think. Seeing that lanky bearded guy hovering again today, I asked Nigel if he knew him. He didn't but agreed to follow him for the day and see where he went. How cool was that – I have an undercover agent! Felt obliged to give him expense money for a burger and a pint. Anyway, it gives the boy something to do. He's a sweetheart. Bit puppyish though.'

'Thought you'd given up men?' I was laughing as our tea arrived, and pastries dripping honey. Two napkin cakes!

We walked over Magdalen Bridge along High Street to

the college's visitor's entrance and spent a few hours in the glorious ancient grounds and building of Oxford's biggest college. Abbie faffed and emptied her entire handbag contents to find her university card for entry watched by an amused porter blatantly enjoying his view of Abbie's low-cut top. On the way out, I had to laugh at a sign saying students could bring in a guest free. My card would have been enough.

While walking round, I read the guidebook. The only famous alumni Abbie had heard of were C S Lewis, Oscar Wilde, and Dudley Moore. We viewed the chapel and ambled along Addison's Walk by the river to see deer at the far side of the park. In the end, we were cutting it fine to return by four, so hailed a taxi to make it back just as Anna, Ramin, and Gwen were arriving. We threw our stuff in my room and met Tilly coming down the stairs.

'I'm off to the Bodleian. And you'll be glad to hear Guy and I are finished.'

I gave her a hug. 'It's probably for the best. Is he upstairs?'

'No. He's gone up to London for a few days.'

I relaxed.

In Jon's room, the folding garden chairs were out again. He booted up his computer, inserted the first disc and copied each file: Chapters, Notes, Glossary, References and Appendices. The book edit was dated the day before Cedric's murder, which delighted Jon. When he inserted the second disc, he scratched his head. 'What is this?' Clicking on each file produced only a box requesting a password. 'Do you know what these are, Gwen?'

She sat down and tried to open the numbered, untiled documents listed in reverse chronological order. 'Funny – these dates might correspond with his Iraq trips. I'll check his diary. Odd they don't have titles. He always gave titles. I often had to correct things he misfiled while working on several things at once. Never seen these.' She sat back.

'Perhaps a police specialist might get into them?'

Anna handed Jon a sealable plastic bag for the discs before putting on surgical gloves and lifting a lidded plastic container with layers of tissue interspersed with cotton wool. From these, she took out clay fragments of various sizes to lay on a tablecloth she'd put on the desk.

'These are Gilgamesh tablets in Akkadian script.'

I felt peculiarly emotional, imagining an ancient clerk prodding away into this clay to write stories centuries before Christ. 'Gosh, some of them are quite small.'

Jon looked down puzzled. 'Where are the main bits from Part Nine? There are four, all a bit larger than these and more oblong.'

Anna looked alarmed and moved around the remaining pieces in the container. 'None here are much bigger.'

Gwen suddenly shrieked. 'Oh, I quite forgot.' Dashing across the room to her handbag, she spilled its contents onto the bed beside a bemused Ramin. From the heap, she handed Anna two large spec cases.

Abbie was muttering at me. 'And you think my bag's bad?'

'Those were Cedric's cases!' Anna looked pleased.

'The Friday afternoon before he died, I noticed some pieces of the *Epic* on the table at the window beside his camera. He'd obviously forgotten about them when he left with Manders. I was worried the cleaners might damage them. These padded glasses cases were on the desk. Silly maybe, but the tablets just fitted in. I popped them into my bag and forgot about them.'

As Anna extracted the clay fragments from the cases to place on the cloth, Jon looked disappointed. 'Sorry, Gwen, these are too small. The little label on the back of this one says IV:28, they're bits of Part Four.' He showed her. 'But what on earth did he do with the rest of Part Nine, the Garden of the Gods? They are priceless and unique.'

Sitting down, Anna closed her eyes and breathed heavily. The room fell silent for a few moments until she spoke. 'I don't know what he's done with them, but nonetheless, these are still precious.'

'I still don't get why he didn't just put them in his display cases.' I shook my head.

Jon answered. 'He was too worried to leave them in the department or the Ashmolean. Instead, he'd photograph them once he'd worked out their sequence, attach identification labels and put them away out of sight. Stupidly, he kept putting off approaching the authorities. Should have done it long ago.'

'Do we take them to the police now?' I asked. Anna bit her lip and looked concerned.

Jon shook his head. 'No. They're too precious to kick about in an evidence room. After Anna phoned, I contacted Charles Clark at the British Museum. He'll be here any minute with a special container to take them to a high security vault before consulting with the relevant authorities. The police can inspect them in the museum.'

Anna nodded and sighed. 'Perfect. And now there are these.' From the large cardboard box she'd put on the bed, she removed a blue velvet bag with a gold tasselled drawstring and emptied out dozens of colourful gemstones. Some I thought were carnelians.

'Over the years, when out East, Cedric collected stones. These are rubies from Iran, turquoise from Najaf, agates and two sapphires. Some valuable, some less so.' She moved them gently. 'He was fascinated by whatever the ancients treasured, including precious stones, and their meanings. Every year, he had a ring made for my birthday. The need to secure these gems was the reason Cedric gave for needing a deposit box. And apart from jewels, discs and *Epic* pieces, he also put in these old photos of my family, smuggled out by my mother.' She handed a brown envelope to Ramin.

191

'I couldn't bear to look at them, but he thought they were important to save so you could understand your heritage, darling.' After stooping to kiss Ramin, she poured the jewels back into their pouch and replaced them in the box. 'These can go back to the bank. That's it, everyone. Now I need to see Mr Steadman and tell him what I know. Please God it might help find Cedric's killers.'

22

Becker, Beardy Man & Lychees

It had been a better tutorial with discussions more in line with what I'd expected of Oxford. Feedback on my paper had been favourable, so I was surprised that Becker asked me to stay back. As the others left, he got up to shut the door and waved for me to sit back down.

'If I may just have a moment, Mrs Frazer?' Smoothing back his thick silvering hair, he arranged his arms across his ample stomach. I noticed for the first time that his arms were unusually short, unlike his hair which needed a cut. I don't usually think such unkind thoughts, but then, his expression, head tilting to the side, suddenly evoked a flashback to 'Uncle' Tom. Years ago, in our old kitchen, after Sunday lunch. My parents next door. Him talking rubbish, ogling my developing boobs, then the *touching, fondling.* I'd fled the room. Dad's old 'school pal' was never re-invited. Becker was beaming. I stared. 'Professor?'

'I see that at last you're settling in, Judith. And the blue of that blouse does suit you.'

'Pardon?'

'I see that you are enjoying the best restaurants Oxford has to offer.'

'Excuse me?'

'Restaurants – I saw you in two over the weekend. And with different men…'

'What?' I decided his face was another that invited a slap.

'I wondered if you had been to the Prince of Wales out at Iffley? I'd be happy to take you next Sunday. They do a splendid fish pie.'

In horror, I felt his hand on my thigh. Swiftly removing it, I stood up. 'Professor Becker, your invitation and this personal touching are totally inappropriate. Be assured, I'm not one of your malleable young undergrads and will have no compunction in reporting you.'

He smiled weakly, raising his hands palms out in appeasement. 'I don't know what you are referring to, but you must know, my dear, that Oxford's a small place where it's only too easy for a woman to get a reputation. You obviously seek out male company.' His fingers went into his waistcoat pockets.

'Join the twenty-first century, Professor – a woman is at liberty to dine where and with whom she pleases. And frankly, my private life is none of your business.'

He pulled out his ridiculous affected pocket watch and looked at it. 'No matter. I only deduced that you preferred a more mature man – and of course, most of our students are so much younger than you.'

The gall of the man! 'Professor Becker, with the rumours I've heard about you, I suspect it would not take much to initiate an inquiry into your harassing behaviour. As of now, I expect our relationship to be completely professional and trust this rebuff of your advances will not adversely affect my grades. Do I make myself clear?' In one swoop, I lifted my bag from the floor, my essay and reading list from the coffee table, and left, banging the door shut.

Outside, I found Abbie and Nigel.

'Hey, Jude – what did Becker want? Terry said he kept you back.'

'Punishment exercise, was it?' Nigel grinned.

I snapped, 'Well, I don't know if he had a whip in mind.'

'Hey, girl, cool it! What happened?' Abbie frowned at

Nigel.

'God, Abbie, he was after a bit of leg-over.' As adrenaline overtook me, my heart pounded, and my eyes filled. 'Bloody chancer implied I was a pushover as he'd seen me out with different men! I mean I've never given him any "come on" signals, God forbid! No encouragement whatsoever. He even insinuated I needed a mature lover since I was getting on and thus obviously too old for most of the students!'

Abbie put an arm round my back. 'Come on, let's get a drink. We'll walk up to the Eagle.'

Nigel made to sidle off. Abbie caught his arm. 'Hey, don't go anywhere! You'll need to tell my friend Judith here what you've found out about Beardy Man. That'll perk her up!'

I didn't take the bait. 'I can't believe Becker just hit on me! After bloody Guy yesterday too – for goodness sake, I'm in my forties! Did Becker think I'd be flattered? Or is he desperate, not pulling in enough youngsters this term?'

'Or did he have them all last?' Nigel piped in.

'You know about him too? I overheard a girl in the Lamb and Flag last term telling her friend he'd grabbed her boob, but she wouldn't report him as it was too embarrassing. To hell with that!' I was almost spitting out my words.

'So, what did you say to him?' With an arm through both mine and Nigel's, Abbie stopped at the kerb edge for a car to pass.

'Essentially, fuck off, leave me alone, or I'll report you.'
'You should.'

'Oh, God. Not sure I can be arsed. There's enough going on. Oh, and I got a message first thing. Keith's phoning after the tutorial. I'd better not drink. Might need to drive to the station. Let's go to Starbucks.'

'OK.' Abbie wheeled her two captives round to head back into town, a confused-looking Nigel meekly allowing himself to be led.

'Do you know what his pickup line was? *That blue*

blouse suits you!' Do I look like a silly girl who'd fall for that?'

'Well, blue does suit you ...' Abbie might have thought that funny, but I glared at her.

Nigel laughed, 'Pretty cheesy!'

'Too right! He's never had to work at it, has he? So many eager nubile young catches hereabouts anxious for good grades. It's the same in the States.' Abbie shrugged.

'It's pathetic.'

In Starbucks, Abbie went to the counter leaving me sitting with Nigel. I tried to banish Becker from my thoughts. 'So, Nigel what are you reading here?'

'Anthropology.'

'And how's that?

'It's great. I love it.'

'I'm glad someone's having a good time here.'

'Abbie told me about the murder. Must be freaky being in the middle of something like that.'

'Especially when, though it's not really anything to do with us, we keep uncovering stuff which leads to more peculiar facts and even more questions. It's a bloody nightmare that never seems to end!'

'Here you go.' Abbie plonked down a tray with two coffees, one tea and three chocolate muffins. 'Drinks and brain food, guys, pile in.'

'Great. Tea! Got any Valium?'

Nigel looked all around before whispering, 'I've got some hash if you'd like it?'

I laughed. 'That's sweet, Nigel. But I'm kidding. I'll be alright after a muffin.'

'Is it vegan?' he asked Abbie.

'For goodness sake, just eat it – you look like you need feeding up!'

Nigel recoiled, dropped his eyes, and sipped his coffee. I squeezed his arm. 'I expect it's fine. Chocolate's from a plant. So, tell me about the Beardy Man Abbie sent you to follow?'

He sat up. 'Right. I watched him till he went to a house in Jericho last night at about six. When he hadn't come out by seven, I went home for tea.'

I was touched: to stand out in the freezing cold that long on the whim of a girl he hardly knew? Devotion!

'First, he followed you two to the Turkish place, then went across the road, sat on a bench and made a call. Then he walked over to Blackwell's. I followed him in. He browsed books then met a plump guy in an expensive coat for coffee. Fortuitously, as it happened, I bumped into a friend as I was skulking behind some shelves. While chatting, Tony looked over at Beardy and the plump character, and said, "Hey, there's Molly Manders, wonder if that's his toy boy?" When I asked who Molly was, he said "A Winston prof who's a puffed-up, pompous git." Nigel smiled.

'Great judge of character, Tony!' I raised my cup to him.

'Then they went their separate ways. I followed Beardy, who walked towards Banbury then round into another street where he got into a van.'

'You listening, Judith? A van! Go on, tell her what kinda van.' Abbie dug Nigel's side with her elbow.

'It was a white Ford Transit, P reg, that's from 1999 maybe? Registration ...' He closed his eyes. 'P449 EGB like "Every Good Boy Deserves Favour", you know?' Seeing my frown, he expanded. 'Staff lines, music? I play keyboard and drums.' He tapped a beat on the table. 'So, right, no company name on the van, but a weird bumpy thing on the roof. Beardy knocked on the back door, a scruffy bearded guy peeked out and let him in. Beardy was inside for eighteen minutes, then came out, walked over the couple of streets to the path for the river, then along it and into the college. Came out in minutes with a small parcel, stuffed it in his shoulder bag, went for a coffee and a macaroni cheese in that brown varnished cafe in Jericho, then went to a terrace house …' Again, he shut his eyes. 'Great Clarendon Street, number 82. As I said, I left him at seven and went home myself after ambling past and seeing him on his sofa watching TV.' He grinned at his companions. 'That's it!'

'My, you've got a great memory!' I was impressed.

'So, what do we think?' Abbie looked questioningly at me.

I muttered, 'God, my phone!' and searched in my bag. 'I forgot to turn it on after the tutorial. There's a missed call from Anna and two from Keith. Shit! Shit!' I hit Keith's number and got immediately connected. 'Yes, I'm fine. Downtown with Abbie and a new friend.' I smiled at Nigel. 'Did you? I'm glad. Yes, we'll be back soon. Tea? Lovely. See you at six.'

Abbie hit a final tap to send a text she'd just tapped out. 'So, what's up?'

'He's seen Anna. Wants to meet me for a chat tonight.'

'I take it alone?'

'You take it right.' I grinned, turning to Nigel. 'You did a terrific job. I want to stand you drinks and a meal out soon.'

'Oh, it was fun. Will I look out for him and follow him more?'

'No, please don't. But would you mind telling a police officer friend of mine all this?' Nigel was looking like a child who had just been awarded a gold star. Tearing a page from my notebook, I scribbled my mobile number and Keith's on it. 'The lower number is his. Can you phone him in the morning? I'll tell him you'll call. Oh, and could you write down that van reg please?' I gave him my notebook and pen. He smartly wrote the registration, van make, model, date, time, road seen in, and signed it with his name, address, and mobile number. Smart boy! I put it away and shook his hand. Abbie gave him a hug and he trotted off.

'Darling boy. And vegan. Interesting.'

'Och, there's a lot of them about.' I swung my bag over my shoulder.

'How about Nigel for Tilly?'

'But he's much younger, Abbie!'

'She's young for her years. He's kind, considerate, and wouldn't feed her Valium.'

'No, just dope,' I laughed, hailing a taxi. 'Come on, I'm too tired to walk home.'

Keith arrived at six. 'Thought we could do a Chinese. I've not had anything all day!'

'OK by me.' I fetched my coat and once in his Audi, asked how Anna was.

'She was fine. Do you mind if we sit here for a moment, Judith? I've some things to say that I'd prefer not to tell you in public.'

'I've got some stuff to tell you too.' I launched into the drunken lunch with Guy, the master key, his security service admission, and my theory about him taking Cedric's computer.

'My God, you've some nerve, Judith! But you must stop looking for evidence. I know about Guy now. Well, what I'm allowed to know.'

I sat up straight. 'Like he's a spy? Oh, don't let me forget to tell you about Abbie's Pentagon uncle who confirms Guy's high-up in intelligence. And also, she had a tail put on Beardy Man, but sorry, go on.'

Keith looked at her horrified. 'Pentagon? A tail on Beardy Man? Who the hell is he? Hang on a minute, let me go first. Totally in confidence, Guy Waller is officially attached to the US Embassy. After being spotted researching him, I got a grilling at Thames House this morning by MI5 who confirm he's got diplomatic immunity. So, if he's up to anything, we can't touch him.'

'Actually, Abbie's Uncle Felix discovered he is part of an offshoot of the CIA attached to the Pentagon called the

Office of Special Plans. They feed raw intelligence to the US Government.'

'Jesus – what else have you found out? Thames House is convinced Guy isn't implicated in Cedric's death, he was only trying to get Cedric to spy for his lot, though in turn Cedric reported Guy's approach to them. You don't look surprised?'

'Abbie had that theory.' I shrugged.

Keith blew out slowly, shaking his head. 'But the master key business is bad. Do you have it?'

'No. I threw it into his room while he was vomiting in the loo. But I locked Cedric's study door to prove I'd had it.'

'Then I'll need to bring a locksmith tomorrow when we go in.'

'Gwen and Anna might have keys you could use, but go back in for what?'

'Seems forensics found a bug inside Socrates. MI5 says it's American but they're sending folk to sweep the Lodge in case there are more. This case is getting too big for us plods so the Met and God-knows-who are involved. Anyway, tell me about Beardy Man!'

'I forgot to mention that Abbie and I have seen this guy hanging about, or trailing behind us, especially near the department at our weekly hand-in times. I wondered if he might've been the man Cedric thought was tailing him, though Gwen never described him and eventually convinced herself that she and Cedric were being paranoid. Oh, you do know she was burgled, and they took her computer – interesting? But I digress. Abbie set a tail on Beardy Man.'

'Oh, come on, you're kidding me? A private detective?'

'No, a young guy from her Pilates class doing anthropology who's sweet on her.'

Keith put his head in his hands.

'Anyway, Keith, he was a totally brilliant sleuth. He tailed him following us to a café down near Magdalen, saw him making a call and then meeting Prof. Manders from the college – who was identified by one of Nigel's mates that he randomly met in Blackwell's – incredible, eh?' Keith now looked dazed. 'Then Beardy walked until he was a few streets from Winston college, got into that white van we keep seeing and met another bearded man for an eighteen-minute chat before walking the back way round to the College, collecting a parcel, going for tea in a café, then home. Nigel saw him sitting on a sofa watching TV in Great Clarendon Street.'

'You've found out more stuff than my team! I'll have to speak to this Nigel. And what has Manders to do with this?'

'No idea. Nigel's ringing you in the morning. I gave him your number.' I delved into my bag. 'Here's the van reg number. I got him to write it down.' Tearing the sheet from my notebook, I handed it to him.

Keith shook his head and took out his phone. 'Hi, Gary. Can you do a DVLA search for me?' He read out the van number and put the note into his inside pocket. 'Yeh, ring me back tonight.' He started up the car. 'Enough. Now dinner – spring rolls, prawn toasts and ribs!'

He swung out into the road and drove to The Peking Dragon in Summertown. I felt as I always did after speaking to him: relieved. He sprang out to open the car door for me, saying, 'You know, this case is the biggest bloody jigsaw puzzle I've ever come across in my life.'

Inside, the restaurant was busy, but a cheerful waiter sat us down with menus, and beamed at Keith. 'So good to see you again!' Taking our order for drinks, he rushed off.

Keith leaned back in his seat. 'That Abbie girl is quite something. How come her uncle could suss out info on Guy?'

'Felix is high up in the State Department and devoted it seems, to Abbie and her twin sister.'

'There's two of them?'

201

I stifled a grin. 'Yes, identical. Not sure I could take two of her at once, but I do love her. She's spunky and intelligent and says she's here to convince her dad she's not a dizzy blonde.'

'Really?' Keith turned over the menu.

'But she's also inspired by Morse.'

'Think even he'd struggle with this one! It's like piecing together a puzzle of shape-changing pieces while simultaneously solving a cryptic crossword. Ah, Mr Chan!' Keith shook hands with a well-dressed gentleman who had appeared with our beers.

'What can I get you, Inspector?' Mr Chan took out a notepad.

'Go ahead, Judith. I'm dithering.'

'Spring rolls and sweet and sour chicken, please.'

Keith paused to answer his phone. 'Typical. Let me know when you have it, Gary.' Closing his phone, he shook his head. 'Van was hired. Need to leave contacting the hire company till the morning. We can do no more.' From the patient Mr Chan he ordered a platter of mixed starters. 'Let's go for broke – then I'm for sticky ribs.'

As Keith deftly poured his beer into a glass, I thought of Guy necking his. My gran always said, "No gentleman ever drinks from a bottle." Reckon she was right.

It was much later when I remembered Anna's missed calls. At eleven, I sent an apologetic text before going to clean my teeth, sorry to destroy the taste of lychees – another delicious new Oxford experience. Looking in the mirror, I decided I had to do something about the dark rings round my eyes. Surprised anyone found me attractive, even Becker.

I'd told Keith about Becker, and he'd urged me to report him. Watching a toothpaste blob whirl and disappear down the plug hole, I decided Becker should go the same way – I would complain. Carefully removing my make-up, I applied oodles of moisturiser to my tired face before getting into bed and pulling up the cosy duvet. A lovely evening out. I put out the light, wondering when I last was kissed good night. I'd forgotten how nice it could be.

23

Bugs, Recipes & Proposals

Morning came very quickly. Around eight, there was a commotion outside my door followed by a tap on it. Blinking into the brightly lit lobby, I saw men in hooded overalls and gloves stripping off the police tape sealing Cedric's study and inserting a whirring implement into the lock. Standing in front of me was the young constable I'd met a fortnight ago, though today her hands were not blue.

'Good morning, we'd like permission to look round your room, if we may, madam? DCI Steadman is on his way with a warrant to inspect all the rooms in this property.'

'Give me five minutes to get dressed.' The girl moved on to Leo's door. From the kitchen came chatter and the noise of heavy things being moved. Thinking there might still be mice under the cooker, I hastily shut the door.

I pulled on the same clothes as yesterday and packed a bag with biscuits, books, pens, a notebook, and a toothbrush for later – the bathroom across the hall being occupied by men with bleeping instruments. Lifting up my laundry, I crammed it into a pillowcase and left it on the bed, which I straightened before grabbing a coat and keys. From next door came angry shouts in rapid Italian. Out in the hall the policewoman stood mute and red. Behind her, Abbie was on the last step, giggling. As Leo slammed his door, Abbie apologised to the policewoman. 'Sorry, he likely has a lady friend in. I'm sure he'll be OK once he's dressed.'

Abbie let the policewoman pass on upstairs and turned to me. 'Leo was absolutely bollock-naked! Got some abs on him, though.' She nodded towards the study. 'What's up?'

'Grab your stuff, Abbie, and let's clear out. Keith will be here soon. They're searching rooms. We should have breakfast over in the dining room. Maybe fetch Tilly to come. She'll freak out at this lot. I'll wait.'

Abbie wrinkled her nose. 'What are they searching for now?'

I put my mouth close to Abbie's ear. 'Bugs.'

Abbie looked horrified and rushed off up the stairs to return minutes later with Tilly who today, I was pleased to see, wasn't looking as twitchy as usual. We passed through the kitchen and down the garden path to walk round to college.

'Did you see they've taken off the wall sockets?' asked Abbie. 'And unscrewed the light fittings?'

'Isn't that where they put them in films?'

Abbie looked puzzled. 'Do you English usually send the police as exterminators? What kinda infestation is it?'

'It's not insects, you ass! It's *listening devices* they're after. Keith says there was a bug in Socrates. There may be more.' I gave a brief resume of Keith's latest information. 'And also, he was well impressed your Uncle Felix got more info about Guy than he got out of MI5!'

'What's MI5 got to do with anything?' Tilly stopped, looking scared.

I put an arm round her. 'Come on, girl. You need a plate of hot porridge.'

'It's nothing. We have a doctor's appointment at eleven, remember.' Abbie walked on.

I kept pace with Tilly. 'That's great. I'm sure he'll have something to help. Anxiety must be difficult to live with.'

'I can't study anymore. Was going to go home to my aunt's but Guy texted last night. He's coming back.'

'What did he say?'

'That he'll take me out tomorrow night, has something for me.'

'He doesn't have anything you need. We'll take you out. And a proper doctor will give you something less dangerous.' I ushered Tilly through the college foyer and into the dining room. 'Sit down and I'll get food. What do you want?'

'Orange juice, please. And porridge is fine.'

I dumped my bag and followed Abbie into the breakfast queue. 'You hear that? Guy's a bastard.' I slammed down a tray at the servery.

'Contemptible! We'll sort her. These searchers – are they police? They have fancy gear.'

'Special Branch maybe – who knows? Keith said Cedric was in touch with MI5 after Guy wanted him to report on folk he met in Iraq. Ugh. I keep thinking this is a bad dream and I'll wake up soon. Today, I just want to have breakfast and lock myself in a study booth.' I selected two croissants, butter, apricot jam and two plates of porridge plus individual milk jugs, and collected the chit from the girl for my monthly Battels bill. Leaving Tilly starting her porridge, I was heading for self-service orange juice and tea when I spotted Manders come in, lift a pastry, and fill a cup with coffee. Ignoring him, I sat down. But he came over.

'Quite a commotion at the Lodge again, I see. Another murder?'

'Hardly. They're searching the place, so we cleared out.' I covered my porridge with sugar, banging the sifter back on the table. 'If you don't mind, we're trying to have breakfast.' At my glare, he aborted an attempt to sit down chummily and marched out.

'That told him! Nosy beggar.' Tilly looked after Manders and laughed.

Pleased I'd amused Tilly, I was even more pleased to see she'd finished the porridge and was nibbling a croissant.

'We're all going out for a meal tomorrow night, so if Guy phones, say no. We know things about him.' I decided not to elaborate. 'He's not a nice person, dangerous even. Anyway, I doubt he'll be around much longer. And if he calls, it might be best not to mention the police search.'

'I won't, then. He said he'd call in the morning.'

'OK, just you stick with Abbie today. I'm going to leave my stuff in the library then nip back to the Lodge to see Keith. Let me know how you get on at the doctor's.' I kissed Tilly on the cheek. 'Stay strong, things will look up! And I may be in the market for some romantic poetry.' Leaving with a wink at a grinning Abbie, I was hailed by Jimmy outside his office.

'Hello, Mrs Frazer! How are ye? Fun and games at the Lodge again, I hear.'

'Yes, the police are doing a search. I'm popping back for something.'

'There's a parcel here for ye.'

'A parcel? I'm not expecting any parcel!'

'Came first thing. Big and heavy.' He disappeared to the back of his room and brought forward a cardboard box which he put on his desk, beckoning me into his inner sanctum.

'Whatever is it?'

'You want me tae open it?'

He produced a sharp letter opener to slit down the wide brown sticky tape securing it.

'Is it some kinda machine?' Jimmy stared at the silver item inside. 'A new printer?'

Pulling back the lid further to look in, I nearly died. 'No, it's not a printer. It's a computer. Who brought it?'

'One o' thae courier fellas dumped it and buggered off on his motorbike without a word.'

'I need to make a call.' I went out into the lobby and dialled. 'Keith? Can you come to the porter's station over at the college? I've just had an unexpected parcel delivered.'

'Don't touch it! It might be booby-trapped. There have been terrorist ones with anthrax in them!'

'Jimmy's opened it. It's Cedric's PC.'

'What the devil?' The line went dead.

Back in the office, I sat with Jimmy who nodded at the box. 'Aye, it's a queer time the noo, right enough.'

I agreed, taking his proffered Polo mint. 'Jimmy, do you keep records of who borrows master keys? Or of any thefts happening in the college?'

'We dinnae usually give oot maisters – there're copies for room keys. We keep a tally o' them.'

'Can you look up lost or stolen keys please?'

He took out a ledger and ran his finger down a list of entries. 'The only time ah mind there bein' anythin' about missing maister keys was when Janice, wan o' the cleaners, lost her lodge key wan mornin' before Christmas. She got a right bollockin' and they were goin' tae change the locks, but the key turned up, handed in next day.' He tapped an entry. 'There, eighteenth of December in the holidays. Disnae say who returned them, mind ye. Why you askin', lassie?'

'Just wondered.' I was spared further explanations as Keith appeared, looking out of breath like he'd run all the way round the path.

Jimmy answered Steadman's questions on the parcel's arrival. 'Couldnae see who he was. He had a visor on his helmet.'

'Right, then.' Steadman donned plastic gloves and tentatively lifted the computer out to inspect it. 'You sure this is Cedric's, Judith?'

'Looks very like it.'

'So, who sent it and why?' At the bottom of the box lay a piece of folded paper. 'What's this?' He lifted and unfolded it. I looked over his shoulder and chortled as he exclaimed, 'For fuck's sake – a recipe for clam chowder, what's that about?'

'Ha! It must be from Guy. He has a warped sense of humour. Long story. He is at pains to convince me America's the home of great cuisine!'

'Give me a break, sweet Jesus!' Keith looked heavenwards.

Instead of going back to the library, I returned to my now vetted 'clean' room and gave a lengthy statement to Keith and Alice, the young formerly-blue-handed policewoman. Having a break for tea and shortbread, we heard a triumphal yell from the kitchen.

We went through. Another bug had been found – in the toaster. I was indignant. 'No wonder the bloody thing never worked properly!' The men grinned.

The searchers' last target was Guy's room. Keith took me up as they worked and pulled open Guy's wardrobe.

'Well, well. It's empty.'

'But there's a few things in his drawers, sir.' One searcher held up the awful green jumper.

'His books and photos have gone.' I pointed to the desk and mantelpiece.

'Done a runner, as they say in the movies!' said Keith.

'Hmm. But he told Tilly he'll phone tomorrow and come to take her out.'

'Really? Make sure she doesn't tell him we've been here.'

'Already done that.'

'In case he does turn up, we'll put someone on watch. We may not be able to charge Guy, but we can quiz him a bit.'

'Just get him drunk and you'll get answers! But poor Tilly. Can't forgive him for the way he's messed her up. How about our other "spy," Baz, in the Hummer or that white van?'

Keith spoke with eyes twinkling. 'We're on all that. The Hummer's got US Embassy plates and the white van renters used false documents. Camera footage from the rental outfit is being scanned. That van was recently acquired from a TV company and is the only hire company one without a logo.

Curiously, it was specifically requested by the renters. God knows why. Or how they knew it was there.'

'Solve one thing, another conundrum pops up.' I exhaled slowly.

'And weirdly, the van hasn't been spotted by any Oxford units or by CCTV or traffic cameras. But we've people watching Beardy Man's house and the Met boys are showing Nigel photos. He's been there since seven this morning!'

'Poor boy – all because he fancies Abbie!' I started down the stairs.

'As for the Manders connection – watch this space!'

'He came over at breakfast to ask what you lot were doing here today. Sent him packing.'

'Probably best.'

'Right Keith, if that's us for now, I'm going to the warm library for a few hours.'

He followed me downstairs, and I opened the front door.

'Thanks for everything, Judith. I can't wait till we wrap this up. Oh, and those numbered files on that disc from the security box? MI5 said not to bother about them. Telling, eh?'

His phone went, and he waved me off.

I escaped to the library, returning for a microwave meal at half six when the police had gone. Abbie didn't reply to my call, so I texted to ask how the doctor's visit had gone. Idly lifting a Guardian from the table, I glanced at the date and realised in horror it was the thirteenth of February – a Thursday!

I just made Life Drawing Class. The night's subject was an athlete with all the muscles necessary for any sport. Very distracting. I switched off my phone.

Friday morning's seminar was surprisingly fun. A visiting scholar from Durham led a hands-on session with his interpretation of *99 Outrageously Engaging Activities to Make Learning Fun*. Abbie and I volunteered to role-play two truants bent on disrupting a class into which they'd been forced. At the end, the tutor led a round of applause for our convincing performance. On the way out, Abbie winked at the tutor. 'Takes one, to know one!'

I professed shock. 'Did you play hooky?'

'If you mean bunk off classes, sure, especially in my rebellious year after Dad forbade me from seeing Brad. He was right, of course. Brad got two girls knocked-up and was expelled for drugs!'

On the way home we detoured to buy some essentials in the Spar in South Parade.

'It's been so hectic I haven't managed a proper shop for ages. Fancy a trip to Witney Waitrose tomorrow, Abbie?'

'Sure!' She was tossing my purchases into a bag at the checkout as my phone rang.

I didn't recognise the number but hit the green button anyway. The caller was surprising. 'Oh, hello. Thanks, but it was nothing really. Anyone would've done the same.'

Abbie was mouthing, 'Who is it?' I ignored her and started walking. When I finally pocketed my phone, she barred my way. 'Stop! Who was that?'

'I have another lunch date.'

'With who, you annoying woman?' Abbie swung the shopping towards me.

'With whom, is the correct grammar.' I smiled. 'It was Prem Kumar, Jared's dad.'

'From the States? Is he over? Where's Jared?'

'Here too, it seems. I had missed calls from Sophie last night. My phone was off for Art Class. I couldn't get her this morning. She only sent a cryptic text: 'Great news! See you later!'

'So, where's this lunch?'

'The Old Parsonage Grillroom, one o'clock. He's staying there, so it must be posh. May I humbly invite you to tart me up again? I really must get new clothes for this busy social life!' Patting my hair, I twisted my neck round. 'And I must get a haircut.'

'You can borrow my new blue top. Becker thinks it's your colour!'

Like two giggling schoolgirls, we made our way back to the Lodge. Sophie was still not answering her phone.

As it was raining heavily, I took a taxi down Banbury Road to the Parsonage. With its mullioned windows and wisteria-clad broad stone walls, it was charming. Professor Google informed me it had been the headquarters to the battling Charles II before his beheading and had hosted Oscar Wilde when he was thrown out of his student lodgings. Round every corner, as Keith had sweepingly asserted, Oxford is linked to everyone who's ever been anyone in England. Entering through the Old Parsonage's gate and garden, I was led into the restaurant where I had no problem recognising Jared's father.

'Mrs Frazer!' He stood, shook my hand warmly and ushered me into a seat opposite his. 'May I offer you something to drink?'

'Perhaps a glass of *Sauvignon*?'

'No problem.' He took a menu from the waiter and ordered a wine and an orange juice.

'Are Sophie and Jared coming?' I glanced at the menu then smiled at my host.

'Jared's with his lawyer at the police station and I suggested to Sophie she needn't miss classes for this. In fact, I was pleased to have a chance to see you alone to tell you how eternally grateful Kamala and I are to you and Sophie for helping Jared when he was in distress. Although I think the flight to Germany was not his best course of action, he should have phoned me. I admit however, that we ourselves did run away – from Idi Amin in Uganda. My wife was entitled to a US passport through her mother, so we headed there.'

'You shouldn't blame Jared. As I know from recent experience, in stressful times we don't always think clearly.'

'Oh, yes, Jared told me you found his professor. A sad business.' He shook his head. 'I have engaged a London lawyer for Jared to challenge the termination of his college contract and the fact that, in my view, his human rights were violated by the US Embassy. So today he is seeing the police, on Monday we have a meeting at the embassy, and thereafter we'll tackle the college.'

'I'm glad he's back. Sophie has missed him terribly.'

'And he has missed her. Our new lawyer, by the way, is hot on human rights and will demand proof of an unblemished record for Jared's future as well as his reinstatement.'

I grinned inwardly, relishing the thought of Manders facing a bigshot international human rights lawyer and this assertive Bostonian physician. 'And how is Jared's mother?'

'Ah, you know she's in the Brigham? Only one last chemo cycle to go. We are hopeful.' He raised his glass in a toast.

'I am sorry.'

'Finding his mother so unwell made Jared keen to come back to sort out this nonsense.'

After we had given our order, soup and fish for me, salad and pumpkin risotto for Prem, the waiter removed our menus. 'Thank you, Professor.'

'Professor? I didn't know.'

'I am a professor at Harvard. They'll have seen it on my passport under "occupation" I expect.' He laughed Jared's laugh. 'But I have to tell you that I'm thrilled your daughter may be joining our family. Jared says he's going to propose this weekend. I hope she says yes.'

'Really? I'm surprised but couldn't be happier. So have you actually met Sophie yet?'

'Jared has talked of nothing else since they met in the fall and last night, she was here waiting when we arrived. He'd phoned her from Heathrow. An emotional reunion! She's beautiful. We talked for an hour then I cited jet lag and left them to it. I hope we can all have dinner tonight.'

I warmed to this gentle, quiet-spoken man. 'Professor Kumar ...'

'Prem, please, Judith, if I may call you that?'

'Of course. Regretfully I have a prior engagement this evening, but perhaps I could take you all out to dinner tomorrow? There's a lovely restaurant just up the road, Gee's.'

'Sure, swell. Ah, here's our lunch. This place was recommended by a colleague. She sure wasn't wrong about the food! I like privately-owned, historic hotels and hate giant corporate ones like Hiltons.'

'I've never stayed in one.'

'Too impersonal. When you come over to Boston you must stay with us. So, where d'you think we should host the wedding?'

I had a pang of sadness. Sophie was flying the nest. But in love. The only way to be.

24

Nigel & Prem

I took a taxi back, musing about how I'd often longed to be a 'lady who lunched', never realising that it meant splitting the day into unusable segments, especially for essay writing. At my desk I scrabbled through the books I'd collected for the wearing weekly polemic and calculated how much time I had to complete anything worthwhile before dinner. I had no inkling where or when dinner was as I'd left it to Abbie. At least I didn't need to think about clothes. My smart *sub fusc* suit and Abbie's top that I'd worn to lunch would do. Eager to know the details of where and when we were going out, I nipped upstairs.

In Abbie's room, Justin crooned quietly as Tilly reclined on the sofa reciting poetry. Abbie lay back on her gold-tasselled cushions munching Jaffa Cakes which had taken over from Oreos – whatever they were – as her favourite 'cookie'. She'd even bought her own!

Tilly looked up to smile. 'Hello Judith. Do you know this poem?'

"Ah! when will come the time, when o'er the plain
No more shall death and desolation reign?"

'Shelley? Is that from *"War?"'*

'Yes! Clever you. Most people only know *To a Skylark.* We were just talking about how even though it's two hundred years since Shelley wrote about the futility of war, he's still relevant. Tragic he died so young and lost several children.

Did you know that?'

'I vaguely think I did.'

'I love his passion on the need to challenge the servile acceptance of authority and aspire to higher goals.'

A new light shone in Tilly's eyes. 'My, you are looking better! What did the doc say?'

'She was lovely. I'm to start a small dose of an antidepressant at night, and she's arranging a cognitive therapist. Talking to her, I felt better immediately – she even understood my fear of psychiatrists.'

'Mightn't one be the best thing, though?'

Tilly shrank into a squashed huddle, shoulders down, book clutched tightly between her legs. 'No. That last one was the end! My aunt wouldn't believe he was a creep. It was awful.'

'I'm sorry, Tilly. Anyway, I'm looking forward to a nice night out. Did you get a table at the Trout, Abbie?' It had been another of Maddie's suggestions.

'All done, seven thirty. Sophie can't come but Nigel will join us there.'

'Grand. I'll take the car and not drink. Shall we leave about seven?'

As Abbie nodded, Tilly opened her book to search its pages. 'Judith, do you know *The Revolt of Islam*? It's not about Islam really, more about oppression. It references the French Revolution, but it has the most wonderful imaginative, musical lines with eagles and serpents and warnings about tyrants. They're still about. I mean, we saw the lunchtime news. That Saddam must be one of the worst tyrants ever. Iraq's in civil war. There's famine – and even plagues he's manufactured for chemical warfare. Guy says …'

I looked directly at her. 'Sorry, Tilly, no more about Guy! He's wrong about a lot of stuff. Anyway, need to cram in a bit more work. See you later.'

As I left, I heard Abbie eloquently change the subject to

Shelley as a beacon of enlightenment, moral dignity, and freedom for all, including free love. Good old Abbie.

As we drove to The Trout at Wolvercote it was raining heavily. I'd looked up directions, but it was easy enough to find. Up Woodstock Road, first exit at the A40 roundabout going over on to the Godstow Road. I'd checked up on the place. Looked like Keith's theory of everything in Oxford having historical associations was right. It was linked to Lewis Carroll, Inspector Morse, Rosamund the Fair (still to be googled) and King Henry II. Sadly, it was too wet to sit out on the Thames-side terrace, but the cosy, beamed restaurant with little aluminium plant pots was charming. We had barely sat down when Nigel arrived, long hair smartly combed and clad in an ironed shirt, chinos, and new parka.

'This is Tilly,' said Abbie. 'She's in our house.'

'Hello, I'm Nigel,' He gave a rudimentary, hip-height wave like a child before sitting. Then he looked from his menu to Tilly's face, to the menu, to Tilly's face. Abbie had given her a make-over and she was looking especially pretty, her cascading hair caught up in two jewelled clasps.

'I think I'll be daring, try a virgin cocktail,' I looked at Tilly. 'What about you?'

'I don't drink alcohol, so I'll try one too.'

'Do you mind if I have a beer?' asked Nigel.

As I was about to say, 'Why wouldn't we?' I realised he was talking to Tilly who laughingly shook her head. From the food menu, I decided on pigeon, which I'd never tasted.

'Great, there're several veggie dishes! Think I'll have wild mushroom risotto.' Tilly put her menu down.

Without looking at the menu and taking his eyes off her, Nigel said, 'That sounds good.'

Abbie's grin couldn't have been wider. 'I'll have that too.'

The waiter left and Tilly spoke. 'What are you reading, Nigel?'

'I'm at St. Hughes, final year, reading Social Anthropology.'

'Fascinating. But I've never been clear, how's that different from Sociology?'

'Well, it's less about how societies are structured, more about how people think, their beliefs and so on, like their view of the world – back through time and across the planet.'

Hearing them chat, I was amazed. For someone who couldn't cope without Valium a week ago, Tilly was holding her own in an animated intense discussion covering religious beliefs, state governance and the influence of literature on societal progress, all during one course! Abbie and I occasionally spoke, but the floor was dominated by the Nigel-Tilly axis.

'Are you going on the march tomorrow, Tilly?' Nigel asked.

'I thought about it, but I'm not keen on crowds.'

'Come with me and my big muscly rower mates from Hughes, then. We'll protect you! I'll come and get you at nine, if you like?'

'Great!' Tilly nodded, moving aside her empty plate. 'What's for dessert?' She was on her second virgin Tequila Sunrise. I was pleased. The evening was a success on several fronts.

As we detoured to deposit Nigel at his college, the back-seat chatter was persistent, both passengers quoting poetry. Tilly was flushed when we finally arrived back at the Lodge.

'Great night, girls! Thanks so much.' Hugging us both, she sped up the stairs humming.

I stood at my door watching her go. 'Your good deed of the century, Abbie!'

'Well, she's still got her black dogs. It isn't only her parents' and boyfriend's deaths that haunt her, there's sexual stuff, like the tutor and that psychiatrist, but I think she's feeling hopeful now. Maybe Nigel can help carry her along.'

'Will he be her *"Star whose wings of light, Speed thee in thy fiery flight"*?'

'Gracious? You caught the poetry bug too?'

'Well, I am an English teacher! Shelley seems to pop into my thinking a lot presently. God knows what else might appear! Night, night. Going to do essay stuff in the morning then take Prem on a whistle-stop tour of Oxford. That reminds me, I need to book a table for dinner at Gee's tomorrow night. You want to come?'

'No, sorry have a date with a guy I met in the library, Douglas, Business School. Never been out with a Canadian!' Laughing, she hugged me tightly and went to bed.

Next morning there was a note under my door.

'Thanks for dinner. Off to St Giles with Nigel. Have a good day! Love, Tilly XX.'

Making breakfast with stale cornflakes and fuzzy raspberries, I realised I still hadn't done a proper shop. I phoned Sophie. 'Hello darling, how are you? Good dinner last night?' I heard the joy in her voice. How much you could tell from the inflection in the voice of someone you loved.

'Great, Mum. You missed a super meal, but hope you had fun whatever it was you did.'

'Had a dinner Abbie arranged to cheer up Tilly and thank her friend Nigel for something.' I realised I hadn't told her about him, now wasn't the time. 'Abbie did some match-making. Nigel and Tilly are off to the *Stop The War* rally together.'

'We're just off ourselves. If we can get on one of the buses, I want to go to London.'

'Oh, be careful, Sophie. It might be very crowded there. Watch your pockets. Stay away from trouble. Mass demonstrations always attract undesirables.'

'Look, Mum, it's all been super-organised by the Coalition with police consultation. There are two starting places finishing up at Piccadilly and they're not allowing anyone into Hyde Park. Folk are coming from all over. It'll be respectable with all sorts of regular national organisations, like trade unions and the Muslim Council of Great Britain. There's a kind of people's revolution all over Europe and the States. This war is wrong. The French see that, but Blair can't. I've resigned from the party.'

'Just be careful, pet. Oh, and you must tell Jared I was mysteriously sent Cedric's study computer. Keith has it. Haven't had a chance to tell anyone, yesterday was so mad, but hopefully between it and the discs Anna gave Jon, they'll be able to finish Cedric's book. We'll discuss everything tonight. I'm taking Prem on a tour of Oxford and will book Gee's for seven. Any change I'll text you.'

'Thanks, Mum. See you tonight. Love you!'

I worked steadily till twelve, then smartened myself up to walk down to the Old Parsonage. For once I was content: my essay in hand, my laundry in the machine, my room tidied, and a shopping list made for tomorrow. To decide what to show Prem, I'd consulted the map. Depending on what he wanted to see, I planned to pass by the Eagle and Child, mention the Inklings, then walk down past St John's and Balliol Colleges to the Ashmolean Museum and St Michael at the North Gate Church before cutting round past Exeter down to High Street. Afterwards, we might go up the tower of the University Church of St Mary the Virgin in Radcliffe Square for the view of the Bodleian, Brasenose College, and a glimpse of All Souls, that funny college with no undergraduates. St Mary's Tower was one of Maddie's recommendations. It was thirteenth century and adorned with gargoyles and grotesques. Prem should love it. Afterwards I planned coffee and cake in the Vaults Café behind and if time permitted, we might go down High Street for a quick look at Shelley's tomb and Magdalen College.

Prem was waiting in the lobby. 'Lead on, Judith. Let's do Oxford!'

By the time we got to the Eagle and Child in the broad tree-lined St Giles, there were crowds of milling people, mainly placard-wielding protestors. Across the road outside St John's College, a man was making a speech, though I couldn't make him out. Large groups stood about chatting. I hoped Sophie was OK in London but consoled myself she had Jared.

'If this were the States, the troopers would be out in riot gear!' Prem asserted.

'Well, I'm glad to say we don't do that much. This is a peaceful march, an expression of opposition to government policy, not a riot.'

Prem looked at a nearby policeman. 'I'm surprised your police can keep order without guns. Is his only weapon that truncheon?'

'Think some forces have Tasers, now. But if they feel the need for guns, they bring in armed squads. I'm glad to say, I've never seen any.'

As we walked down towards the town centre, two beautifully groomed police horses went sedately by. The crowd thinned in Broad Street. At the Radcliffe Camera, Prem enthused over its iconic dome-shaped Palladian roof and his camera clicked away nineteen to the dozen. I was sorry it was so busy: waving placards spoiled the shots. We'd walked quite a while when I suggested we do the café before attempting St Mary's Tower. It wasn't too busy in there despite the High Street crowds. Guessing from his lean physique Prem wasn't into sticky cakes, I ordered cheese scones. He exclaimed, 'Kamala would love these!' and took a photo of his, half-eaten. We climbed St Mary's tower after Prem insisted on paying the small fee, counting the one hundred and twenty-seven narrow steps leading up. Fortunately, today visitors were few. The crowds had a different agenda from sight-seeing. Still, it was a tight squeeze at the top until an American couple left, declaring it a 'swell view!'

Looking down, I was surprised the mass of people in the High Street were drifting towards Iffley and surmised there might be an afternoon rally down at the university sports area. There were all ages, from toddlers in prams to silver-haired oldies. If it were like this in Oxford, London would be even more mobbed. I hoped Jared and Sophie would make it back in time for dinner. As I pointed out the sights my voice was drowned out by police sirens.

Over to our left there was a commotion at the Shepherd & Woodward corner where Sophie had bought my birthday sweatshirt, but I couldn't clearly make out what was happening.

'Perhaps there's been an accident there?' Prem pointed.

'No ambulance though. Who knows? Time's getting on. If you still have the stamina, we could make for Magdalen's Chapel and deer park?'

'I'm up for it, Judith. Then we can get a cab back and have another chinwag before dinner.'

'Sure!' I had planned to go home and change into my one and only frock, smart by my standards, though not Abbie's, and heels instead of the comfortable trainers I'd worn for walking, but you couldn't resist this charming man. I was happy that Sophie was going to end up with his son. Well, unless she turned him down …

Prem was entranced by the choir rehearsing in Magdalen Chapel. During a lull, Prem asked the choirmaster if he could take a photo. Hearing he was a visiting professor from Harvard, we got a conducted tour and history lesson. By the time we made it to Addison's Walk, it was misty and getting dark, but Prem managed a photo of two deer. He seemed tireless, but I was flagging, and delightedly fell into a taxi.

In the bar of the Old Parsonage, I accepted a hot chocolate as Prem took his coat to his room. At six, I phoned Sophie, only reaching her answer machine. As I left a message hoping they'd make it in time for dinner, I wondered if Jared had popped the question.

We spent a pleasant hour chatting. I even found myself telling Prem about Steve. Prem's comment was, 'Tough times, Judith. But here you are, making a new life. Bravo! I know Sophie is proud of you. It's a big thing to come to Oxford in midlife for a masters. I quite fancy a sabbatical myself.' He looked at his watch. 'I'm gonna call Jared again. They should be back.'

It was the first time he'd uttered an American-English 'gonna.' He was such a contrast to Guy. I fleetingly wondered what Gee's maître'd would think about seeing me with a different American.

'That's weird, his phone's gone straight to voicemail.' Prem looked at it in puzzlement. 'He always has it on. Are there many locations without signal in England?'

'Not sure.' A call again to Sophie went unanswered so I texted, 'Where are you? With Prem at the Parsonage.'

The waiter came to ask if we'd like a drink, our chocolate being finished.

'Sure, I think for once I'll have a wine with my friend.' Prem smiled at me and then at the waiter. 'White as long as it's French or Italian. Did you know they put chemicals in some white wine in the States? It's one of the reasons I stopped drinking wine.'

'We have a Loire that seems popular.'

'Great. This place is buzzing today – Simon, isn't it? I couldn't believe how many people are out in the streets marching against the war.'

'Yes sir, it's all over the news. I heard on the radio in the kitchen that there's been huge marches in many countries. And with people pouring in from all over, London's at a standstill. Lots of politicians and celebrities are speaking out against the war. If you like I could put on the TV news in here?'

Prem nodded. 'Sure, let's see what's happening. Our young people are there.'

The waiter disappeared behind the bar and in minutes the TV on the far wall, which I hadn't noticed, sprang into life. The waiter switched channels until it showed BBC News.

A flutter of anxiety crossed my breast as I checked my phone again.

25

Missing

By a quarter to seven, with still no sign of Jared and Sophie, we left a message with the Parsonage's reception and walked up Banbury Road to Gee's where, if Edward thought anything of my different dining companion, he made no comment.

Once seated at our table, Prem said to him, 'I'm afraid my son and his girlfriend are delayed. They've been in London all day.'

'No problem, Sir. Shall I organise drinks and leave your order for a little while then?'

'Thank you. I'll have a gin and light tonic. You, Judith?'

'The same, thanks.' Prem must be anxious: he'd told me he rarely drank alcohol. The menu was excellent, but my stomach was churning. It no longer seemed important that I was under-dressed. Nor lacking high-heeled shoes. What had happened to Sophie and Jared?

'I'd hoped we'd be having champagne tonight, but there's always tomorrow. I wonder if Jared has proposed yet. Do you think it's too soon?'

'Oh, I don't think so, Prem. She's missed him so since he left. But I can't shake off the feeling something's wrong. Even if the crowds delayed them, why haven't they phoned?'

Prem turned to the menu and started explaining how diet influenced diabetes, his medical speciality. I recognised a diversionary tactic. The drinks came. We ordered our food.

It was such a waste; I only pecked at my halibut. When

my phone rang, in my haste to grab it I almost knocked my wine off the table. Normally I'd have switched off my phone at dinner – or at least, excused myself to go outside.

'Hello? Is that you Sophie?' It was not. 'No, I'm at Gee's in Banbury Road having dinner with Jared's father. Yes, we've eaten. Why? OK, meet you there, then.'

Prem looked expectantly at me. 'What's happened?'

'That was Keith Steadman, the detective investigating Cedric's death. He wants to meet us at the Lodge. I'm sure something awful has happened. He won't tell me on the phone but is asking for photos of Sophie and Jared.' I bit my lip hard, too numb to cry. They were dead. Crashed in a motorway accident, crushed in a crowd …

'Photos? Did he say why?'

I could only shake my head.

Prem called the waiter for the bill and asked for a cab. Within minutes we were in my room at the Lodge. As requested by Keith, I collected a photo of Sophie from my desk before showing Prem into the kitchen and putting on the kettle.

'Tea or coffee Prem?'

'Tea's fine.' Prem looked round. 'This is kind of quaint and old-fashioned, isn't it?' He patted the oilskin tablecloth I'd bought first term from the Covered Market to hide the stained old wood table. 'Makes me think of my grandmother in Kampala. She had this kind of cloth. But why two cookers and two Frigidaires? Does someone not cook for you?'

'Seven of us share the two cookers and two fridge-freezers. We have a wall cupboard each, plus a shelf in the walk-in larder.' Seeing the larder door open, I quickly shut it, current whereabouts of rodents still unknown. 'It works quite well. When I've had time to go shopping, that is. But, if necessary, we can go through there,' I nodded at the back door, 'and cut along to the college dining room.'

'So, who all rooms here?'

226

I told him all about my eccentric housemates in some detail until the bell rang. Putting down the kettle. I dashed to open the door and was surprised to see Keith accompanied by a smartly dressed older woman.

'Judith, this is ex-Assistant Chief Constable Margaret Webb. I thought bringing her would save time. Can we come in? '

'Please!' I led them across to the kitchen. 'This is Professor Prem Kumar from Harvard, Jared's father.' I bent down to pick up Selassie who was weaving in and out of my legs. 'And this is Selassie, Cedric's cat.'

'He's very unusual, isn't he?' Steadman stroked the chirruping cat in my arms.

'Yes, it's an ancient breed, traceable back to the pharaohs. But what's happened Keith?'

He sat down and looked at the wall clock. 'About five hours ago, around three-thirty, Margaret here, who lives just off High Street, phoned in to report a possible abduction opposite her house.'

'An abduction?'

Margaret nodded. 'Well, that was what I thought. Looking out from my first floor flat to watch for my friend walking round from the bus station, I saw an attractive tall couple being ushered along the pavement towards a girl sitting at the kerb, head on her knees, looking ill. The tall blonde girl bent down to speak to her, egged on it seemed, by a dark-skinned shorter man. Then the wide back doors of a van beside them opened. It was difficult for me to see exactly what was going on behind them, but within minutes, the doors were closed, the couple were nowhere to be seen, and the van had sped off after the short fellow jumped into the passenger seat. The girl on the pavement sprang up, dusted down her coat and walked off briskly in the opposite direction towards the High Street. She was pale, Caucasian, but the man who lured them was possibly Asian or Mediterranean, as were the van occupants, though their hands and the back of one neck were all I could see.'

'Sorry, where was this exactly?'

'In King Edward Street where I moved after my husband died. I'm only yards along from Shepherd and Woodward. After the van left, I took a call from my friend. Elizabeth had heard the town was mobbed and had decided to come tomorrow instead. Worrying about what I'd seen – I suspected the abduction of a young couple for robbery – I phoned in. The incident had all the hallmarks of a set-up with the girl as lure. Almost immediately, officers arrived, spoke to me, then tried to find someone else who'd seen anything. Apparently, no one did! Extraordinary considering it was a busy afternoon.'

'Ah, we saw police from up St Mary's Tower!' Prem nodded at me. 'How could this happen in broad daylight?''

Margaret raised her brow. 'It was quick and, on reflection, well-rehearsed. We've seen similar before, haven't we Keith?' She addressed him as he returned and accepted a mug of tea from Prem in Jon's new mug, proclaiming, 'Running is Cheaper than Therapy.' Crazy. I sipped from my time-honoured 'Keep Calm' one. Impossible presently.

'I only heard about this after Greta – you've met her, Judith – was told at a canteen break about Margaret reporting a possible abduction of a young couple in broad daylight. With a white van being mentioned, mindful of our interest in one, she phoned me. I obviously thought of Sophie and Jared and called Margaret myself for details.' He looked at her affectionately. 'She's my old boss. Her description of the couple sounded like Jared and Sophie – especially her cream coat and Youngman College scarf.'

'I went to Youngman too,' said Margaret. 'Its scarf is distinctive – purple, green and cream. And I could confirm the van I saw was identical to the hired one in Keith's photos.'

'Right, Judith, do you have a photo of Sophie to show

228

Margaret?'

I got up to fetch my photo from the worktop. 'Here.'

Looking carefully at it, Margaret nodded. 'Yes, that's her. She's very pretty.'

I felt my throat closing. 'That was last summer at my cousin's wedding …'

'And here's my son.' Prem took a photo from his wallet of Jared and Kamala.

Margaret looked at it. 'That boy in the mortar board was the young man.'

'OK. Now, the office is having trouble locating any mobiles. Can I have their numbers?'

'They have pay-as-you-go "burner" phones, as they called them, bought after Jared was being bugged by the CIA and they wanted to be off the radar.'

'Jesus!' exclaimed Keith.

We scrolled our phonebook lists, offering them to Keith who copied the two numbers.

'Well, well. CIA?' Margaret raised her eyebrows. 'Things are certainly more exciting than in my time, Keith.'

'You've no idea, Margaret. The murder next door to here has been an absolute bitch. I think the guys who've got the kids might be the ones who came here. All we know is that they speak Arabic.'

'What's up?' Abbie appeared in joggers and a T-shirt.

'We think Sophie and Jared have been kidnapped.'

'Jesus!'

'We thought they were in London, but now we don't think they went.'

Abbie was white. 'No, they didn't. They heard how many were expected there and decided they might not get back in time for dinner with you guys.'

'When exactly did you see them, Abbie?' Keith opened his notebook again.

'I didn't see them – it was Nigel and Tilly. They stayed in

Oxford as well. Nigel worried London would be too crowded for her. Mind you the city here was jumping as well.'

'What time did Tilly meet them, do you know?' Steadman asked.

'I don't. Let me go fetch her.' Abbie left.

'Might one of these men be Beardy Man?' I asked Keith. 'Are you still watching him?'

'We were, but when they went to pick him up, the flat Nigel spotlighted was empty.'

'Heavens, didn't anyone watch the rear of the premises?' Margaret was incredulous.

'A good question, Margaret, one that you can be sure I will be asking.' Keith's phone rang again, making him go out to the hall as Abbie returned with Tilly huddled inside a big cardigan, PJs, and slippers.

'This is awful, Judith.' Tilly hugged me then sat. 'Sorry I'm a bit groggy. Had one of my new pills.'

Prem got up and put the kettle on. 'Coffee?' He held up some ground Arabica he'd found in the cupboard. Tilly nodded and yawned as Keith returned from taking a call in the hall.

'Tell me, Ms Prendergast, where and when did you meet Sophie and Jared today, and exactly what did they say?'

'Like us, they didn't go in the buses to London in the end. Nigel and I hung about listening to the speakers at St Giles and then went up to Carfax. We met them when we came out of the Vaults, you know, the tearoom? As we'd had lunch, it must have been around two thirty. Nigel may know better. He's very observant.'

Keith smiled. 'He is an exceptional young man.'

She smiled shyly, twining hair behind her ear. 'They looked so happy, and Sophie said they were going to look at engagement rings instead of going on the bus. I was so pleased for them. We told them we were off to hear speakers at the sports ground and they left, on their way to a jeweller

230

in the High Street, don't know which. We only spoke for a few minutes.'

'Thanks, that's all extremely useful.' He took another call at the table. 'Right.' He turned to address me. 'There have been technical issues, but the van was spotted by cameras on the Abingdon Road at Hinksey, so that's a start. There are teams out. We may do a media appeal. I'm taking Margaret back to the station to look at photos. We have identified your Beardy Man. Nigel picked him out – a Hamza something or other. His photo is in every car now.'

I moved to shake Margaret's hand. 'Thank you so much. We'd have no idea about any of this if you hadn't called the police.'

'Try not to worry. Keith was the best officer that ever served under me. He'll find them.'

At the front door, Keith allowed Margaret to step out first and turned to me.

'I'll keep you posted. One good thing is, at no time during all this have these guys appeared to have firearms. The only weapon we know of was Anna Gilbert's kitchen knife found in the back garden here with unidentified prints and her dog's blood.' He gave me a half-hug and a brief kiss on the cheek. 'Hang in there.'

As Keith's car sped off, Jon came downstairs and found me crying at the door. He guided me back into the kitchen where Prem introduced himself and Abbie got him up to speed with developments. Jon then looked round the table. 'I guess we can only wait.'

'I'm certainly staying for a few hours until the police phone back. I wish I knew what the hell this is about.' Prem folded his arms.

'Greed, Professor Kumar. On balance, my view is these men are agents for a private collector or Saddam's henchmen. It's about *The Epic of Gilgamesh* or I'll eat my hat. Anyone fancy something to eat? I'll make some toast.' Jon got up and looked round. 'Where's the toaster?'

'The police took it since it was bugged,' I said.

His face was a good study for my art class. 'What? Who on earth by?'

Abbie put her feet up on a spare chair. 'Take your pick, Jon – the CIA, MI5, Mossad, Saddam's sons or maybe Molly Manders? But perhaps if we're going to be stuck here, you can explain this bloody Gilgamesh thing properly. We may have all night.'

'Hang on,' Jon left the room, squeezing my shoulder as he passed, to return minutes later with five crystal tumblers and two bottles. He poured himself and Prem a generous Islay Malt. Abbie and I took some Courvoisier. Tilly was already asleep on Abbie's shoulder.

Jon lounged back and put his feet up too. 'Right, Gilgamesh. So, in the beginning was the word and the word was God? No. As far as written stories go, in the beginning was Mesopotamia, the land between two rivers, the Tigris and Euphrates. Bit like Oxford – we're on the Thames and Cherwell, and incidentally, we have our own Mesopotamia, an island in the Cherwell!

'Mesopotamia roughly corresponds to modern Iraq, another one of the British Empire's cock-ups', muddled together after the First World War out of bits of the Ottoman Empire. As bad – if not worse – than our balls-up partition to form the new Israel and Pakistan after the Second World War. You with me so far?'

'But surely this Gilgamesh thing isn't modern history?'

'No, Prem, but the two are intertwined. Bits of these old poems have been turning up in Iraq and Anatolia since the 1800s. In 1840 a clerk, not an academic, managed to translate some in the British Museum. So, the story?' He poured another whisky. 'Gilgamesh was King of Uruk, a city state in Sumer. The first version was a religious text from around 2000 BC with bits on the netherworld and ogres like Huwawa – all good stories have ogres! This too has a Bull of Heaven et cetera. Later, about 1600 BC, a clerk called Sîn-lēqui-unninni – not great ones for short names, these ancients – wrote an expanded version which Cedric was obsessed with. It was preserved by a King Ashurbanipal who wanted a copy of everything ever written – a bit like the British Library.'

'Gee, you don't say?' Abbie looked fascinated.

'This second version's stories re-appear in the *Odyssey,* the *Bible* and *One Thousand and One Nights*. There is, indeed, *"nothing new under the sun,"* as Ecclesiastes 1:9 so succinctly says. The *Epic* even has parallels with Oxford mythology. For example, the Eagle and Child pub takes its name from the Crest of the Earls of Derby whose ancestral lore includes the story of a noble baby being found in an eagle's nest. Personally, I fancy it a tall tale to explain a bastard child, but Gilgamesh too, was rescued by eagles, having been conceived while his mother was locked up by her father who was anxious about a prophecy foretelling that he'd be deposed by a grandson, bit like one of *Grimms' Fairy Tales*.'

I had never seen Jon so effusive. Prem was shaking his head. 'And we Americans think history starts at the Pilgrim Fathers! Did Gilgamesh exist?'

'Yes. You might like to know too, Professor, that there are bits of the *Epic* in the Smithsonian and at Yale. Its story has a gazelle made from clay, a common ancient idea, then the God Anu makes a wild man called Enkidu to teach Gilgamesh a lesson as he's too harsh a king and his female subjects have complained about wedding night rapes by him – the original *droit du seigneur.* There are twelve tablets: the first on Enkidu, the second on his strength trials with the king after copulating with a prostitute for seven days and nights. Resonates with biblical earth creating!'

'What an extraordinary set of stories.' I helped Abbie

successfully lean in to get another drink while trying not to let Tilly fall.

'Then Gilgamesh refuses the advances of a goddess, Ishtar, who sends a Bull of Heaven – precursor to the Minotaur – which Enkidu kills. After this he gets ill and dies. Gilgamesh has a meltdown then goes in search of Utnapishtim, a man given eternal life after some great flood, same as Noah. Gilgamesh wants the secret of immortality, gets a plant for it, but it's eaten by a snake monster. There's loads more, but that's the gist.' He downed his whisky and sat up. 'It's got horrific bits, like Gilgamesh knows Enkidu's dead when a maggot drops out of his nostril.' I was glad Tilly was snoring. 'And beautiful bits, like the Garden of the Gods with carnelian-jewelled trees, expanded in Cedric's recent tablets. Cedric feared Saddam wanted it all back. Seems Mr Hussein models himself on ancient kings like Gilgamesh and Sargon. He's built monuments to himself and wants to be the centre of a new Arab world. I know one of Saddam's sons offered Cedric a job. He refused. Cedric was more into showing how the *Epic* illustrates the tension between the natural and civilised worlds, the potency of true love, and morality and what makes a useful life.' Jon reached for his whisky bottle.

I sat silent. More pieces of the jigsaw. But how was our saga going to be resolved? And would there be more deaths?

26

Taken for a Ride

The vehicle had suspension problems. It was awful travelling in the back of a van without a seatbelt while propped up, hands tied behind, ankles duct-taped together and no hope of bracing yourself to avoid being flung about on corners. Their two 'minders' sat across the rear doors of the van through which they'd been so swiftly tossed. Each guy had had duct tape in his hand to clamp over their mouths before twisting their arms behind them and bundling them in. Within seconds their legs had been bound together. After seeing Jared hit while struggling, Sophie had passively succumbed. Now they were sitting on vinyl padded benches inside what resembled an old ambulance, though Sophie had no notion what its black boxes with knobs, switches and dials were for. Nor the coiled wires dangling from the roof above them.

Sophie remembered her grandfather (a police officer) telling her as a child that should she witness a crime or be kidnapped by 'bad men' she should memorise faces and details to help the police later. These two big, sweaty guys in black hoodies were definitely 'bad men.'

One was six foot, thirtyish, with a scar from left eye to temple, a black moustache, and short curly hair. The other was about twenty pounds lighter, younger, twenty at most, acne-scarred with a thick chin-edge-only beard and long dark hair straggling over his collar. Neither reminded her of anyone special, another of Grandpa's exhortations. On the floor were two zipped Adidas holdalls. Bulging. Guns? Suicide vests? Drugs? Best not to speculate. Two other bundles looked like sleeping bags. A Tesco carrier spilled out bread and milk. Possibly not staying in a hotel, then? Confirmed by their odour: no showers for a while. It wasn't the stale muskiness of the permanent street-dweller she'd encountered in casualty, but more like stale testosterone sweat from a male athletic kit. All distracting thoughts. But she was angry at herself. Fancy her falling for that con artist in the street?

She'd been a bit flattered when 'Trojan Man' came up, addressed her as 'Doctor' and said he recognised her from being treated in Radcliffe Casualty. And he'd looked so concerned as he'd pleaded with her to check his girlfriend. 'She is just up here, feeling faint. But she will not let me call an ambulance,' he'd said. 'Can you tell me if it's safe for me to take her home? It will take one moment.'

God, she'd even echoed his patter to the reluctant Jared. 'It'll just take a moment.' They'd been near the lovely top-notch jeweller, Reginald Davis, with whom Jared had made an appointment, obviously confident she'd say yes to his daft proposal proffered down on one knee on Folly Bridge with passing students cheering and clapping as she'd said, 'Yes!' And now, here they were, minutes later, facing death at the hands of these men in the very white van (by the look of it) that her mother had worried about. Her stupidity gave her physical pain.

She knew Jared was trying to be reassuring. Lacking speech and the usual body language of arms, he was nodding, trying to transmit with his eyes all the love he could muster. They were helpless. What did these guys want? If it were only robbery, they could already have stripped them of phones, watches, and cash. Looking out of the small back windows, she thought they'd gone down Abingdon Road but now the glass had steamed up. Disorienting, travelling 'blind.' And nauseating. She prayed she wouldn't be sick. With thick tape sealing her mouth, aspiration, asphyxiation, and death were not impossible. Were these Cedric's killers? Might they have been following the other housemates since his death? But the 'Trojan Horse' that led them to the girl looked quite different from these guys. He'd looked more like her classmate Hassan from Tangier. A useless observation.

Their companions sat staring straight ahead. She had no idea of the time. Unlikely they would have been missed yet. That would be dinnertime. Ages away. A lot could happen by then. The men hadn't taken their mobiles, not that they could reach or use them anyway. And with a sinking heart, she worried that their pay-as-you-go phones were likely to be untraceable.

The rhythm of the vehicle changed. It veered left then slowed, bumping along a rough road – an unmetalled track maybe? Blobs of rain now further obscured the back window. All she could make out was a grey, darkening sky with an expanse of green below. So, they'd reached countryside. Great. No one would hear them even if they managed to scream. Jared looked drowsy. An alarming bruise had formed over his left eye. Christ, had they punched him so hard he was concussed? Or worse, was developing an extradural haematoma? The van stopped. Metal grated over metal. A shutter or a garage door? They lurched over a bump. More metal grated before they were encased in darkness. The driver and passenger doors opened and slammed shut. Jared lolled forward; eyes closed.

Their van companions sprang up to open the doors. Light flooded in. Sophie was dragged out, slung over a shoulder, and dropped onto a folding chair at a cheap picnic table beside three other folding chairs and an upturned crate supporting a microwave plugged via an extension cable to a power point high on the wall. There was a brown plastic tray emblazoned 'HOVIS' that held mugs, plates, cutlery,

KitKats and foreign-labelled packets and tins. This must be their hideout. She tried to memorise everything as Grandpa had recommended, a water tap stood against the corrugated metal wall, along the wall, tubular metal gate partitions stuck out at regular intervals, opposite, coils of narrow hosepipes with nozzles lay in tangled heaps. The smell was excruciatingly rancid. No wonder the guys were unaware how badly they smelled themselves.

As Jared was half-carried, half-dragged from the van, his eyes opened, and he mumbled. Please God he was OK! Acne Youth tore off Jared's mouth tape. She winced as her lover screamed. A red weal and blood appeared on his upper lip, chin, and cheeks. Some of his beard had been torn off. Remembering her one and only leg wax, she knew Jared's facial epilation must have been very painful. Instinctively she tried to rise to comfort him but was pushed back by Scarface who tore off her own mouth tape. She considered lunging to bite his hand but thought better of it: God knows what she might catch.

'You can scream all you like. No one will hear you here.' Scarface's mouth formed a yellow-toothed smile that conveyed pleasure at his own cleverness.

'You can't keep us prisoner. They'll be looking for us.' Sophie tried to look dignified, hard to do when in control of nothing but your voice.

Opposite, Jared blinked before saying weakly, 'Come on, guys – what is it you want? Money? Let me call my father!'

At that Scarface sprang to search their pockets, confiscated their phones, turned them off and threw them down with a cackle. 'We do not need your father's money. We will have plenty soon.'

Acne Youth flexed his head sideways, shoulder to shoulder. 'Our leader pays us much.'

Sophie quietly asked, 'Who's he?'

Acne Youth started, 'My Uncle …'

Scarface barked, 'Quiet, Fakhir! It is none of your concern, girl. We are loyal to our Leader. *"Allahu Akbar!"'*

Fakhir echoed him, adding in English, 'We have been sent for the tablets.'

'Which tablets?'

Scarface moved to stand over Jared. 'Of Gilgamesh, of course. The ones illegally removed from our country. Our Leader requires them.'

'I don't have them.' Jared swallowed. 'And can't get them. They are locked up in the British Museum in London.'

'But we must have them! Our Leader must know what they say!' Scarface's voice was loud as he stood erect, legs apart, arms folded. 'We do not believe you. Professor Clark's Office in the Museum was searched. They were not there.'

'Of course not. They'll be in a locked vault, a secure place we can't get at.'

Fakhir swaggered back to put his face inches from Jared's. 'I think you will be able to think of something if we start cutting off bits of your lovely girlfriend – eh?' Returning to Sophie, he grabbed a handful of her hair, took a knife from his pocket, sliced off a four inch chunk and raised it aloft like a trophy. 'Such golden hair! And my knife is sharp, eh?' He pretended to run his finger along the blade.

Sophie froze. This creature was a psychopath. Trawling her brain for any psychiatric lessons in handling psychopaths she remembered little of use except that they were incapable of sympathy for others' pain. Other unhelpful exam pointers included their faulty brain-programming, often after adverse early-life experiences, inability to reason and lack of compassion. Common sense suggested it was best not to argue. And didn't they 'get off' by eliciting fear? So, smile, detach, think yourself elsewhere. Hard. At least Jared looked awake now.

'Look guys, if it is what these tablets *said* that you need to know, I can get the transcript of the whole *Epic of*

239

Gilgamesh with all the new parts added, something no one else in the world has at this moment in time. But please let this lady go free.'

Seeing Scarface processing this but looking somewhat puzzled, Jared repeated it in simpler language. He was unsure how good their English was.

Scarface waved the youth over. Jared's Arabic was sufficient enough to understand the question Scarface put to him. 'I think a transcript would be better than nothing, Fakhir, wouldn't it? We could say it came with those other tablets.'

Fakhir nodded rapidly. 'Good idea. Shall I ask Uncle?'

Scarface waved permission to do so, then snapped his fingers at the other two men from the front seats who'd been lounging against the van. He ordered them to come and stand over their captives as he retreated with Fakhir to a far corner.

Unable to follow the conversation, Sophie looked about and became convinced they were in an abandoned milk shed. The hoses were for milking and the smell must be cow dung and stale milk. She looked up as a new figure loomed over her and was shocked – it was none other than Beardy Man, whom her mother had pointed out once in Summertown. At least the police knew where he lived – hadn't Abbie's friend followed him home? With any luck they might even be tailing him. Any hope was better than none.

Sophie could see Jared was straining to follow the Arabic discussions across the shed. After Fakhir made a brief phone call, he and Scarface debated animatedly until Scarface took a return call during which he nodded furiously, concluding '*Alhamdulillah.*'

Scarface returned to point at Jared. 'OK, you get us transcript.'

'And you will release my fiancée?'

'Ah, fiancée? This is to be bride?' Fakhir came up to leer at Sophie before looking over at Jared. 'Our girls not

240

good enough for you, brother?' He pawed Sophie's face and hair. With every bone in her body, Sophie willed Jared not to react.

Scarface snapped his fingers. 'Enough! The girl stays until we have the transcript. Bring him!' He pointed at Jared and jerked his arm towards the van. Trojan Man and Beardy Man got Jared onto his feet and Fakhir walked away from Sophie.

*

In the kitchen at Winston Lodge, Jon had finished his account of Gilgamesh and was on to discussing George W Bush with Prem. By now I'd lost any concentration and was making futile circles on the cloth with my brandy glass. Beside me, Tilly suddenly slipped off Abbie's shoulder, heading for a slump towards the floor. Jon was round in an instant.

'Come on pretty lady, let's take you to bed.' Scooping her up, he followed Abbie upstairs.

Abbie lifted Tilly's duvet for Jon to deposit her gently on the bed and turn her onto her side. Removing her slippers, Abbie covered her. 'It's not that warm in here.' She went to adjust the heater.

'Tilly is very pretty, isn't she?'

Jon was gazing down at her and for a moment Abbie wondered if he was having an epiphany about his sexuality, until he said, "She is a classical Titian beauty with russet hair and milky skin. And brilliant brain. I've read her first thesis draft which is remarkably superb and insightful, embracing all the emotional facets of war highlighted by her beloved poets. Writes splendid poetry herself, too.'

'Really? She does love poetry. She read some Shelley to me yesterday.'

Jon patted Tilly's shoulder through the duvet. 'But such a damaged soul. She's confided in me a bit. God knows what she's been through. Sweet dreams, princess.'

241

Abbie felt teary. Must be tiredness. Nice to see Jon had a soft side. At the door he looked back. 'I hope Guy doesn't return.'

'Yeh, so do I. You do know he's CIA? Oh, and he's sent Cedric's PC back to Judith. The police have it.'

'Excellent news if he's gone. Hope we can soon get the computer to check whether Cedric added anything after his Gilgamesh disc from the security box. Have they deciphered the funny numbered files on the other one?'

'No idea. Gosh, look at the time – it's after eleven already.'

'Oh, heavens, I was meant to phone Caleb. I'll let him know I'm still up if he wants to come over. He's been on 'lates' this week. Be down in a minute.'

Abbie returned to the kitchen and took a glass of tap water. 'Tilly's snoring comfortably and Jon's on his cell to Caleb.' She sat beside me.

I was becoming impatient. 'I can't stand this waiting!' Lifting my phone, I called Keith who answered immediately.

'No, Keith, no one's turned up. Really? You think? But you'll let me know the minute… OK, fine.' I dumped my phone down. 'Keith thinks we should get some rest. Not that I'll sleep.'

'I'm gonna call for a cab back to the Parsonage, Judith. You'll keep me informed of developments?'

'Sure, Prem, absolutely, of course. I'm so sorry. This was meant to be such a lovely night!' I lost it. Tears fell. Abbie got me a tissue.

Prem stood up, clenching his jaw before saying, 'We mustn't assume the worst. They'll find them. And there's been no ransom demand so far.'

The doorbell rang. We heard Jon come running down the stairs to greet Caleb.

*

Sophie was sitting in darkness, angry that the bastards couldn't even have left a light on when they went. But they hadn't replaced her gag which suggested one of two things: either shouting was pointless, or they were idiots. Or both! On balance, apart from the doubtless rehearsed grab in the street, the rest of their activities, like their lack of masks and pathetic hideout facilities, were decidedly amateurish. Yet thinking on Fakhir's knife, they were still dangerous. Would they return to free her and let them both go once they had the manuscript? The jury was out on that. If she was spared, Scarface and Fakhir would haunt her dreams as long as she lived. But live she would – to get that engagement ring!

When the shed had been illuminated, she'd noted that one set of protruding metal gates was severely damaged with sharp-edged metal poles sticking out. With her eyes now accommodated to the low light, she reckoned she knew exactly where that section was. The moonlight seemed to be getting brighter; it seeped in round the gaping door edges. The sharpest looking broken gate was third on the left counting from the door on the opposite side of the cowshed and only accessible across the dirty, smelly floor. The putrid smell was enough to put you off milk for life.

She rolled herself down onto the floor. More evidence of the thugs' incompetence: she'd have tied a prisoner to a chair. The floor was disgusting, but she succeeded in rolling across and down towards her chosen spikes. Blessing her yoga flexibility, she managed to assume a sitting position, but getting her hands at the correct height for sawing her bonds was awkward to say the least. Linking her elbow round one metal bar, she found a standing crouch gave most purchase, and started to work at the thick resistant tape. The gap left between her wrists allowed some leeway, although she did stab herself once and cried out. She paused in terror in case they'd left a guard outside, but hearing no one confirmed her thoughts that they definitely weren't bright: she'd have left someone behind as a guard. Though might this indicate that they had no intention of returning? More determined than ever, she resumed sawing away at her bonds. It seemed like hours before she managed to pull her wrists apart.

Trying to cut through the tape wound tightly round her boots was more difficult, both because it was difficult to apply pressure and also difficult to get in the right body position to use the metal edge. Eventually, she'd dislodged enough tape to allow her to get at the zips to remove her boots and stand up. Unsteadily, she made her way to the door, groping round its left side where she knew it had been closed until she found a hooked handle. Putting both hands on it, she tugged. Creakily, it moved two inches. Great, they hadn't attached an outside padlock! Cursing her lack of muscle power, she closed her eyes to concentrate all her effort on tugging, eventually managing a gap big enough to slip through, whereupon she paused in shock. Not only from the sight of nothing for miles bar flat fields, but also from a weird, warm, pulsing sensation developing in her right wrist. Was that a pool of blood gathering on the ground? There was enough light to discern some colour. A pattern of scarlet roses was spreading over her jacket.

Arterial blood! She'd seen enough in casualty. God, her right radial artery must have been damaged by the metal cutting shard and further ruptured by her exertion on the door! Unwinding her scarf, she bound her upper right arm as tightly as she could using her left hand and teeth. The tourniquet wouldn't stem the flow completely, but it might buy her time. Comforted by past teaching about farmers who'd successfully walked miles for assistance carrying limbs severed by agricultural machinery, she started out.

Though the rain had stopped the ground was muddy on the surface with frost-hardened ridges. Her socks were thick, but boots would have been better. With her good hand, she zipped her jacket to her chin and tightened the traction on her tourniquet. The moonlight was a godsend. She assessed that the welcoming lights to the left though distant, were nearest, and set off across the fields. To her right, a shot rang out. A bullet whistled past. Her heart almost stopped as she tried to speed up. Thinking first principles, she elevated her right arm as far as her makeshift tourniquet would allow and made for the shelter of a hedge. God, they must have had guns in those bags. And they hadn't all left in the van! Feeling increasingly unsteady and unwell, she tried to move along the hedge while crouching low. Tears were forming. This was it. She thought of Jared's smile, of her mother's irritating, if well-intentioned, fussing.

Now there was a gap in the hedge with a track leading out of the field. She followed it. Ahead, she could see a wood. Her vision was becoming blurred. She tried to focus. Damn, there was a wavering torch. And a male figure moving towards her.

27

A Long Night

As Prem left in his taxi, Jon shut the outer storm doors, locked them, and went to bed with Caleb. I put the mugs and glasses in the sink to wash in the morning while Abbie lifted the almost empty whisky and brandy bottles and put them on Jon's larder shelf.

'Amazed we left any! What a night. I'm off up, but if you hear from Keith, come and get me immediately, won't you?' Abbie put her arms round me and kissed my cheek.

'Sure,' I said, putting off the kitchen light and following her out of the kitchen. But before we reached the stairs, two loud bangs sounded on the front door, making me clutch her.

'Don't open it, Jude. I'll go get Jon and Caleb!' Abbie ran for the stairs.

'Wait!' I waved my hand, palm down. 'Shhh! Listen.'

We heard a voice – a tired, desperate voice – entreating, 'Judith! Judith! Can you hear me? Let me in, it's urgent!'

After a panicky run back into my room for the key, I flung open the front door.

'Oh, Jared. What's happened? Where's Sophie?'

I helped him into my room and laid him on the bed. With a raw weal across his right cheek, a missing strip of beard, and bruising round his left eye and cheek, he was a sorry sight. His jacket was soaked, his trousers torn and muddy. His lips were cracked and blistering, his tongue dry and parched as he croaked, 'Water!'

I gave him the glass of water from beside my bed, reckoning he wouldn't care it had been there for twenty-four hours. As he was gulping it down, Abbie arrived with Jon and Caleb.

'Jesus, what happened to you?' said Abbie.

Caleb took his pulse, felt his hands, and looked at his eyes and tongue. 'He's exhausted, dehydrated, and getting hypothermic. More water Abbie – take it lukewarm out of the kettle, not the cold tap. Jon, bring your electric blanket. Let's get his wet things off. And Jon …' he called after his partner, 'bring down a sweatshirt and joggers, please!' Caleb set to, removing Jared's muddy trainers, socks, sodden jacket, and trousers.

Jared suddenly propped himself up on an elbow. With wide eyes he looked round at us and shouted, 'They've still got Sophie. I need a transcript – they want all of it!' As he fell back onto the bed, I caught his head to prevent him banging it on the headboard.

'What transcript?' I asked. His blue hand clutched mine as Caleb pulled up the duvet.

'The *Epic*. With the missing bits. They're Iraqi. They need it for their Leader.' Jared groaned, closed his eyes, and lay back.

Abbie returned to hand Caleb the kettle plus a glass of water. 'Where's your phone?' she asked. I pointed to my desk. She grabbed it, running into the hall saying she'd phone Keith.

I pulled the duvet further up over the shivering Jared, now stripped to his underpants. Caleb was throwing his wet clothes into the corner when Jon returned with thick towels and an electric blanket.

'Good thinking, Jon!' Caleb raised the weak Jared to rub his torso and arms vigorously before helping him into the fresh dry clothes. Meanwhile, I slipped the electric blanket into the bed and plugged it in before we eased Jared back down on it.

'If he doesn't warm up soon, he'll need a doctor. Anyone got a thermometer?' Our shaking heads gave Caleb his answer.

'Let's get the proper story first!' Caleb looked startled. Realising that I had shouted. I softened my tone. 'Sorry, Jared, can you tell us where Sophie is?'

A screech of brakes outside interrupted his answer. Keith sped in through the unlocked front door to usher us out into the hall, but I hovered at the door, listening as he questioned Jared. An accompanying young detective took notes. This was a new Keith: urgent, intense, demanding. 'Why have they let you go? Where is Sophie? How long do you think you were travelling to get there? How many of them were there? What did they look like? What did they want? What are your instructions for handing over this ransom manuscript?'

When pushed for more details about their place of captivity, Jared became upset. 'I tell you – I don't know! It was a large metal building. The van went right into it. It had a sliding metal door, smelled of animal shit, had electricity, bits of metal fencing sticking out. They had a picnic table, some chairs, a microwave. They trussed us up like fucking turkeys!' He held up his wrist to show inflamed grooves and waved at his damaged face.

'I'm sorry Jared, we just need as much information as we can get so we can find Sophie. I must ask you one important thing, did any of them have guns?'

Jared was now sobbing but shook his head. 'Not that I saw. But one guy had a knife – he used it to get us into the van. And on Sophie. He cut off her …' On the other side of the door, I felt my knees buckle. I slid to the floor where Abbie joined me as Jared yelled out, 'her hair, a big chunk of her beautiful hair! The one called Fakhir, he thought it was bloody funny, the bastard! Oh, and the other main one had a big scar on his face.'

Outside in the hall, Abbie stood up and made for the kitchen, scrolling my phone's address book before making another call. 'Professor? Jared's here at the Lodge. He's OK.' She came back to help me up. 'Prem's coming. I'll make some tea.' She collected the kettle from my room as I stood on the threshold.

Caleb was touching Keith's arm. 'I think Jared's had enough for the moment, Inspector.'

'Sorry, and who exactly are you?'

'I'm Caleb Nelson, Dr Jonathon Wolsey's partner, Senior Charge Nurse at the Warneford in Headington – the Psychiatric Hospital.'

Keith rose from my desk chair to shake his hand. 'OK, let's take a break.' He handed Jared the glass of water he was shakily reaching out for.

'When did you last eat, Jared?' Caleb asked.

'Seems an age.'

'Reckon you must need food. I'll make you something.'

Keith looked at his watch. 'This transcript, Jared, can you have it by the time they've stipulated?'

'Jon, I need Jon. Get him! He can do it. Quite quickly, I think. He'll have it on his computer. There was a version on my laptop when it was stolen. I wonder if it was them who took it? But I took computer security at Harvard, so probably they couldn't get into it. Or maybe they can't read English? Christ, will they want it in Arabic?'

Keith patted his shoulder. 'Let's try to stay calm. I'm sure English will be fine.'

'We have to get the manuscript done immediately – it's Sophie's only chance!' Jared sat up, took a deep breath, and said, 'Get me Jon, now – I need him more than food.'

As Caleb left, Keith asked, 'Now, exactly when and where do they want this thing?'

'By eight-thirty this morning at 82 Great Clarendon Street. I'm to put it through the letter box. They said they'd let Sophie go once they had it, but I'm not so sure they will. That Fakhir, the way he looked at Sophie!' His voice broke. 'But it's really the tablets themselves they want. Isn't there any way we can get them from the British Museum?' He clutched Keith's forearm.

'I doubt it, and anyway there's not enough time. You get the document from Jon. Then let us worry about Sophie. You've done your best. Where did they dump you, by the way? If you can tell me that, we might get witnesses.'

Jared shrugged. 'Oh, somewhere in Summertown. They had decided police might be hanging about here. They gave me back my phone for some reason. But I wasn't sure where I was exactly, I got all disoriented and panicky. The sidewalk was icy. I fell a couple of times. Lost my phone, hurt my elbow.' Pulling up his sweatshirt he exposed a raw abrasion with a sloughed area of skin. 'Ouch, now I've seen it, it hurts!'

Caleb had returned. 'Heavens, I didn't notice that when I undressed you! There's a first aid kit in the kitchen. I think it's best we put a dressing on that, then I'll get you something to eat. Here's your man for your transcript.'

Jon came in to sit on the bed and listen to what Jared needed before racing upstairs. By the time Prem arrived for an emotional reunion with his son, the boy's elbow had been dealt with and he was eating toast. Caleb disappeared upstairs followed by Abbie and I, leaving Prem with Jared.

In Abbie's room I lay down on the sofa. Abbie lay on the bed. We were exhausted. Caleb appeared to ask for paper.

'Jon says he doesn't have enough. You OK, Judith?' he asked kindly.

'I will be when we get Sophie. Pity Guy's gone. I could do with some of his Valium.'

'Don't even joke about them. Our unit's full of student benzodiazepine addicts. If it's not that, it's speed. Downers and uppers, Oxford's full of folk trying to stay up all night studying or wanting oblivion. Then there's the drink – we've got one of the longest waiting lists for alcohol and drug dependency clinics in the country. Dreaming spires? At times it's like working in a dystopian madhouse!'

He was on a roll, but I was slowing to a standstill and yawned. 'Who'd have thought?' Yet so many kids dream of getting in here.'

'Oxford may have given us world leaders and scientific breakthroughs, but if you can't take its pressure, it's hell. The suicides! Sorry for ranting. Anyway, Jon needs paper.'

Abbie came from her cupboard with a ream of paper. 'Best Ryman's cheapo – that do?'

'More than good enough for these bastards!' Caleb took it and left.

Closing the door, Abbie gave me a hug. 'I'm sure Keith will sort this. He's smart, a swell guy. Like Caleb. And Jon's turned up trumps. Oxford's not all bad. Come on, let's leave that lamp on, put off the ceiling light and get some rest.' Lying down on the bed, she patted it. 'Come on, it's comfier here. I promise not to hit on you despite your gorgeousness!'

Weakly, I obeyed, lying down and closing my eyes. But my mind still whirred. The umbilical cord never breaks. I lay awake beside Abbie, who was soon quietly snoring.

Abbie had no bedside clock. Eventually, I sat up to grope on the bedside table for my watch. Then realised I was still wearing it. Five past six. A dull headache and heavy chest reminded me of the desperate situation. Outside it was dark, cloudless, the moon large. I looked out. The police car at the gate had frost on the roof and steam on the windows. Keith had said he'd be back at seven. I decided I might as well get up and do something. Perhaps make tea for the poor souls in that patrol car? I crept down to the kitchen to put on the kettle. Caleb appeared.

'Any word?' One look at my face gave him his answer. 'Did you get any sleep?'

'Maybe dozed a bit. Going to take tea out to the guys in the police car.'

'Good idea. I'll make toast too.'

'You can't – the police have the toaster. It had a bug under it.'

'What's this, then?' He pointed at a silver Russell Hobbs appliance I'd never seen before.

'Where did that come from?'

'No idea – but it works. I gave Jared toast, remember?'

I hadn't twigged. 'How is he?'

'Sleeping fitfully. I'll need to see if we have some other clothes he can wear. The police took his wet ones and Jon's joggers are so big they'll be round his ankles in no time.'

'Why don't I go round to the college and get some of his own from his room?'

'We don't have his keys.'

'The night porter will let me in when I explain. They have master keys.' As do other people, I thought, opening the mug cupboard: empty. I rinsed and dried some from the sink, jiggled teabags in boiling water and used Abbie's milk. Caleb was buttering toast.

He fetched a tray from the larder and filled it with mugs and a plate of toast.

'Thanks. I'll grab my coat and head for the college.' I tiptoed into my room. Jared was sleeping. Prem dozing in my chair. Lifting my boots, I took my coat from behind the door and keys from the desk and sat down at the kitchen table to zip up my boots. Softly, I closed the back door and set off.

At the college, Jimmy was sitting in his office with a steaming mug and book, feet up on a chair. 'My, you're up early the day, Mrs Frazer!' He held up his book. '*Lanark*. You read it? Night shift's great fur catchin' up wi' yer reading!'

'No, I've never got round to it.' I'd never have put Jimmy down as a reader. Prejudice. This sabbatical was teaching me so much.

'What's wrong, lassie? Ye OK?'

'Not really, but can you let me into Jared's room, please, to get some things? He's escaped from kidnappers and has to meet them again, but the police took his wet clothes.'

Jimmy was round at once clutching a key. 'Gawd. Right. Ah'll tak ye along. So, how's yer lovely daughter?'

'Still with the kidnappers.'

Nothing else was said until we were in Jared's room. As I looked around bewildered, Jimmy opened Jared's wardrobe. 'It's parky oot.' He selected a thick flannelette shirt, a pair of jeans, and a woollen jumper that he laid on the bed. 'He'll be needin' smalls tae, eh?' Diving into a drawer he took out socks, pants, and a white T-shirt. 'Noo, hoo aboot shoes?'

'Yes, his are soaked.'

Jimmy flung orange Nike trainers onto his pile. 'Terrible garish things these kids like!' Then he grabbed a holdall and stuffed everything in. 'Anythin' else?'

'He'll need a jacket. Does he have a spare? '

In the wardrobe the only jacket hanging was the thin jerkin he'd worn setting off for Berlin. I thought of his gentle smile when I'd urged him to buy something warmer. Poor Jared. Rummaging in another drawer, Jimmy produced a ski hat and gloves which he put into the black Puma bag before zipping it up and handing it to me. 'There ye go, lassie. That'll keep him warm till they get the buggers! Ah assume the polis is goin' wi him?'

'I expect so.'

He walked me to the front door of the college and gave me a hug reminiscent of my dad consoling me as a child. 'It'll all work oot. She's a smart lass, that Sophie! Ah'll be sayin' a wee prayer, though.' He returned to his lair and Lanark. Only the moon lit my way back along the icy path.

Caleb was in the hall with Abbie and Jon, who was holding a thick brown envelope.

'Is that the *Epic*?' I asked.

Jon nodded. 'Steadman and another guy are in with Jared.'

'Is he up to this, Caleb?'

'Sure, Judith. He's determined to get Sophie back as soon as possible.'

'I only hope they keep their side of the bargain,' said Jon, pacing up and down the hall.

'We've no reason to suspect otherwise.' Caleb nodded at my holdall. 'Those his clothes?'

'Yes. Think I'll go and sit down.' I handed it over.

Abbie and I went into the kitchen with Jon and Prem. Minutes later, Keith appeared. I didn't mind the lack of a hug from him: he was in full professional mode. My eyes went to his bulletproof vest.

'We aren't taking any chances. An armed response unit is standing by. Plain clothes officers have subtly removed the nearest neighbours. There's no sign of life at the house, so it's likely they'll not come until after the manuscript deadline. We think that as there's been no sign of the van since the sighting in Botley Road yesterday, they may have another car.'

'Doesn't sound as though you could do any more.' Abbie looked at him. 'How do you think they'll let Sophie go?'

'The usual is dumping someone on a road somewhere. All police units will be out with her photo, and those of the individuals picked out by Margaret and Jared as the kidnappers. Gary is off to talk to the mosques. He wondered if a mosque might be the only thing these men have in common as Jared thought they weren't all Iraqi. It's a long shot, but it might help us identify them.'

'You shown any pics to Anna?' Abbie had an arm round me as I sat looking at the floor.

'Not yet. Will do after we sort out this drop. You OK, Judith?'

Looking up, the concern in his eyes made me teary. I could only nod. As Jared appeared at the door, I mustered a smile, 'Jimmy selected your wardrobe – hope it's OK.'

'Thanks, Mrs F!' He donned the ski hat. 'Never got that ski vacation with Sophe, but we'll get there yet!'

I tried to match his attempt at levity. 'You look fatter. Must be all those layers.'

Jared grinned. 'But I didn't realise Kevlar was so light.' He thumped knuckles on his chest to demonstrate his protection and walked over to give me a hug. So many hugs today! I held in my emotions. The boy had to be strong and so did I.

'Time to go son,' Keith held out his arm and ushered Jared out of the door. Turning to me, he added, 'I'll phone with any news.' As they walked out, I heard him say to Jared, 'Remember, walk up, push it through the letterbox, then back in the taxi, stop for nothing.'

They were gone. Abbie was at the kettle again. The rest of us sat down. Silent. We waited.

28

Rabbits & Guns

An hour earlier, three miles away in Headington, Casualty was quietening down after the usual chaotic Saturday night into Sunday morning shift. The waiting injured drunken cyclists, victims of pub disagreements, and occasional genuinely sick patients, had been dealt with. Tea was on the brew when the doors swung open to admit a blood-spattered patient on a trolley being rapidly propelled by a paramedic. Immediately following them came a trundled wheelchair bearing an armed man. A policeman who'd been lounging at the door counting the minutes till the end of his shift, sprang into action to wrestle with the wheelchair occupant who was hell-bent on retaining his weapon.

Ignoring the altercation, staff sped after the bloodied patient into the resuscitation room where the paramedic rattled off pertinent patient details to a young doctor still clutching undrunk tea. A nurse checked that a drip set up in the ambulance was running freely into the woman's left arm then lifted the blood-soaked blanket covering her right and recoiled in horror.

The young doctor stepped over and smothered a smile. Apart from the blood-saturated dressing on the woman's lower arm and the tightened BP cuff constricting the circulation of her upper, two pairs of lifeless eyes stared up. He nudged the nurse. 'It's OK, Sandra. They're just dead rabbits!' But turning to the paramedic he pointed at them.

'What the fuck?'

'Sorry. The lad rushed in to snatch the offending leather strap and its corpses. 'Old Thomas used this as a tourniquet. He learned first aid in the TA. It worked well, but he didn't waste time unfastening his game. She was so poorly that I dropped this caboodle beside her as we worked.' He lifted them up. 'Not fancy rabbit pie then?'

The look Sandra gave him would have curdled milk.

The paramedic continued. 'The old boy needs a check over. Got chest pain when we cut her coat off, and he saw her injuries properly in the light. Might have had an MI. Given him GTN and aspirin.'

'What happened to her?' The young doctor nodded at the woman.

'God knows. She hasn't spoken. An old guy saw her staggering along a lane like something from a zombie movie then collapsing under a hedge. Saw no one else about. Police are on their way. Base got through to them but couldn't get through here to warn you about her. Busy night, eh?' The paramedic left with a parting shot, 'Hope they get the bastards that did that to the poor lass.'

Sandra gazed at the raggedly torn flesh. 'What on earth could have caused this?'

'Give it a quick clean and I'll get theatre teed up. The limb viability is well compromised and that's a torn radial artery or I'm a monkey's uncle! Let's get a vascular guy in.' The young doctor rushed off.

A student nurse helped Sandra, the Staff Nurse, to change the woman into a theatre gown. The student picked up the blood-stained clothes. 'Where will I put these? Shame, this has been a lovely jacket.'

'Best get a Patient Effects bag. Put everything in it. The police may want it.'

The girl started stuffing it and the other clothes into the bag and asked, 'What'll I put as the name?'

The young blonde doctor returned. 'She'd no ID. You could put "Rabbit Lady" on it!'

Sandra glared. 'Not funny doctor!'

'Sorry. I've put "Hinksey Lady" on her blood forms for the mo. Right, Theatre Two's ready, vascular surgeon's on his way. Just let me just get blood for haemoglobin and cross-matching.' He inserted a needle into the woman's elbow and filled several sample bottles. 'Can you phone for two units of O Neg from the bank?' he asked the student nurse, handing her the blood samples. Then without waiting for a porter, he grabbed one end of the trolley and wheeled it off. 'She's lost a lot of blood. Think the old guy found her just in time.'

Three hours later in the surgical ward, a white-coated medical student was checking vital signs. Recording 7.45 a.m. from her watch onto the chart at the foot of the bed, she added heart rate, BP, and oxygen pressure from the bleeping machine at the bedside. The blood drip was flowing freely. The exposed fingers of the patient's right hand were peeping healthily pink from the bandage-swathed hand and the arm was safely elevated on a pillow. All good. The student's eyes travelled up to the tangled, long, muddy blonde hair lying over the patient's face. That hair was going to be a bitch to brush later. The visible cheek area was badly lacerated. The notes said she'd fallen into a thorny hedge, poor thing. After gently sweeping the hair from the patient's face, she drew back, startled. Despite its puffiness, bruising and scratches, the face was instantly recognisable! Kneeling, she rummaged in the bag of personal effects slung in the corner. No bag, no phone. Pity, as she knew her password – the patient's birthday, 1407. Rushing to the duty room, she wrote Sophie's name, date of birth and address on her until now anonymous case record and presented it to the sister in charge. 'Didn't you recognise her? She's been in this ward a few times. Sophie's in my year! You phone the police. I'll try to get her mother. She's at Winston College.'

*

In Winston Lodge, only the clock's visibly jerking second hand showed me time hadn't completely come to a halt. I didn't know what to do with myself. Jon was trying to distract us with a story about how he met Caleb. Jon had apparently taken a suicidal student into the psychiatric ward when Caleb was on duty. Next day at visiting, Jon had asked Caleb out, but he'd refused, reckoning Jon was a pompous twit. But after a chance meeting in the Turf when he saw Jon fall off a bar stool laughing, he had agreed to a date. I couldn't raise a smile. Abbie suggested we go out for some fresh air.

'Sorry, Abbie. I'd rather stay here.' At that, my phone rang. 'Bugger, it's not Keith, it's an unknown number. It had better not be some double-glazing company! Hello who is this? Oh, Chloe? What? Are you sure? Of course, sorry! That's marvellous! Thank you so much! I'll be right there!' I turned to clutch Abbie's arm so violently she yelped.

'Sorry! Sophie's in the Radcliffe! Let's get the car. Or should we get a taxi? Shit, I need the loo. Call a taxi!'

On return, Abbie was standing in her coat and boots holding mine. 'The cab will be twenty minutes.'

'Twenty bloody minutes? We could almost walk there by then!'

'Sorry. Jericho Cabs says there's loads stuck in jams on the A34. Some pile-up in ice.'

'Fuck that – cancel it. We'll get the car!'

We rushed round to the college and were in the car before Abbie could ask me, 'So what's happened to Sophie?'

'Her friend Chloe recognised her in a ward. Some farmer shooting rabbits found Sophie unconscious under a hedge injured with no ID. She's had surgery but is OK. '

'Do the police know?'

259

'She didn't say. Can you mibbe phone Keith?'

Driving as fast as the traffic allowed, exceeding speed limits and jumping a red light, I arrived at the hospital to find an empty car-park. 'There'll be no wardens about this time on a Sunday. I'm not wasting time getting a ticket. Sorry about doing a Stirling Moss!'

'Who's Stirling Moss?' asked a baffled Abbie. I've still never told her.

At the A&E desk, we were sent to a surgical ward where we found an ashen Sophie asleep. Oxygen cannula sprouted from her nose, a blood bag dripped into her left forearm and wires from under her loose gown were connected to a machine exhibiting ever-changing green numbers, while traces of electrical life pulsed in zigzags. Her right arm, expertly bandaged from fingertips to elbow, lay elevated on a pillow. A white clip oximeter was clamped on the only finger of her left hand which didn't look swollen and scratched.

'Oh, God, Sophie, what have they done to you!' My hand flew to cover my mouth.

'Hello Mum!' Sophie croaked, opening one eye groggily. 'God, don't cry – I'm fine.'

'Did they torture you?' I was scanning all visible parts of my daughter.

Sophie smiled. 'No, of course not. It's all self-inflicted!'

I had to gasp. 'Look at your hair. God, they've scalped you!'

Abbie interjected, 'Not sure it'll catch on Sophie, long one side and short another!'

'Haven't seen in a mirror. No idea how bad it is.'

'Trust me, it's bad!' Abbie laughed.

I kissed Sophie's head. Everywhere else looked too sore.

'Know any good hairdressers, Abbie?' Sophie yawned with heavy lidded eyes.

The door opened and a small dark-haired girl in a white

coat entered, checked the monitor, and wrote on a clipboard. 'All good, Sophe!' Then she spoke to me. 'Hi, Mrs Frazer.'

'Chloe! I can't thank you enough for phoning.' I gave her the bear hug I couldn't give Sophie.

'No bother. The college porter gave me your number when I phoned. She'd no ID, no phone and was unconscious when she arrived. Most of the staff on shift were new and didn't recognise her. By the way, she's not allergic to any meds or anything, is she? You might have a quick chat with the doc on the way out to give some history. She hasn't been able to say much, and now she's on diamorph.'

'She's not allergic to anything.' I looked at the now sleeping Sophie. 'Do they know what happened?'

Chloe shook her head. 'Not really. Notes say she was found by an old guy shooting rabbits. Her arm was all cut up, I believe, so she's had stitches in a cut artery and a wee tuck in a tendon. They had a proper vascular guy in, so it'll be perfect. Likely be a scar, but otherwise, hopefully hunky-dory. They didn't see any nerve damage.'

'Thank God.' I sat down at the bedside as Sophie started mumbling. 'What's she saying?'

'Where's Jared? What have they done with him?' Tears were running down her face.

Chloe looked surprised. 'Was Jared with you?'

I nodded at Chloe. 'Yes, they were together.' I bent to speak to Sophie. 'Jared is fine, darling. He's had a sleep in my bed and is with the police now. He's safe.' Without thinking, I squeezed her left hand.

'Ouch! But what – Jared was in your bed? Ridiculous!' Sophie breathed more than spoke the words. Smiling she added, 'We'll go for the ring tomorrow!'

'Ring, my girl? You said nothing about a ring!' Chloe clapped her hands. 'Fantastic news! But that left hand's not going to take an engagement ring for a few weeks. *Mrs Kumar*, what a thing!'

261

'The police are helping Jared deliver the *Epic* copy and waiting to catch the bastards.' But my words fell on unhearing ears as Sophie relaxed into a sighing opiate sleep.

There were footsteps and murmuring outside. I heard a familiar voice saying, 'I'll interview her. You can …'

Chloe moved to the door. 'I'll deal with this.'

Abbie followed. I heard her saying, 'Hi, Keith. This is Chloe, Sophie's friend who identified her.'

Without waiting for him to reply, Chloe firmly said, 'I'm sorry Sophie Frazer can't speak to you at present. She's recovering from her anaesthetic, and although she has managed a few words to her mum, it'll be a good few hours before she can give you anything worthwhile.'

'And are you her doctor?'

'Not exactly, I'm in final year with Sophie. We do weekend stints, especially in Casualty, helping out and getting experience. You want me to get her proper doc for you?'

'No need if you can fill us in on anything she's said.'

'Only know what's in her notes. Brought in by ambulance along with a farmer who found her under a hedge out Hinksey way, unconscious and with blood spurting from her arm. He tied her arm up with a leather strap and phoned for an ambulance though took unwell himself and is in Coronary Care. My friend there says he wasn't helped by some A&E policeman who thought he'd shot Sophie and tried to get his gun off him. Poor chap's apparently had an MI.'

'MI?'

'Heart attack. Be nice when you see him – he saved Sophie's life.'

'Sure. We'll speak to him later.'

'Though mibbe she saved his too. They say he had heart damage already but didn't know. The hospital gossip wagon has Sophie's arrival like a comedy film. She had a tourniquet on her arm with dead rabbits attached. Makes a change from vomiting drunks who've fallen on broken bottles!'

I heard Keith talking to (presumably) his sergeant. 'Go find that duty police guy if you can, Gary, and get a statement. And arrange to see the farmer. And Chloe, has she said anything about where she was held?'

'She woke up a bit after transfusion pre-theatre, said she'd injured herself. Her feet were in ribbons, covered in mud and dung. She'd no boots. That's all I heard.'

'That's terrific, thanks.'

'Think you should leave her for a bit.' Chloe was about to shut the door when Abbie opened it again and ushered Keith in, waving her back. 'Give him a minute.' They watched from the door as Keith embraced and kissed me.

I heard Chloe say to Abbie, 'Aw, a bit of Mills and Boon to add to the *Kidnap* and *Escape with Rabbits* movies we've had so far! Who needs cinema living in Oxford? Sorry, got to go check some other patients.'

After looking at the sleeping Sophie, Keith nodded at me. 'Right, off to see what's happening with Jared.' As he took off, phone at ear, Abbie returned to sit down opposite me. I leaned back in my high-backed vinyl bedside chair and closed my eyes. I suspect Abbie did the same in hers.

29

The Drop, the Kiss, & the Gems

Feeling every beat of his heart and every twitch of his hand muscles clasping the envelope, Jared breathed in slowly. He had never felt so wide awake, so attuned to all his senses. With every sinew of his being, Jared was willing this over. And Sophie back in his arms.

The voice beside his was calm. The words were measured, reassuring.

'Before we set off, I'll recap. We drive to Jericho, go slowly past the house, as if I think I'm lost, then do a circuit so all our guys know we're there, then I'll stop just past the door and let you out. The engine will stay running and the minute you are back in your seat, we're out of here, OK?'

Jared nodded.

'Intel suggests no one's arrived there yet. We can't be sure of their setup, but there are no signs of any snipers. *Caution* and *quick* are the bywords. Any questions?'

'No. That's fine.'

Out of the taxi, up to the door, back to the taxi – what could be simpler?

*

Keith was in the station control room. There had been no sightings of the white van. To his 'Any activity?' question, each unit replied 'Negative.' He updated them with Jared's movements. 'Romeo now on his way.' As acknowledgements crackled back, his mobile rang.

'Yes, Gary, what've you got?'

'The old farmer has suggested two possible barns near where he found Sophie. Been to both. One old milking shed contained items as described by Mr Kumar i.e., the microwave, plus blonde hair and outside there were some pools of blood and van tracks, plus a few cigarette stubs that we've bagged. SOCO are on the way.'

'Good lad. Come back in.'

He itched to be out with the teams. Paperwork wasn't his forte. He was more 'hands-on' than most at his pay grade. With the need to get Jared up and out, there'd been no time for a briefing meeting. He picked up the pile of Greta's memos; she knew he preferred important emails typed-up and he let her screen his to extract them from the excess departmental spam and waffle. So, the boy who lured Sophie, as identified by Margaret, had been spotted by a patrol outside the Central Mosque, but, sadly, they'd lost him. Mosque security cameras had shown the white van in the car-park several times in the last few weeks, though it was interesting how it had got there without triggering traffic and CCTV cameras. Greta and a DS were off to Cowley to see the Imam with images of Hamza, the putative 'Beardy Man,' and the 'Luring Youth' in the hope the cleric might know them and potential associates. He stretched back, realising he'd now been awake for a solid twenty-nine hours.

*

The armed police driver returned Jared back to the Lodge and sped away, declining breakfast. Caleb managed egg rolls for himself, Jon, and Jared, but there was little else in the fridge, so Abbie persuaded me to run her along to the Co-Op. On return, I dumped the shopping on the floor and sat down wearily. Jared was sipping hot chocolate.

'Once you've got that down you, Jared, I'll phone to see

265

when you can visit Sophie.'

'Thanks. Can I borrow your phone to let Dad know Sophie's OK? Maybe I should have gone back to the hotel?'

'Don't worry, he knows,' I said, as the doorbell rang. 'Bet that's him!'

'Maybe you should take off that Kevlar thingy?' Abbie tapped Jared's chest.

'Yeh, right. Good thinking, Abbie.' He took it off and stood to greet his father who hugged him closely.

'Mum sends love. She's doing good. Filled her in once I knew you and Sophie were safe.' As Prem sat down, Abbie triumphantly plonked down a mug before him.

'It's decaf coffee. Jude and I got some at the store.'

'Excellent.' He looked from Jared, to Abbie, Caleb, and I in turn. 'Where's Jon?'

'Out running. Be back soon,' said Caleb.

'Have they got them yet?' Prem asked.

Jared shrugged. 'Police said they'd call Mrs F when anything happened. They can't call me. I lost my cell somewhere in Summertown. '

'Oh? After we've been to see Sophie, let's go pick you up a new phone. Then you can come back to the hotel for a rest.' Prem had a hand on Jared's shoulder.

'Right, I'll call and see when we can get in to see Sophie.' As I went out to the hall for quiet, Abbie was pestering Jared with questions. The bell rang, and I had to open the door again. On the doorstep was Keith. I gripped his arm, clutching my phone to my chest. 'You got them?'

'Not quite. Come in here for a minute.' He led me into my room, released the Yale button to lock the door before sitting on the bed, patting it for me to join him. As I sat, our knees touched. The resultant tingle was startling. Might there be something in that reiki treatment Maggie used to rave about? I'd scoffed at energy transference between two human beings. Nonetheless …

'We picked up your Beardy Man when he cycled to the back of his house. Warned he faced charges of aiding and abetting murder, kidnap, grievous bodily harm, and umpteen burglaries, he started talking. We can't shut him up! I believe he's truthful. First thing he said was that they hadn't intended to return to pick up Sophie, but he gave us directions to the barn that we had just worked out might be their hideout.'

'Well, one down. Three to go.'

'"Beardy Man" is one Hamza Dogan, a Turkish immigrant, who met two Iraqi guys at the mosque a month ago. They wanted a driver and seemingly liked that he'd been inside for housebreaking and had lock-picking skills. Hamza recruited a buddy he'd met inside, Ishmael Tazi, to help. He's a street robber from Essaouira in Morocco who was likely the guy that duped Sophie in the street. Anyway, the two Iraqi gentlemen asked Hamza to find a van, then a big hiding place on the outskirts. They wanted to move about avoiding cameras as they'd been told at home that we used them a lot. As a housebreaker working in the wee small hours, I reckon Hamza's a dab hand at sneaking about. We should pick his brains about the gaps in our coverage of Oxford!'

He was holding my hand. I felt the heat from his clasp.

'Hamza says the Iraqis told him they were doing surveillance on people to find and recover stolen property. They didn't say what and he never asked. The targets were Cedric and Gwen, then you and Sophie – probably in the hope you'd lead them to Jared.'

'Horrible to think we were being followed.' I shivered.

'The white van's a funny one. Likely Hamza spied it while subcontracted as a cleaner at the hire firm. The bold boy thought it had surveillance equipment they could use, but it's out-of-date broadcasting equipment, according to the hire company. The thing on the top he thought an aerial is the old fixing for a broadcasting satellite dish. The barn Hamza

267

found through the paper. His English reading isn't great, but he phoned the estate agent and learned it'd been empty for months and they said it might be demolished soon if not sold. He was offered it cheap, declined to buy the place but broke in to use it anyway.'

'It's all pretty unbelievable!'

'And then the chloroform's interesting. Hamza's post-prison DSS pad in Clarendon was sad. He only had an old sofa, a TV and a bed, plus a bag of bits I'll tell you about later. And chloroform. He'd nicked that from another cleaning client, a plastic-film factory on the industrial estate, thinking it would be useful to use on Cedric's family when told of the plan to kidnap Cedric. He appears genuinely upset at Fakhir roughing up Sophie. Think it was getting a bit hot for him and he's relieved to be in custody!'

'Ah, Sophie wondered how they got chloroform when no one uses it nowadays.'

'Hamza said Ishmael told him it didn't work like in the movies!'

'Like lots of things!' I did smile, thinking about useless glasses held at walls to eavesdrop.

'In the end, Hamza wasn't with them when they took Cedric. He had to work or risk losing his probation. One bit of good news is that Hamza says they don't have any working guns. Coming in via Heathrow, they couldn't bring arms. Ishmael only procured a useless jammed sawn-off shotgun. We are inclined to believe Hamza. He's not a totally bad lad.'

'Sounds like a *Carry On* film!'

'So, we've stood down the armed teams in Clarendon, but are still watching the house and the barn in case they return there. Hamza called the kidnappers Abdul and Fakhir, surnames currently unknown. He's looking at mugshots. He's keen to cooperate fully and stay in custody while they are at large. Couldn't be better.'

'That's something.'

'So, off home for a shower and a rest, but there was something vital I had to do first.' Leaning forward, he put his hand gently behind my head and drew me in. The kiss was long, rhythmic, and slow. I felt light-headed, enveloped in warmth drifting up from my pelvis to my throat. As he drew back, he slid his fingertips slowly round to caress my face, neck, shoulder, and arm, before finally taking my hand. 'I've been wanting to do that all week.' His eyes smiled. I expect mine did too.

My lips were tingling as I said softly, 'Don't think I've ever been kissed like that.'

'I know it's only been a couple of weeks, Judith, but I've begun to care deeply for you. I was hoping if we can get this wrapped up quickly, we might go away somewhere nice and quiet next weekend – or is that too presumptuous?'

I squeezed his hand, laughing. 'Well, we've only had one "not-a-date" and one date!'

'Seeing those two young lovebirds who could have had their happiness snatched away so quickly reminded me of what my wife said, "You've only got one life." She always hoped I'd find someone else, but I didn't believe her.'

I broke the spell by standing up. 'Right. I'm going to phone the hospital to see when I can take Prem and Jared to visit Sophie.'

'By all means, do phone – but I think you should rest. Let them get a taxi. And I'll need Jared tomorrow to look at more mugshots so we can properly identify these two men. Sophie's not up to it yet. Oh, and we've got Ishmael's girlfriend, the one pretending to be ill. Poor thing's already in withdrawal. She has a serious drug problem.'

Flicking my door catch back on to avoid getting locked out, I followed Keith whilst ringing the Radcliffe. I was sitting in the kitchen by the time I got through to the ward. 'OK, I'll tell them half an hour. It'll be her fiancé and his father.' I nodded at Prem.

'You not coming?' Jared asked.

'Keith reckons I'm so whacked that I'm probably not safe driving. I'll get you a taxi.'

Abbie cleared the table and Caleb went upstairs to wait for Jon. Keith left me on the porch with a hug and a nuzzle at my neck that almost made me cry out and sink to my knees.

With a 'See you tomorrow!' he left. I felt dizzy like a daft schoolgirl.

In minutes, the taxi arrived, and I saw off Jared and Prem. 'Tell Sophie I'll see her tonight!' I turned to find Abbie standing in the hall, arms folded, and one eyebrow raised.

'I saw you earlier, madam! Locked-door *tête-à-tête*? What was going on in there?' She nodded towards my now open door.

'They've got Beardy Man. He's called Hamza and is singing like a canary, Keith says. The boy who tricked Sophie is his friend, Ishmael. They've also got the girl that lured Sophie into the van.'

'That's great,' said Abbie. 'But what about Keith?'

I felt crimson but didn't care. 'We hope to go away next weekend …'

'Right on, result!' Abbie gave me a high-five and ran upstairs, calling back as she went, 'Get a snooze, if you can. Forget the essay!'

I tried lying down but was too full of adrenaline: that kiss! I got up to switch on my computer.

*

Jared and his father found they weren't Sophie's only visitors. Beside her bed was an elegant lady, talking quietly. Sophie was sitting propped on pillows and beamed as Jared walked in.

'Oh, Jared – your poor face!' Lifting her left arm with its drip, she tried to touch him.

270

'It's OK. Gee, your arm's so swollen, darling!' Jared sat on the bed,

'Those are just thick dressings. They're happy with it though.'

'Are you in a lot of pain?'

'I'm getting stuff. It's fine. But it was all my own fault. I'm an idiot – can't even hug you!' As if to demonstrate, she raised her right, white-bandaged arm, and her left, drip-attached one in a feeble attempt. Jared dropped forward to take her gingerly in his arms. Prem and the lady visitor sidled back out of the room, closing the door.

'Let's give them a few minutes, alone.' He extended his hand. 'I'm Prem Kumar, Jared's father.'

'And I'm Anna, widow of Cedric Gilbert, Jared's professor.'

'I am sorry for your loss. Are you very friendly with Sophie?'

'I know her mother better, at least lately I do. I've only met Sophie a few times, but I have got to know Jared well over the last eighteen months. He shares my husband's passion for ancient texts. The detective inspector telephoned to tell me Jared was safe, and Sophie was in here, so I came along to see her.'

'Kind of you to come.'

'When Mr Steadman told me the lovely news that Sophie and Jared had become engaged, I thought I'd offer some of the gems Cedric collected on his many journeys to the Middle East. I expect he would have offered some himself for their ring if he were here. It is a great sorrow to me though that the university have dismissed Jared and Cedric's secretary. Quite ridiculous with the book in its final stages.' She shook her head as a boy appeared in the corridor with two lidded hot drinks.

'Here, Mum.'

She took one and gestured to the boy. 'This is my son,

271

Ramin.'

'Good morning, Ramin.'

The boy smiled shyly. 'Would you like me to get you something sir. There is a machine in a waiting room at the end of the ward.'

'No, thank you.'

Anna looked at her watch. 'They said only half an hour visiting – my time is up! Please tell Sophie I will be in touch, and she can let me know what they decide about the stones. I will quite understand if they feel they would rather not have a reminder of this sorry business.'

The mother and son were almost at the end of the corridor when Sophie's door opened, and Jared emerged beaming. 'Come in Dad!' He looked up the corridor. 'Where's Anna?'

'She said her half hour was up. How's Sophie?'

'See for yourself!' He took his father back into the hospital room.

Prem noted the girl's pink cheeks and happy eyes. Thank God she'd managed to escape, however severely injured. 'How are you feeling, my dear?'

'Better and better! But the opiates are making me a bit sick, so I reckon they won't let me out till I can get by on something less.'

They chatted for a time about Jared's "drop" in Great Clarendon Street, the lack of police news, and the offer of Anna's stones.

Sophie took Jared's hand. 'How about Cedric's gemstones – what do you think, Jared?'

'It's up to you, darling.'

'I know you were fond of the old guy. Might be nice.'

'Most of his gemstones are mentioned in the *Epic*. There's a lovely bit in Tablet Nine, "*A carnelian tree was in fruit, hung with bunches of grapes, lovely to look on. A lapis lazuli tree bore foliage, in full fruit and gorgeous to gaze on.*" It can be interpreted differently. You can't really

272

distinguish between "look" and "gaze" in cuneiform. Sort of thing Jon advises on – making it poetic whilst being true to the symbols' meanings.'

Prem pursed his lips and shook his head at his son. Sophie looked too tired to be discussing ancient texts, but she laughed.

'If you say so! But when I'm up and about, let's go visit Anna and choose some stones.'

A plump, older nurse entered, shaking her head. 'Two visitors and two just gone, I hear? Like Piccadilly Circus, Sophie!' She set down a tray bearing a syringe and swab. 'Sophie's due a jab so you lot will need to make yourself scarce!' She waved them out of the door.

Jared snatched a last kiss.

'Ah, so this must be the lucky young man? Congratulations! But we should let her get some rest. No one else till seven tonight – or else!' Laughing, she closed the door firmly after them and activated the louvred facility in its little window.

Prem walked back to the hospital entrance, arm round his happy son's shoulders.

30

Manic Monday

Looking at his reflection in the secretary's glass door at his side, DCI Keith Steadman straightened his tie and smoothed down his hair. The office was locked, the room empty. In front of him was a solid wood door with a brass plate proclaiming *'Assistant Master Professor T. Manders'*. A heated discussion was going on within.

Still tired despite having had some sleep, he was gearing up for a heated confrontation himself. This was likely an acerbic and wily adversary: you didn't make a senior post in an Oxford college without an ability to wriggle out of tricky situations. He knocked. At the peremptory, 'Enter!' he did, and a tall figure rose to walk towards him, hand outstretched.

'Good morning, DCI Steadman. '

'Good morning, Dr Wolsey.' Steadman smiled, shaking Jon's hand.

'I'm just leaving.' Turning to the still seated figure behind the desk Jon Wolsey said, 'Think on it, Timothy. It is in the college's interest – and you know it.' Looking serious, he nodded at Steadman and left, closing the door firmly.

Keith Steadman moved to sit in a chair opposite the sitting man.

Manders barked, 'Sit, why don't you?' with a wrinkled brow and a look of irritation. 'Now, what is this about? I hope it won't take long. I'm a busy man. In fact, I have an important meeting with an American benefactor in …' He looked at his heavy Cartier watch, readjusting his sleeve to make it more visible, 'thirteen minutes.'

Thinking the man must be deluded to imagine Kumar would donate a cent after the way his son had been treated, Steadman was cool. 'I know Mr Kumar is due, but I would suggest you cancel any other engagements you have for today. I see your secretary is not in her office.'

'She will be here presently. But your request is very arrogant and presumptuous.'

'Not when the alternative is being charged as an accessory to murder, abduction, grievous bodily harm, housebreaking, and theft, to name but a few, Professor Manders. I am happy to bring in your Master whom I briefed ten minutes ago.'

For the first time in the last two weeks, Keith Steadman felt amused, really amused. He had never seen anyone pale so swiftly or drop all facial animation so completely. The man's fingers twitched on the desk, his eyes darted about, as if trying to collect thoughts, and his nostrils flared as he countered with, 'This is preposterous! I demand you leave at once! I will be consulting my lawyer to sue you for slander!'

Keith looked at the man's mouth, a 'little mealy mouth,' as Judith had described it. He was sorry she wasn't here to see his arrogant bubble being well and truly burst. God, what a contrast he was now to the doubly life-size, ridiculously smug, formally red-gowned, portrait behind him.

'Taking legal advice is entirely your prerogative, but we have reason to believe you have been colluding with foreign nationals involved in crimes which include the murder of Professor Cedric Gilbert and the abduction of Miss Sophie Frazer and Professorial Assistant, Mr Jared Kumar. We have a witness – indeed we have two.' He suddenly realised Nigel's friend, Tony, who'd identified Manders in Blackwell's would also have to come in to make a proper statement. 'Professor Timothy Manders, you are not at present under charge, but I require that after your next appointment you present yourself for examination at the station today.' Somehow, he felt *examination* more apt than the less intimidating *questioning*. 'You will be accompanied there by the two officers you will find in the corridor after I leave. Feel free to bring your lawyer. I'd recommend you advise him that we have evidence that you provided misappropriated and valuable archaeological artefacts to a certain individual for a fee and that we know your bank account has received several large sums from questionable overseas sources.'

Keith Steadman stood up and bowed his head formally. 'I look forward to seeing you later. If you have any more Sumerian tablets, I exhort you to bring them with you.' He left Manders staring into space.

Out in the corridor, Professor Kumar had arrived. Shaking Steadman's hand warmly, he introduced his lawyer, Mr Peter Quiller, who looked exactly like the kind of unflappable, intimidating, single-minded, silver-haired barrister that Keith hated facing in court. Excellent! At Prem's other side, Jared looked smart in a white shirt, black suit, black tie and black shiny shoes, the university *sub fusc,* or 'under dark' uniform Oxford had always traditionally insisted on for matriculation, examinations, and graduation. Keith remembered a poor Ugandan in his first year who'd been sent away from the Examination Hall by the proctors as 'improperly dressed' for his history exam by dint of brown shoes. The hapless scholar had rushed back to Baliol, swapped his shoes for the porter's one-size-too-small black polished ones, and still passed despite missing thirty minutes of the exam. Keith baulked at such heavily imposed rules – even under the guise of tradition. Tradition once burned witches. God, he was thinking in tangents. But he was tired. And had more to do.

'If you like, Mr Kumar, I could send a car to bring in Jared later for his mugshot session?'

'Most kind, Chief Inspector, but I've hired a limo for the

day. Didn't take a self-drive. I reckon mastering Oxford's crazy one-way system on the wrong side of the road was a step too far for me!'

An older woman in large tortoiseshell glasses pushed past them to unlock her door. 'Excuse me gentlemen, some of us have work to do.' Pausing, she peered at Prem. 'Mr Kumar?'

'*Professor* Kumar. From Harvard. Here to see Doctor Manders about my son.' He waved at Jared and then the brief. 'And this is my lawyer, Mr Quiller, QC.'

Drawing herself up, she ignored Prem's deliberate demotion of her boss, and bustled into her room saying, 'I will check if the *Assistant Master* is ready to greet you.' She lifted her telephone but paused mid button-push before returning to close the door in their faces.

The lawyer moved to the front of the little party, nodding at Manders' door. 'Is he like his Dragon Lady, Jared?'

Jared smiled. 'Cedric's secretary, Gwen, didn't get on with either of them. '

'Shouldn't think that woman gets on with many people. By the way, Jared, I am pressing Gwen's case too and aim to speak to her later today. Compensation is due. I'll do it pro bono, especially if that rude woman has had anything to do with her not being redeployed or given redundancy.'

Keith moved to shake Prem's hand again. 'Sorry, I must go. Good luck.'

As he left, he heard Quiller say, 'Now, remember, Jared, let me do the talking.'

The secretary came out, opened Mander's door, and announced them as if they were being granted an audience with the Queen. 'Mr Jared Kumar, Professor Kumar and their lawyer.'

As she left, Quiller immediately sat directly opposite Manders, Prem chose the chair to his right. Jared had to fetch a seat from beside a coffee table at the far end of the room. He placed it to the left of Quiller as the lawyer whispered,

277

'Let battle commence.'

At the far end of the corridor outside, Keith had a conversation with two police officers clenching hats under their arms, before he skipped down the stairs two at a time, restraining himself from whistling. The only thing marring his enjoyment of the current proceedings was that he had kept Judith in the dark. But there were still a few loose ends.

*

At the Lodge I worked away in my room until around half past eleven when Abbie rapped on the door, sticking her head round it in her customary fashion, to enquire, 'You wanna come with me for some fresh air and a walk down to the department? We could leave a note for Becker, The Prince of Darkness, excusing you from essay drudgery this week.'

'No need, I've just printed mine out. Only need a paper clip.' I attached a large red one to my stack of paper, inserted the assembled sheets into an envelope with my name on it, then leaned over to hit 'Print' for another document as I put on my boots.

'You up all night, you mad woman?'

'No, not all night, Abbie. But I was wide awake by evening. When the hospital phoned to say Sophie was sleeping and I should give visiting hour a miss, I decided that I'd just march on. Inspired by events, I've twisted the remit to look at assimilation and integration of minority groups in inner city schools – citing several authorities not on Becker's hallowed prescribed reading list. Dangerous territory, but after all, it's a free world. Plus, I'm feeling bolshie!'

I scanned the last single sheet from the printer tray, signed it, stuck it into another envelope, sealed it, and tossed it into my bag beside the essay. Putting on my coat, I pulled the door shut. As we marched companionably down to Norham Gardens in the cold, I asked Abbie what she had planned for the rest of the day.

'Nothing much!'

'Going to come with me to get Sophie a new coat? Chloe said hers is unsalvageable. Though I'd try M&S, then its's easy to change it if she hates my choice!'

'Any word when she'll get home?'

'They said to phone at one after the ward round. Oh, and I called the bursar first thing to take on Izaak's big room. Sophie can stay there for a bit when she comes out, then I'll relinquish my small one and move into it myself when her flatmate's home. She's in Bristol for a funeral.'

'Cool! We'll be neighbours! Means you won't fall downstairs again after six cocktails!'

'Hey, I only tripped on the last step! And it was three. Have you seen Tilly, by the way?'

'Ah, love is blossoming all around! There's you and Keith, Jared and Sophie, and now Tilly. Went off yesterday to Nigel's pad at St Edmund's and haven't heard a peep since. Hope she's taking her pills – contraceptive and anti-depressant. I'll try phoning her later.'

'You sound like a mum! Maybe she won't need antidepressants long. Nigel might be great therapy.'

Essays safely deposited in our respective tutor's pigeon-holes, we'd started downstairs when I had a thought. 'Hang on a minute, Abbie.' I turned back to the office and asked, 'Is Professor Becker in?'

'He's in a departmental meeting.'

'Can you tell him that there is an important letter here for him? I don't want to leave it in his pigeon-hole in case it gets lost in the essay pile.'

'Sure, leave it here.' A young girl with red talons and cascading blonde hair took the envelope that I retrieved from the course pigeon-hole. As she typed on, I wondered how she coped with those nails! Abbie was standing at the door looking quizzical. She wrinkled her nose. 'Why are you sending him a letter when you're seeing him at tutorial?'

She looked wide-eyed at me. 'You're not resigning from the course, are you?'

'Anything but. It's a letter setting out what is unacceptable behaviour for a tutor in 2003. It says I've copied it to the Dean of The Faculty, though he won't know that I've not sent that one yet. Shut your mouth Abbie, you'll catch flies.'

'Thought you'd decided not to report his advances?'

'Changed my mind. Kept thinking about that young lass from before. That's why this kind of thing is perpetuated: no one says anything, so they get away with it. All teaching comes with responsibility for the education and welfare of students whatever their age. They mustn't be exploited, bullied, harassed, or made uncomfortable by sexual advances or demands.' I hadn't moderated my voice, and behind me, the two office girls burst into spontaneous applause.

'Nor hit on the staff!' called the secretary, waving my letter aloft. 'We'll make sure he gets this!' I laughed and moved off down the stairs.

'My God, Jude, you are on a roll today!'

'That's what love does to you!' I stopped so suddenly that Abbie cannoned into me. 'There, I said it!' We looked at one another and fell down the last few stairs giggling.

'Anyone'd think you were a teenager, Judith Frazer. Manic on a Monday – think we need to get you a drink!'

'Too early. I'll settle for tea and carrot cake in the Vault after we get something nice for Sophie. She deserves it. And later we can discuss where might be a good place for Keith and I to go for a quiet romantic weekend. Need a bit of Googling maybe? Now I've got that song in my head, you know it? "*It's just another Manic Monday, wish it was a Sunday ...*" Can't remember the rest. Oh, I know – da, da, "*fun day ...*"'

Abbie put her hands up as if in surrender. 'Enough! Or I'm not with you.'

Laughing, I stopped singing, took Abbie's arm and

walked down into town.

*

In Divisional Headquarters, the interpreter sat with a transcript in front of him listening intently. After twenty minutes he switched off the CD player, removed his earphones and looked at DCI Steadman.

'This transcript is pretty accurate, though I'd disagree with the odd phrase here and there. This is a recording of an altercation between several men – likely three – speaking a mixture of English and Arabic. Two seem to be coercing an Englishman – who speaks presentable, though not perfect, Arabic – into giving them something. I agree where the transcript says it sounds like they're moving furniture about after one says, "Look under the desk." But there's a crucial bit. If you listen carefully, you can hear the exact sequence of events just before the murder."

Steadman looked taken aback. 'I just asked you to check that this transcript accurately reflects what's being said as I don't know if we can trust the translator. I never said anything about a murder, Constable!'

'I read the press, Chief Inspector! This is likely a recording of the murder of that Assyriologist at Winston, isn't it?' Referencing the transcript timing, he set the CD player to play at it a certain point and increased the volume. 'Listen to this … One man has just insulted a wife – the Englishman's, I presume – calling her a "whore." The translation has question marks at it – but I am sure they say "ghaba" which I've heard my mother's cousin use. He's a hothead from Mosul. These guys might be Iraqi, though I'm no linguistic expert. The English guy knows the word though, but retorts in Arabic "You bastard – leave her out of it!" He uses "*zawjataa*," my wife, that's clear. Then, there is this …'

Listening intently Steadman catches little squeals. The

281

boy stopped and replayed it. 'The transcript queries "animal noise" then the professor softly says, "Guard this little one."'

'He's putting the key in the cat collar!' Steadman slapped his palm on his thigh.

'Was there a key in a cat's collar? Maybe this is when it was put there, then. This next section is mostly fuzzy whispering with that sort of echoey quality you get when talking too near a microphone. It's hard as the guys are arguing at the same time. The transcriber has missed the "guard this" comment. Then here are more squeals and an Arab voice saying, "Leave that *(swearword)"* then possibly "cat,' alone." Then the English-accented Arab voice calls someone *"a pig for kicking a defenceless anima*l." Squeals don't sound like a cat though, do they?'

'It's an Abyssinian, they make an odd noise. They don't miaow.' Steadman shrugged as the constable paused the tape. 'Go on.'

'Then comes this angry Arabic reply. All expletives not needing translation! Then this loud thud and rustling, is that the poor soul being bonked?'

'The mike was in a china bust and it was the murder weapon.'

'Right, fits. Now there's distortion, crackling, all sounds get quieter then louder again. Frantic chat. Most significant is that the murderer is named, I think, in "What the fuck have you done, Fakhir?" There are lots of different Arabic ways of saying "fuck," depends on the occasion and to whom you are talking. This usage is likely aimed at a friend who's being a dickhead, sorry sir… Fakhir's friend doesn't sound a happy bunny at the turn of events; obviously, the murder wasn't planned.' He pushed fast forward, then hit stop. 'There you go.'

'That's terrific. Thanks for coming up, PC Zarif, I appreciate it. I didn't know we had an Arabic speaker in the station till Gary Mitchell told me. Not knowing the source of this, I worried the transcript could be saying any old thing. You've saved me waiting on an interpreter.'

'My pleasure. Where did it come from?'

'The mail. Anonymous, but think I know who sent it.'

'Think I'd like to join CID. This is much more interesting than being on the beat down in Cowley!'

'As it happens, Zarif, one of the DCs is taking his sergeant's exam this week. Apply in the next round and give me as a referee if you like.' The beaming constable left with a bit of a swagger. Steadman smiled, thinking that at least he had made one person happy today. He lifted the phone. Time for the call upstairs.

'Superintendent Mason?'

'Keith? How are things going on with the college murder?'

'That's what I need to talk to you about. Have you got a minute later? In the meantime could I impose on you to phone the US Embassy and ask if they'll let me talk to a Mr Guy Waller sometime soon? I think he's sent me a murder recording. I must flag up a PC Zarif, by the way, whose help has been invaluable with the recording which is likely from the device we found in the china bust that was used as the murder weapon. But when you phone about Waller, don't mention the recording. Just say we need to clarify a few points with him about the murder of one of his neighbours.'

'Waller, the US military historian with the CIA links? Is he not still in the college?'

'Think he's gone to ground, perhaps in the Embassy. Thank you, sir. And lastly, I'm formally interviewing the Winston College Assistant Master, Professor Manders, later today about his involvement.'

'What involvement? College staff? By God!'

Hearing his boss's dismay, Steadman kicked himself. 'I'll explain later. Yes, a rum do indeed sir. But at least now I know the name of the murderer.'

'You do?' Mason's voice rose an octave.

'Fakhir, sir.' He'd barely replaced the receiver when the phone rang again.

'It's a Mr Clark, sir, from the British Museum returning your call.'

'Put him through. Ah, good morning, Mr Clark. This is Detective Chief Inspector Keith Steadman from Thames Valley CID. I believe you gave Dr Wolsey startling news last night.'

'Indeed, I did.'

'With that in mind, I was wondering if you could manage to come to Oxford later today or tomorrow and look at some artefacts that we have recovered? They may be what you are looking for.'

31

Molly Manders

His lawyer looked aloof and indifferent, but Manders' eyes were blazing with anger as he entered the police interview room.

'Good afternoon, Professor Manders. Thank you for coming. As you know, I am DCI Keith Steadman, and this is DS Gary Mitchell.'

Manders' lips tightened. Steadman knew this was not going to be an easy interview.

'I would like to ask you about your meeting with a Mr Hamza Dogan in the coffee shop in Blackwell's Bookshop in Oxford on Monday the tenth of February at approximately two o'clock in the afternoon.'

'I do not know whence you got this information, but I know no Mr Dogan!' Manders spat out the words sitting bolt upright, forearms straight out on the table, palms down. His lawyer whispered something to him. He shook his head.

'Well, I am prepared to believe you might not have known his exact name, but we have two witnesses who testify that this meeting happened. Perhaps you can tell me what you discussed one February day in Blackwell's with a young man wearing a shell suit? '

Manders glared. 'Well, I did speak with a young man in Blackwell's one day, I have no recollection of exactly which…'

'What about?'

'I went after receiving a telephone call.'

'What was the purpose of the meeting?'

'It was said to be of "mutual benefit".' Manders stared above Steadman's head.

'And this was?'

Manders looked at his lawyer, who nodded encouragingly. 'He said he knew I had been sent some artefacts for appraisal, though as his appearance suggested he was a low-class, unemployed sort of person, I wondered how he could possibly know that. He asked what I had done with them. I said that I'd been terribly busy but would be taking them to the police.' Glances exchanged between Manders and his lawyer told Steadman he'd said no such thing.

'Where did you get them from?'

'They arrived by courier, but after I emailed the sender that they were fakes, I heard no more. When I enquired some weeks later what I should do with them, the email address was invalid.'

'And how did this youth know you had them?'

'I have no idea. He merely said he had friends willing to pay good money for them and he wanted to come with me to collect the pieces.'

'So, you agreed to sell fake antiquities?'

Manders shrugged. 'It was their money. Perhaps in hindsight I should have declined to get involved.'

'Anyway, what happened next, Professor?'

'I was reluctant to be seen on college premises with such a disreputable fellow and told him that I would leave them with the college porter for collection the next day. He gave me an envelope with some money and promised the balance in twenty-four hours. After my return to college, I left the objects for collection at the porter's desk, but I believe the boy arrogantly came later in the afternoon and the stupid man handed them over. Since then, I have had no further contact with him. I really do not see what the point of this inquisition is. I have important meetings to attend.' He looked at his watch.

'Bear with me. So next day, your bank account was credited with a substantial sum, wasn't it?' Manders shrugged. 'As it had been previously on occasion from other overseas sources with such monies being immediately transferred to an offshore account, is that not so?'

'No comment.'

Manders' lawyer intervened. 'Chief Inspector, we will require to see your evidence of wrongdoing before my client says anything further. Are you bringing charges against the Professor?'

'Not at this point in time, but further investigations are underway. I must counsel you, Professor Manders, for your own sake, to tell us everything you know about the people who sent you these objects and those who later bought them.'

Manders shrugged. 'I had an online request for evaluation. A package arrived with an invoice from a London antiquities dealer though I eventually discovered its telephone number and address were false and it is not listed at Companies House. My only communication with them was online. I admit it was foolish getting involved this single time.'

Steadman again noticed Manders exchange glances with his lawyer. Single time, my ass! Closing his notebook, Steadman leaned back. 'But why should they ask *you* to appraise these and not Professor Gilbert? I thought ancient artefacts would have been more his field?'

'Although now more known for modern Middle Eastern studies, in the past, as a former Assyriologist, I have published papers on cuneiform tablets.' He shrugged minimally, pouted, and sneered. 'Who is to say why I was asked?'

Steadman noticed Manders inserting a finger inside his collar to loosen it. The man was riled. He pushed on. 'Do you think they felt the opinion of any Oxford professor in the Department of Oriental Studies would be prestigious enough to deceive unwitting gullible, lay buyers? Is it not true, Professor Manders, you have a track record in certifying fakes?'

'Nonsense. In any case, these particular tablets would have fooled no one, not even a virgin lay collector since many modern resources and international databases like the Cuneiform Digital Library Initiative offer accessible pictures of genuine artefacts. On these tablets some lettering was gibberish, even upside down. Many were much too thick for the real thing or bore no comparison with the certified replicas on show in the British Museum. I would not tarnish my name by verifying them.'

'But have you passed other fakes?'

Manders unblinkingly held Steadman's gaze. 'I certify genuine antiquities. There are dozens of real and fake antiquities on the market, especially since the Iraqi troubles. Mesopotamia was, and Iraq is, a land of waters and clay. Anyone can attempt to get rich quick by crafting objects from its earth to fool naïve, untrained eyes. People do desperate things when they need money.'

'Indeed.' Steadman smiled. 'Your tablets were passed by this Turk to some Iraqis.'

'A Turk dealing with Iraqis? I doubt that – they loathe the Ottomans!'

'Perhaps it's merely a case of convenience and money.' Keith shook his head. 'But you've had no meetings yourself with Iraqis in the past?'

'Not as far as I know.'

'Thank you, Professor. You may go, but we will be in touch.'

On his feet, Manders suddenly turned. 'I had my differences with Gilbert, but I hope you know that I didn't wish him dead, Mr Steadman. I had nothing to do with his murder.'

'Perhaps not, Professor, but you have complicated a murder investigation and there will be consequences. The London Antiquities Unit will be in touch with you and the college presently about the antiquities.'

Manders sighed. 'Then I suppose I must fall on my sword and resign. Good day.' Head held high he strode out with his lawyer who closed the door quietly.

'So, what did you think of that, Gary?' asked Steadman, standing up.

Removing the interview recording from the machine, Gary bagged and labelled it. 'Pompous lying bastard! He's been at it for a while. Let's get a coffee.'

'See you in a minute. I need to make a call.'

'Keith! You, OK? Anything happened?' I answered immediately.

'Still not caught the buggers. They've not been back to the Jericho flat. Have you seen Jon?'

'Not since yesterday. Mind you, I've been busy. Was up working early, out shopping with Abbie then at the Radcliffe to see Sophie. She might get out tomorrow. I'm just in. It's gone five. Are you still at work?'

'Yes, waiting on Dr Clark from the British Museum.'

'Why's he coming?'

'That parcel that Hamza, your Beardy Man, fetched from the Winston porter's desk was found in his house, wrapped in brown paper and bubble wrap, as Nigel described. It contained cuneiform tablets. Hamza confirmed it was Manders he met, having identified him from a photo on the college website. Told us Abdul and Fakhir took the big bits from the parcel, reckoning they'd be something to take back. Jon kindly came in first thing to have a shufti at what Hamza had left and reckons they're all fakes. Clark's coming to corroborate that and give a statement about Cedric's fake ones. We're not sure where his came from.'

'Cedric's fakes?'

'Yes, sorry. Jon heard last night from Clark that when he decided to catalogue the deposit box tablet fragments at the museum, he confirmed some Part Nine ones were missing, but found others were fake. God knows what Manders has been up to, but his bank records show he's had multiple unattributed large payments over several years and has been squirrelling money offshore. The Antiquities Unit will be after him and the Tax folk if he's been dealing – fake tablets or not.'

'How odd Cedric had fake tablets. You'd think he'd have spotted them a mile off!'

'Clark thinks the only explanation is that someone swapped or stole some tablets just before – or I suppose even after – Cedric packed them into his Tupperware for the bank. We know Cedric packed up in a hurry as he forgot the ones Gwen found on a table. I spoke to Anna earlier and she said that after Jon noticed the bigger Part Nine ones were missing, she didn't take the remaining smaller ones out – is that right? You were there.'

'Yes, I think some were still in amongst the cotton wool. What a thing!'

'God, I'll be glad when we get to the bottom of this. Fake tablets being bought as real? Genuine ones being substituted with fakes? Important ones missing? Tablets everywhere! I've got the Met Police's Art and Antiquities guy coming tomorrow. Surprisingly, he reckons our UK market in antiquity and art theft is the second largest in the world after the US. And he thinks it likely Cedric's genuine Gilgamesh stuff will be repatriated to Iraq if it was exported without permission. Not sure how that'll go with a war coming. If it still is, haven't seen the news for days!'

'You sound tired.'

'I am a bit. But fancy a drink? I could call past the Lamb on the way home?'

'Sure, what time?'

'I'll text once I'm free of Clark. You may have to get used to such vague and ever-changing arrangements – such is the life of a policeman! But I'd appreciate if you'd keep all this to yourself. Oh, one good thing – Manders is resigning.'

'As he should. He's a disgrace to the college! Bye, darling.' God, I'd said it. Darling.

*

Next morning, Abbie was sitting with a peanut butter sandwich. 'Wonder why you don't get walnut or hazelnut butter?' she mused, flicking through a pile of research paper photocopies.

'Think you get hazelnut. But I can't stand even the smell of that peanut gloop! You Yanks put weird things on bread, I mean, marshmallow paste?' I made a face while munching cornflakes.

'Love that! Can't find it here.' Abbie looked sad. 'What time are you fetching Sophie?'

'They phoned. She'll be out earlier than expected. Any time after eleven if her drugs are ready. Thought I'd dash over to college, get Izaak's old key from the bursar and make up the bed for Sophie before fetching her. Should be plenty of time before my tutorial. I'll need to get her a kettle and some dishes too.'

'Oh, I'll get them, and mibbe a rug for lying on the bed? She'll be pooped. I'll pop over to Jimmy's Treasure Room!'

'What?'

'His room beside the pantry, full of stuff left by temporary students and academics. Like things they don't want to take home or can't be assed selling. That's where I got the toaster.'

'Oh, I wondered!'

'You pick up items for a donation to college funds. Like I did for my golden cushions. Jimmy said a Greek woman left them, along with an Ouija board. Sadly, it had gone.'

I chuckled. 'Spirited away? But great if you could pick

up some bits for Sophie. I'll phone Jared after I get her. He can come and keep her company until I'm back. He'll want to see his dad off tonight, though. Not sure what time his flight is.'

'Reckon Sophie's worst problem will be going to the loo.'

'Why? There's nothing wrong with her kidneys.'

'You ever tried pulling up your pants with one hand? God, it's hard as hell! Had a hockey injury once. Eventually just wore a skirt for the week and nothing else ...'

'Bit draughty here in February! I've got her a loose jogging suit, thought that would be easiest. Gosh, she is going to need a lot of help for a few weeks till it's less sore and she can grip, isn't she? Anyway, be great to have her here till her housemate gets back.' I leaned against the door. 'Thank God this murder thing is almost over!'

'Well, it will be once they've got the other guys. Hey, howzabout last night? You do the deed?'

'Don't be ridiculous, it was only a quick drink! He was knackered. It's a tough life being a detective. Ah, one top secret titbit you mustn't repeat yet – Manders is resigning!'

'No? How come? Spill!'

'My lips are sealed! He's a naughty boy. You, however, are Keith's golden girl since your Nigel offered such great info! Right, I'm off to get that room key.'

*

DCI Keith Steadman was adding two new photographs to the wall boards at his Tuesday briefing. 'This is Fakhir Husseini, age twenty-one, and this, Abdul al-Hamdari, age thirty-four, Iraqi nationals who have been in the country for twenty-one days on tourist visas. Photos come courtesy of our security services who've had them on their radar as persons of potential *jihadi* interest as they were rumoured to be close to a preacher now in custody. Hamdari is a favoured member of Saddam's Republican guard and Fakhir a relative of his commander. It seems they were sent to get important bits of the Gilgamesh *Epic* that Hamdari's boss had somehow sussed Cedric smuggled into England. Jared's identified them as the kidnappers, though to date we have no evidential DNA or fingerprint records to link them to the murder.'

Steadman tapped the photo of the white van. 'Their elusive white Ford van was finally picked up by a patrol in the early hours in an industrial estate off the ring road. It had deflated tyres. Brought in and forensics are on it. Our concern is that now we have no idea how they're moving about.' He pointed at two officers. 'Jed and Rick, photos to all hire companies, usual stuff, all ports alert, patrols down at bus and rail station and consider cab companies They might make a break for Luton as a springboard, thinking it's an obscure airport. Check they're not booked on any flights home, or even to Europe. Pity they didn't come to Jericho for their manuscript, but we haven't given up hope. Discreet surveillance there continues.' He picked up a transparent evidence bag containing a jiffy bag. 'We may not have fingerprints or DNA, but we do have a voice recording on this CD which may give us voice recognition, or whatever they call it, if it's allowed as admissible evidence. Thanks to the clever PC Zarif,' to whom he bowed, 'we can confirm that this records the murder of the poor professor after an exchange of insults about pigs and whores and the impulsive murderer being reprimanded as ...' He tapped a photo, 'effing Fakhir!' There was a small cheer. 'By the way, PC Zarif has been seconded to us for a week as an interpreter should we need one. Don't put him off. He wants to be a detective.' One of the DCs shook Zarif's hand which pleased Steadman.

'Who sent the recording, sir?' A voice came from the back.

'Arrived in the post anonymously, but it's likely from a Lodge housemate, Mr Guy Waller, attached to the US Embassy-oblique-slash-CIA who's bunked off. The Super was trying to get us access to him for a chat, however he's been met by blank denial that Waller's even in the embassy, so I'm not holding my breath. He has diplomatic immunity anyway. And the toaster bugging device we found was like the one in Socrates – both US types, both probably his.' He tapped Guy's photo. 'MI5's take is that the Yanks thought Cedric Gilbert was close to high-ranking Iraqis and wanted him as a spy. My take is that he did stuff for MI5 instead, what with those numbered files Cedric had on that disc that MI5 dissuaded us from asking about. However, I've no idea guys why this guy, Guy,' he paused for laughter, 'should be wanting to help us by sending Cedric's computer to the Lodge and the CD to the station, but it has certainly been handy in helping us to bark up the right tree.'

Several constables cried 'Woof! Woof!'

'Steady lads, there's still a lot of work to do to get this lot strung together into a case. Now, if you are all still with me …' he lifted a photo and started a new board section.

'This is Winston College's Assistant Master, Professor Timothy Manders, who has admitted receiving dodgy antiquities and has confirmed he met and gave some to Hamza. Enquiries continue. But moving back to Professor Gilbert.' He walked back across to the wall. 'Before this poor soul hid away his own illegally imported artefacts, some clever dick had nicked and possibly replaced some with fakes. Was it Manders? If so, how? When? One for you Greta.' She lifted her hand up to acknowledge. 'Secretary Gwen as first port of call, I think. Who had opportunity? And Gary, look out for and brief the guy from the Met's Art and Antiquities Unit, due in at two. See if he thinks Cedric's fakes and Hamza's are like the same batch or anything, while you're at it.' He paused to scratch his head. 'Now what else?

This case is like a bloody octopus! At least Miss Frazer is coming out of hospital today, which is great, while her boy's got his job back. His father brought in a big cheese lawyer. I like tying up loose ends!'

'Are we any clearer on the actual murder motive, Boss?'

'The recording suggests anger, not pre-meditated, Gary. Think they were after these bloody clay fragments to further their careers, maybe? Could be all down to a kick at a cat that upset the prof who went off on one. So, let's find the bastards anyway and wrap this up before Friday. I want a weekend at the seaside!' Waving them to their feet he pointed to the door. Within minutes, PC Zarif arrived with a coffee and donut.

'Thanks, Constable Zarif, just as I like it. You could go far in here!' He was laughing as he returned to his desk. But not for long. His phone rang.

'What? Are you sure? Who saw them? But I didn't think they had any working guns, Jesus! Get armed response, the Super, the sergeants, my office in five. Is Judith there?' He was about to hang up when he retrieved and shouted down at the phone, 'And bring a hostage negotiator and Zarif. We don't know how good their English is. We can't risk misunderstandings.'

His coffee went undrunk.

32

Terrible Tuesday

Ninety minutes earlier

Sophie staggered over to the bed and lay back in relief. 'You don't think our roads are that bad till you have stitches and find yourself bouncing along. Sorry, can I have some water to take my painkillers?' She checked her watch. 'That's over four hours.'

Abbie took the pharmacy bag and tore it open to remove the pills. Sophie picked up a bottle of water and asked me to open it. 'Sorry, Mum, I can't do it with only one hand!' She sat back on the bed abruptly. 'Feeling a bit dizzy, weird. With this sling on, I feel all to one side, like I'm going to fall over.'

'Oh, God, do be careful, we don't want you to injure anything else. The hospital car-park's too expensive for a start!'

'Thanks, Mother. Glad to know how much I mean to you.' She laughed and downed her pills. The doorbell went. For once, Abbie rose.

I sorted Sophie's pillows. 'That's probably Jared. I called him to come and stay with you till we're back.'

'Thanks, Mum. He's going to see his father off at Heathrow later. A car's coming at five.'

'Don't worry we'll be back by four. There's a plate of sandwiches for now and I thought we'd get pizza for tea.'

'Save some for me!' Jared rushed in and headed for the bed to hug Sophie. 'Hello darling – how are you feeling?'

I felt quite emotional seeing the love sparking between them. 'Right, we'll leave you to it. Sandwiches and pills, Jared.' I pointed at the little table under the window. 'Next lot of painkillers isn't due for four hours. We should be back by then. Kettle and coffee there, bananas in the bowl ...'

'Stop fussing mother! We'll be fine. Get off to your tutorial and do battle with Becker. Dying to know what he says after your letter!'

'What letter? What have I missed?' Jared sat on the edge of the bed. Sophie started telling him as Abbie and I left. On the way out, I knocked on both Jon's and Tilly's doors without response.

Abbie said, 'Haven't seen Jon today, but Tilly went out early. Said she was up for a heavy day in the library. Looked pretty upbeat. Nice.'

'I'm glad. Jon must still be at the police station. If I tell you why, you mustn't let on to the others, promise?'

'Ooh, I love a good secret!'

'I'll tell you on the way. Let me grab my stuff and meet you at the door.'

*

I was almost disappointed. The tutorial was taken by a carmine-haired academic in Doc Martens and yellow tights. The contrast couldn't have been greater.

'Dr Becker sends his apologies. So, for today you're in the hands of me, Dr Maria Weston. Some great essays you have handed in this week, guys. Let's start!'

She thought my essay 'illuminating' and 'progressive,' Terry's made 'several incisively valid points' and Fred's was 'refreshing reading.' I lingered at the end, asked a desultory question then threw in, 'Is Professor Becker unwell?'

'No, I believe he's had to return to Germany because of a family illness. You may have to put up with me again next week. Not sure how long he'll be away.'

'Right,' was all I said.

Abbie was waiting outside. Tilly and Nigel were approaching us.

'What did Becker say?' Abbie asked eagerly.

'Nothing. Absolutely nothing. He wasn't there!'

'What do you mean?'

'We had a funky new tutor. Said Becker's gone home to Germany for "family illness."'

Abbie grinned. 'Pecker between his legs! Result, girl! Hope he stays there.'

'Be better if he got an official reprimand. Decided I will post that letter to the Dean. Hi, Tilly.'

'How about we all go for coffee?' asked Tilly, now beside me, Nigel's arm around her.

'Sorry, Tilly, I can't. Sophie's at home and needing a lot of help. Jared's there but has to head for the airport to see his dad off. Why don't you go, Abbie? I'll order pizzas for half six. Sophie may well want an early night.' Lifting out my phone to turn it back on after the tutorial I was surprised. 'There's a dozen missed calls from Keith!' As I hit dial, a police car sped up and an anxious-looking Greta got out. Keith's phone was engaged. I aborted the call as the answer machine came on. 'What's up?'

'Ms Frazer, could you come with me in the car? And,' she turned to Abbie, 'your friend too?' She swept us in, closed the door and the car drove off speedily, leaving a startled Tilly and Nigel on the pavement, holding hands.

In the police car, Greta explained the situation.

Back in Keith's office, I admit to falling into his arms, not caring who saw. As Abbie hovered at the door, I clutched Keith's arm and asked, 'Have they made demands? Why? I mean it's crazy – haven't they got the transcript?'

Keith was momentarily confused. 'How would they know about the CIA tape, Judith?'

'What CIA tape?' It was my turn to look bewildered. 'I mean the *Epic* transcript.'

'Oh, that. The manuscript! They haven't collected it.'

'Couldn't we give them Beardy's, sorry, Hamza's, clay tablets and say they're Cedric's?'

Keith sat me down. 'We've had no demands yet, Judith. Stay calm. Here's the story. A 999 call came from an elderly neighbour directly opposite Winston Lodge, who saw two tall men in hooded jackets force their way into the Lodge, after the door was opened to their ring. She said they'd driven past earlier, twice, in a dark blue Mercedes saloon – she identified it as the same car as her brother's. There were two men in it, foreign, dusky, bearded, like the men who forced entry. Think she spends all her life at the window, bless her. Better than a CCTV camera!' I didn't move. Keith was holding my hand. But I sobbed. 'Be strong. So, what alarmed her was that the first man pushed back the boy who opened the door. The boy looked like he was shouting something. Then the second man took a long gun, whether a rifle or shotgun she didn't know, but not a small handgun, out of a holdall he was carrying and threatened the boy – hence they got in. Then the neighbour phoned us. No one has come out since. We have men there now, keeping out of sight, watching the house and river path. They've identified a blue Mercedes parked near the end of the road that they've immobilised. An armed response team have just arrived so I'm going down there.'

'Have you tried phoning Jared and Sophie? Should I try?'

'They aren't answering. We also got the landline numbers from the college and phoned all the rooms but there's been no answer from any. Not sure if that means no one else is in apart from Jared and Sophie. Is she in your room downstairs at the side?'

'No, she's in Izaak's old room upstairs facing the back garden. Tilly is opposite, but not in. Guy was next door to Izaak at the back, but he's buggered off as you know. Abbie's room is next to Tilly's at the front, but she's here. No idea about Jon.'

'He's here – still closeted with Dr Clark from the British Museum. I've warned him not to go home. Nor can you two, obviously. We've cordoned off the street and warned the college to get all students to remain in their rooms or the refectory. They're faxing me through a plan of the Lodge as well.'

'So, what next?' My knees were knocking together uncontrollably, and electric shocks coursed up the inside of my wrists.

'We wait.' Keith looked so calm.

I lost it, standing up to shout, 'We wait? Is that the best you can do – we wait?'

Abbie told me my eyes glazed over as I sank to the floor. She tried to hold me up but was prevented by Greta, who put me flat and elevated my feet.

'Leave her down, please. It's a faint, she'll be OK in a minute.'

As Abbie sat on the floor beside me, a lad at the door beckoned Keith into the communal office. He hesitated, but Abbie waved him away. 'Go on. But shouldn't we call Jared's dad? He'll be rolling up at the Lodge soon to take Jared to Heathrow with him.'

Keith nodded, telling her to tell me when I came to that they'd caught Hamza's friend, Ishmael, when he'd arrived at the rear of the Jericho house in the morning. 'Think that's why they grabbed Jared and Sophie again, knowing we were watching the house and they couldn't get the manuscript.'

Outside the room, he had an animated discussion with the new arrivals. Abbie told him about Sophie mentioning bulging bags they'd had in the van and barn which might have held weapons. Keith assured her they thought they had all the bags from the barn but would keep an open mind.

I have vague memories of Abbie sitting beside me giving a quiet running commentary as the police put on body armour and Keith returned to tell her Jared's dad was on his way into the station. I was trying to open my eyes and focus as he was telling her to get someone to make me hot sweet tea. She laughed, saying I'd hate that as much as coffee! I was too weak to get up as he left.

33

Coping with Kidnap

Within ten minutes I was sitting sipping tepid tea. Without sugar. Out in the main office, Greta was on the phone. Another policewoman was collating and stapling papers. A youth clutching a memo wandered in and ambled off. Life as normal in the station? But from my previous visit I knew there were more empty desks than usual. I took comfort that their occupants were all out helping. Abbie asked me how I was feeling.

'Stupid! What must Keith think of me fainting like a silly schoolgirl?'

'Come on, honey, it's kinda normal, isn't it? You got a real shock. Don't beat yourself up.' She looked at her watch. 'Say, shouldn't we phone Tilly in case she goes home?'

'She won't get near – didn't Keith say they'd blocked the road? Oh, I wonder how Sophie's coping? She's so frail after her op – and to be facing mad gunmen? Bastards! God, I feel so helpless.' I was crying again, fumbling in my bag for a hanky when my phone rang. Grabbing it clumsily I knocked it off the desk. Abbie swept down to pick it up before shouting, 'It's Jared!' and thrusting the mobile at me. 'They must've got them out!'

'But why is he phoning me? 'I was feeling very exhausted and confused as I put the phone to my ear. 'Hello, Jared, are you OK? What – Jon? He's here – well, around. Hang on, I'll get them to find him.' I looked angrily at the phone. 'He's hung up! He wanted Jon's number. I don't have it. But wait a minute, he knows Jon's number, he phones him all the time. What's he playing at?'

But by this time Abbie was off and within seconds, Greta appeared with Jon to take the phone. Abbie suddenly exclaimed, 'He's phoned you as he lost his phone, remember, so he's lost all his contacts! Silly, you even put his new number on yours this morning as *Jared New Number* when he took your number for his!' Abbie laughed.

I sighed, closing my eyes. 'Of course. I'm brain-dead.'

Jon returned the call and strolled into the corner to talk. 'Yes, Jared. It's me. No, of course, whatever you have to do, that's fine. It's in *Documents*, under *Gilbert's Book*, labelled *Final Gilga Text*.' He smiled. 'Password? *Ashurbanipal*. Yes, capital A and add 35, asterisk. No, why would I use *Istenarmu*? Who's he? Never mind. Plenty paper in the cupboard behind the door. Luckily, I never gave it back to Abbie. Print out should take ten minutes, max.'

I was thinking how amazingly calm Jon was and how good he must have been with that poor distressed student he'd taken into Caleb's ward as he added, 'Oh, and to save them smashing in my door, there's a spare key for my room under the vase on the hall table which I leave for Caleb. He lost his last week. Must get a new one cut. Right. Good plan. Stay safe.'

Greta stood at the door. 'Well?'

'They want him to run off another transcript. No police to be involved. They know the Jericho house is being watched. Sophie's OK, just gagged.' He glanced over at me holding a soggy tissue to my face. 'But she's OK. He had trouble convincing them he couldn't get into my computer without a password. Funny he should think my password would be *Isten Armu*. Any idea who he was, Charles?'

Dr Charles Clark, who had been patiently standing at the door since arriving with Jon, came in. '*Isten Armu* isn't

303

a person, it means "one weapon" in Akkadian. "*Armu*" is more a sheathed knife weapon, kind of thing, but of course they didn't have guns three millennia ago!'

'Clever boy!' shouted Greta, speeding off, dialling on her phone while yelling at the desk occupiers to phone 'ART' and various other acronyms. 'Tell them – ONE gun.' She smiled back at us. 'Every little helps!'

I brightened up. 'Please God when they get this damned *Epic* copy, they'll let them go!'

Abbie nodded. 'Sure!' Later she told me she'd had fingers crossed behind her back.

Greta returned to whisk Jon and Charles outside for a rapid discussion about the possibility that *Istenarmu* might mean something else. Hearing, 'unlikely,' she left.

Charles walked over to shake and clasp my hand. 'Worrying time for you, I'm so sorry, Mrs Frazer. You know, Gilgamesh was a terrible king. It's unbelievable his legacy's travelled down through the centuries and still wreaks havoc today!' I was unable to form words to reply. 'But that boy Jared is bright. Clever to use Akkadian. Jon's is adequate now, but Jared's is spectacular. I was thinking, once Cedric's book finishes, Jared might like a job at the Museum in the Assyrian Department or to do research at SOAS. Tell him to contact me when he feels up to it. I'm sure everything's going to be all right.' He patted my arm and handed over a card.

Thinking this would be great, and result in Sophie staying in the UK and not going to live across the Atlantic, I thanked him profusely, hoping something good might come out of this nightmare.

Greta brought more tea. I decided after this was all over, I would never drink it again.

*

Sophie was beyond worried. She was angry. Lying back on

304

the bed helpless, she heard the men arguing next door in Arabic. She had no idea what the words meant but thought perhaps that they were of the "What-do-you-think-we-should-do?" and "No-that's-a-dumb-idea, let's-do-this-instead," variety. Like kids, these two clowns. They'd taped one of her wrists to her hip with three loops of duct tape wound round her body. When they'd grabbed her bandaged arm, she'd screamed so loudly, despite the gag, that they'd simply left it in its sling, obviously thinking she couldn't use it at all. And this time, when she'd pretended to swoon, they hadn't taped her legs together but just tossed her onto the bed. They were more intent on getting Jared organised for their bloody manuscript than bother with her.

Her face itched under the tape. There were still painful grazes on her cheeks from last time. God, how many times could a girl be expected to be held up? She wondered about these men. Who were their paymasters? They seemed like idiots. Was clobbering Cedric and harassing Jared their first mission? Surely this carry-on couldn't all be about Garden of Eden monster stories? One thing she didn't share with Jared was his love of ancient mythology. She thought the 'here and now' was enough to contend with, but she respected his work. He didn't deserve to be involved in all this dangerous drama.

That gun Abdul was waving didn't look up to much. Doubtless he could shoot, but the thing looked antiquated. Bit like the old sawn-off shotgun Uncle Archie kept for vermin on his farm at Uplawmoor. She wondered if they had cartridges. She knew such a gun took two. In her teens her uncle had shown her how to load one and suggested she try shooting rabbits. Bunnies weren't vermin! Thank goodness she hadn't seen the dead ones that had featured in her last rescue. Appalling, even if Chloe said the whole hospital thought them hilarious. Tilly would understand how she felt. Funny Tilly wasn't home by now. No one seemed to be. These guys were taking a chance coming here in broad daylight. Mum and Abbie might be back soon. She felt brief panic but quashed the thought: they would have been here by now, surely? Perhaps the police knew what had happened? A more pressing concern was the here and now: the two of them with Abdul and Fakhir. God they were even so stupid they called one another by name! And didn't wear masks. But if they weren't worried about being identified, might the plan be to kill them anyway? Sophie's heart raced.

Fakhir had left a kit bag on the dressing table stool. It wasn't one she'd seen in the van but longer and thinner. The babble next door continued. Rocking back and forth in ever increasing arcs (while vowing to do more core muscle exercise) Sophie achieved a sitting position and threw her legs over the edge of the bed. Bending down at an odd angle, she used her few free bandaged fingers to explore the bag. It held an odd assortment of items: several pairs of undergarments, crusty socks, and prayer beads. She moved aside a novel in Arabic but discovered no cartridges. But of course, there would be some in the gun. Or their pockets. Ah, there was a knife! Sheathed in a leather holster with a strap big enough for an arm or ankle. If she'd been a captor, she'd have been wearing it. Pain made her wince as her fingers explored further, locating two thin notebooks. Gingerly teasing them up, she found they were passports with Turkish airline tickets tucked inside. At that moment, something caught her eye from the window: a flash of movement to the right as a helmeted head briefly popped up, and an arm gesticulated across the garden to another head that transiently reared, accompanied by a thumbs up. The cavalry was here! She smiled, having had an idea. A daft idea, but it appealed. What else was there to do?

The printer had started up next door. Surely, they'd not be back for a few moments? With excruciating difficulty, she grasped the passports and the knife strap, leaned over the dressing table, and dropped them out through the slight gap provided by the latched window left ajar by Mum, who bless her, felt the recently unused room was 'musty.' Never again would she complain about her mum's fussing. Now both heads outside bobbed up again, and Sophie drew back to swiftly re-zip the bag, using her two exposed fingers whilst biting her lip against the pain. Staggering the short distance back to the bed, she collapsed on it and closed her eyes. God, it must be more than four hours since her mother had left: her nerve endings cried out for codeine.

*

Next door, Jared sat back and watched the printer whirr through its task.

'Where are you from?' asked Abdul.

'I'm from New York.'

'But where is your homeland, brother?'

'America, the United States.' Jared wondered where this was going. The man seemed to be trying to be affable. Why?

'But your homeland, where is that?'

'If you mean of my ancestors, many places. Syria, Pakistan, then Africa until Idi Amin threw us out and we went to relatives in America.'

'I am glad you are not Iranian. They are not Arabs.'

Jared drew in a deep breath while picking up a second pile of typed sheets. This was dangerous ground. He was ignorant of the finer details of current Iraqi foreign policy and relations but knew enough not to admit his maternal grandfather's name was Tehrani. 'Iraq is of course, the cradle of civilisation – Akkadia, Sumer, Babylon, eh?' Safe topics, he hoped.

Abdul grinned, watching Jared cross to the wall cupboard for a folder to encase his growing paper pile, unaware the boy was calculating the possibilities of success should he wrestle him for the gun. Jared assessed the odds as unfavourable with two adversaries in the room. Perhaps if it were Abdul alone?

Trying to ignore the pulse in his throat, Jared asked, 'And where are you from, Abdul?'

'I was born in Mosul, but now live in Baghdad.'

'Is that better?' To his surprise the big man made a face.

'As good as anywhere if you do what you are told.'

'Not the best way to live, perhaps,' said Jared, squaring up the last of the papers and adding them into the expanding plastic folder.

Abdul put out his hand for it. 'But with this we will live better. Have more standing. Our Great Leader is obsessed with these ancient fathers. He is reburying old kings, reconstructing our glorious *ziggurats* and temples.'

Thinking of little else safe to say, Jared handed over the folder with a bow, trying to be super-polite, but wondering at the mellowing of this guy's demeanour – was he simply happy to be getting his bloody *Epic* manuscript? Anyway, 'befriend your captors', he remembered reading somewhere.

'There you go.'

Abdul clasped the folder. 'Our mission has been accomplished.' But his smile faded on turning back to Fakhir, currently standing chewing a fingernail on one hand, and scratching his backside with the other. Abdul sneered, 'This one, however, has been a liability. His uncle does not realise how useless he is!'

Fakhir stopped scratching. 'Hey, but my English is perfect, man, no?' Looking at his watch, he flicked his hand in impatience. 'Come on! People return soon. We need to get to airport.'

'We have plenty of time till the flight.' Abdul turned back to Jared. 'My wife expects a baby in July. I hope for a son.'

Jared felt his forced smile waning and wished they'd just go. How was this to end?

'*As-Salamu-Alaykum*. I hope your dreams are fulfilled,

308

Abdul. My plan is to marry soon.'

Abdul was nodding. 'That is good. Now we must take this home for the Great Leader.'

'You do know the man who translated this met your Leader several times and was a great authority on your ancient history.' Jared couldn't help saying it.

Abdul put the file under his arm. 'His death was unfortunate.'

Fakhir scowled. 'The professor would not cooperate and insulted my mother.'

Abdul and Fakhir stood glaring at one another, making no move to leave.

'I don't know anything about that, gentlemen, but now that I have cooperated and you have your information, please let me return to my fiancée who requires her medication.' Jared took a deep breath. '*Inshallah*. I hope there will be peace and I may visit Iraq one day. Safe journey.'

Jared had moved slowly to place himself between Abdul and the open door. Now he rushed out of the room. Behind him, there was a rapid exchange of words and glancing back, he saw Fakhir receive a cuff on the head.

Next door he was barely at Sophie's bed when Fakhir ran past him to pocket Jared's phone from the dressing table where he'd put it after letting Jared call Judith. Within seconds, Abdul had taped together his wrists and ankles yet again, though leaving his hands in front and not doing it as tightly or roughly as he'd done in the van. Looking at the sores on his face, Abdul pocketed the roll of tape and yanked the landline for the bedside telephone out of the wall saying, 'Keep the faith, brother,' Abdul lifted the zipped bag and clumped out to have an argument with Fakhir on the landing.

Opening one eye, Sophie saw Jared biting at his wristbands, working to uncurl the barely overlapped tape. Sitting up on her free, sore, right elbow she whispered, 'Close the door, jam the desk chair under the handle and move the desk over in case they come back.'

'Why should they?'

'They might not get out – we're surrounded by armed police!'

34

Abdul & Fakhir

Keith was getting a headache. He put down his binoculars, rubbed his eyes and pinched his nose. There was only a certain amount of time you could peer down those blooming things. How his father had done it for hours on end during wartime convoy watches he didn't know. Granted, there you were liable to die if you didn't spot the enemy before they spotted you. Yet here it wasn't his own life, but the lives of two young people that were at risk. Then there was Judith, back in the station, breaking her heart. He turned to Gary.

'What's your take on this, Detective Sergeant? Like me, would you go in now, or wait to see if they put on a light so we're sure what room they're in? Tactical firearms advice is to wait and see.'

Gary consulted the floorplan. 'Are we sure whose room is whose?'

'No, to be absolutely honest. Let's try a double-check.' Scrolling his mobile, he tapped a call. His taut face relaxed when it was answered.

'How are you? I'm glad. No, we haven't got them yet, but run it past me again. Exactly which is Izaak's old room?' He nodded several times and patted his hand on the map. 'Right, then chances are they're at the back left upper room, Izaak's, where Sophie was or in Jon's room next door at his computer. Though evidence points to one firearm, the powers that be are fixated with possible *jihadi* connections and fear grenades or bombs or whatever.' He clenched his jaw, instantly regretting this disclosure as he heard Judith's sharp intake of breath. 'Sorry, I do think they're wrong and, in any case, Hamza thinks the gun they have doesn't work. It'll be fine, Judith. I'm sure. Sorry, there's the radio, got to go.'

The ART Commander sounded pleased. 'News from the rear, Chief Inspector. Our boys sidled up close in at the wall and recovered a knife, passports and airline tickets from a flower bed.'

'How did they get there?'

'An officer saw them dropped from an upstairs window.'

'Which one? And who dropped them? It's so frustrating that with that bloody river at the back there's no feasible point to clearly observe the property from the rear.'

'Sergeant Michaels thinks it was a blonde woman with a sling. He saw her briefly look out of the upper back – left to you – window, then slip the items through a window gap.'

'So, Sophie's likely OK.' He exhaled deeply. 'And the passports?'

'Iraqi. One Fakhir Husseini and an Abdul al-Hamdari. Contain airline tickets one-way Turkish Airlines to Baghdad via Istanbul.'

'In their real names! Excellent work, Tom. So, as we thought, they've been in this chap Izaak's old room. The one next door, Dr Jon Wolsey's, is the one with the computer they need. Looks like they must both be in there with the boy if she's chucking things out of windows. Standby. Can your guys effect entry without being seen by those upper back windows?'

'Affirmative. The only side windows are ground floor and we've already sussed those rooms as clear. We have a college key for the patio doors at the back and a master key for all other rooms in case they've locked them. Be great if we don't have to announce ourselves prematurely by blasting locks.'

'Swift, silent entry, then? The Super's gone. It's up to us.'

'Agree.'

'Let's go for it!'

As Keith returned to the window, Mrs Malone brought in a tray of coffee and newly baked scones. 'I hope you like cheese scones ....' Her next words were drowned out as Keith shouted and bent forward to grab the radio from the ledge. 'Go, go – they're coming out the front!'

Dark figures wielding guns swarmed from nowhere to encircle the front garden. A shot rang out. The two kidnappers fled back inside the house and slammed the door shut. One armed police officer could be seen dragging a colleague back, blood seeping from his neck. Two others, crouching low, lifted the injured man to carry him off out of Steadman's vision.

'Man down! Shit – bloody Hamza! That fucking gun wasn't jammed after all.' He raced downstairs muttering to Gary at his side. 'The Super should be here and not at his bloody *Policing Today* conference. What a bloody disaster!' As he opened Mrs Malone's front door, another shot rang out.

*

Jared had a problem moving the old desk. He had to sit on the floor, spine jammed against it, to try to walk it back. Luckily, he'd succeeded in freeing his ankles. Sophie sat on the edge of the bed, willing him on but unable to help. Even though Jared had undone her taped left arm, her hand was weak and full of pins and needles as it had been bound so tightly. Sophie was concerned their assembled defences might not hold, though the solid, if antique padded tapestry desk chair had its back jammed firmly under the handle. The heavy desk was next in line and should hold out for a bit until the police got them, hopefully.

313

Rolling over to look out of the window, Sophie saw dark figures swarming across the lawn. 'Jared, armed police are moving in!'

'Thank God!' He leaned back against the desk, confirming it was hard against the chair pinioning the door handle. 'Now for your tablets!' He got up, and as he tried to push two tablets out of the foil packet, he found his hands shaking. 'Why do they make it so difficult to get these little babies out? Here.' He handed her the pills and an opened bottle of water.

'It's to deter suicides. A dozen paracetamol can kill you.' Snatching the pills from Jared's outstretched hand, she quickly swallowed them. 'Thanks, darling.'

Jared stooped to kiss her before looking out of the window himself. 'Can't see anyone now. It's getting dark. What time is it?'

Turning her left arm to look at her watch, Sophie said, 'Five forty-five, why?'

An explosion blotted out Jared's reply. In the silence that followed, loud voices could be heard and heavy footsteps on the stairs.

'Bloody hell, here we go again!' Sophie collapsed back onto the bed as Jared knelt rocking and muttering with his eyes closed. Praying? She really must learn Arabic.

There was a muffled indistinct shout followed by banging on their door. As it shook, Jared clutched Sophie. The bangs became frantic. Multiple shouts suggested that the police were in the building. Hearing, 'Halt, armed police!' Sophie did not feel reassured. The door was moving. The back of the chair splintered slightly, but the heavy desk moved only a few millimetres. Sophie thought of Jared's modern college room with its flimsy built-in desk and furniture. There, they'd be dead by now.

Jared stroked her hair as she laid her head on his chest. 'I love you, darling. Now, likely they'll be wanting one of us as a hostage to negotiate out of this mess.' He turned her face to kiss it. 'If they get in, I'll go. Actually, it might be best if you lay on the floor down there behind the bed?' Without waiting for her consent, he rolled her over the edge. Even doing it as gently as he could, she whimpered in pain.

Jared jumped at another bang, much, much louder and not on, but outside the door. At the same time there was a thud and a foreign curse. Sophie was looking up at him from the floor, her dark eyes wide and her pupils large. She had never looked so beautiful.

They heard crying from outside, followed by barked orders, 'Hands up, behind your head, lie down, face to floor!' Then came brisk knocking on their door and a voice shouting, 'Police! It's safe to open your door!'

Jared rushed across and started trying to haul the desk back from the doorway. He managed a few feet while calling, 'Hang on! I've got furniture in front of the door!' There was obviously force from the other side as the chair splintered and the desk moved enough for an armed officer to enter.

He pushed back the desk to allow clear entry for another colleague who sped round the room looking inside the wardrobe and cupboard, then behind the sofa and bed. He stepped back in shock as a wraith appeared from the floor to crawl up onto the bed on one elbow, her curtain of uneven long blonde hair dishevelled, one arm cradling the other in a sling. The checking policeman said, 'Clear,' nodding at the first who looked from Sophie, now on the bed, to Jared sitting on the floor. He smiled. 'You two OK?'

Jared gave a short laugh. 'Nice to see you, officers. What took you so long?'

Both men laughed and one helped Jared to his feet. In the hall, he could see a paramedic kneeling at a groaning figure. Both Iraqi men had been dressed identically in black jeans, grey hooded sweaters, and Timberlands. From his viewpoint, he couldn't tell whose boots and trouser legs were lying on the floor. Nor whose blood was in a large puddle on the carpet. Their other captor was nowhere to be seen. Jared went to hug Sophie. The officer who had helped him up lifted his transceiver. 'Romeo and Juliet safe and well.'

Sophie laughed, 'What?'

'Sorry, it's our lads' name for this op. Do you need anything immediately, sir?'

'A phone, to call our parents, please. The men took our mobiles.'

From his back pocket, the officer handed over his own. 'Here you go. But the bosses will be onto them, I'm sure. I'll get the phone back before I go.'

As Jared typed in his father's number, Sophie tried to rise from the bed. 'God, I'm hungry. I need a sandwich!'

She got a kiss. And then a sandwich as Jared found his father's number engaged. He then said 'I'm going to see if your mum has a beer in the fridge!' He didn't get far, the officer on the landing stopping him. 'Best stay inside, sir – I'll go look.'

Jared returned and wolfed into a smoked salmon sandwich before the police officer returned with two beers. Grinning, he saluted the officer with his bottle. 'Here's to the great British Bobby – you've even taken the caps off – great service!'

Though worried about her painkillers, Sophie swigged some beer too before lying flat back down on the bed exhausted.

*

Keith congratulated every officer he could find and reassured Sophie and Jared, telling them to wait for a medical check. He sped back to the station where he found Judith, Abbie, the Heathrow-diverted Prem, and Jon waiting in his office. Charles Clark had returned to London.

'Both the kids look OK, but they're being checked

by a police doctor. We'll need to arrange temporary accommodation for everyone in the Lodge until forensics sweep the house. It's a precaution to ensure they've not left anything nasty, but from my first brush with the boys, I'm not too worried myself. They don't look too tech savvy to me.' Keith rubbed his palm over the side of his jaw. Judith thought he looked completely shattered. 'So, turns out the gun Hamza got them did work after all. One policeman down.'

'Oh, dear!' Abbie put her hand to her mouth.

'Luckily, it looked worse than it was. Bleeding was due to surface lacerations from scattered shotgun pellets. Thank God for body armour!' He made to remove his. 'The other casualty is Abdul. Got it cleanly in the shoulder when he raised his gun at one of our guys outside the kids' room. Not sure how, but he ended up shooting a hole in the ceiling. Scared the crap out of his mate, Fakhir. Literally. Not a nice sight I believe. So far, they've been unable to make head nor tale of Fakhir whose English seems to have deserted him.' He slapped his hand on his thighs and stood up. 'Right folks, you can all go home now if you can find a bed! Thanks for your patience. I'll tell you now – this was my first siege and I hope it will be my last!' He shook Prem's hand then came to hug and kiss me before Abbie flung herself at him. Laughing, he peeled her off. 'Enough! Now for the paperwork mountain. Maybe call you later, Judith? Where should we take the kids? Need to get them out of the Lodge soon.'

'I'll get a car, Mr Steadman. They can come to the Parsonage. In fact, I'll get a room for Judith and Abbie too for tonight – Jon too if he wants.' Prem offered.

'I can stay with Caleb,' said Jon.

'Can we go for our things?' Abbie asked.

'Sorry, not today.' Steadman shook his head.

'Right, Jude, let's get a taxi over to Boots and M&S for

essentials! Shall we see you at the hotel, Mr Kumar? It's real generous of you.'

'No problem, Abbie.' Prem turned to Steadman. 'Chief Inspector, do we know who sent these men on this ridiculous mission? Our embassy says the Iraqis deny knowledge of these clowns.'

'Would they admit it though? Once we know more, we'll make sure you hear.'

Clapping Prem on the back, he returned to his desk to switch on his computer. In minutes, coffee and digestives arrived. 'Brilliant timing again – got that CID application ready, Constable Zarif?'

*

Later, Abbie flung her carrier bags on the floor and flopped on the bed. 'Prem's swell, isn't he? What a great room!' She was stroking the burgundy silk cushions and velvet coverlet when the phone rang. 'Hi! Yes, this is Room Ten. Oh, hello! We were just saying how kind you were to get us this room for the night. Say, what a great idea! I'll tell Jude. See you!'

'Was that Prem?'

'Yes sirree, and he's got a buffet laid on in a private room downstairs from eight as he thought we'd be too tired to dress for dinner. Think he's forgotten we don't have anything to dress into! Thank God I've at least got my make-up with me today.'

'You go, Abbie. I'm too tired.' I sat on the chair by the window and unzipped my boots.

'You need to eat, honey. Or is it the food of love you're living on?' She made a pouting face, lowering lashes and looking down to the side, which made me laugh.

'That's music, idiot! Well, Keith might phone. I'll get room service if I need anything.'

Abbie was rattling in the minibar. 'Here we are, perfect. One G&T coming up. I'll pay for these though, we can't let

318

Prem pay for everything.' She ticked her selected items off in the desk bar list, mixed two drinks and handed one to me before lounging back on her chosen twin bed and flicking on the TV. It was the seven o'clock news on Channel 4 with a picture of Keith, Gary at his side, fending off reporters outside the Lodge.

'Gee, look – your boy's famous.' As Abbie turned up the volume on the remote, a group photo appeared, circled then enlarged to show Sophie as a portrait. That was from Youngman College matriculation. Next came a photo of Jared, so young it was likely from High School.

'The young lovers,' warbled the presenter, 'were snatched from their dire predicament by a team led by Detective Chief Inspector Steadman of the Thames Valley Police aided by armed officers who stormed the building. One kidnapper is in hospital with gunshot wounds and the other is in custody. A police officer who was wounded in the incident has been released from hospital. The men arrested are believed to be Turkish nationals involved in a *jihadi* plot and have been under surveillance for some time.'

'What nonsense!' I almost choked. 'You should never believe what you hear on the news!'

'It's all about viewing figures.' Abbie's shoulders came up to her ears in a shrug. 'I reckon if you said the gunmen were after mouldy old ancient tablets wanted by a lunatic in the Middle East who thinks he's Nebuchadnezzar that viewers would turn off. Oh, shoot – there's Keith again.' The programme had cut to a press conference where Keith sat sombre and mute beside a braided officer who was talking volubly with peculiarly emphatic hand moves that I suspected came from some PR training course.

'I must commend the bravery of the young couple caught up in the middle of this drama. Investigations continue, but the public can be assured that due to the efficient tactics shown under my command today, everyone in Oxford can sleep more soundly in their beds.'

'Gee, Keith looks moody-blues, doesn't he? Who is that guy, Jude? We haven't seen him, have we?'

'Must be Superintendent Mason. Keith says he does zilch but takes all the credit. Typical.'

'But reporting it as a *jihadi* plot!' Abbie put her drink on the bedside table and sighed. 'It's only when you're involved in something you realise how false a lot of news is.'

I turned my chair to put my feet up on the bed. 'Keith did look cross there, didn't he? I'll phone him later.'

The screen now shifted to outside the Lodge, where a reporter said two Turkish men were being charged with kidnap and reckless endangerment. I drained my glass. 'Enough!' Pressing buttons, I channel hopped, but found only game shows, home makeovers and Coronation Street. 'Oh, to hang with this.' I threw the remote on the bed. 'Let's go down and see what they've got at Prem's buffet. Be rude not too. Besides, last time I ate here the food was excellent.'

Abbie jumped up and sped into the bathroom clutching her make up, emerging after five minutes looking like she had been in a beauty salon. Then she hustled me in, not leaving until she'd 'done' my face too. I was too tired to argue.

'You gotta make an effort, Jude. Keith might drop by!'

Before we left, I laid out my new nightdress on the bed and my new toothbrush in a bathroom glass. 'This is in case I'm too drunk to find my stuff when I get back.'

'You're something else, girl.' Abbie laughed all the way down the stairs.

35

Pledges of Blessing

In the private function room, Prem rose to greet us with
a hug and kiss. 'Come on in! As I have to go back home
tomorrow – the hospital's all horns and rattles – Jared got
me to ask Anna and Jon along tonight, and I hope Cedric's
secretary, Gwen, can join us after she's finished at the police
station. Sit down and help yourself to the buffet!'

Side tables held a mix of cold starters and hot mains which
looked delicious. I took a plateful of smoked salmon and
salad. Since the kidnap news, I'd suffered waves of anxious
nausea, but suddenly I found myself starving. Sophie and
Jared were well and truly safe. And happy. Sitting down, I
asked where they were.

'I've sent a car – they should be here soon.' Prem glanced
at his wristwatch which I saw was a Breitling. Like the
one Steve bought when we couldn't afford a new boiler. I
congratulated myself: that was the first time I'd thought of
him for days. Progress.

Accepting the offer of wine from a waiter, I looked round.
Amazing how close I felt to these people who until recently
had been strangers. Beside me, sat Jon. Opposite was the
lovely Prem sitting beside Anna. Next to her, Abbie, currently
swilling a glass of wine while flirting with a mesmerised
young waiter whose 'French' accent was slipping into West
Country.

Jon turned to me. 'You, OK, Judith? It's been a bit of a

321

trial for everyone lately, but especially you. Thank God it's over. And I'm so glad Jared's back to help get the book out.'

'As am I. Oh, and by the way, I must give Jared Dr Clark's card. He wants Jared to work with him. And we must have an engagement party in the Lodge once Sophie's arm is better.'

As if on cue, the door opened and in walked Sophie, surprisingly now wearing jeans and a different top. 'Hey, how come you got fresh clothes?'

'Hello Mum! Don't I get a "How are you, have you recovered from being held at gunpoint?"' She laughed, stooping to give me a one-armed hug.

'Sorry! Did you get to the shops, darling?'

'No, I'd left stuff in Jared's college room, so we diverted for a change and toothbrushes.'

'Room here OK, son?'

'You kiddin' me, Dad? It's palatial! Bit premature booking the honeymoon suite – we haven't even got a ring yet.'

'Aw, if a father can't spoil a brave son, who can he spoil?' Prem lifted his glass. 'A toast to the happy couple.' Everyone raised their glass. 'And great news. Your mom just had a scan showing the tumour's dramatically shrunk. We'll schedule a call tomorrow before I go.'

Jared clapped Prem's shoulder. 'Terrific!' He helped Sophie to a seat before heading to the buffet.

To my astonishment, Sophie didn't look tired. She was glowing and sparkly-eyed and gave me that little smile of primary schooldays, like *I've-done-something-clever-and-you-should-be-pleased-with-me,* perhaps after getting a gold star from the teacher. Who'd have thought that smug little person was soon to be a doctor – and a wife? Leaving her mum on her own. But I no longer feared it.

Anna was asking her which gemstones she'd like for her ring.

Sophie glanced at Jared. 'If it's all right with you, Anna, may we have the carnelians?'

'What the heck's a carnelian?' Prem wrinkled his nose.

Jon put down his fork. 'It's quartz infused with iron oxide. Can be flecked with yellow, orange, or red. The pharaohs thought they symbolized the setting sun and used them for seal rings. Mohammed and Jewish priests wore them. Queen Victoria was a fan. The name's from Latin "carnem" meaning "flesh." I believe it's a birthstone for July.'

'Perfect. My birthday's Bastille Day!' said Sophie. 'I'm impressed – you know a lot about gems, Jon.'

'My favourite uncle was a jeweller,' he replied.

Abbie added, 'They say carnelians give confidence and promote creativity. Is that one?' She pointed to Anna's ring.

Anna twirled it. 'Yes. Cedric was a bit of an old mystic about his gems and crystals. You should put carnelians outside your front door after marriage, Jared. They're said to attract prosperity and abundance.'

'Abundant what?' asked Sophie feigning horror. 'Not kids, I hope? Two's plenty!'

We laughed as the door opened to admit Keith. I managed (just) to refrain from rushing over to throw my arms round him in public.

'I just came to say goodnight. My ear's sore from being on the phone all day! The desk said you were having a party, but if I could just speak to Judith for a minute…'

Prem stood. 'Oh no, I should have phoned you too. Sit, have a drink and some food!' Going out into the corridor, he summoned a waiter to get another place setting. The young man scurried in with a seat and looked admiringly at Keith. 'Say, was that you on the telly at teatime? I bet that pompous git beside you didn't do a thing – did he?' The boy was instantly shuffled off by his boss, but Keith smiled.

Abbie rose and nodded at me. 'Hey Jude, you sit here with Keith.' She took my place beside Jon.

'So, what was so funny when I came in?' Keith asked as he sat down.

'We were hearing about carnelians, Mr Steadman.' Sophie grinned.

'And what are they?'

Anna said, 'Treasured ancient stones. Apart from being featured in the *Epic of Gilgamesh*, which I think we're all now a bit sick of, ...' sighs round the table signalled agreement. 'Goethe wrote a lovely poem about them called *"Pledges of Blessing."*'

Carnelian is a Talisman,
It brings good luck to child and man.
If resting on an onyx ground,
A sacred kiss imprint when found.
It drives away all evil things
To thee and thine protection brings.
The Name of Allah, king of kings,
If graven on this stone, indeed,
will move to love and doughty deed.
From such a gem a woman gains
Sweet hope and comfort in her pains.

We all clapped but Sophie frowned. 'After this week think I'd prefer codeine for pain!'

Jared laughing, hugged her gently. I'd watched them throughout the meal: Jared topping up her glass with water, checking his watch before giving her painkillers from his pocket, cutting up her food for eating one-handed. Exchanging glances, secret smiles. This was love. A human constant, unchanged for millennia. Glancing to my right, new eyes met mine. A hand reached out. Sometimes touch is enough. Emotions can flow without words. I felt more relaxed than I had done for years.

Jon was in his element, ridiculous red glasses on his head, elaborating yet again on the ancient story that had caused all our recent troubles. How wrong I'd been about him –

and the others. He wasn't buttoned-up and cynical. Abbie had recently told me it was compassionate hospitality to a homeless drug addict, careless with cigarettes, that had cost him his home. I could hear my father. *Judge as ye would be judged.* I'd learned many lessons this term.

Jon was in full flow. 'Forget you've been told the *Epic*'s about kingship, scorpion trees, heavenly bulls, angels of death, magical cedars and eternal life ...'

'Is that all?' Prem looked amused.

'Pretty much. But do you know the greatest irony of Gilgamesh's story?'

'No, but I think you're going to tell us,' laughed Prem.

'Right, here's this chap, monarch of all he surveys – bit like Tony Blair.' He paused for groans. 'Ghastly Gilgamesh goes around raping virgins on wedding nights, pillaging, plundering, being a right all-round bastard. When the girls complain, what do the gods do?'

Jared smiled. 'They send a wild man, Enkidu.'

'Correct! And how do they civilise *him* to meet the king?'

'They send a prostitute!' Jared was now shaking with laughter.

'Yes, Shamhat who bonks him for a week, cuts his hair, and gives him seven beers to make him sing.'

'Is that your seventh wine, Jon? Are we expecting a song?'

'I'll ignore that, Judith! Then this randy bugger's meant to go and persuade Gilgamesh to stop bonking virgins? I ask you, some plot! Mind you, they had a goddess of beer ...'

In the doorway Gwen appeared. 'Hi everybody, sorry I'm late.'

As Prem rushed off for another seat, Jared waved Gwen into the seat Prem had vacated. Patting her hand, Jared said quietly, 'But there's more to it than sex and drink, Jon. Cedric's latest translation shows the poetic imagery of the *Epic*. "A *carnelian tree was in fruit, hung with bunches of grapes lovely to look on.*'''

Jon sat erect. 'Yes, but sadly, it's the only known copies of that part that are missing.'

'Perhaps not.' Keith smiled broadly.

Anna put a hand to her mouth. 'You've found them?'

'We hope so. Some we found today appear to match the Part Nine Garden of the Gods tablets seen in photos on Cedric's camera that Gwen remembered about and brought in. I'm taking them up to Charles Clark in London tomorrow for confirmation.'

'Where did you find them?' Abbie clapped in appreciation.

'This morning a team found them in a locked room at Manders' home out at Boars Hill. You should see it! A six bedroom mansion he'd never be able to afford on a don's salary, groaning with a treasure trove of antiquities from statues and coins to stone bulls and cylinder seals. We found Gilgamesh fragments inside an old briefcase that Gwen identified this afternoon as the one he had with him when he visited Cedric the day before he was murdered. Gwen thinks it's possible Manders might have taken the Garden of Gods ones out when Cedric left his box open on the desk as he went out into the hall to take a call. She was sitting with her back to him. Possibly he added the fake ones then too.'

Jon was shaking his head. 'Surely, he'd know Cedric would spot fake or missing ones? Or wait – he had a meeting up at the British Museum on the Monday. D'you think he wanted Cedric to be shown up when he couldn't produce Part Nine? He was taking a chance though!'

'God knows. My bet would be he took the Part Nine tablets to sell himself and replaced them with fakes for spite. The Art and Antiquities Unit are going to have their work cut out at Boar's Hill sorting out what's real, what's not, what's "hot" even – and what he's flogged. If he kept records.'

'So, where is he?' asked Abbie.

'In custody.'

'And the Arab guys?'

'Abdul's in High Dependency, but Fakhir's a gift now we've got him an interpreter. The guy translating his tapes is doing overtime. Fakhir's afraid to return after their failed mission, He wants asylum and will happily do time here if given assurances he won't be deported.'

'So how did these guys find out about the prof?' Prem asked.

'As some of you know, Abdul's boss in Baghdad heard from dodgy antiquity-dealing friends about potentially important *Epic* pieces given to Cedric. They then easily traced him to Oxford. Knowing Saddam's obsession with Gilgamesh, the Colonel sought to curry favour, so gave Abdul leave and donated him the services of his supposedly English-fluent nephew, Fakhir, to come to the UK and retrieve the pieces. But as inexperienced lone wolves, their whole operation was shambolic. They couldn't even tell fake tablets from real. Anyway, turns out Fakhir hates his bossy Colonel uncle. But he's a big cheese in Iraq, so our security services want a chat with Fakhir, about how things are out there. Expect he'll be taken off our hands soon. Fakhir alleges Abdul killed Cedric, but our Socrates bug tape shows he did. The boy's bitter, ranting about Saddam wasting money re-building old temples and re-burying ancient kings when his people are starving.'

'And Beardy Man?' Abbie smiled.

'Ah, Hamza? He's trying to bargain too. Says Abdul arrived with Manders' mobile number, implying past Iraqi deals. Fakhir says Abdul got fed up chasing the tablets and wanted Hamza to get any old ones from Manders to take home. Meant they could blame him when they were found to be the wrong ones.'

Jon frowned. 'So, Manders has been at it a while?'

'Seems so. One last thing – tonight Jimmy the porter got another parcel for you, Judith, and phoned me.' I felt a squeeze on my hand. 'This one contains an Apple laptop and someone's juicy diary.' As he looked round the table, Jared perked up. Abbie reddened. 'Laptop I guess, might be Jared's?' He nodded at him. 'Anyway, if anyone would like to come and identify them tomorrow, please do.' Turning to me he said, 'And there was something else in your parcel.'

'What?' I asked.

'*A Guide to New England Fishing* and a US phone number.'

I chuckled. 'God, I'd have thought Guy was too drunk to remember! In the taxi home he suggested taking me fishing in New England. Nutcase. Have you seen him?'

'Nope. And doubt we will. MI5 suspects he's already back in the States.'

'Anyone for dessert?' Prem gestured to the replenished buffet table.

'No thank you, Mr Kumar.' Keith stood and shook his hand. 'Safe journey home. Hope we meet again under less stressful circumstances. Good luck you two.' He waved at Jared and Sophie before offering me his hand. 'Going to walk me out, Judith? I'll have to get a taxi.'

Out on Banbury Road we stood with arms entwined. 'Think you can go back to the Lodge late tomorrow afternoon, Judith. I'll phone to confirm. But it's in a bit of a state. The top landing carpet's been removed and there's a hole in the ceiling!'

'I don't care. Just be nice to get back to my own stuff.'

'How does Dorset grab you?'

'Dorset?'

'I've found a lovely country house hotel near Bournemouth for the weekend.'

'Oh?'

'I thought I'd pick you up at six on Friday. We'll be late for dinner, but reckon we can recover over the weekend, is that OK? Course, if you've not done your weekly essay, I won't take you …'

    'Och, it'll be a quickie this weekend!'

    'I hope not!' With amused eyes he bent down.

    The long kiss only ended at the taxi's toot.

36

Dolphins, Old Masters & Carnelians

Lying waiting for sleep at midnight, I was anxious. It had been some time since I'd been intimate with anyone. I hadn't planned a new relationship, but then life planning was never my strong point. My quiet year down in the dreaming spires of Oxford cocooned from the harsh realities of teaching had not materialised. Bloody ancient kings, modern security services and dangerous Iraqi hoodlums had put the kibosh on that. Although I had acquired an unexpected education in literature and ancient history – and learned not to judge on first impressions. Looking fondly across at Abbie – snoring like a machine gun after multiple wines and brandies, I rose to turn her gently onto her side. The snoring abated. Slightly.

*

Next afternoon at three, I ordered my essay reading list online and went up to check on Sophie, who was sitting at the dressing table forlornly trying to pin up her ragged hair.

'Hi darling. I've booked an appointment at Abbie's hairdresser on Friday. Shall I try to get you fitted in?'

'Oh, yes, please!'

'Where's Jared?'

'Gone to get some of his stuff. He's coming to stay at Cowley Road to help me.'

Abbie swept in, grinning.

'What are you looking so pleased about?' I asked.

Her reply was to unbutton her cardigan and expose the back of her shoulder. 'Ta, da!'

'Oh, you got your tattoo! Was it sore? It looks a bit red.'

'It wasn't too bad. They say it'll take a few days to settle. I chose a dolphin – intelligent and cute – like me! Off to do some work, guys, see you!'

Sophie shook her head as she left. 'What next? You going to get a tattoo too, Mum?'

'Never! A new hairdo, maybe.' My phone rang. It was Anna.

'Hello, Judith. I was wondering if you were in after school today?'

'I can be, why?'

'Ramin wants to bring Selassie home. He was only in college because he and Eli used to fight, but with our poor dog gone, we'd like the cat home.'

'Of course! I'll get everything together. He's got a new bed and litter tray.'

'See you at four?'

I hung up and kissed Sophie before setting off to collect my essay paraphernalia.

*

On Friday morning, I was sitting in Popham's hairdresser with Sophie, who was smiling at the mirror. 'Think it's been an ill wind. This short cut will be easier to manage as a junior doc!'

'What do you think of mine?'

Regarding my newly layered hair with highlights and feathery fringe, Sophie gave a thumbs up. 'Keith will love it. Much less eighties!'

'Very funny. Are you up to a quick shop downtown? '

'Great idea. Time you got some new clothes. Phase Eight, I think. Spoil yourself!'

An hour later, I threw four carrier bags in the boot, aware I'd never have spent so much money if I'd been alone. 'Right Sophe, let's get you home to rest. And I have to pack!' Looking over, I grinned at her. 'God, Jared's going to love that hair – you look like a model!'

Sophie giggled all the way home.

*

On Friday afternoon I distracted myself from by spending time in the company of Old Masters, finally taking up Maddie's offer and visiting the Ashmolean. I felt like Alice in Wonderland as I was ushered through a door hidden behind a velvet curtain. A girl led me down a small winding staircase to a large magical basement room lined by hundreds of flat drawers. These held extraordinary unframed drawings by Renaissance and Dutch masters. I felt in awe touching – albeit gloved – the actual work of Michelangelo, Leonardo, Rembrandt and Reubens on centuries-old paper and parchment and marvelled at their brilliant portrayal of character and anatomy in so few strokes. How privileged was I? Oxford was an extraordinary treasure trove of a place.

*

By late Friday evening, I knew I'd been worrying needlessly about making love with a new partner. It was a completely different experience with a man whose main aim was my pleasure. Unlike what's-his-name to whom I was once married. History.

Next morning, I returned from the shower to find a small Reginald Davis gift box on my pillow. It held a pretty silver Tree of Life pendant encrusted with carnelians. Keith looked a bit sheepish.

'I hope you don't think this too cheesy, but when I saw it in the window, I couldn't help thinking that while jewelled trees were kind of the end of Gilgamesh's journey, maybe

they might be the beginning of ours?'
    We missed breakfast.

The End

Acknowledgements

The book is entirely a work of fiction but atmospherically authentic as I attended Oxford for a sabbatical Masters in 2002-3. Thankfully, no professors were murdered during my stay, nor did I meet any dodgy characters as portrayed in *The Carnelian Tree*...

No book is written by one person, and I must thank many people for their suggestions and red pens: Polly Beck and Grace McKelvie for comments and advice, Garnethill Writers Group, mentor Dr Cathy MacSporran and Greenock Writers Club for encouragement, Siobhan Hamilton and Isobel Freeman of Ringwood for editing, Skye Galloway for the fantastic cover art and Ruthvika Sankineni for support. Thanks also to Ringwood CEO Sandy Jamieson for his faith in publishing.

Last, but not least, thanks to my long-suffering brilliant husband, Norman, who is not afraid to tell me what he thinks of anything I write – and can cook when I lose track of time!

Thanks also to the many readers who've attended events, bought, or borrowed my previous books and taken time to write reviews or send website messages. Every one of these is much appreciated.

About the Author

Scottish author Anne Pettigrew is a former doctor and journalist who has published two medical novels, the SAW and Bloody Scotland prizewinning *Not the Life Imagined* and the critically acclaimed *Not the Deaths Imagined.*

She is also a book reviewer and blogger interested in anthropology, art, history, and travel.

Royalties from Anne's books benefit charity PlanUk International who support girls' education and welfare world wide.

If you have enjoyed this book, why not leave a review on Amazon, Goodreads, or your preferred bookstore site to help others discover the novel?

For future publications, news and extracts, sign up for her newsletters at her website
http://www.annepettigrew.co.uk

or find her at
Facebook @annepettigrewauthor
Instagram anne.pettigrew.author
Twitter @pettigrew_anne

Blogs/book reviews on her own website
and https://annepettigrew.literaryglobe.com/

Other Titles from Ringwood

All titles are available from the Ringwood website in both print and ebook format, as well as from usual outlets.

www.ringwoodpublishing.com
mail@ringwoodpublishing.com

Not the Life Imagined

Anne Pettigrew

A darkly humorous, thought-provoking story of Scottish medical students in the sixties, a time of changing social and sexual mores. None of the teenagers live the life they imagine.

In *Not the Life Imagined*, retired medic Anne Pettigrew tells a tale of ambition and prejudice that provides a humorous and compelling insight into the complex dynamics of the NHS fifty years ago.

ISBN: 978-1-901514-70-4 £9.99

Not the Deaths Imagined

Anne Pettigrew

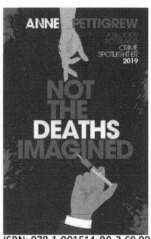

In a leafy Glasgow suburb, Dr Beth Semple is busy juggling motherhood and full-time GP work in the 90s NHS. But her life becomes even more problematic when she notices some odd deaths in her neighbourhood.

Is a charming local GP actually a serial killer? Can Beth piece together the jigsaw of perplexing fatalities and perhaps save lives? And as events accelerate towards a dramatic conclusion, will the police intervene in time?

ISBN: 978-1-901514-80-3 £9.99

What You Call Free

Flora Johnston

Scotland, 1687. Pregnant and betrayed, eighteen-year-old Jonet escapes her public humiliations, and takes refuge among an outlawed group of religious dissidents. Here, Widow Helen offers friendship and understanding, but her beliefs have seen her imprisoned before.

This extraordinary tale of love and loss, struggle and sacrifice, autonomy and entrapment, urges us to consider what it means to be free and who can be free – if freedom exists at all.

ISBN: 978-1-901514-96-4
£9.99

ISBN: 978-1-901514-43-8
£9.99

The Ten Percent

Simon McLean

An often hilarious, sometimes scary, always fascinating journey through the ranks of the Scottish police from his spell as a rookie constable in the hills and lochs of Argyll, through his career in Rothesay and to his ultimate goal: The Serious Crime Squad in Glasgow.

We get a unique glimpse of the turmoil caused when the rules are stretched to the limit, when the gloves come off and when some of their number decide that enough is enough. A very rare insight into the world of our plain clothes officers who infiltrate and suppress the very worst among us.

ISBN: 978-1-901514-88-9
£9.99

Cuddies Strip

Rob McInroy

Cuddies Strip is based on a true crime and faithfully follows the investigation and subsequent trial but it also examines the mores of the times and the insensitive treatment of women in a male-dominated society.

It is a highly absorbing period piece from 1930s Scotland, with strong contemporary resonances: both about the nature and responsiveness of police services and the ingrained misogyny of the whole criminal justice system.

ISBN: 978-1-901514-90-2
£9.99

Murder at the Mela

Leela Soma

DI Alok Patel takes the helm of an investigation into the brutal murder of an Asian woman in this eagerly-awaited thriller. As Glasgow's first Asian DI, Patel faces prejudice from his colleagues and suspicion from the Asian community as he struggles with the pressure of his rank, relationships, and racism.

This murder-mystery explores not just the hate that lurks in the darkest corners of Glasgow, but the hate which exists in the very streets we walk.